Red I

Susan Pritchard

Copyright © 2023 Susan Pritchard

All rights reserved.

ISBN:9798359051026

Acknowledgement

To everyone who has ever had to listen to me, for more than a decade, going on and on about 'when I write my book', thank you, thank you for listening, thank you for your endless and ongoing encouragement. None more so than my children, who have always pushed me to do what they know I love, and thank you Stacey for bullying me daily to get my book finished and into publishing ! I would never have gotten this far without you !

Chapter 1

Reasons not Excuses…

    I don't remember exactly when it became my responsibility to keep my mother sane, it just became the 'norm' I suppose, while my life appeared, on the outside, to continue as normal, it was there, in every action, every counter action, trying to protect her from what she already knew.

    So today I'll go to school, I have just one year left, so she knows where I am, and I'll be straight home, so she doesn't worry. She'll make sure she's home from work, I can't remember a day when she was never there when I got home, she'd never allowed us to come home to an empty house, or flat as it was now. She needed to know at least one of her sons was safe, and if that was all I could ever give her, then I would give her that. So, I'll help with dinner in our tiny, faded and spotlessly clean kitchen, she will sit in *her* chair, at the two seater blue formica table, that I swear my grandmother used to own, and tell me about her day, and she'll do it with that not quite there smile, while we both wonder if he'll make it home tonight. And she'll pretend she's ok, and I'll know she's not. Eat…Sleep…Repeat !

    The reason for her pretence, for the nervous smiles, for the lifetime of looking over her shoulder, began with our dad, and now continues in his namesake Joseph Doyle, the only difference between them, dad got the shortened version, Joe, he was THE Joe Doyle. Joseph was like him in every way, he inherited dad's good looks, if a man could be beautiful, he was. They were built the same, tall, lean, with just enough muscle to make a suit fit perfectly, dad always wore one, Joseph never did, but he always wore the best, jeans of a perfect cut, slim fit plain T-shirt, shoes or trainers, that you couldn't buy on the high street, he dressed impressively well for a man with no legitimate form of income, he wore his fair hair in a brush cut, but never looked harsh, I think it was the smile, it started at the corner of his mouth and ended in the bluest of eyes, and he wore them all with an air of confidence, that could make any one feel more than just a little uneasy.

Unfortunately good looks and exceptional dress sense were not all he inherited. Joseph could charm the birds from the trees, he was surprisingly intelligent and articulate considering his lack of formal education, he was used to getting anything he wanted, with the least amount of effort, and was genuinely astounded if he didn't get his own way first time, he always got it eventually of course, one way or another. The reason for my mums failing mental state…was…that just like our father, Joseph was also arrogant, conceited, and a bully at times, but just like our dad, he was never, ever that person at home, split personality, Jekyll and Hyde, or just plain manipulative, who knows, I'd like to think it was love and respect for mum, for the family, but could it be, knowing the pain it caused ?

I never saw it as a kid, our dad was the best, we wanted for nothing, he provided for mum and us in every way, we lived in an amazing home, holidayed abroad several times a year, our rooms were filled with all the latest toys and technology, he never missed a school play or football match, we watched WWF on TV, then wrestled on the floor on Sunday afternoons, I can still hear the laughter, the three of us in a tangled mess on the floor, catching the beaming smile on my mothers face as I glanced up from beneath the mess of arms and legs, still makes me smile now.

The love he had for our mother made my heart literally shift in my chest, the way he held her so tenderly, talked to her so lovingly, the way he looked at her with such utter reverence, it was such a beautiful thing for a young boy to see, and a wonderful experience to learn from. Only now do I remember the look on my mothers face whenever dad left the house, that same look she wore now, whenever Joseph left, the fear in her eyes, almost pleading with him not to go, but never quite able to say the words, she knew it would be futile, she would just have to wait, and hope that he returned safely.

I felt a physical pain in my chest at that moment, to think how she had lived all those years. I'd never noticed, never seen the sadness, the pain, and now it was all flooding back, her crying in the dark, always watching the door, checking at the windows, looking at her watch, waiting, always waiting, never knowing if dad would come home safely, or come home at all. There was a mixture of guilt and anger, anger that I'd never realised my oh so perfect father had put her through so much anguish, and guilt at my complete ignorance and inability to help her. And yet for such a tiny woman, she is the strongest person I know, I'm very like my mother, physically at least, which is really unfortunate, small, slim, pretty, the most beautiful green eyes, tumbling curls of the reddest hair, every inch the product of her Irish roots, and all of which would look perfect on any woman…not so much on a fifteen year old boy ! A skinny little redhead, with not an ounce of muscle on this tiny little frame, definitely not a good look in my books, my mother promises I will grow into my looks, but I'm yet to be convinced.

Joseph was the 'real' boy growing up, always active, climbing, running, getting into mischief, hated school, played truant at every opportunity and … was loved by everyone who knew him. I was the quiet one, I loved to draw, read, help mum in the kitchen, I can cook like a pro, I loved school and hated sport, nothing like the grandfather I was named after. Conal Matthew Davies, my mothers father, Conal apparently meaning 'strong wolf' was a name my grandfather carried well, he was a big man, and not just in stature, and although he was a mans' man in many ways, he was nurturing and gentle, just like my mother, he was a good man, and I always enjoyed being in his company, I suppose I'm more like him than I realised. I loved my dad too, but now when I think back, I always felt just a twinge of discomfort around him, I smiled sadly to myself as I realised just how much I was my mothers son.

"Ahh, yer home," the Irish lilt lingered on Cait Doyles voice, even though she'd left her homeland, more than twenty years earlier. They may have been just three little words, but they meant so much more, her eyes wide with a mixture of adoration and relief, much more than was necessary to greet your childs' return from school. She was always in the kitchen it seemed, and I took my place in the chair she was eagerly pulling out with one hand, whilst patting it with the other, "There ye go," she said, "Sit yerself down son." There were two cups of tea and a plate of chocolate digestives on the table in less than two minutes, she took her seat, opposite me, and we did as we always did, she told me about her day at work and I told her about my day in school. I tried dropping in a few comic anecdotes, I liked to see her smile, occasionally it was genuine, but the anxious look would quickly return, it was good to take her mind off things for a while though. The conversation would always end with the same question, "Have ye heard from your brother today ?" I paused for a moment, I had, he'd sent a text to me earlier that day, offering a lift home from school, this roughly translated as he needed someone with him on his next run, the reasons were never clear to me, surely one drug sale was pretty much like any other ? But then how would I know, I'd accepted that lift many times, but today seemed different, I'd thought a lot about him lately, about what had happened to dad, and how all of this had affected our mum, maybe it was just that I was growing up, but it had all started to become so much clearer. I was remembering things I'd never given a thought to, so today I decided I wasn't going to make her wait.

She listened, nodding, her face expectant, then just as I knew she would, she said, "Did he say what time he'd be home ?" I honestly don't know why she asked, every day, like every single day, she never got any other answer than, "No." I wanted to shout, 'Why do you care, he doesn't give a shit about you, couldn't care less that you sit here every night praying he makes it home,' but I couldn't do it. "Oh you know Joseph, he just doesn't think, he'll be fine," I said, trying to reassure her as I pushed my chair back, scraping it along the floor as I stood. I put our dishes in the sink, put my arm around my mother and kissed the top of her head, as I did, she reached up and patted my arm, and I headed to my room, guilty at my need to escape her sadness.

I listened to the floorboards creaking each time a car could be heard outside, I knew it was her checking at the window, and every time she walked across that room, the noise seemed to get louder and louder, creaking and squeaking with each and every step, until it felt like it was all I could hear, why couldn't she just accept what he was and get over it ! It literally drove me insane ! I threw myself face down onto one pillow and pulled the other tightly over my head trying to drown out the noise of car doors and the damn fucking creaking, squeaking floor !!

Mum left before me the next morning, I was glad, although she couldn't read my thoughts, I still felt guilty for being so angry with her. She left for her job as a cleaner, or 'Sanitation Technician' as the job was originally advertised, at our local hospital, she loved it, she loved the people, the patients, the staff, she loved her job, she was very proud of her independence, loved being out of the house, but most of all she loved not having to think about what might have been and what may be. She'd never worked when dad was here, not because she didn't want to, but dad was a bit old school, in his opinion a mother should be at home with her children, and not in a chauvinistic way, but simply because he thought that was were she would be happiest, and in all truth he was probably right.

We lived a few miles out of town back then, in a village called Cohm, there were only about twenty houses in the village, a tiny pub, and an even smaller shop, but we were literally just twenty minutes drive to the town centre, and yet you couldn't see another house from ours, I loved it there. It was a huge, monster of a red brick house, with an oversized bright red front door inviting you in, six bedrooms, all equally huge, that's what I loved most, the space, I could be alone at any time. It was an old house, mum had had it refurbished beautifully, she'd kept all the old traditional features, she'd kept the decor light and neutral, the only room being super modern was the kitchen, it had every available gadget, but I highly suspect that was more dads doing than hers, they liked to cook together, and I smiled as I remembered them, singing and laughing as they chopped vegetables and mixed ingredients, dad would grab mum by the waist, regardless of what his hands were covered in, and swing her into a dance, she would throw her head back laughing, when I think of her now…in our little flat, well, how things have changed. Our flat was above the newsagents on the high street, two bedrooms, hers and ours, the neighbours were pretty quiet, but the shop opened till late, although we never seemed to hear the comings and goings much any more, and I doubt it affected mum, she rarely sleeps till the early hours any way.

It's so easy to let your mind take you back, remembering all the good times, unfortunately it always comes hand in hand with how the good times ended.

I was eight years old, almost nine, and apart from a general feeling of underlying uneasiness, I was happy, we had such a good life, Joseph was thirteen, and I suppose, thinking back, he knew a lot more than I did, he was always so much more astute than I was, I could see it in his eyes, he didn't miss a trick, always watching, making a mental note of everything he saw, questioning the things he didn't see, his mind holding on to all that information for future reference, ready to recall should he ever need it. Maybe he knew even then, that everything could change in the blink of an eye.

Chapter Two

Sunday 2nd November 2008. That day is seared into my mind, my eyes, my heart, forever, I've re-run it in my head a million times, it never changes.

Joseph thought he was too old for wrestling, I mean he was thirteen !! He was practically a grown up ! But dad and I knew he wouldn't be able to resist, we were practising for WWE Raw, I was Chris Jericho, and dad was The Undertaker, Joseph said he was being himself, cause he could take down any one of them anyway, and the way he stood in front of the two of us on the floor, he looked for all the world like he actually could, such an air of confidence. I'd sighed with a mixture of jealousy and admiration, as I turned toward dad, with my elbow in his ribs, and caught that look of utter pride in his eyes, as they met with Josephs, it was fleeting and forgotten as Joseph dived in to complete the tumble of arms and legs on the floor. We laughed a lot that day, mum had made a great lamb roast, big brother spilled mint sauce right down the front of his new navy t-shirt, he was just about to blow his top, when dad leaned across and licked it off, we sat in silence for a second or two, not knowing what his reaction would be, till he burst out laughing along with the rest of us. A regular Sunday afternoon, full of family fun, love and laughter.

If only we'd known it would be the last.

Six thirty that evening, a good friend of dads called in, they often did, dad was a, 'slap on the back' 'how the hell are ya' kind of man, today was no different. Nell Quinn had been a regular visitor for many, many years, as long as I could remember, he wasn't a big man, in fact he was a little scrawny, always looked like a good wash wouldn't have gone amiss, never, ever did find out if Nell was his real name. Mum had answered the door, and shown him into the lounge, I remember he'd brought the cold air in with him, the temperature dropped so suddenly, it had made me shiver, at least I think it was the cold. Dad jumped from his seat, and Nell gave him a light punch to the upper arm, Joe Doyle, being Joe Doyle, returned the favour by taking on a boxer's stance, and punched him full force to the stomach, laughing the whole time. Sometimes dads over zealousness in these situations scared me, I was never sure how the other person would take him, but, not with Nell, I'd never liked him, trusted him or felt comfortable around him, I wasn't sure of the reason, simple childish intuition I suppose. I think he knew how I felt, he never tried to interact with me, Joseph always got the hand ruffled through the hair treatment, I stayed well out of arm's reach, he made no attempt to acknowledge me, not a smile or even a nod in my direction, and I was happy with that. I'd sat in silence, my eyes fixed on his face, trying to see what was inside his head…if only I could've seen, if only I could've known why he came for dad that day.

Dad took him off into the 'office,' arm around his shoulders, joking and chatting as he went, nothing unusual, he did this with most of his 'friends'. Mum went off to the kitchen, presumably to get them drinks. But dad was back within a few minutes, meeting mum on her way back to him, I saw him put one hand round her waist, he bent in and whispered something in her ear, she quickly leaned back, looked straight into his face, fear telling, and started to speak, dad placed a finger over her lips, then pointed towards the room we were sitting in, he saw me watching them, and gave me a massive smile, mum didn't look my way, in fact she didn't do much at all, she just stood looking into dads face, beers still in her hands. Dad placed his hands on either side of her face, with a pained look on his face, eyes closed, he kissed her gently for the longest time, it had frightened me at the time, but I'd never known why, I understood now... he was saying goodbye.

The feeling passed as soon as dad and Nell left, he'd always made me feel uneasy anyway so I'd just put it down to that, he was gone, the threat was over...or so I thought. Mum made dinner, I can even remember what we had, sausage, beans and mash, she'd made a circle with the mash, poured the beans in the middle and halved the sausages to stand them on end in the mash potato, to make a fort. She gave nothing away at all, just carried on as usual, bath time, bed time, there was no sign she knew what was coming, not that day anyway. Although the fact that there was none of the usual concern should have sent alarm bells ringing, she was obviously hiding something.

He didn't come back. We didn't notice at first, he was often 'at a meeting,' 'out with friends,' 'sorting business,' he was going to 'be back soon,' 'be back later,' 'be back tomorrow,' somehow we had always 'just missed him,' and to be fair it wouldn't be the first time he'd disappeared for a few days and come home looking like he'd had a run in with a bus, in fact it was so 'normal' we didn't even question it, now when I think of what it must have taken for her to keep up that facade, to keep smiling, laughing, caring...I was never sure whether she knew he wasn't coming back, and couldn't bare to tell us, or whether there was a glimmer of hope that he would return. It wasn't something we ever talked about, but I wanted to know now…I needed to.

The disappearing act usually lasted about four or five days, that came and went, we were oblivious, there was no real reason for us to doubt what mum said, and it was a few more days yet before we started asking questions, none of which were answered conclusively. Our mum had always cried… a lot… when dad came back bruised and broken, she fussed over him, tended his wounds, made him soup, she was by his side no matter what life threw at them. So her sadness now gave us no cause for alarm.

It was raining on the way home from school that Friday, almost two weeks after dad left, the sky was so dark it was almost as if night time had come early. Mums friend Sara, picked us up from school, she hadn't done that for a while, but we loved her, so were delighted to see her, she was like the fun aunt, she was tall, slim and blonde, always played games with us, told us all her secrets, although I realised a long time ago they were mostly fabricated, she once told us she had been the curator of the World History Museum in New York, she told us all the crazy tales of how she and her colleagues used to get all the exhibits out when it was closed, they'd have sword fights, and dress up, they'd climb statues and dinosaurs, it sounded like the most magical place on the planet. Today she made small talk as we both sat and stared out of opposite sides of the black saloon car, watching the rain pour down the windows, two small boys, no cares in the world, whose whole lives were about to be turned upside down. I loved pulling into our driveway, seeing that big, bright red front door felt like arriving at the safest place in the world, the car had barely come to a standstill, before the two of us were out the doors and running, paying no attention to the protests of Sara.

It was in the air, the minute I entered the house I could feel it, I slowed till I was barely moving, heading cautiously for the kitchen, Joseph felt it too, he was a step behind me, looking from side to side... then there she was, she jumped up from her chair when she saw us, I think we startled her, Sara came behind us apologising to mum for some reason. I ran to my mothers arms, I couldn't remember ever seeing her so sad, she'd obviously been crying, and still had a damp tissue in her hand. I can still feel that hug she gave me, the one that told me something terrible had happened, she didn't want to let go, but she reached out one arm to Joseph, who had stopped by the door. He took a step back, but didn't speak. Mum called him to her. "Joseph come here," but he just shook his head slowly, "I need you to come over here Joseph, there's something I need to tell you," he shook his head again, took another step back, bumping into Sara, who was just behind him. I thought for a minute he was going to turn and run, Sara put her arms around him and he turned into her chest, I'd never seen him look so vulnerable, Joseph never needed comfort, from anyone. Now I was truly scared, me being worried was one thing, but if Joseph was worried then there was something horribly serious to worry about !

I can't remember the exact words my mother spoke, she barely managed to get them out, she looked and sounded like her heart was completely and utterly shattered, the pain in her voice, showed on her face, after the first few words, nothing really sank in, she held my face with one hand, and rubbed the tears I didn't know I'd cried, with her thumb, she sobbed through the words, "I'm so, so sorry boys ..." my stomach churned, and the panic inside me rose until I thought I would be physically sick. I could feel my heart pumping so hard in my chest, I thought I would see it visibly pounding through my shirt, the pain was physical, everything inside me felt like it was too big for my body, I knew he was gone, I knew he wasn't coming back, but I wasn't really sure why, I don't know if she didn't tell us or I just didn't hear, what I mostly remember was Joseph tipping the chair up as he stood … punching the door open, and running. I never knew where he went, but it was hours before I saw him again. I was still crying when he came to my room, not sobbing, no noise, just silent tears that I couldn't stop, in that moment I thought I might cry forever. I felt the bed move as Joseph climbed in, and pulled me to his side, not sure if the comfort was for him or me, I took what I could, while my tears continued to flow, he lay in silence with me in his arms. I didn't realise at the time, but he'd just took his first steps to becoming the man in my life. My father was gone, my mother was broken, my life, my wonderful carefree life, had changed forever.

The days that followed were the quietest they had ever been, there was no laughter, no music, nobody spoke, except my mother, to the noticeably few visitors to the house. The quiet made me feel so uneasy at first, that I spent much of my time alone in my room to escape the obviousness of it. There was no funeral…there was no body to bury, there was no 'closure'. I was too young to realise what all this meant back then, but it became apparent over time. The difference it would make to our lives became very evident, within a year, our mum, who had been there every day of our lives, was working two jobs to pay the rent on the little flat we'd been forced to move into. All those promises that she'd be taken care of, long since forgotten, all those 'friends' who would always be there for her … gone. To be honest I preferred it like that, and maybe she did too, but at the time I'd never given any thought to how it must have hurt her, to lose so much, her home, her income, her friends, and most of all the only man she had ever loved... gone... poof... just like that.

You've probably heard it said many times, 'children are so resilient' and for me this was true, I actually feel a little guilty when I think back to how quickly I settled into our new life, maybe it's because there had been many times when dad wasn't around for a while anyway, or maybe it was because we never really knew for absolute certain what had happened to him, or maybe I was just kidding myself, either way I settled into a new school, made some good friends, and sure it was hard seeing mum still looking so sad and working so hard, but I kind of got used to that too...resilient...like I said. I guess I was lucky I was a little younger than Joseph, I didn't fully understand the implications of what had happened at the time, and I didn't ask questions. Joseph on the other hand knew exactly what dad's disappearance meant, and although it didn't change him completely, it exaggerated who he was, to the extreme. These days he seemed a lot older than the five years there were between us, I had been allowed to continue to be a child, and he, sadly had not.

And so, here we are six years down the line, so many things have changed, others not so much.

It's literally only been in the last year or so, that my past life has started to make sense, I've been gradually putting the pieces together, listening, remembering, and coming to the very stark reality, that the very 'normal' life I thought I'd had as a kid, was anything but normal.

The things I've learned :-
As I mentioned earlier, dad wasn't just the fun loving super dad I thought he was, he was a violent and by all accounts callous man.

Dad definitely wasn't a 'business man' unless full time drug dealer, fraud, money launderer etc, etc, are considered 'business'.

Dad didn't have friends, he had acquaintances, apparently he trusted no one. In fact he had enemies...many enemies.

Dad didn't just disappear, someone or many someones, made him disappear, for reasons I can only imagine, given his 'business' dealings.

And it would seem that as soon as big brother was old enough, he'd been trying to find out exactly who 'disappeared' our dad, and why !

The events of my whole life just fell into place, all those times I'd felt uneasy, all those times mum had been so nervous, all the watching and waiting, dad leaving the house at a minutes notice no matter what the time, it's surprising how many things come back to you once you've figured it out. I now know why I never liked Nell, it was more than a little likely he had something to do with dad being on the missing list ! The hairs on my neck still stand on end when I think of him, he always gave me the creeps. I remember we were always being shuffled out of the room, whenever dads 'business partners' came round, I can still see the not quite there smile on my mums face, the one she still wears now, as she'd sweep us along with promises of ice cream, obviously I know now, she was just getting us out of dad's way, but hey we got ice cream, so ! While I spent my time giving all of this some quick, quiet contemplation, Joseph, being Joseph has been out manhandling his way through tips, and suspects, through rumours and suspicion, part of me wanted to ask what, if anything, he had learned, but another part of me wanted to carry on with my life pretending none of this had ever happened. I mean seriously, what's he going to do if he does find out what happened to dad, he might think he's some tough guy, but the fact of the matter is, he's just a hard-headed twenty year old, who's angry and out of control. A disaster looking for somewhere to happen.

Like most people, regardless of what's going on in your life, day to day you just get on with it, some days it doesn't cross my mind at all, and others, it's all I can think about. I've had a lot of those days lately, watching my mum with that same look on her face, waiting for Joseph to come home, just like she'd done with dad all those years ago, the only difference being I now understood why. I'd assumed she was scared he was going to take a beating, or hurt someone else, but now I knew, she was terrified he wasn't going to come home at all.

Chapter Three

I'd always known the day would come, and so had she, I'd enacted it in my head so many times, and I knew she had too. I'd been through every scenario, the 'what ifs' and the 'maybes'. I'd dealt with it many times…in my head. I'd felt the panic, the nausea, the numbness, always preparing ourselves for the inevitable, maybe in the hope it would somehow lessen the pain when dealing with it in reality.

It didn't.

I had this tornado ripping through my head, not allowing for any one thought to surface, just a riotous mess inside my brain, whilst I stared at, but didn't see, the space where my mother was, or had been, just a blur of movement that my eyes could make no sense of. And while I tried to pluck information from the riot, grab some sort of reasoning from the whirlwind in my head, my hearing kicked in again, from the pandemonium of confusion inside my body, to…nothing… silence, it made no sense, two yellow coats in the corner of the kitchen, working their pens, my mother in her chair, still and noiseless.

I'd stood there motionless, waiting for my body to catch up with my brain, or was it the other way round, it made no difference, there was no connection between the two. How long it lasted I don't remember, but in one single second, a million points of chaos dragged themselves at lightning speed into their rightful place...and the devastating reality was restored.

We all have those points in our lives where we change, a pivotal point, not just become more aware, or decide to do things differently, but chemically, physically, our brains completely rewire and we become someone new, someone who can never be the person they were before, this was my point, I would never, ever be the person I had been for the previous fifteen years, never, ever again.

Rewired.

I'd always been the laid-back brother, calm, contained, patient, but I was different, something had gone from me, I didn't know what it was, I just knew it was gone. I should have been an emotional mess, but I was more together than I'd ever been in my life. My mother, my beautiful, heartbroken mum had sat in silence, only then could I see the tracks of her tears, the wet drops leaving her face, falling to her chest, she made no attempt to stop them, the silence she made, gave a pain to my heart that I will never forget.

The only thoughts in my head...someone is responsible for that hurt, and someone should pay, someone must pay. Whilst some sane part of my brain reminded me how ridiculous that sounded, I mean seriously, who the hell did I think I was, and what the hell did I think I was going to do.

Now that I'd regained some level of consciousness, I went to where she sat, placed my hand on her arm, I could feel her shaking, whether through shock or cold I wasn't really sure, I took the pale blue cardigan she only wore around the house, and placed it gently over her shoulders, she held it in place with one hand, whilst her other hand sought mine, she held on so tightly I could feel the energy from her fear transferring to me, she didn't look at me, and the silent tears continued.

Joseph William Doyle, had been shot twice in the head, the officers told her, her precious boy, had 'most probably' died instantly, but we would know more from the coroner's report. He was unceremoniously shot down as he left the house of a known drug user, he had just a few hundred pounds worth of heroin on his being at the time, he was known to the police as a dealer, but had never been caught with anything more than personal use cannabis on him before now. All of this meant nothing, it was nothing we didn't already know, just like we knew this day would come, it was always 'when' never 'if'.

Once or twice before, I'd wondered, whether, it wouldn't all be a relief, when we didn't have to worry any more, when we could get on with our lives, without waiting for that knock on the door, when my mother could smile, and mean it, before she said goodnight.

It was not a relief.

The rest of that Friday night, had drifted by with no sense of time, we'd nodded in all the right places, shown the officers whatever they wanted to see, gave them what little details of who, when and where, we knew, they were going through the motions, just as we were, they knew who and what Joseph was, and although they seemed to have some genuine sympathy for my mother, there was to be no real enthusiasm in their search for the murderer of a drug dealer, a fact which they barely managed to disguise. When they finally left in the early hours of that Saturday morning, the heavy weight of their disdain left with them, and my mother was free to release her emotions, and she did, she sobbed uncontrollably in my arms, but now that initial pain of her heartache had left me, I felt nothing, no sadness, no sense of loss, no anger, I held her in my arms because it was the right thing to do, she needed to be comforted, and I could do that...physically, I didn't want her to hurt, but she was going to anyway, so what was the point. I held her till her sobs quietened, till she had no more tears to cry, as the sun came up that morning, I put my mother to bed, emotionally exhausted, in the clothes she'd worn the day before, her damp handkerchief in her hand, I watched as she closed her now swollen, red eyes, and already in my head I'd begun to plan ...

I should have been exhausted, but it seemed like an impossible feat to get my eyes to close, a million different scenes flashed through my brain, people in cars, people on corners, people in houses, people selling drugs, people buying drugs, people using drugs ! How the hell was I supposed to make any sense of it all, right now I couldn't remember where I'd seen one single one of those people, let alone who they were, there had been no reason for me to get involved in anything Joseph was doing, in fact, I'd always purposely tried to stay out of his business. I tried to reason with myself, this has to stop, leave it to the police, they would make sure justice was served, but even as I thought those words, I knew they were not true, no one was looking for Joseph's killer.

Rationally, I knew my priority was only to take care of my mother, and the thoughts I was having were not conducive to looking out for her at all. I wanted to stop myself, I'd convinced myself over and over that it was not my place, not my responsibility, to look for...well, I don't know who, but whoever it was. Only to find, thirty seconds later, I was once again trying to figure out how to find them, and what to do with them when I had. I was driving myself insane with the constant back and forth. I prayed for my brain to switch off, for sleep to come, so I didn't have to think about it for a minute longer. For what seemed like an eternity I lay staring at the ceiling, my mind spinning with contradictory emotions, until at last exhaustion joined forces with sleep and they came to my rescue.

I knew instantly when I opened my eyes the following morning, I had made my decision. I understood, I understood the burning desire to find the truth, the need to know, and the overwhelming compulsion to make someone pay. Only now did I understand the desperation my brother must have felt, the overwhelming need to know who was responsible for our dads 'disappearance'. And now, that desperation was mine. Sadly my mother would more than likely become collateral damage in this urge to find the truth. Mentally she would not cope, she would not manage, she would not keep moving forward. She could not lose anyone else, and so my underlying aim would be, to make sure that didn't happen. Of course at nearly sixteen I had absolutely no idea what I was doing, no idea where to start, I knew very little about what Joseph was doing apart from the obvious. But... I did know faces, and due to my occasional lifts home from school, I knew some places too. That was it, that would have to be the start. I shouldn't have, I know, but I felt exhilarated, maybe even excited. My brother was barely cold, we hadn't even planned a funeral, and yet here I was seriously contemplating, no not contemplating, the decision had been made, seriously planning to go down the exact same path as he had. I had no intention of selling drugs, but I had to find a way in, if I wasn't in, then I would never find out what happened that night, that had all but ended my mothers life in the process.

It would be another month before my mother finally got the chance to lay her son to rest. It seemed bizarre to be doing this so long after he had passed, but my mother needed this, more than she had ever needed anything. She didn't get to do this for our dad, and that had left her with a huge open wound that could never, ever be healed. She would never get over the loss of Joseph, but she would have 'closure' she would know where he was, she would have somewhere to visit when the overwhelming urge to be with him hit her. She'd had none of that with dad. We didn't have a big family, or a lot of friends, since dad 'went' we had kept our circle small, well we had tried to, Joseph had opened that up to some degree, but we had just a few real friends. Mum's good catholic roots shone through, Joseph's funeral was perfectly planned, it was going to be a long, and not pleasant day, the only thing I cared about was making sure my mother was ok. With this in mind, I hoped beyond all hope, a string of arse holes from the drug scene did not descend upon us.

Thankfully the day went as she planned. There were a couple of unknown faces, faces I suspected knew Joseph from 'work' but they stayed respectfully in the background and only for the service. Mum had put on a 'spread' afterwards, sandwiches and tea. I was so proud of her that day, she stood tall and proud, even with her tiny stature. She was not ashamed of her son, she knew some had thought she should be, but my mother was the kindest, most forgiving person anyone could ever meet. She knew Joseph was guilty only of looking for answers. She'd known long before I had, just how much Joseph had struggled with the loss of his dad, and she knew someday, he would want answers. The anger that had kept me searching for those same answers for the last few weeks, crept up in me again. I quickly pushed it away, my mother did not need my anger today, today she needed only my love.

It helped that she had been able to bury her child. It had always seemed quite a benign thing to say, 'oh at least they have closure' but I got that now, mum was a different person once she had lay her boy to rest. Quite literally overnight, a huge shadow lifted from her, she was lighter, she was composed, all of the things she had not been since the night he died. I wondered if I was doing the right thing, dragging up the past, being the new person in the family trying to seek answers. Let sleeping dogs lie they say, looking at her now, I thought I could see a time when my mother may just recover from this. Could I let things go ? When they were just beginning to get started. The answer should have been, without a shadow of a doubt, YES, let it go, get on with your life, be a son to your mother, and live the life you always intended to. And that is what I wanted to do, more than anything. I'd always asked myself how Joseph could've hurt our mum the way he did, how could he put her through that every day, and now I knew. While part of me knew the immense heartache I could cause her if she found out, the compulsion to know the truth won out in the end. I had always told myself I could never be like Joseph, I could never, ever hurt my mother the way he did, but then I had never lived inside Joseph's head before, and now that I had, there was no way out.

Shortly after Joseph had died I'd made numerous ingenious plans for how I would find out who was responsible for his death. But in reality, there was nothing ingenious about it. It was just watching and waiting. I'd been watching someone for weeks now, and although I'd not had an actual conversation with this guy, I only knew him as someone Joseph had met when I'd been in the car with him, I wondered if he remembered me ? Or whether I was just another face he couldn't give a crap about. I hoped it was the latter, I'd prefer he didn't make the connection between Joseph and myself. I'd made eye contact once or twice in the last few weeks, a couple of nods of acknowledgement as I'd passed, I didn't want to become too obvious, this was going to take time, but then time was something I had copious amounts of. I still had no set plan, but I vaguely knew what I would do, I needed to know who did what, the when, where's and why's, I could keep a dossier then take it to someone, who would know what to do with it. I had no real idea who that someone would be, the police maybe, I just didn't know, I'd not looked that far ahead. Now, was all about finding out who, and this guy definitely fitted in there somewhere.

I started spending my days wandering around the area, watching, making mental notes. I recognised a few of the people I'd seen while out with Joseph, but most of them could have been anybody. Two weeks passed before I had my first breakthrough, I stopped at the kerb waiting to cross the road, nerves building, for no real reason. He stopped his car to let me pass and put his hand up to acknowledge me, what seemed like such a small thing, was, for me, huge, it was a start, it was the beginning, now that he had made the first move, I could build on it, this was all I needed, what I been waiting for, yes, it had taken a while, but this way there would hopefully be no suspicions. Here I was running my own little undercover operation, the only downside was, I was enjoying it just a little too much, it took a lot to keep reminding myself just why I was here !

I'd noticed most of his 'customers' came to him, but he did have a couple of houses I'd seen him stop at, Home Delivery ! I was curious as to why, there was one particular house he went to, it was just around the corner from where he'd stopped to let me pass. I'd seen what I thought was a young girl answer the door, she didn't look much older than me, sometimes he was at the door for a minute or two, while she nervously scanned the road behind him, she always looked scared, and sad, and without even knowing her, my heart ached for her. Some days he went inside, stayed around fifteen minutes, then left, I wondered if she 'sold' for him too ?

Today he didn't stop there, he pulled over at the end of the street, custom was steady, I could see who came and went from my seat in the window of the cafe over the road, I'd gotten to know the old guy in there, a lovely man, always smiling, kind and always a nice word, sometimes he gave me a free biscuit with my cuppa, I wondered what it would have been like to grow up with a dad like him, I had great memories of my dad but let's face it, it's become increasingly obvious that he was not a nice guy out in the real world, I wish I knew what had happened to him, who was responsible. In that moment I thought of mum, of how much she must have missed him being around, how lonely and sad she must have become, and yet after the initial shock, *we* barely noticed, at least I didn't, now he was gone, and Joseph was gone, and the sadness I often felt for her washed over me. It still hurt, deep in my heart when I would catch her deep in thought. I knew she would be going over everything in her head, I'd done it myself so many times. It solved nothing, it changed nothing. But it was unavoidable.

Most of the things I saw, I knew I'd remember, the things that happened on a daily basis, the people/customers he served throughout the week, but occasionally there would be someone new, something a little different, then I would take note, real notes, keeping it all safe in my little notepad. I didn't have names, so I used a more descriptive method, like, big chin guy, shirt guy, ridiculous tan guy, they were essentially young to middle aged men, I'd not seen any women go to his car, the only girl I knew of was the young, sad one he visited, she never came to him.

Chapter Four

And so this is the way life continued, whenever I saw him there was always a wave, well maybe not a wave, I don't think drug dealers wave enthusiastically at people on the street, more a raised hand of acknowledgement. I had no idea how I could take this forward without seeming like I was trying to interject myself into his life, which I was, but I didn't want him to know that, I always wanted any interaction to come from him. It was another three, painfully slow weeks before that day finally came. I was walking, not even really thinking about him, I heard a car slowing beside me, at first I didn't want to look, my pulse quickened as it dawned on me, this could be it! I carried on walking, not daring to look to the side, I wasn't sure what I was more afraid of, it being him…or not being him, this was what I'd been waiting for, but now the thought actually filled me with terror. My pulse raced and my hands sweated as the car pulled up right next to me, to a point where I had no choice but to look, I turned my head not knowing what to expect, I mean for all I knew it could have been someone looking for directions. It wasn't, it was him. "Joey's brother ?" he said, before I had a chance to react. I'd never heard anyone call him Joey before and I didn't like it, it really pissed me off,

I'm not sure why, I had the urge to shout a correction at him, 'His name is Joseph!' Of course I didn't, I smiled a huge welcoming smile and nodded, putting my hand out towards him, waiting, hoping for him to accept it, he did. As soon as his hand touched mine, I had the overwhelming urge to pull away, but I had to remember, this is what I had been working towards, all of these months, I had hoped he hadn't known who I was, and I felt sickened that I was touching the hand of someone who could've played a part in the death of my brother, I mean I realise it was far from likely it had been him who pulled the trigger, but it was possible.

He placed his other hand around our hand shake and actually had the gall to tell me how sorry he was about 'Joey' how they were great friends, and how he was deeply missed in the 'community' part of me wished he would stop saying his name, stop pretending they were friends, pretending he cared, but he almost seemed genuine, I'd not contemplated this meeting being so complicated, my emotions were all over the place and I was scared I was going to say or do something that would blow my cover, I needed to get away, and fast...emotions are such arseholes! I nodded quickly, and slid my hand away from his, backing up away from the car, panic seeping in, 'don't blow it' I told myself, 'don't blow it.' "Thanks," I said quickly, before turning, my body still full of so much adrenalin my fingers were tingling in pain, breathing so quickly I thought I might pass out, I walked away. Elation, anger, guilt and relief all rolled into one.

I ran up the stairs to our flat, two at a time, fumbling with my key, desperately seeking the safety behind that old, red door, eventually managing to open it, inside I leaned against the door I'd slammed shut, still trying to catch my breath, head back I looked at the ceiling, looking for answers as to why the hell I was doing this. How far would I need to go into Joseph's world to find out what had happened to him, to find out if there was anything anyone knew about our dad. Could I do it ? If I couldn't handle someone stopping to say 'hi,' how the hell would I manage to find a killer !

I had to get myself together, I knew mum would already have the kettle on the minute the key went in that door. I stopped to compose myself, hoping she wouldn't see the panic I was trying to recover from. With my usual smile, I hoped, I walked into the kitchen, " Hello son, sit down," she said, placing a small plate of biscuits onto the table in front of me. I sat, relieved to be off my feet, I took advantage of her going back to the kitchen counter to finish off the tea, to take a deep breath. Two minutes later I was joined by my mum. She sat opposite and started to ask about my day, where I had been, who I'd seen, interjected with stories of her day. Every time we sat like this I still expected the question she had always asked 'Have you seen your brother today ?' But she would never ask that question again, she would think it, I know she would, she would probably almost say it some days, but I would never hear those words again. All the panic and stress from earlier events vanished, and determination returned. And there I was back to my usual self, a little bit of banter with the mother, a cuppa and some sugar, and I was right as rain. Didn't really take that much I told myself, not much at all to quickly bring me back to knowing I was doing what I had to do, that I was doing what was right. This feeling I had, the one I now knew Joseph had for so long, would never go away. The overwhelming urge to know, would overcome any other feelings that came my way. Even the guilt of knowing I was betraying the person I loved most in the world, my mother.

Mum had left long before I was awake, these days I liked that, I didn't have to feel bad about what I was doing, I didn't have to worry that I looked guilty, or worried, or a little detached from the world around us. I could just focus on the job in hand.

Just before lunch time, I walked out onto the landing outside our flat, and for the first time in a long time I felt positive, I felt good, maybe even happy…ish. I'd walked this route so often now I did it without thought, down the stairs, through the front door, turn left and head towards the high street, some days I went to the little cafe with the lovely old guy, sometimes I went through the park, depending whether or not I had any cash, that day was a no cash day, I really needed to look into a part time job, but I'd been so wrapped up in my new mission in life, I'd not really given it that much thought. I went through the park today, it reminded me of being younger, playing there after school with my mates, strange how long ago that all seemed, I'd not seen that much of them since Joseph died, not because they hadn't kept in touch, but more because I had other things on my mind. My best friend Carl still came round at least once a week, he knew nothing of what I was doing, but he always brought back a touch of normality to my life, and that of my mum, she loved having someone to look after, so he was always plied with drinks and sandwiches and cakes or biscuits. She loved it, and so did I, I loved seeing her smile, and looking just like the old Cait Doyle. It was a chance for her too, to be a normal mum, not someone whose husband disappeared, or whose son was shot, just a mum looking after her son and his friend, normal and happy. For me it was a blessed relief, a small space in time when neither of us had to put on an act. On those days, I wished it could stay that way forever. But all too soon, Carl would leave, and we would both go back to the quiet distractions of our past.

I came to the opposite side of the park, through the gate, and onto the High Street I looked left, then right, apparently there is some sort of scientific evidence that suggests, we instinctively, or was it intuitively, well one or the other, either way we generally choose left, I turned to the left, looking into the sun, squinting a little as I did. I knew I would see him today, and I knew he would make some form of contact, whether it was a nod or a 'wave,' I think we have already discerned that drug dealers don't wave, but for all intents and purposes that's what it is ! I didn't see him every day, but I had convinced myself I would today, maybe not even convinced, I just knew, I had willed this to happen so much, it really did have to happen. I walked to the far end of the high street, once you reached the end there was nothing much to see, it was quiet, the shops ended and opened up onto streets. That was the 'posh' end of town, now I'm not saying posh people don't buy drugs, but drug dealers don't tend to hang out there so much, I crossed to the opposite side, and began my walk back along the road I'd come along. It was about ten minutes from one end to the other, the other end being nearer to our flat, I did this several times, I was all but giving up hope, I couldn't believe it, I was so absolutely certain I would see him, I waved at the old guy in the cafe as I walked past his window, he always looked so genuinely happy to see me, I mean I'm sure it wasn't just me, but still it was real nice to be greeted with such a smile. I'd barely finished waving through the window, when I saw his car coming down the opposite side of the road, I couldn't cross now, it would look too obvious, I was furious with myself for being on the wrong side of the road ! Shit !

I was gutted, so close, and yet so far ! He drove slowly, like he was looking for someone, I walked straight ahead, glancing every couple of seconds to the side to see what was happening. Someone was waiting at the side of the road, he pulled in right across the road to me, as a guy in his twenties walked towards the car, already half bent, looking towards the open car window. There was a beep, I glanced to the side, but couldn't see properly, he beeped again, I looked up and across the road, he beckoned for me to come over, the guy was still waiting at his window, looking if possible, even more agitated than he had thirty seconds earlier. I surprised myself by not getting into an inner panic, I didn't feel any anxiety at all, I have no idea what had happened over night, but it was certainly beginning to feel like I had turned a corner in my life, I was taking control. As I checked the road for traffic, he 'served' the agitated guy, and sent him on his way. Walking around the back of his car, I thought to myself, I knew it, I knew today would be the day, and I knew something else…one day I **would** find out who killed my brother.

I took the place where 'agitated guy' had stood a few seconds earlier. Today he shook my hand and asked where I was going, like we had known each other for years. I instantly knew what was happening, this was exactly how you get silly little kids to do your dirty work for you, he assumed given my brother's history, I would be up for it, what he didn't know, could never have imagined was, the reason why I would be up for it. I didn't want to help him sell drugs, but I did need him. For a fleeting moment, what this would do to my mum, flashed through my mind, but I was getting real good at swiftly pushing those thoughts aside. This time it was my turn to cup our hands as we shook, we small-talked for a short while, he asked if I was working, I said no, at that moment I really thought he was going to ask me straight out, there and then, whether I wanted to 'work' for him. He didn't, he told me if I ever needed anything to just let him know, I thanked him and he drove away. And I was left on the pavement, a little bit deflated, a little bit bewildered, I knew I would see him today, but what the hell was that, it was a nothing, a big fat zero, nothing had happened, nothing had changed. I mean I know I'd told myself this needed to go slow, but now that we were on speaking terms I felt the need for things to speed up a bit. I walked away reflecting, negatively, on my lost chance. What if there was never another one ? I shook my head a lot on my journey back home that day, I'd had such hope for the day, and there it was, poof, gone in less than a minute practically. It took me a good hour or so to stop kicking myself, metaphorically of course, although if I could've kicked myself up the arse, I would have !

All my evenings were the same, mum waiting for me to get home, cuppa, dinner, TV, bed and a couple of hours of tormenting myself over that day's events. The monotony was killing me. Maybe I should just ask him straight out for a 'job' I mean I wouldn't, mainly because I wouldn't ever give anyone the satisfaction of thinking I needed them. Anything that came from our encounters had to come from him, I mean he hadn't even given me his name yet, how could I not even know his name. Damn I was so crap at this, yet another evening of arguing with myself over whether or not I was doing the right thing. I don't know why I did it, the outcome was always the same, always ! And so our little encounters continued. I saw him most days, sometimes just a wave, sometimes he would stop for a minute or so, but never for any longer. I was getting nowhere...fast, frustration was eating me up, I felt like I'd come so far and yet gotten no further. I'd plateaued and I had no idea what more I could do, maybe I should look for someone else ? Thing was, I presumed this guy must have taken over from Joseph, yes I'd seen him before, but not that often, now he was working the exact same route Joseph had, that told me something, they were both working for the same guy, and that was a connection I couldn't ignore.

Chapter Five

It happened on a Saturday afternoon. I took my walk down to the old guy in the cafe, his name was George, but I'd just gotten so used to calling him the old guy, it kind of stuck. I was there for over an hour, I'd ordered a cuppa, he always told me how he liked that I ordered a cuppa, most of the young ones ordered soft drinks, he thought that told him something about the way I'd been brought up, he didn't say what, but it obviously meant something to him. He always gave me a cake or a couple of biscuits 'on the house'. The trouble with that was, sometimes I really wanted to go in there for a cuppa, but I wondered if he thought I only went in for the free cake, it made things a bit awkward. Today I was thankful for the Bakewell Tart he gave me, I'd not eaten breakfast, and it was almost three pm. I'd not seen Carl since the week before, when he came round to our flat, and I'd not been out anywhere with him for a long time. Today we were meeting in town, he was on his way home from his dad's house, and was meeting me at the bus station in the city centre at four. My bus was due around 3.45, luckily for me the bus stop was just outside the cafe. At 3.40 I said goodbye to the old guy, thanked him for his kindness, and stood outside on the pavement waiting for my bus. It was late and at 3.50 it still hadn't arrived, I'd have to text Carl to say I may be a little late, it was only about a ten minute journey into town, so I wouldn't be long once my bus arrived.

In the middle of writing my text, a car pulled up into the bus stop. I knew who it was before I looked up. Not now I thought, my bus is bound to come now ! I looked along the street for any signs of the bus, hoping, praying it was not on its way. "Where are you off ?" he said, "Just into town," I told him, "Jump in, I'll give you a lift." Like seriously, this was how easy it was, after all this time, all I had to do was wait at a bus stop ! My stomach lurched, and my heart beat a little faster as I thanked him and opened the car door. I had waited what felt like an eternity for this moment, and yet it felt wrong, so intrinsically wrong. I almost jumped back out, but I held my nerve, and kept my arse glued to that seat. "What are you going into town for ?" I told him, and we talked. I was surprised by how natural conversation came with him, within seconds I felt at ease, like I'd known him for years. It was just ten minutes, but it's surprising what you can learn in such a short space of time. Yes ! I thought at last I did it ! His name was Sam, all those weeks and months, and I was just now finding out what his name was. He didn't ask me straight up if I wanted to earn any cash, but I knew it was coming, I knew he would, he asked had I finished school, what was I doing now, what do I do for money, he asked how my mum was, and told me it must be tough on her having to support us both on her own now. I was pretty certain he didn't realise I knew exactly how this would go. In my head, Joseph was the one who knew it all, who could see right through people before he barely knew them, but now I was thinking that maybe it was a family trait, I hoped it came from my dad, if it was from mum I was in major trouble. I prayed she had no idea what I was up to. He dropped me in the city centre, I thanked him, and he drove away with a smile. I wanted so badly, to fist pump the air, but I just about managed to control myself, I put my hands in my pockets, just in case I was tempted.

God I wished I could tell someone, I was desperate to have a release, I needed to talk about everything that had happened these last few months, all that I'd done, about finally making a connection with this guy. I shouldn't have been proud, but I really did feel it was a massive achievement. It was something I'd worked hard for, for a long time, and I was, at last, getting somewhere. I was in good spirits when I spotted Carl, he beamed a smile at me, he always did, and today he got a real one back. We had a good day that day, it felt more like the times before Joseph died, than it had since, we laughed and joked, reminisced about school. I wondered if my life would ever be like that again. Yes, we worried about Joseph making it home, but my days were generally happy, spent in school with my friends, but the emptiness of being just me and my mum was something I could never have imagined. Days like this were a blessing, thinking of the past brought back memories of dad, and how life was when we were kids, I could never, ever have even begun to imagine it would end up like this. But hey, it did, and now we just needed to get on with it.

It took just two more excruciatingly long weeks before Sam did what he had wanted to do from the first time we met, he asked me to work for him, I honestly believe he thought he was doing me a favour. He knew mum wasn't making much money and he wanted me to be able to help support her, I wondered if this was how it had gone for Joseph, he would have wanted to support her, probably more than anything else, he would want to do what our dad couldn't. "So, I might need someone to run a few errands for me, and I wanted to ask you first ?" I began to shake my head saying, "Errrm, I don't know, you know, my mum would be gutted if she knew, I mean I'm not sure it's me to be honest." And I really wasn't sure, after all this time, when it finally came down to it, I really wasn't sure I could do it. "I'll look after you," he said, "You're mum will never know." He seemed so genuine I was already beginning to calm, "I don't know," I said again, "Like, she kinda knows these things, and she knows I don't have money." He looked down, thinking, "I know someone who has a shop a bit further out, you could tell her you work there, listen I only want to help, you wouldn't be doing anything too heavy, and there's absolutely no pressure." I couldn't look at him at this point, suddenly things had gotten way too real, and I wasn't just acting when I looked terrified and couldn't decide whether to take him up on his offer or not. He could see I was struggling. "Listen you don't need to decide today, it's all good, take this, and I'll catch you in a day or so. "He handed me a small bundle of cash, my eyes widened in horror, I didn't want money from him, shit, shit, shit what the hell was I doing, who the hell did I think I was, I was not Joseph ! Never was, never would be, not even remotely, I shoved the money away, like he was trying to hand me a fresh turd. He laughed, "It's just a gift mate, no strings." He pushed it in my direction again, but I was already turning for the door, "Thanks, but I'm okay." I climbed out of the car so quickly I almost fell over my own feet. I didn't even turn to say goodbye, I didn't wave or nod, nothing. I shut the door and I walked away without looking back. I could feel the tears burning my eyes, trying to escape down my cheeks, I was furious with myself. What I hadn't realised at the time was, a few months is not long enough to get over the death of your brother, emotions would continue to run high, some days would be better than others, and the thing about today was, I had just re-traced my dead brother's footsteps.

Back at home, in the safety of my own bed, after putting on a brave face for my mum, I let the tears flow, I cried until my chest hurt, and my eyes were sore, I felt sorry for myself, I felt sorry for my mum, I was angry with myself for almost ruining her life even more, I was angry with myself for being a coward and not finding out what happened to Joseph, I was angry and I was sad, and I was angry that I was sad, and I had no idea how to make it all go away. I didn't move outside of my front door the next day, in fact I didn't move out of my bed, not until I knew mum would be coming home, and I had to put on a show once more. I showered, dressed and put on the Tv, put the kettle on as her key went in the door, just as she would for me. She asked about my day, I told her I'd been cleaning my room, watched some Tv, she raised her eyebrows as she asked, "So you've not been out ?" She knows I rarely stay at home, I loved being outdoors, I loved the fresh air, the wind, the sunshine and the freeness. "I had a few things to do," I said with a smile, I could only hope she couldn't see through me. Inside my head I was a mess, I was on the verge of tears every five minutes, I'd have to go out, I couldn't keep this up for much longer in front of her, I would have to get away. I held myself together long enough to get through dinner, then I made my escape.

It was cool when I stepped outside, not cold, but I was glad I'd grabbed a coat on the way out, I zipped it up, pulled up my hood, and walked quickly, going nowhere, with my hands tucked into my pockets, and my eyes on the floor. My brain quite literally had not stopped for twenty-four hours straight, I had drifted in and out of sleep, but my mind was constantly flipping from one disastrous episode to another. My dad, my brother, my mum, Sam, I was so confused, totally frustrated, I couldn't figure out which of my thoughts were wrong and which were right. I had no idea where my life was going, which direction I should go in next, I was lost, I felt so completely lost, so lonely, there had been times when I had felt nothing, when I'd not cared about anything, I hated that time, but now I wished for it, I wished nothing, for my mind to stop just for a minute. My wishes were not answered and my mind continued to race. I had no idea how long I'd been walking, but I'd come almost full circle, it was purely instinct for me to head home I suppose. My dad was gone, my brother was dead, my mothers life destroyed in the process, and I was a mess, I had no answers, no one was accountable, we were sad, lonely, heartbroken, and there was no one to blame, the injustice was inescapable. One thing was for sure, no one could rely on me to find out what had happened. How embarrassing, I was embarrassed by my behaviour, ashamed that I'd even thought about doing it to start with, practically betraying my mum, and I was ashamed that I couldn't go ahead with it and have justice for my family. There was no way forward, no way back and no way out, none that I could see.

Before I even realised, I was once again standing at our front door, a dull red plain front door, but, I'd always loved this moment, finally getting home to mum, no matter what had happened during the day, being here made it all go away, but now whenever I got to this point, I dreaded walking through that door, and having to endure her trying so hard to put on a brave face, to carry on as she had before, trying the only way she could, to keep getting through the day. She had always been the solution to all my dilemmas, and now she was my dilemma… and I had no solution. No one could ever have a solution to someone losing their child, it's unnatural, it's devastating, it's insurmountable, I had to accept at some point, that I could never, ever, put that right. Joseph would always 'not be there' there would forever be another great hole in both of our lives. That was something we would not overcome, it was merely something we must learn to live with. I realised it was early days for us, but I knew my mother, probably better than anyone, and no matter how many days, weeks, months or years passed, she would live in a perpetual state of sadness.

I knew now that I couldn't add to that sadness, and so, as put the key in the door to our little flat, home to just us two now, I resigned myself to the fact, there would be no answers, I was not made for that sort of lifestyle. I would concentrate only on doing all I could to give my mother some small degree of happiness in her life. Making that decision drenched me with relief, I'd expected to feel angry with myself, but a massive weight lifted from my shoulders, I felt instantly lighter than I had done. My mum had no-one but me, and I would be there for her, always. I paused for a moment at the front door of our flat, I smiled, genuinely smiled as I put the key in the door. In approximately two minutes, I would be sitting at our table, with a cup of tea and some digestives, ready to resume some form of normality.

Something was wrong.

I knew it the minute I stepped through the door, mum always called out when she heard the door shut, she always shouted, "Hello son," or "Come sit down son," anything but silence, in a panic I ran to the kitchen, half expecting to find her laying on the floor, hurt or sick. I hoped she was just late home, or hadn't heard the front door, It has always amazed me just how many scenarios you can run through in two seconds of sheer panic. She was home, but I wasn't relieved. Standing either side of her were two men, possibly in their late twenties, one was much bigger than the other, and they most definitely were not there for any good cause. "What the fuck's going on?" I screamed, trying to reach my mum, she looked so scared, I couldn't bear to see it. I was no match for them, before I got anywhere near my mum, the big guy had my arm up my back and his hand on the back of my head pushing it onto the table. "Mum, are you ok ?" I begged, hoping they'd not hurt her in any way. To my surprise, even though she'd looked absolutely terrified less than ten seconds ago, she sat up so straight, she held her head up high, and she spoke so strongly, my fears were almost forgotten. "I'm just fine son, don't you be worrying about me." She did that far too easily, I thought, and in that moment I knew she had done it before, dad, she'd done this for dad. What a life she'd had, had she ever experienced any peace in her life ? Had she ever gone to her bed without a worry ? I doubted she had, but in that moment, she gave me strength, if my mother could sit there, pull herself together and be strong, then I was damn sure I could too. I stopped struggling, and calmly asked to be let go. Give him his due, he released me immediately, and I sat at the only other chair at the kitchen table.

I hadn't even wondered why they were there, I knew, we both knew, it had something to do with Joseph. What a legacy to leave your mother.

"So, one of two things are going to happen here, either you're going to tell me Joey has left our ten grand with your good selves, or... *you're* going to give us our ten grand." Shit! What the hell Joseph, what the hell have you done, I thought. "We're not going to waste our time looking round your house, we will leave that to you, but we will be back to see which option you will be going with." And that was it, they left. There were no threats, no one got hurt, they hadn't touched the house. But both mum and myself were painfully aware that if we didn't find them their money, they were not going to tell us not to worry about it and to get on our way. There would be a price to pay, and the thought terrified me. As soon as they left the room I jumped up from my seat and went to my mum, I threw my arms around her and hugged her tightly. Would this never end for her, living in fear, never knowing what the day will bring, it devastated me that she had barely known peace in her life. "Come on son," she said, showing no signs of being beaten. "Let's see if we can't find this money they want so badly." How I prayed while we searched our home, looking in absolutely every nook and cranny for the money that would get us out of this mess. Several hours in we had looked everywhere imaginable, and it had become increasingly obvious we were not going to find any money. Either way they wanted it back, and we had now inherited his debt.

Chapter Six

It was time for a cuppa, obviously, tea was my mum's answer to pretty much everything. Sitting watching her with that cup of tea, looking slightly flustered from the searching, but otherwise looking just like the amazingly strong woman she was, I couldn't have been prouder. Nothing stopped this woman, yes she would be sad, yes she grieved, yes there were times when she was incredibly quiet, but she never stopped, she never gave up and she never, ever let anyone else bring her down. I loved my mother for who she was, how she had overcome so much, but where the hell were we getting £10,000 from ! And why the hell was she looking like we didn't have a problem. I watched her from the corner of my eye, she had a wry smile on her face, and I started to wonder if she was about to have a breakdown or something or maybe this was just where her comfort zone was, this was what she knew, she knew how to do this, and that for her was like a warm blanket, taking her back to the old days of her and dad against the world. That's what that smile was, I recognised it now, it was for dad, she'd had a little slip back in time, and whilst it was a crazy and terrifying situation, it still, in all the madness, brought her comfort.

The tea was drunk, the biscuits eaten, and the memories faded, it was back to reality, we spent the next hour or so discussing just how we could get hold of that amount of money. Mum had about a thousand in savings, I had nothing at all, in Joseph's stuff we'd found odd bits of cash amounting to just over £300, that left us with just under £8700 to find. Mum said she could get another job, but she already worked two, I would need to find one and quick, but let's face it even then it was going to take a while, and we had no idea how long they were prepared to wait. Mum suggested a bank loan, as a last resort, but with her income, the chances were slim. Surprisingly, both of us were remarkably calm, so much had happened in recent months, I think neither of us was surprised at yet one more spanner in the works. We were pretty much numb to anything at that point. Mum started to laugh, shit I was right, she really was having a breakdown ! She laughed so hard, and I couldn't help smiling myself, I quite literally couldn't remember the last time I'd seen her laugh like this. "Jees son, what the heck did we do to deserve this eh," she said, still laughing, I laughed as loud as she did, at the ridiculously awful situation we found ourselves in.

We spent the night reminiscing about the old days talking about dad and Joseph, when you've been through so much trauma, you really do begin to lose track of any of the good times, after talking for a few hours, we realised, we'd had a lot, we'd been a perfect little family unit, regardless of what was going on in the outside world. Mum may have had to learn to live on her nerves, but she'd loved her husband and she had loved us, and that was all she ever needed from life. By the time we were ready for bed we were high from our memories, and still had no idea where we were going to find the rest of the damn money ! I didn't even want to think about what might happen if we couldn't get it, to be fair I didn't need to think, I knew, and it would not be pretty. Sleep came quickly to me that night, probably for the first time in a long time, and despite the dramas the day had brought, I still slept feeling good about my life, seeing mum smile and laugh like the old days, was all I needed.

I didn't leave the house for the next two days, I didn't want mum to be alone if, or rather when those guys came back. A tiny little part of me thought maybe they wouldn't come back, but in reality I knew that was never going to happen. I had been filling in online application forms for work, mum had been looking for work she could fit around her existing jobs, that wasn't that easy. We had both applied for credit cards, with no success whatsoever, so it was very unlikely mum would get the bank loan that was our last resort, still neither of us was half as concerned as we should be, life was a bitch, but it couldn't affect us any more. Of course there was no mistaking the seriousness of what was happening, and sooner rather than later we would have to pay up. I'd thought of all the very different things that could happen if we didn't find the money, none of them good, and yet I could not muster up one tiny, iota of fear. I was as I'd always known, my mothers son. And that thought filled me with absolute pride, I smiled as I sat with my thoughts. Waiting as we had done for so much of our lives, for something to happen.

Mum came home beaming, as I put on the kettle and told her to take a seat, she slammed a mini statement on the kitchen table, "There you go son." I stepped over to the table, there was a deposit amount of £3000, she was beaming, "Half the battle eh son." I loved my mums accent, no matter how bad I felt, those beautiful Irish, dulcet tones would always lift my spirit. She was so pleased with herself, I think a little part of her felt like she was doing this for Joseph, paying off that final debt, and doing the only thing she could for her son felt good, it satisfied her craving to be there for him, in the strangest possible way, this was the best thing to have happened to her in a long time. She had felt helpless for so many years, and now she was gaining just a small amount of control, just enough to make her feel useful, needed, wanted, all of the things she'd been unable to be. So, for all the wrong reasons, my mum was happy, if she was happy, then I was too.

I picked up the tiny slip of paper, and grinned at her "You're amazing mum, what would we do without you." Once again I was standing behind that chair hugging my mum, we might be a smaller unit now, but we were still a unit, and a tight one. That left us with more than £5000 to find, which in this day and age is not considered a huge amount of money, but to most working class people, it is an amount they will probably never even dream of having, to us it was going to be an almost impossible task to find. I'd not heard anything back from any of the jobs I'd applied for, and even if I had, it would take months to save that amount, mum still hadn't found anything that would fit in her time frame and again, it wouldn't help if she had, we needed the money now, not in three months time ! We were losing hope and yet still, somehow, we were calm. "We will either have the money, or we won't son," Cait Doyle said, being just as laid back as she had the last few days. "There's very little we can do son, we'll have to just face the consequences, when they occur." Once again my heart swelled, pride overflowed in me, this woman was the bravest, most amazing woman I had ever met. But, I didn't want her to face the consequences, in fact I was going to make damn sure she didn't. I knew tomorrow would bring the pair of goons back, I was surprised they'd taken this long, and I would not have my mother hurt, yes she'd been hurt emotionally many times, but I couldn't and wouldn't sit back while someone hurt her physically. We had nowhere else to turn ... nowhere except Sam, and I knew exactly where to find him.

"I'm just nipping out mum, I think I might know someone who can help," "What do you mean you might know someone," she said, concern filtering through her words, "Nothing dodgy, mum, just some guy who runs a cafe, you never know, these old guys always have loads of cash stashed away, it's worth a go mum." I think that was the first time I had ever told my mum a bare-faced lie, like a real lie, like a big one, a serious one, and I felt totally shitty, but there was no other choice, we didn't have time to get the cash any other way. I knew Sam would be more than happy to finally get what he'd wanted all this time, and now that it was my only option, I really didn't feel so bad doing it. 'Needs must' my mum had always said, and that had never been more true than it was at that precise moment. As I left the house that evening, I felt different, it was as if I had aged overnight, I felt like an adult, like a man, not the little kid I really was. I had a job to do, and I was going to do it. I had no shame in what I was about to do, I didn't feel guilty, apart from the lying of course. When I was doing this for myself, because I wanted answers, it felt so completely wrong, but to do it to protect my mum, well then hell yes I would do it in a heartbeat, without a second thought. No one was going to hurt my mum, not while I could stop them.

Coat, door, stairs, door, turn left. I'd done this a thousand times, but never on a journey like the one I was about to embark upon. Usually it would be hood up, hands in pockets, hunched over trying to look inconspicuous, today I needed to stand out, I needed to be seen. We probably had about twelve hours or so before they were back demanding what they thought was theirs. I walked with an air of confidence that evening, the confidence of a 'man' who knew exactly what he wanted, and would get it at any cost. And there was to be no mistaking, I knew there would be a price to pay. I smiled and nodded at the old guy locking up his cafe door. He beamed as he always did, I knew he would want to talk, but I didn't have time today, I felt bad about that, but I simply couldn't stop, "I'll call in tomorrow to see you," I said, keeping up my pace so he knew I wasn't stopping. "Yes, Yes you do that," he didn't look disappointed, for some reason that gave me a huge sense of relief, I really was no good whatsoever at letting people down. I walked on, scanning the road for the car I'd spent months watching. I'd walked the full length of the high street with no sign of him, not tonight, I thought, please god not tonight, surely this couldn't be the only night of his life he wasn't going to be on this road at some point. I always felt a bit ridiculous reaching the end of that road, trying to look real casual as I turned around and walked the other way, I found crossing over and using the other side of the road just a tad less conspicuous ! Twenty minutes later I'd walked the full length of the high street again, I would walk up and down all night if I had to, so that's what I did. I waited at one end for about fifteen minutes before making the return journey, I even walked back into the park, just to cure the boredom and monotony, and of course to not look like an absolute nutcase.

It would be almost two hours before I could breathe a massive sigh of relief as I saw his car in the distance, making its way down the road, stopping a couple of times to 'serve' some young guys. I hadn't decided whether to put my hand out to stop him, or be a little less forthcoming and wait to see if he stopped, I felt like waiting was a bit of a gamble. I'd already made it pretty clear to him I wasn't interested in 'working' for him. But on the other hand I didn't want to come across as the desperate kid I really was. I'd no need to worry. He pulled up next to me with a smile and a raised hand, he wound down the window as he came to a halt. Walking across the road, no signs of the palpitations I'd felt in the past, I bent forward towards the window and smiled as I reached in to shake his hand. Now I was going to be the one taking control. "So about that little 'job' you needed doing ?" His eyebrows raised, and he nodded in acknowledgement. "Jump in," he said, "Let's talk." It's no surprise how two guys coming to your house, threatening your mother and having you hunting for ten grand for two days, can change someone so much, but it had. I was not the boy I was just a few days ago. I felt no guilt doing this, I felt no shame. It would be a means to an end. And that was something I could quite easily live with.

The hard part was going to be getting five grand cash out of him before I'd even started! He drove to the end of the high street, continued on until we came to the park, five minutes later we reached the far side of the park, it was quiet, no people, no cars. He pulled the car in towards the kerb and came to a stop. "So what's changed ?" he said. "Nothing," I lied, trying my hardest to appear super casual. "So, let me get this straight, last week you practically fell out of my car, and ran away when I asked if you needed a little work, but today you're like all Mr Casual ?" "It was just a bit of a shock last week, but now

I've had time to think about it, you know ?" "No, I don't know. Tell me, tell me what's changed and I'll think about it." I was having the usual exchange in my head, like I did about everything, trying to weigh up all the odds for both arguments, trying not to look like I was having a full scale debate with myself ! Do I tell or do I keep schtum ! Would letting him know how desperate I was, put me in debt to him, or would it make him a little more inclined to help. Come on brain, I need an answer and I need it now ! I realised I hardly knew this guy at all, but I hoped my instincts were right, and he was an ok guy, as ok as he could be given what we were doing. I took a deep breath, "Two guys came to our house, they say Joseph owes them ten grand, and they want it back, we have five, but there's no way we can get the rest in time." He didn't look at all surprised, in fact I suspected he already had an idea what I was going to say. Of course he did, these things get round, I mean that's the idea isn't it, intimidate people and let everyone know, then if they don't get what they want, we get hurt and everyone gets the message, you don't mess with them! "I'm guessing, from the look on your face, you already knew," I said, "I'd heard something, wasn't too sure how true it was though, how's your mum?" I liked that he asked, it gave me some faith in him, "Surprisingly good," I smiled as I thought about how she'd been these last few days, sure I didn't want her to go through all of this, but it was good to see her so strong, so determined, and even a teeny, tiny bit happy. He pulled his mouth into a tight smile, with his eyebrows raised again, he nodded his approval. "I heard she was a good one, Joey loved his mum, was always telling us how amazing she was, bringing you boys up."

Chapter Seven

All this time I'd imagined Joseph out doing his thing, without a care in the world, especially not one for our mum, who was inevitably at home worrying, I'd never imagined he would talk about her in that way, big, tough Joseph, I felt bad for always being so angry with him for treating our mum like crap, he was obviously supporting her in some way financially too. Shit, how could I have not known that, it was all just too obvious now. I realised neither of us had spoken for a couple of minutes. I was staring at the glove box, with my hands clasped together in my lap, I looked up and to the side. "So," said Sam, he paused for a moment, "Let's see if we can't get you some cash, how long do you have ?" "I don't know, they came two days ago, so I'm guessing they'll be back real soon." He was thinking now, I could see his brain tick, tick ticking away, for the first time that night, I felt nervous, I prayed he would find a way, I had to have that money, and I had to have it soon. "I can get you the money for tomorrow, but I'll need you to work tonight, you'll need to prove I can trust you, no questions asked, ok ?" Gone was the attempt to act all cool and casual, my gratitude shone through, nodding way too quickly I practically shouted, "Yeh, yeh of course, anything, I'll do anything."

He started to laugh, "Ok, calm yourself down and let's get something sorted." I had never felt relief like it, my whole body melted into the car seat, I lay my head back against the headrest, and I thanked god that my mother would be safe.

I didn't realise he was still talking, I was so wrapped up in my own thoughts until I felt a whack on the top of my arm, "OW !" I shouted, rubbing the spot where he'd punched me, I mean punched maybe a little bit strong, it was one of those moments where you shout 'ow' more out of shock than any actual pain. "Wakey, wakey mate," he was smiling, obviously finding my trip into another universe amusing, "No time for sleeping now, we've got work to do."

Each time the knowledge that I was moving further into a world I had never wanted to enter hit me, I waited for the rush of adrenalin that told me fear or guilt had kicked in, to arrive, it didn't. I was in this world now, and I felt no anxiety whatsoever. For now.

I realised I hadn't been home for a good few hours, "Hey Sam I know this sounds really cheeky after all I've asked from you, but I really need to get home and check on my mum before I get to work." He was weighing up what I had just said, looking straight ahead as he thought, then he nodded, put the car in drive, and said, "Let's go then." Once again relief washed over me, it would only take five minutes to get home, I could check she was ok and be back out before you know it. We pulled up outside, before I'd even put a key in the door I felt uneasy, they were here, I knew it, I raced up the stairs two and three at a time, and burst through the front door and into the kitchen, mum was there just as she'd been two days ago, with what I now affectionately called 'the dicks' either side of her, she didn't look scared today, she looked downright furious, she went to stand as I flew through the door, but a hand was placed, thankfully perfectly gently upon her shoulder. These guys might have meant business, and there was no doubt they could and would hurt us, if it was necessary, but they had respect too, that kind of made me respect them a little too. "I have your money," I gasped, "Well, I will have it, I can't pick it up till tomorrow." There was no argument, in fact they said nothing at all as they moved towards the door. Only when they were pulling the door shut behind them did we hear, "Tomorrow, same time." Then they were gone.

My mother was livid, and I mean she was insanely furious, "Twice !" she yelled, throwing her arms in the air, "Twice !" she repeated, "I can't believe I let the little buggers in twice." I tried hard not to laugh but couldn't help myself, I thought she was angry they'd come twice, but she was just pissed at herself for letting them in. God I loved this woman, she was all I had, and she was all I needed. I explained to her that the guy from the cafe was giving me a loan, that I would be working there to pay it off, I kept on lying as I told her I'd promised to go in that night to help him do a stock check. I couldn't decide whether she believed me or not, she nodded in what I assumed was approval, but her statement of 'be careful' made me believe she wasn't quite sure. It's surprising how, once you've started lying, it all comes so much easier the next time, and the time after that. She hugged me, a little tighter than in recent weeks, she kissed me on the cheek and sent me on my way. "Don't be out too late now son, you wouldn't want me worrying now," "I'll be back as soon as I can." That part wasn't a lie, I really would get back to her as soon as I possibly could, unfortunately, I had no idea where I was going, what I was doing or how long it would take, but I could do the one thing she had asked, I would be as careful as it was humanly possible to be.

Climbing back into his car, I wondered if he would mention 'the dicks', they weren't his problem of course, but he may have been curious. He asked whether everything was ok, I told him yes, and that was the subject closed. As I thought, he was making it clear he would not be getting involved in any way, other than allowing me to do his dirty work for cash. And that was just fine by me, I wanted his money and nothing else. As soon as I had paid this guy off and worked off the loan, I would be out of this game and looking forward to going to college, I'd signed up for a Psychology course before I'd finished school. I'd not told anyone, not even my mum, I'm not sure why I hadn't, maybe because it didn't seem like the type of thing someone from our family would do, I know mum would be delighted no matter what I was doing, but it was just so different from anything anyone I knew was interested in, plus, mum had had a lot on her plate lately, and it just didn't feel right getting excited about the future, while she was still struggling so much with the past.

Soon we were racing through the streets, heading towards god knows where, ready to do god knows what. It would be almost half an hour later before we pulled into a really flashy looking estate, big houses, but way too close together. We drove slowly now, until we pulled up next to what I presumed was our destination.

"Stay there and take note," Sam said quietly. This was the first time I'd ever heard him sound serious, he had always been so blazé, like he didn't have a care in the world. So this change in his tone and manner made me sit up and do exactly that, take note. It was dark outside now, so I had to watch carefully, he shut the car door quietly and walked quickly but casually to the front gate of the house we had parked near. The gate didn't open straight away, so I presumed there was some sort of electronics to it, a camera maybe, but definitely an intercom of some sort. I was better at this than I thought ! I could see the front door and one side of the house from where I sat in the car. Sam's parking had been done with precision, he wanted me to have a full view of what was happening, and probably more so, who he was seeing. A minute or so later the gates slowly opened, Sam didn't walk in until they were almost completely open, I thought this strange for a moment, but it was more than likely a precaution, he could observe, and ensure nothing untoward was waiting for him, I'm guessing in this game, you trust no-one, not even the people you like, which meant he also didn't trust me. To be fair there was no reason that he should, we barely knew each other, and we were only where we were right now because I needed a large amount of cash from him, fast. He walked along the gravel path towards the front door, he didn't knock, and he didn't go right up to the door either. He waited about two feet away, it was just a couple of moments before the door opened. The guy who greeted him did not smile, Sam nodded towards him, and he nodded back, gesturing for him to go in, the guy stood to the side dressed only in a white vest and white underpants, he was overweight and bald, and had no tell tale signs of any sort of emotion on his face, it was the face of a 'gangster,' in the sense, he looked like he could have walked straight off the set of the godfather. This was bizarre, the oddest thing I had ever seen. Sam walked inside, keeping as much space between him and 'white vest guy' as he could, without it seeming too obvious. The door shut, and memories of all the different men who came to our house when we were kids came flooding back to me. Is that how they saw our dad, was he someone to be feared, did he hurt people, did they have good reason to be afraid, I'm guessing the answers, sadly, would be yes.

Sam had given no indication of how long he would be, I started to question how long I should wait, what should I do when I'd waited long enough ? Who could I tell if he didn't come back, whilst I started to work myself up into a lather, Sam was finishing up his 'business', my worries were over less than two minutes later when the door opened, with no sign of anyone else around, and shut behind him as he walked quickly back down the path, this would, I should imagine, be the most dangerous time, the gate was shut, so there was no way out until someone let you out, which meant if they didn't want you to leave, then you weren't leaving. Sam stood by the gate looking a little edgy, the gate started to open immediately, and I could see him physically relax as it did so, he was even quicker now, back to the car, in the seat and driving away without saying a word. I didn't speak. One, I didn't know what to say, and two, he didn't really seem up for conversing !

We left the estate, and drove back towards our own side of town. I was beginning to feel really uncomfortable, a little bit like I was intruding on something that had nothing to do with me. We'd driven for around ten minutes, when Sam eventually broke the very awkward silence, "You don't drive do you ?" "No," I told him, "Got a bike ?" he asked, "Errmm, no I don't," "We'll get you one, unfortunately, just for tonight, you'll have to walk." As soon as we got back into an area I started to recognise, he pulled over, I was looking around from side to side, trying to make out in the dark, just where exactly we were, I knew the place but I wasn't too familiar with it. As we came to a stop, he pulled a parcel from the inside pocket of his coat, for all the drama it had caused to get it, it seemed very insignificant. It wasn't a big fat bundle of 'stuff', just a pack about eight inches by four, and about an inch thick. I took it as he handed it to me, I turned it around and around in my hands weighing it up, there was nothing written on the brown paper, it was packed perfectly neatly considering what it was, or what I assumed it was. He gave me an address, it was a street I knew, he told me to take it there, they would give me a new package, and I was to meet him on the high street with that one, he would be waiting where he had picked me up. Nerves almost began to hit, but the massive rush of adrenalin that followed, quickly washed away all fear, and left me only with excitement, that excitement closely followed by shame, I was not supposed to be enjoying this !

I didn't have an inside pocket, but zipped up my coat and placed it inside with my left hand, while I placed my other hand in my pocket, ready to hold it in place, hopefully the band on my coat would help, it seemed a snug enough fit to do that, I'd have to be more prepared next time. With a quick nod of my head, I said my silent goodbye, and went on my way. I knew the street I was going to, the houses there were nice, nothing fancy but they were in a good neighbourhood. I walked quickly in the chill of the now night air, wondering as I went, about where I was going, who I would be meeting, what the 'new' parcel would be like. I thought about Joseph, and how easy it must have been for him to get into this game, he was confident, he had no fear, and he loved a challenge. He would have done all of this without a care in the world, I think, maybe I was totally wrong, I mean let's be honest, he could have started this doing exactly what I was doing now, not the bit about making money, but looking for answers, trying to find out what exactly happened to our dad. Maybe, just maybe, we had all gotten 'Joey' very, very wrong and sadly no-one would ever know now. Just fifteen minutes later I found myself at the end of the street I'd been looking for, I hadn't been exactly sure where I was going, my plan had been to walk in the general direction, until I came to some more familiar places, it had worked, and here I was, Baymont St, now I needed to get to number 52. I turned into the street and started checking the door numbers, the first couple didn't have one that I could see, then I found number 5 which meant, 'my' house was on the opposite side, I checked the road and crossed to the even side of the street. It was just a short walk before I was standing outside number fifty-two. No electric gates or intercom here, just a good old doorbell. I pressed the button for the bell then stood back a couple of paces from the door itself. There was a small glass panel to the side, it was frosted, so although I could see the shadows of someone appearing, I couldn't make out who they were.

As I stood alone, waiting for the door to be opened, I understood Sam's nervousness, I had seen someone near the door but it remained closed, and at that point I began to feel more than a little vulnerable. I stepped back a little more, and looked from side to side, checked over my shoulder, I checked out the upstairs windows to see if I was being watched, it was hard to tell as the rooms were all in darkness, anyone could have been watching me, I'd never have known. I was almost at the point of turning and running, when I heard bolts being moved and locks being turned on the other side of the front door. I took a deep breath whilst I waited to see who would be on the other side. He wasn't like 'white vest guy' he looked just like any regular person, he dressed nicely, was clean and tidy, looked like any other person on this street could have done. I was surprised when he spoke with a somewhat more affluent tone to his voice, this guy was posh, a posh drug dealer, who knew eh ? "Hello, " he said in his lovely 'posh' voice. That voice made me feel less scared, less intimidated, less concerned in some way. No real idea why, I didn't know the guy from Adam, could've been a serial killer for all I knew. As the words went through my head, my blood ran cold, I realised any of the people I'd seen tonight could have killed Joseph, or, had him killed. I suddenly became very defensive, I stood up straight, raised my head, and showed no emotion whatsoever. "You have something for me ?" he asked. Without speaking, I took out the package, from beneath my coat, I looked him straight in the eye as I handed it to him, still saying nothing. He took it, turned it over once or twice, then reached behind the front door, my eyes widened, what the hell was he doing, I took several steps backwards, before his arm appeared holding what looked like an identical package, with his outreached arm he said, very, very politely, "Young man, you wouldn't want to be forgetting this now would you ?" I walked cautiously towards him, took the parcel gently from his hand, he smiled and nodded as I did so. I said and did nothing, except turn and walk away, back down the path, and out onto the street.

    I walked quickly now, god I needed to get back, get rid of this parcel and go home. I was not Joseph, and I could only do this for one reason, and one only, to get that money for my mum, once I'd worked that off, I would never, ever do this again. Sam was waiting exactly where he said he would be. I didn't wait to be invited in, and I certainly didn't want him to know I'd practically ran away. I composed myself as I approached his car, swung open the door and jumped into the passenger seat. With my biggest smile, and a cocky look on my face, I handed him the parcel I'd been given. First job done! He smiled and nodded, "Good job mate," he said, ruffling my hair. "How was Professor Plum ?" Making the very obvious assumption he was talking about the posh guy, I said, "Yeh, he was good, didn't say much, but he was very polite." I laughed thinking of how terrified I'd been at that door, I really had thought he was going to reappear with a gun ! I mean these things happen right? I didn't tell Sam any of that of course. "I'll have your money first thing, that ok," "That's perfect," I said, "Thankyou," he turned in his seat, "No problem, best getting it back to your mum soon as, get rid of them 'dicks' once and for all eh ?" Just one more day and mum would be safe, I know I still had a few more jobs to do, but it would be worth it. And if I'm being honest, now that the night was over, I didn't actually hate it !

I said my goodbyes and made my way back towards our flat, in twenty minutes I would be in my bed, resting, ready for a new day tomorrow, if they were all like today, I could do this with my eyes closed ! I heard sirens in the distance, and instead of taking not very much notice at all, as I would have normally, I hoped they weren't on their way to Sam, I needed that money, so him being arrested would not be good right now. I laughed a nervous laugh to myself. How my whole line of thinking had changed over the last couple of days, if you'd told me six months ago, I'd be selling drugs to pay off my dead brother's drug debts, I'd have been furious, disgusted that anyone could think that of me. Today, I was thankful I had access to that life, it wasn't like me and mum hadn't tried other ways, it was just that sort of money wasn't available to people like us. Just a couple of months and it would all be over. We could move on. Life would be good one day, I was sure of it.

Chapter Eight

I was just five minutes away when I first saw the smoke, I couldn't smell it but I could see it, grey-white against the night sky, I wondered where it could be. Just a few minutes later the smell hit me, now I knew what all the sirens were about. I hoped it wasn't serious, and nobody had gotten hurt. Probably kids setting fire to something, little shits, I have to say, I never did any of those sort of things when I was younger, I was always shocked when other kids did, like, I didn't vandalise things, or write graffiti everywhere, all my mates loved to write their name on just about anything that didn't move, but I really just couldn't see the point. I didn't steal things, I didn't let car tyres down for the fun of it. I really could never quite understand why all of them did. But hey, takes all sorts I suppose. I knew when I was just a couple of streets away, that wherever that smoke was coming from, it must have been near to home, Mum will definitely have been at the window, and will be able to give me a full run down when I'm back, I smiled as I thought of her, waiting to give me all the gossip.

I don't know what feelings hit me first when I turned the corner to be faced with the illumination of flashing blue lights, right outside our flat. Confusion ? Intrigue ? Realisation came slowly at first, panic building like a volcano preparing to erupt, and then it hit me like a ton of bricks, and I ran, screaming for my mum as I went, there were people everywhere, I was still screaming as I pushed through them, trying to get to the front of this mass of people, desperate to know my mum was safe. I burst through the other side into the full glare of our flat and the shop below, fully ablaze, flames leaping from the windows, black smoke from every orifice, I desperately scanned the street, side to side, trying to spot mum in the crowd of people that had accumulated. Panic was ripping my body apart, my brain couldn't think, my legs didn't work, I could no longer speak, I stood mouth gaping, terrified of what I was seeing in front of me. A police officer appeared to my left, and tried to move me away, my legs wouldn't move. "My mum," I whispered, I looked at him, eyes pleading with him to tell me everyone was safe. "Come with me son," he said, "We don't know anything just yet." I let him guide me away, half carrying me, as I was unable to support my own body weight. I couldn't take my eyes off the flames, as I was moved from the carnage. I was taken to an ambulance and given a seat and a blanket. No-one spoke, nobody knew what had happened. If my mum was in there, then she was gone, she couldn't have survived, no one could have. I waited in silence for someone to come and put me out of my misery, still staring at the blaze, I almost stopped breathing when one of the 'dicks' appeared at the back of the ambulance, the smaller skinnier one, "I want my money, or your next," that was all he said, he smiled and he left. It took just a split second to comprehend what he had just said. I ripped off the blanket and ran screaming towards the fire. I fell to my knees, head in hands, "Nooooooooo, please god no."

When I awoke, I was looking at the roof of an ambulance. The doors were shut and we were moving, it wasn't like in the movies, I didn't try desperately to get up and escape the situation, I just lay there. There was no reason for me to move, there was no reason for anything anymore. No reason to be, no reason to breathe, no reason to live, I was alone, I had nobody. Silent tears rolled down my cheeks. I must have been given a sedative, there was no way I could've remained this calm. It was just money I thought, and not even that much money either. Whilst my body had no reason to move, my mind could not find a reason to stop, I went over and over in my head, what those guys had said. They'd never seemed that threatening, not to the point of murder, it made no sense, and the more sense it didn't make, the more my brain overcompensated trying to make it do just that. No one gets murdered for that sort of money, even these guys don't kill women, do they ? Only then did it dawn on me that she might not have been home, I mean there would be very few reasons why she wouldn't be, and why hadn't they waited to see if we had the money, had they asked her and she'd said no, was she not home and they'd burned the house down as a warning, was mum there wondering where I was, I had no answers, not a single one, but although I hardly dared to believe it, I did have a tiny glimmer of hope that my mum was still ok. Now all I could do was pray, like I had never prayed before.

Now I sat up, waiting while the dizziness slowed. Finally I could see straight, "My mum ?" I pleaded with the paramedic sitting across from me. "You lay down son, I don't know anything at the minute, but I'll check when we get to the hospital, what's your mum's name ?" He was softly spoken and sounded genuinely concerned. I lay back down "Cait, Cait Doyle, C-A-I-T, she's Irish," I've no idea why I felt the need to tell them that, maybe because she'd always been so proud of her roots, and I needed them to know, I needed them to know what a proud, good woman she was. I thought I'd known emptiness in the past, but only now did I truly understand what it really meant. The minuscule amount of hope I had, was not by any stretch enough to keep me going. I was nothing, I felt nothing, I was a body with a million thoughts in my head, but no feelings about any of them. It seemed like an eternity before we pulled up outside our local hospital. I wasn't even sure why they had taken me there. But I didn't care, I went along with whatever they said. "Don't forget my mum," I said as I was wheeled from the ambulance. "Don't you worry, I'll find out what I can." I lay my head back down, I was so tired, I was physically exhausted, mentally shattered, I knew I would sleep soon, even though I desperately needed to stay awake.

The next time I came around, there was a man in the room who I didn't know, he wasn't a doctor, he was dressed casual, and was wearing an overcoat. I stared at him, trying to figure out whether maybe I did know him, I didn't, for a moment or two he hadn't noticed I was awake, he had something in his hand, a notebook maybe, he was looking intently at whatever was written on those pages. Suddenly he looked up, as though he had felt my eyes on him, he said nothing, but rose slowly from his chair and walked towards the right hand side of my bed. My eyes followed, this was the man who was going to tell me the best thing I had ever heard, or the news I never wanted to hear. "You want to know about your mum ?" My eyes filled up and I couldn't speak, I nodded instead, "She's doing ok at the minute." That was all I needed, my emotions exploded and the sobs rose, as the tears streamed down my face, I had my head in my hands, my whole body heaving as I tried to control myself, whilst he finished speaking. "You can go see her soon, but you've had some pretty strong meds so they need to make sure you're ok, now I said your mum's ok, but she will be in hospital for a while, the nurses will give you more info when you see them. She thought you were at home, she's a tough one, your mum, as soon as the firemen's backs were turned, she went straight in there looking for you." My brain stopped dead there, I didn't hear another word he said, mum had gone into a burning building looking for me, while I was out selling drugs, or god knows what. She almost died, because of me. Strangely, on top of all of this, I was a little relieved that the 'dicks' weren't as bad as I'd thought, they'd set fire to a house, not my mum, to me in that bizarre moment, that seemed like a good thing, you know like 'Oh well at least they weren't as bad as I initially thought' it's crazy how irrational your brain becomes at times like this.

I needed to see a nurse, I couldn't think straight till I knew where mum was. I shuffled to the end of the bed, feeling like I weighed twice as much as I usually did, I didn't make it very far, my head was swimming, and I almost fell before my feet even touched the ground.

"Whoa !" said Detective whatshisface, "Steady on there, let me get a nurse for you." A nurse appeared from nowhere just in time to help me back into a much more comfortable horizontal position, she told me I should feel much better in the next hour or so. "Could you find out how my mum is, and where she is, please ?" "Of course honey, let me just take her name, and I'll see what we can do." She had such a lovely smile, I couldn't help smiling back at her, even though it seemed very wrong to smile at a time like this. I gave mum's details, and she promised to let me know as soon as she could. There was no more I could do, I just had to lie there and wait for whatever they had given me to wear off.

As I lay, I thought about all the things that had happened over the last couple of months, how much life had changed, how I had become a person I never dreamed in a million years I would become. I hated myself, I hated that I'd taken such an easy way out of this mess, granted, the other options weren't any better, on account of there not being any ! Yesterday we didn't have the money, today I'd earned that money, but we had no home, no belongings, nothing, just each other, barely, but I suppose that's all we'd really had for a long time. We didn't really have a 'home' we just had a place where we lived, ate and slept, it had never felt like home to us. I had to hope some things had survived the fire, mum would be heartbroken if she'd lost photographs, she kept all our baby things, she'd be devastated if they were gone.

My head was starting to clear, my mind was slowing and didn't seem quite so chaotic now, I was managing to think more clearly, piece together what had happened. With some effort I tried sitting up again, it wasn't so bad this time, moving my legs slowly off the bed, I waited while I got my bearings. At the door, I poked out my head, looked up and down the corridor before deciding to go right, it looked busier up there so I guessed that was where the nurses station was. I'd taken just a few steps when I heard a contrived cough, "Ahem ! Where do you think you're going ?" I knew the voice, and it made me smile, I turned to see the same nurse who'd promised to find out where my mum was. "I'm feeling ok now, I really need to go find my mum, she's hurt and alone and… " she interrupted, "I know where she is, I just wanted to wait until you were fit enough to move before telling you !" She beckoned for me to follow her, at the nurses station she took a piece of paper from behind the desk. "There you go, she's still in resuscitation at the minute," she must have seen the look on my face when she said 'resuscitation', she quickly added, "That doesn't mean she needed to be resuscitated necessarily, it means there was a possibility, and that was the safest place, as far as I know she is awake and talking, and asking for you, so that's a good sign, yes ?" It was, it was so much more than I had hoped for, "Thank you, thank you so much." I almost cried again as relief flooded my body, the physical changes of our emotions had never been more noticeable to me than in these last few months, our bodies react so dramatically, chest tightening, palms sweating, pulses pumping, numbness, I mean there's a feeling for every emotion, guess that's why they're called feelings eh? I took the paper she'd given me, listened to her directions, I needed to go out towards the main entrance before I could access A+E. With a smile and a nod I thanked her and left.

Every staff member I spoke to was so kind and understanding, I was guided through two sets of doors, by a lovely older nurse, she reminded me of my mum a bit, she was small and warm, and had the same beautiful red hair. "Your mum's doing well, all things considered," my heart skipped a beat, and I gave a sceptical glance towards the lovely nurse. "Burns are difficult, and a patient's prognosis can change quickly, but she's doing well at the minute, she's going to be with us for a while, but you know what, she's strong, willed I mean, I'm sure I don't need to tell you that !" She laughed, a lovely little laugh, and I did too, she'd known my mum just a couple of hours, and she had her summed up already, that gave me comfort, comfort in the fact that they were obviously watching her intently, to have learned who she was so quickly, and that mum was obviously being her very capable, independent self ! She stopped outside a door, and now she got serious. "Your mum is on a lot of pain medication, which I have to say, she's handling extremely well, but she does have some obvious burns, and you may be shocked when you see her for the first time." I shook my head from side to side, how the hell had it come to this, how had I allowed this to happen, in the midst of blaming myself I was also angry, angry with my dad, angry with Joseph, how could they do this to us, how dare they leave us to face all of this alone. "Would you like a minute or two to compose yourself," The lovely nurse was still there, whilst I'd been lost in my thoughts, I'd not noticed my body betraying my emotions, my fists were clenched, my body tensed, my mouth twisted into an angry grimace, with silent tears betraying my pain. I nodded, and she led me to a room just a few feet away, "You get yourself a warm drink, come find me when you're ready and we can go in together." Everyone being so kind wasn't helping my emotional rollercoaster one little bit, and the tears continued to stream down my cheeks.

Now that I knew where she was, knew she was just a few feet away, knew she was alive, and awake, I could relax, sort of, I made myself a cuppa, there were some digestives near the kettle, I wasn't sure if I was allowed to have one, but I was so hungry I took one anyway. People came in and made tea, everyone sat in silence, which was a mixture of being a little awkward, and a relief, I wasn't up to a conversation at this point, and being amongst strangers at such an emotional time, felt so very strange. I wondered who they were visiting, what awful scenario was playing out in their family. A sense of quiet angst filled the air, it was time to leave, I finished my tea and left the room with a silent nod in their direction. I found my lovely nurse just a few feet away, and she immediately came to my side. "You ready ? I've just been in and she's comfortable at the minute" Everything was 'at the minute' or 'for now' it scared me, the uncertainty, to wonder what the future would hold. As it happened, no amount of tea, or time, would ever have prepared me for seeing my mum. Her hair was almost black, burned almost to her head on one side, her beautiful red hair. Her face had been cleaned, I could see where they had cleaned to, along her hair line, one side of her face was red and blistered, but it was nothing compared to the charred marks along her shoulder and arm, I couldn't even bear to imagine what the rest of her looked like. I couldn't cry in front of her, I wouldn't. I walked, not quite able to smile, towards her bedside, she smiled faintly, with such relief on her face. She grimaced as she lifted her hand towards me. I couldn't touch her, I was too scared, what if I hurt her or made things worse. "Hey mum, how're you doing ?" It was obvious how she was doing, it was a stupid question, but the only one I had for her. "She smiled her beautiful warm smile," her voice tired and hoarse. "I'm ok son, just happy that you're alright, Conal, I thought you were in there, I thought I'd lost you." She began to cry, deep heavy sobs, and now I held her, I held her gently for fear of causing her pain. "Oh mum I thought you were gone too, I'm so sorry mum." I wanted to curl up next to her in that bed like I had when I was a kid, I wanted her to cradle me in her arms and comfort me, in a way only a mother can do, now I had to be the adult, I had to think of her, I had to care for her, I had to grow up.

We stayed in that embrace for what seemed like an eternity, and even though I knew she must be in pain, I selfishly held on for as long as I could. When she could finally take no more and her arms loosened, I stood and wiped away the tears that had flowed. We might have had nothing else, but we had each other, and that for now, was enough.

I had no idea where I would be sleeping that night, but mum would be safe at the hospital, and that was what mattered more than anything to me. It was going to be a couple of hours before she was sent to a ward, they needed her to stay there, where they had all the equipment she needed should she deteriorate. She looked good, she looked strong, and I wasn't worried when I left her to go back to 'work'. I gave my mobile number to the lovely nurse, and told her I'd be back later that day. Sam had called, he was picking me up, he didn't have to, and although I'd not known him long, it was good to see a familiar face when I walked through the hospital doors, out into the cold, fresh air. The usual nods were exchanged acknowledging each other. Very little else was said. Not for a little while anyway, and I appreciated the fact that he understood that I wasn't yet able to talk.

Chapter Nine

We reached the high street in no time, Sam quickly pulled into the kerb, I stayed in my seat looking at my hands in my lap, as I'd done throughout the journey. Sam turned, leaned his back against the driver's side door, and said, "Well ?" I shook my head slowly, I didn't know where to start. "Come on mate, tell me what's going on." Before I realised, I was racing through the horrific events of what had just happened, I barely took a breath as the words kept spewing from my mouth until eventually I needed to breathe. I stopped, he'd said nothing, I waited for some sort of sign he'd at least heard me, and maybe even understood. He sat straight in his seat again, still saying nothing, and started the car up again. "Where are we going ?" I asked, "Work of course," I looked at him, confused, was he taking the piss ? Why would he ask what had happened, then say nothing at all ? I'd expected something, even if it was just a few words of comfort, but nothing ? I stared at him for a moment trying to figure him out, I suppose, we're not friends, he owed me nothing, he'd just wanted to know what happened, maybe more for his own safety than mine, I mean depending who these people were, I could be bringing more trouble to his door than he needed. I needed to stop thinking everyone was like me, that everyone was my friend, and we all look out for each other, because that's the absolute one thing I should have learned by now, no one looked out for my dad, no one looked out for Joseph and no one was looking out for me or my mum. My hands were clenched again, and then there was a hand in my hair, with a ruffle Sam said, or more he told me, "Hey mate, you and your mum are ok, it'll all be good." That one short sentence, that would mean nothing to most people, gave me a small glimmer of hope that people did still care, that people could still be kind, and they could have compassion. I had no idea what time of day it was, or even what day it was, it was dark and I had work to do, that's all I knew.

"When you knock, no one will answer, wait five minutes and someone will come to meet you, I'll be in the next street when you're done." This was bizarre, I mean who on earth did these people think they were, I swear they thought they were on the set of some sort of Hollywood movie, I shook my head in utter disbelief at the way they did things. It simply didn't cross my mind that handing a letter to someone could be a problem, I had no concerns as I left the car, "Oh by the way, do not under any circumstances, go into that house, or get in anyone's car, ok ?" "Ohhhhkaaay," I said, just a touch of impertinence in my tone, "I'm serious, you hand over the letter and you walk away, no conversation needed," he wasn't messing around, he really was deadly serious. My mood changed instantly, so, now I was concerned, now I realised this was serious, whatever was in that envelope, one thing was for sure, it was no love letter.

Standing in front of the door with my heart racing, was a wake up call for me, this was dangerous, all of this was dangerous, anything could happen, at any time, I was a seventeen year old kid, and not a big one, there wouldn't be a thing I could do if anything went wrong, what if they made me go in, I couldn't stop them. Shit ! Shit ! Shit ! God I was saying that more and more. I chose that moment to remember my mum was laying in a hospital bed because of all this shit ! Right, deep breath, deep breath, here goes, I took a step forward, knocked on the door, and stood back, and just like Sam said, nothing happened, I looked down the street to where Sam had been parked, he was gone, I looked to the other end of the street, I saw nothing, I looked behind me, there was just a couple of cars parked across the road, it began to feel very, very dark, I kept thinking I could see things out the corner of my eye, I was so completely unnerved by it all, I almost died when I did hear a car driving at speed into the street, it flew up onto the kerb next to me, so much so that I had to jump back against the wall of the house. WHAT THE FUCK WAS HAPPENING !! Oh shit, were they gonna kidnap me ? The window came half way down on the passenger side of the car, which was the side that was just about a foot away from me. A hand appeared through the half open window, and a voice said, "You got something for me ?" I handed over the letter, completely forgetting for a moment what Sam had said, 'walk away,' I didn't walk away, I stood, in shock, dumbstruck, as I watched the car race off, bouncing off the kerb as it went. I hadn't realised I'd been holding my breath until I gasped in air as I bent down to put my hands on my knees. I had no idea what just happened, but now I remembered to walk away. I didn't walk slowly, in fact I didn't walk at all.

To be fair, once I'd got back in the car, and partially over the shock, I told myself it wasn't bad pay for an hours work, I had to tell myself that otherwise there would be no way I would be going back ! "What's next ?" I asked, trying as much as I could to seem underwhelmed by what had just happened. "Nothing for tonight mate, you get back to see your mum, I'll drop you off." I was finding it difficult to make Sam out, couldn't quite figure out if he was a good guy or not, I mean selling drugs is not good, obviously, but was he a good person, like deep down, on the inside. At the minute, I really didn't know. He dropped me right outside the hospital doors.

Walking back in reminded me how real this situation was, and the sick feeling in my stomach returned. She was still in the same room, and thankfully sleeping. I liked that she was asleep, she looked so much more peaceful than she had when I'd seen her last. Seeing someone you love in so much pain is one of the most difficult things anyone can ever experience, whether it be physical or emotional, and

I'd watched my mum go through both. So much shit this beautiful woman really did not deserve. She was a good person, a good, kind woman, who would do anything for anyone. Life really was a bitch, a big bastardy, shitty, twat of a bitch. I slept well in the chair next to her bed, knowing she was safe.

I woke in absolute terror, leaping from the chair, as alarms were screaming around the room, as soon as I stood, they stopped, she was sleeping peacefully, there was no noise, everything was quiet, just a dream, an awful, horrible dream, I wiped away the sweat from my forehead, and dropped, relieved, back into my chair, my heart continued to race, adrenalin still coursing through my body. Then and there I had been given just a little taste of how I would feel if anything happened to the only person I had left in the world. I rubbed my eyes and my face hard, I needed to wake myself up completely, I couldn't risk another nightmare ! I took a deep breath, and sighed, mum was ok 'for now'.

Sam was true to his word, he called me later that day, he had my money, "Cheers mate," I told him, with no enthusiasm whatsoever. "Whats up mate?" he asked, I explained that the £5000 he was giving me was neither here nor there any more, I couldn't get the rest of the money, I had no idea when they were going to come looking for me, right there and then, I felt hopeless, feeling desperation was one thing, but saying it out loud made it all hit home, I was up shit creek with no sign of a paddle. "Listen, I can get you the money, but this is a lot of money, and your gonna have to work it all off, I feel bad your gonna be working with no income mate," "Sam I don't care how long I have to work, or what I have to do, I've got to make sure my mum's safe, she's all I've got left in the world." I was deflated, and it was obvious. "You'll have it today, no worries mate." I didn't feel any better, in fact I only felt worse, I was simply digging myself a deeper and deeper hole. "Sam, I, I don't know what to say, I can't thank you enough, I thought it was all over, there was no way out, but now, well, yeh I can only say thank you." And that was it, he was gone, I still had the phone to my ear, taking in what had happened, I was now in debt to the tune of £10,000, I could pay off the debt, but I felt no relief whatsoever.

My days passed in a blur of hospital visits, and 'working' for Sam, sometimes he would take me, and sometimes he would only give me the address, he was being good to me, I knew that, he took me back and forth to the hospital, he made sure I was fed and watered, I couldn't have asked for more from him, he was quickly becoming a good friend. I'd been staying at the hospital when I finished 'work', I slept on the sofa in the visitors room, we weren't supposed to stay, but nobody brought it up, so I would do it for as long as I could get away with it.

Over the last couple of weeks I'd come to realise how serious mums injuries had been, she had serious burns right down her left side, head to toe, her lower leg was causing her the most pain, and she had been told it would require several operations, but you know Cait being Cait, she was in good spirits, all of the nurses loved her, just like anyone who ever met her did, and she treated them with the utmost respect, she'd worked in this hospital for a few years, some of the staff she already knew, and they had been especially good to her, popping in to see how she was getting on, and bringing in little treats, it took some of the pressure off me too, I didn't feel so guilty when I had to leave, knowing she was being so well looked after by people who genuinely cared, was a huge relief for me.

It's funny, peculiar, not haha, how quickly the strange life of working for a drug dealer becomes not very strange at all, in fact it becomes so normal it's quite ridiculous. I can see why they call it work, cause it does in fact feel just like that. I was doing a lot more now for Sam, which in a way was good, because it meant I was working my debt off quicker. Sam had told me how much I'd earn for doing what, and to be fair, it was only going to be a couple of months before it was paid. I had no idea what the going rate was, but I trusted Sam, I couldn't complain, he was feeding me and being my chauffeur, so I needed to just keep on going. Remembering how scared I used to get doing this at the beginning made me laugh to myself, now I gave it very little thought at all, which made me wonder, why, after all this time Sam was still so wary of 'white vest guy.' Sam still hadn't divulged his name so he would remain 'white vest guy' until I knew otherwise, and maybe even then. I was getting used to the people I delivered to, they were all quite similar, liked to keep things short and sweet, well maybe not so sweet, I'd never been back to the house on the terraced street where the guy mounted the pavement, and as that was the only one I'd felt truly scared about, that was fine by me.

If any one knew, I did, that life can change at the drop of a hat, like one minute you have a dad, the next minute you don't, one minute you have a brother, the next you don't, I'd learned the hard way to never rely on things to stay the same. Fate would always come along and smack you straight in the face, just to let you know it could, so I never took anything for granted, I was always aware of what I could lose at any given time, and tried my best not to get close to anyone else, it's way easier to lose people you don't care about ! So when I arrived at the hospital one night, to be told mum had taken a turn for the worse, I didn't react the way I should have. I should have been distraught, I should have run to her side. But I didn't, I accepted that this was what life brought, and I followed yet another lovely nurse to the room where my mum had been staying. I was shocked at how pale she looked, at how ill she looked, but it was just momentary, I very quickly composed myself. I went to her side and took her hand, she was sleeping, and didn't wake when I touched her, I leaned in and whispered, "I love you mum, I know you can do this, you're the strongest person I know." I swear I saw her lips shape into an ever so slight smile. God I loved this woman. I had never been this calm in such an emotional situation, I was more controlled than I had ever been. I had been warned several times by doctors and nurses, that the injuries mum had sustained were life threatening, she was at great risk of infection, and she was at the very least at risk of losing her leg. I knew there was a possibility that, at some point, I would have no family, but it didn't scare me any more. She had been doing so well, and I knew my mother, she would not give up without a fight and wouldn't give up hope, no one knew her like I did. She would not let go.

Chapter Ten

I sent a text to Sam, it read 'won't be out mum not good' there was a ping as he replied, I didn't read his message, it didn't matter what it said, I would be by mum's side till she got through this. And she would. For now I was going to hunker down next to her, and make sure I was there by her side when she woke. I'd been warned yet again, that there was a chance mum wouldn't survive, again they informed me that infection is the biggest risk to life for any burns victim. I wondered if I was kidding myself, apart from the obvious injuries, she looked pretty good, well she had done, before this infection took hold. Now, she did look seriously unwell, the more I looked, the more I saw, the more I realised just how different she looked to when I'd last seen her before the fire. She was thinner, paler, she didn't move so much, she tried to stay up beat, but it wasn't the same, had I been kidding myself ? Yes ! Yes I had, I didn't want to believe it, because if she was doing well the risk of losing her was slim. Sitting beside her now, the gravity of the situation kicked in, I was instantly overcome with fear, terror, I was utterly terrified she was going to die, in the space of less than fifteen minutes, I had gone from 'my mum will get through anything' to 'oh god I could really lose her'. The thought wouldn't leave me, 'my mum could die' it was an actual possibility, maybe even a probability. Of course the nurses had been telling me this all along, I'd just not been ready to listen. That night I grieved for the mum I might just lose, I grieved for myself for the loss I could already feel, and a hatred and a need for revenge that I'd not felt for some time…returned.

I felt so sad for myself, or maybe I felt sorry for myself but just didn't want to admit it, it had been three days and mum had shown no signs of waking up, and the fear kept on creeping in, it was going to keep on, crawling all over me until it had consumed me completely. That awful pent up pain you get when you lose someone, had kept my body tense for days. I ached all over, every little ache and pain reminding me just how bad things were. Headache…your mums dying, stomach ache…your mums dying, legs aching…your mum is dying.

My mum was dying, I could see it now, she was all but gone. I'd always thought I'd be angry if mum ever gave up on life. But I knew, if she could stay she would, and all I could do now was pray, pray that she could.

My prayers were not answered, and mum never did wake up. She died in intensive care, infection caused by her burns, destroying her body, causing her organs to fail, and her blood to become poisoned. I was numb, there were no more tears left for me to cry, feelings were for those people who had someone to share them with, and I no longer fell into that category, they were useless to me, and caused me only pain, for now, I did not need them. I needed a good head, a strong mind and determination, and of those, I had all three.

Sam, as always, had been good to me, once again making sure I was fed and watered. He had found me a place to live, it was ok, just a small bedsit, but I liked it, it was small enough to keep me safe, I'd only been there once, just so he could show me around, it was clean and tidy, had a modern look to it, it would have everything I'd need now it was just me. I had no idea what to do next. Mum had sorted pretty much everything for Joseph's funeral, the lovely nurses had told me not to worry, someone would be available to guide me through it. How frickin' wonderful, I thought !

I hadn't seen the 'dicks' since the fire, I'd only been out with Sam and he had picked me up at the hospital door and dropped me off in the same place, they wouldn't wait forever though, as soon as they found out where I was living they'd be back. I didn't want to pay them, it would feel like I had paid them to kill my mum, and ok they couldn't have known she would get in there, but if they'd not set that fire, she would still be here, with me. The police had been into the hospital several times to speak to me, and I had been more than honest with them. I'd told them exactly what had happened, I couldn't give them any names for the 'dicks', but I gave them a pretty accurate description, and "Yes," I was more than prepared to go to court and give evidence if I needed to. Now that mum had died things got a bit more serious, they wouldn't face a murder charge as mum hadn't been in the property when they'd set it alight, but the fact that she had died, and because of the circumstances, they assured me that if they could find them, they would serve long sentences due to extenuating circumstances. This was all so different to when Joseph was killed, there was little compassion from the police, and we barely saw them after that first day, this time they'd come each week, now that I think about it, they were just waiting for mum to die. Everyone knew, everyone but me. I'd been playing at 'drug dealing' and all the time my mum was dying before my eyes. Hindsight, as they say, is a wonderful thing.

And then there was one, me, just me.

I kept myself busy, and was hardly ever by myself, physically that is, but as we all know, loneliness has nothing to do with the actual presence of another person, it's about feeling mentally that you have no one. I was sad, so extremely sad, and whilst I'd told myself for months I'd only 'worked' for Sam as a means to an end, to enable us to pay off the 'dicks', in reality, if I didn't have that work, I'd be lost, that loneliness may have pushed me over the edge. Once again my mind was drawn back to Joseph, I was learning more and more about why he did the things he did, and this was yet another, he did this 'job' so he didn't have to think about dad, he didn't have to think about the life we had lost, he didn't have to think about mum working two jobs to make ends meet, it was his escape then, just as it was mine now. I lived from 'job' to 'job' and in between, I walked, I went to the cafe, with the lovely old guy, I did anything that stopped me from being alone, feeling so deeply sad that I had been left behind.

At mum's funeral, Sarah had reminded me that she would always be there for me, but she'd said that after dad was gone, and we'd barely seen her, I kind of couldn't forgive her for that. Mum's funeral had been so beautiful, it was simple and whilst there wasn't a mass of people there, there was a lot more than I thought she knew. They were good people, people she had worked with, people she had worked for, people she'd met at the shops, people she had met on the wards, they all remembered her, because once you met Cait Doyle, you didn't forget her, she stood out in a crowd, well she would have, had she been a foot taller, she was beautiful, her magnificent red hair her crowning glory, and her smile shone so brightly it lit up any room. Saying goodbye to her, with so many people telling me how kind she was to them, filled me equally with pride and utter heartbreaking sadness.

The 'dicks' never did come for their money, I couldn't figure out why, why kill for something you never came back for, it made no sense. I didn't touch the money, mum's money was still in the bank, most of it would pay for her funeral when it was released, but the rest stayed in the bottom drawer of the kitchen cabinet at what was now my home. And that was where it would stay, I could never spend it myself, it was blood money now. But neither would I give it to THEM. And so my new life began, I did as I was told, I paid off my debt and I earned my own money. It wasn't the life I had ever dreamed of, and if mum had been here, I wouldn't be doing it now, but she's not, and I am. Sam was a big part of my life now, we spent most of our days together, he had been there for me when I had no one else, and I would always be thankful for that. So life went on. I lived each day as it came, I slept and started again. But I couldn't remember the last time I had smiled at something, or laughed out loud, or even had a happy thought, I had no feelings, not happy nor sad, I just was, and right now that was ok, it meant I could think, when you don't feel you think more clearly than you have ever done. I was watching, I was noting, once again I was on the track of who killed Joseph and while I was at it, I was going to find out what happened to dad, and where the 'dicks' where now. I was going to do it all, no matter how long it took.

Once a week, Sam went to an aesthetics clinic, just on the edge of town called somewhat imaginatively The Aesthetics Clinic. Apparently it was high class, very expensive, with quite a distinctive clientele, footballers wives and the likes, have to say, I'd not seen one person I knew going in there but hey, what did I know. Sam never once said what he was doing there or who he was going to see, he took his package in, and he came out with nothing, same thing every week. Sam worked a lot more than I thought he did, I mean I slept, but I have no idea when he did, I couldn't see when he would find the time. Sam had all his regular clients, but there was always something new to do, someone new to see, I tried not to get involved with any of them, some liked that, others would try to make conversation, probably because the silence made things a little awkward. There was one more place Sam went every week, and that was a rundown terraced house, on a run down street, in a rundown part of town called the Nethers, never knew why it was called that, it just always had been. This house had dirty net curtains on windows that looked as if they'd never been cleaned, the wooden frames were decayed, with parts of them so bad it looked as though the windows could fall out at any minute. In this house lived Fiona, she was so small and dainty, she looked like she could be a child, her hair was always tied up in a dirty blonde mess on the top of her head, you could tell she was pretty, but drugs had taken their toll, her face was thin and drawn, but what stood out more than anything was, her sadness, I'd never seen her smile, then again I only ever saw her for a brief moment now and then, so hey, maybe she was having a ball the rest of the time. I seriously doubted it though. I found it odd that he had never asked me to go. Usually these were the type of 'sales' he'd expect me to do. Once in a while he would go inside, he wouldn't be long, maybe like five minutes, ten tops, never had a clue why, but that's not my business, one thing I'd never needed to learn was, don't ask questions, listen, learn, but don't ask.

I don't know what it was about Fiona that intrigued me, but I found myself thinking about her more and more, maybe it was how lonely she looked, how sad she seemed, I could see myself in her, an affiliation with her isolation and desolation. I wondered where her family were, was she alone, or was she lonely. I wondered a lot about her life. She was the only person I'd ever asked Sam about, that's how I knew her name. She was eighteen, but looked like a kid, he said she was a heroin addict, you could tell, I felt nothing but sadness for her, you had to wonder what had driven her to this life of solitude. I assumed I would never know. Until, one day Sam sent me to her house. I was obviously surprised, but excited too, finally I would get the chance to see her up close, something I had wanted to do for a long time. She opened the door, and almost shut it again when she saw me standing there, I held up my tiny pack, and placed my hand on the door, she looked past me, over my shoulder towards Sam's car, I turned to look in the same direction, she was up on her toes looking at him, he nodded, and she slid back onto her feet, she was so nervous, wringing her hands, looking around, she said nothing, but kept looking over towards the car, I kept looking too, usually it would go like this, here's your stuff, here's your money, bye, I had no idea what was going on. The next time I turned to look at Sam, I shrugged my shoulders, her delivery still in my hand, he shook his head and climbed out of the car. He did not look best pleased. "Not again Fi, come on, let's' not start making a habit of this !" She looked utterly humiliated, and it suddenly dawned on me, she didn't have the money. She looked down at the floor, getting more and more jittery, obviously waiting for Sam to do something. "Fi, this has got to stop ok, you know I don't like this," she nodded and walked back into the house, Sam followed, I didn't know what to do, I tapped him on the shoulder and passed him her stuff, he took it, handed me the car keys and said, "I won't be long." In that split second everything I had ever thought of Sam changed, as I realised how she was going to pay for the drugs she so desperately needed.

My stomach churned and the blood drained from my body. I didn't know whether to stay where I was, go back to the car or just run away, I wasn't sure I could ever look Sam in the eye when he came back. How could he do that, how could she do that. This was sick, what the fuck was up with these people. I turned to face the street, so thankful I could hear nothing coming from inside the house. Just a few minutes later Sam appeared at the door, pulling it shut behind him, he ran his hands through his hair, straightened his T-shirt, and returned to the car. Neither of us spoke, I was thankful he hadn't come back looking pleased with himself, I couldn't have coped with that. He looked genuinely gutted. I waited, knowing I should say nothing, but I had to ask, "Why do you do it if you feel like this ?" I half expected him to be furious I'd had the audacity to ask, but he looked more relieved that I had actually spoken to him. "She needs it," he said, "I know she needs it, but how could you do 'that'." I gestured with disgust back towards her house. "It's like this, I could give her it for free, it wouldn't hurt my earnings, but if word got around I did freebies cause I felt sorry for someone, they'd all be at it, and, she won't take it for free, what most people can't see in her is, she still has her pride, she won't take nothing for nothing, this was her suggestion, I didn't mind before I got to know her, but she's a good kid, and it can't carry on." I had no answer to that, whilst I found it difficult to personally condone what he did, I could see how in his eyes he was trying to do his best for her. What a twisted, fucked up world we live in.

We didn't speak of it again, but I couldn't get it out of my mind. I did the rest of my jobs for the day, then returned to my bedsit till the night shift started. I missed putting that key in the door and hearing my mum's voice, I think I missed that more than anything, no matter what had happened, no matter where we had lived, she would be there to greet us when we came home, but, I *was* coping much better at being alone now, I could watch Tv without my mind drifting too much, the thoughts were still there at the back of my mind waiting for an opportunity to shine through, ready to question why I had no answers yet. One day I told them, one day.

Every week from then on, I had that one thing to look forward to, my visit to Fiona, she knew me now, although she definitely didn't trust me, she still looked past me to see where Sam was, I think it comforted her knowing he was nearby, she craved that familiarity, in a life where she had no one, he was her constant. It saddened me that the only person in the world she trusted was her drug dealer. I wished so hard that there was something I could do for her, but there was quite literally nothing, not now anyway. I could only hope a point would come when she learned to trust me, maybe even enough to become her friend. She looked like she could do with one, and if there was one thing for absolute certain, I could too. She took her drugs and gave me the cash, I'd been coming for about five weeks now, and I'd barely even had eye contact from her, I smiled at her as I always did when I took the money she offered, for the first time, she looked up and straight at me, my eyes widened, it was the first time I'd really seen her face, like properly seen her, up close, even with her drawn cheeks and dark rings around her eyes, she was beautiful, she gave an ever so slight nod as she started to shut the door, and I could swear there was just a hint of a smile in there. I was still stood, looking at her door, with a rather inane grin on my face, when I was brought back to the real world by Sam beeping his horn. That was the first time in such a long time I had felt happiness, like genuine happiness that slight nod, and that almost there smile, were like my greatest achievement in life.

Chapter Eleven

My mum always used to tell me, 'you always need to have something to look forward to in life, it keeps you going son.' She couldn't have been more right, Fiona kept me going, I lived for Thursday afternoons, when I could see her again. It had taken weeks to gain her confidence, but I had cracked it, that first real smile, one you couldn't mistake for anything else, it totally took my breath away and melted my heart all in one go, if she only knew what seeing her meant to me. She even spoke to me now, I'd ask how she was, and she would tell me she was ok, and would ask me the same, she was obviously still wary, I couldn't imagine when the last time she had been close, mentally I mean, not physically, to anyone. But each little thing she did, each smile, each nod of the head, every tiny thing she said, made me feel like I'd overcome some massive hurdle in both of our lives. We were healing each other, and I desperately wanted her to know that I would be there if she needed someone, I'd given her my number and told her to call if she ever needed something, or if she just wanted to chat. She'd taken it coyly, and slipped it in her pocket. She didn't call, but I wasn't surprised, it would've been a massive step for her to take, reaching out to someone, when you never wanted to rely on anyone but yourself, well, I'd been there I knew how that felt. It was exhausting and lonely.

Sam picked me up early today, it wasn't unusual, he did that from time to time, what was unusual was his mood. He was angry, he didn't say so, but he had a face like thunder and his white knuckles were tight on the steering wheel. "You ok ?" I asked, knowing perfectly well he wasn't. No answer. I didn't push it, I simply sat in silence wondering what the hell was going on. When we left early it was usually just for some early drop offs, but this time we went straight through town, I knew where we were heading, 'White vest guy.' Sam was never the happiest when we went there, but this time he was more than uptight. He was driving way too fast, another thing he never did, he was always super keen to stay under the radar, well that was the idea anyway, in reality, you'd only have to sit on the high street for an hour to see what he was up to, but hey, whatever makes you feel good. Five minutes faster than usual we had pulled up outside the fancy house we had visited many times. I was still confused as to why he even brought me here, he'd never asked me to go in, or even get out of the car. Maybe it was just for back up if he needed it, moral support, a witness maybe, although he may just have picked the wrong guy if he thought there was any chance I could do anything to save him !

As Sam left the car I realised he had no parcel today, that was the first time he'd ever gone empty handed, he'd also parked a little further past the gate than normal, usually I would have been able to see what was happening at the door. Although it was always really tense when he came here, it was also pretty amicable and straight forward.

BANG !!!!

The loudest sound I think I've ever heard shattered my thoughts, I was so startled, I banged my elbow on the door as my arms flew upwards protecting me from some invisible danger.

BANG !!!!

Shit ! Shit ! Shit ! My blood ran cold, literally cold, I was covered in a cold sweat, I grappled with the door handle trying to get out, what the hell was going on, I finally managed to swing the door open and start running towards the gate, I barely made two steps when I heard Sam's voice screaming, "Get in the car ! Get back in the fucking car !" I was back in the car barely before he'd finished the sentence, followed seconds later by Sam himself. "What the fuck Sam ! What the fuck ! What the fuck have you done, shit, mate what have you done ?" He said nothing, he didn't take his eyes off the road, he raced out of the street, screeching around the corner, then immediately slammed on and slowed to the speed of the general traffic. If I had to guess, I'd say it wasn't the first time he'd done this. He didn't like it, I could see that, but he *had* done it before. "Did you kill Joseph ?!" I yelled at him, "Did you ?!" He looked at me now, a mixture of fury and disbelief written all over his face, "Fuck mate, really !? Are you fucking kidding me !" I'd offended him, I didn't care, but I had. "I can't believe you even thought that, Fuck." I was the quiet one now, I'd never asked him the question, I didn't want him to know that I was looking for answers, but now it was time. "Who did then, Sam ? Who did ?" I knew I was pleading, and I didn't care, if a guilt trip got me the answers I needed, then I would beg on my knees if I had to. He didn't answer, and that told me a lot more than he thought it did. He knew, and he *would* tell me…eventually.

For the next two days, I feigned illness, I couldn't face Sam, not after what I'd witnessed, and the truth was, if today wasn't Thursday, I'm not sure I could ever have faced him again. Thursday as you know is the day I see Fiona, the only day I ever really looked forward to, and a part of me was beginning to think she was starting to look forward to it too. She always had a smile for me now, although she still checked Sam was around before I could see her physically relax, I was waiting for the day when it would be knowing I was there that made her feel safe, but, it was going to take time, fortunately for me, the one thing I always had, was copious amounts of time. To say it was awkward getting into Sam's car, was an understatement. He was leaning against the driver's door looking at me, waiting for something, approval ? Forgiveness ? Acceptance ? An apology ? I couldn't give him any of those, so I gave him all I had which was a rather uncomfortable nod. He sighed, but said no more, as he pushed down on the accelerator and took us to our first job. One thing for sure, we were most definitely not going to see 'white vest guy'. I'd gone over and over in my head what had happened that day, it made no sense whatsoever. What could have changed ? What could he possibly have done ? It was obviously not Sam's idea to go smack him with a couple of bullets. It made the news, I heard it on the radio, probably because he lived in such an affluent area, I don't remember hearing about Joseph's murder on the radio at any time. I wondered if my dad's disappearance had ever hit the news, I was too young to have noticed at the time. Not like I could go ask mum or Joseph, every time I had those thoughts my heart sank, my memories just reminding me how alone I was. But I did have 'google' It had never crossed my mind to look before, maybe because mum had always been so honest with us, she'd always answered any questions we had put to her, plus it was so long ago, I wasn't sure there would be anything at all to find. I quickly hit the search box on my phone, and typed in 'Joseph Doyle' I hesitated, placed my phone between my legs, whilst I debated with myself whether or not I even wanted to look, it had been such a long time since any of us had talked about what happened to dad. Maybe I had enough on my plate right now, this was something that could be left for the future. I hit the enter button and closed my eyes knowing there may or may not be something about my dad on that page. It was just a few hits down. MISSING COHM MAN JOSEPH DOYLE. It went on to tell the story of known drug dealer Joseph Doyle who was known to the local constabulary who was last seen by his family on November 2nd 2008. They assumed his disappearance was connected to his illegal activity. They didn't say it exactly but what they assumed was that he was dead, and he was dead because of what he did, which in all fairness was completely true. Nothing I hadn't already figured out for myself ! Seeing it in black and white though, made it all so real.

The atmosphere inside the car was strained to say the least. I couldn't think of a single word to say to him, I still hadn't completely grasped what he had done, I mean surely I wouldn't be sitting here if I had ? I had one goal today, to go see Fi, she didn't love her name, so she'd shortened it to Fi, that was probably the longest, most personal conversation we had ever had, but it gave me hope. Sam and I finished the rest of our jobs, and made our way to Fi's house. For the first time ever she didn't look for Sam, I literally melted inside, she trusted me, after all this time, she trusted me, I was enough for her, she smiled the most amazing smile and invited me inside, I was puzzled, I looked back at the car but Sam was busy on his phone. I didn't know what else to do, so I followed her inside. We had barely gotten through the door, when I realised what was happening, she was already heading upstairs. Oh god no, my stomach turned, and I started to shake, my nerves in pieces. I didn't know what to do, rejecting her was going to make her feel utterly ashamed, but this was more than a step too far for me. "Fi, no, I'm sorry, I can't do that," my voice trembled. "Don't you like me ?" she asked, she looked just like I knew she would, hurt, humiliated and ashamed. "Of course I do, but I can't let you do this to yourself." Her face hardened, "Well, it's either you or Sam, it's up to you." The pain I felt in my heart was culpable, I felt like she was the only person in the world I had, and I couldn't bear to think of her living like this. "Fi, I'll give you the money," I said, pulling cash out of my pocket as I spoke. Wow, I knew she wouldn't be happy, but I couldn't have imagined the angry outburst I did get. She stormed back down the stairs, shoving my handful of cash back towards me as she did, yelling as she went, "I don't want your money, I don't need your charity ! You people think just cause I take drugs I can't pay my way, I take nothing from no-one !" How the hell did this happen, now I understood just how Sam had gotten into this mess ! "I'm not just anyone Fi…am I ?" She looked up, surprised at what I'd said, she didn't answer so I went on. "Fi, I thought we were friends, you have to know I care about you, what if I loan you the cash and you can pay me a little bit back each week, I know you have your pride, but let me do this as a friend." She slumped onto the stairs and sat with her head in her hands, and sobbed. I couldn't help but go to her, to hold her, I needed to do that for her, just as much as she needed comfort from me.

I'm not sure how long we sat in silence in each other's arms, while she continued to sob, and I continued to hurt for her. Our moment was brought to a sudden end, by a car beeping outside, I gave her the drugs, and reminded her she had my number, "You don't need to be alone any more, neither of us do." I kneeled before her and took both of her hands in mine, letting go with one hand for just a moment while I wiped away her tears, "I'm your friend Fi, don't ever forget that." She nodded through her tears, and gripped my hand a little tighter, I knew that was her thanks, and I was grateful that she could give me that. With a deep breath, and an immense sense of relief that she finally understood how much she meant to me, I turned and walked away. Sam as always in these situations said nothing, my business was my business and his was his, unless either of us wanted to share, nothing was ever said. This, I definitely did not want to share, I knew what he was thinking, he thought he knew what had just gone on inside that house, and I was more than happy to let him continue with that thought. Although I'd left her with tears still streaming down her cheeks, I couldn't help but feel elated, she had finally let me in, she couldn't possibly know how much that meant to me, she was after all, all I had left in the world.

To my surprise, and horror, I had almost forgotten that Sam had killed someone just a few weeks ago, it barely crossed my mind, nothing else changed, except 'white vest guy' was replaced by 'crazy hair guy.' Sam didn't seem even half as anxious going to see this guy, he lived in a different area completely so it took a bit longer to get there, but they were the same type of houses, big, gated, full of security. And it was still one of the two jobs I wasn't allowed to do. Fine by me, if it all went tits up, there was absolutely no way whatsoever I would be running in there with a gun ! Yep, suits me just fine.

This guy had the reddest hair, and each time I saw it I thought of my mum, hers was beautiful though, long soft curls, his was wild, I swear it had not seen a brush in...well...ever, it stuck out in every direction, at every angle, and the whole, be it short time Sam was at the door, he ran his hands through it, somewhat pointlessly from what I could see. Sam definitely got on with this guy much better, we had only been twice, but he was so chilled when he got back in the car, I never knew what the problem with 'white vest guy' was, maybe one day I would get up the nerve to ask.

Chapter Twelve

Four months passed and it was all but forgotten, life was good, Fi had completely let me in, and it was the best feeling in the world. I'd never told her, probably never would, but I loved her, I loved her strength, her pride, her ability to keep going in the face of every adversity, but most of all I loved her smile, probably because it took me so long to earn one, now they came freely, and naturally, and each one melted me to the core. It wasn't often she didn't have the money for her drugs, but when that occurred, she was happy to ask for a loan, and she always paid it back in full. I didn't want her to, but I knew it wasn't about the money. And so this was my life now, and strangely, given my history, I was thankful for it. I had not found out anything significant in my search for answers, but all those small things I had learned, would eventually add up to something, I was sure of it.

Sam had bought me a bike a few months back, which meant when he was busy, I could do some jobs on my own, like Fi's, the people he knew he could trust me with, and regulars who weren't phased by me turning up at their door, and that definitely did not include whoever the guy at the aesthetics clinic was, which was frustrating, because for some reason I felt sure that's were my answers lay.

No-one it seemed, knew who the guy at the clinic was, or if they did, they weren't saying, I'd tried bringing it up in conversation with Sam, he seemed surprised that I knew of him at all, he tried not to show it, but I saw his eyebrows raise a little just before he got them under control. "Heard of him…" Sam said, "…couldn't tell you anything about him though." He looked out of the driver's side window as he spoke, I'd suspected he was lying, but this proved it, he couldn't look me in the eye. I didn't have any use for an aesthetics clinic, and I really wasn't their *type* of client, so that wasn't a route I could go down to get in there. I racked my brains trying to think of a way, there wasn't one, and anyway, it's not like the guy was going to be sitting in the back room watching his cash go through a counting machine like the good old days of the movies. This was so much harder than I ever thought it would be. No one in this business could ask too many questions, and no one answered them if they did. I wondered how old I would be before I eventually had a breakthrough. I imagined myself as a little old man, hunched over on my bike, balding and wearing glasses, still racing around doing jobs for Sam, and searching for answers along the way. I actually tickled myself a little at the thought. I did amuse myself sometimes.

One day, after my regular Thursday visit with Fi, they were getting longer so I could genuinely call it a 'visit' now, it dawned on me that she only bought drugs once a week. I don't know why this had never crossed my mind before, I wondered why, but I didn't ask her. I took my bike home before Sam picked me up around tea time. "How come Fi only buys drugs once a week ?" I asked, there was a pause, obviously something he didn't want to share, normally I'd have just let it go, but not when it was about her. "Sam ? Why ?" I waited, not very patiently for the answer. "You won't like it mate." I was already becoming uncomfortable, now I wasn't sure I really did want to know, but I had to of course, "I don't care Sam, just tell me," he paused a minute longer, "She has another…erm…dealer." His lips were pursed now, like they were trying their best to keep the information in, I could see this was going to hurt. "Go on," I said. "So most people just have the one dealer Yeh?" he waited "Yeh ?" "And usually they wouldn't want another dealer stepping on their toes, but I like Fi, everyone does," "Hold on ! What do you mean everyone ?" I shouted now, fear showing in my voice. "She gets drugs from other guys…" he waited, expecting me to get something that I didn't. "Why wouldn't I like that ?" I asked, a little bit pissed that he'd made me worry for absolutely nothing! "Well, you know how sometimes she can't pay…"

Oh god no, oh shit, why was I always so fucking slow. I needed to get out of the car. "Pull over Sam," "Mate you'll be ok," he urged, "No, Sam pull over now !" He flew into the kerb looking at me like I'd lost the plot. I flung the car door open and immediately threw up all over the pavement, by the time I'd finished I was on my knees heaving nothing up from my stomach. How could she not tell me I thought, she didn't trust me after all, I was devastated.

I was sickened, I was angry, but most of all I was hurt, a part of me wanted to go straight to her house and have it out with her, but I really didn't have the right, did I ? I sat in my bedsit, coping the way I always did, by replaying everything over and over again in my head. She'd never even slightly indicated that she even saw anyone else, let alone…had sex with them for drugs, the thought of it sickened me all over again. It wasn't what she was doing that was the problem, it was her life to do with whatever she wished, but she hadn't told me. She was, I assumed, too ashamed to tell me. This alone saddened me to the core. Or maybe, she rightly assumed it was none of my damn business. The thoughts kept on coming, and I prayed for sleep. When it came it should have left a message…all thoughts of desolation will resume promptly at awakening, cause that's exactly what happened. Sam was due to pick me up at eleven, I sent a quick text, 'won't be in till later' I got a ping straight back, 'cool'. Pretty sure if he knew where I was going he wouldn't be quite so cool with it.

I wasn't in any hurry to get to Fi's, in fact a great deal of procrastinating was done before I even left the house. So much so that Sam had text to ask if I was ready yet, 'Not yet' I replied. I took my bike, carried it down the three steps outside onto the street, checked the brakes, checked the tyres, I'd never done this before in my life, and I knew I was simply delaying the inevitable. I haven't been in to see the old guy in a while, I thought, I really should, he's always been so good to me. I loved my mind some days. I rode off in the direction of the high street, looking forward to a catch up with my old friend.

Just as I thought, he was thrilled to see me, "It's been far too long," he said, his arms open ready for the hug he always demanded from me. It had been too long, and I felt guilty at the reminder of neglecting him. Today his hug was more than welcome. I really will have to make the effort to see him more often, I thought. Soon we were sitting together, with a cuppa each and a plate full of assorted cakes and biscuits. He asked how I was, how I was feeling about mum, whether the police had caught the guys, they hadn't, those guys had disappeared off the face of the earth. I'd expected them to make themselves scarce for a while, but something wasn't right, they should have reappeared by now, I'd still not touched the money. The money they would never get from me. We talked about his daughter and his grandkids, he lit up when he spoke of them, and it was wonderful to see someone so happy with their life, quite literally bubbling over with joy. I hoped there would come a point in my life where I could feel just a little of that. People give you different things in the course of your life, you collect all of these little lessons along the way, and what he always gave me was hope. I left his cafe with hope, and that was a pretty amazing gift.

I seriously hoped Sam was wrong, I knew he wasn't, but all I had was just that faint glimmer of hope, I clung on to it like my life depended on it. I couldn't remember the bike ride to her house, my mind had been coming up with so many other explanations for how she got her drugs, none of them a realistic possibility. By the time I reached her front door, I had resigned myself to the fact that she had no choice but to sell herself for drugs, the only speck of good to come from this was that I had been able to stop her sleeping with Sam. I reached up to the knocker, but before I managed to touch it the door opened, standing before me was a guy, around forty years old, looking extremely flushed as he was pulling the zipper up on his jeans. My initial reaction was to smack him right in the face, until I saw the look of shock on Fi's face. She was horrified, it was then I realised I should never have come, what she did with her life was not my business, it was private to her. I had no right to question what she did with herself, except, it hurt, it hurt so much my heart ached. I turned, tears welling in my eyes, ready to climb back on my bike and leave. "Wait !" she cried, and of course I stopped, I couldn't look at her, I couldn't bear to see her in pain. She was crying now, trying to explain, I saw her face, full of shame, in my mind. Never, ever would I have wanted her to feel that way because of me. I turned, thankful that the guy had already left, the hurt, the pain I thought I had felt, was nothing compared to what I felt now, I almost crumbled at the sight of her, and for the first time since we had met, I gave no thought to how she would react, I gave her what she needed, what we both needed, I wrapped her in my arms, and held her until her tears subsided.

I took her inside, and did what my mother taught me, I made tea, before sitting beside her and trying awkwardly to apologise. I succeeded only in making her cry even more, she sobbed into her hands, the piece of loo roll I'd given her was soaked, and she was struggling to control the mixture of snot and tears. My heart was breaking. I couldn't bear to watch, I pulled her close to me, she cried for so long. Maybe she was crying for all those years she had lost to drugs. Sam had text many times, I'd answered none of them. I couldn't let Fi go until she had cried all of her pain away. Even then, I didn't move, emotional exhaustion took over, and she fell asleep in my arms.

Two hours passed, and my phone had vibrated at least five times, and now someone was calling, no matter how many texts I missed, it wasn't like Sam to ever call, but my phone was in my pocket under Fi, and she was in an emotional coma. I didn't want to wake her, but something wasn't right. I tried to slide out my phone without disturbing her, it was never going to work, and it didn't, she woke, eyes still red from all her tears, and looking as exhausted as she had before. She gave me a faint smile as she sat up, as I apologised for waking her. Sam had called four times and I hadn't realised, I smiled at her, held up my phone and headed to the kitchen to call him back. "Where the fuck are you !" he yelled, Sam never yelled, something was very, very wrong ! "I had something to sort out Sam, what's going on ?" "Get to number ten, I'll pick you up there." He was so angry, like even more angry than when he had to go shoot 'white vest guy'. I went back to Fi, made my excuses, and headed for the door, she thanked me, then hugged me like she never wanted to let go. For fuck sake Sam, why now I thought, but this was serious, and I had to leave.

I couldn't for the life of me figure out what had got him so wound up, fuck I hope he hadn't killed someone else. Number ten, was one of the guys he sold drugs to, it was near the high street, secreted away up a little side road. When I took the corner, Sam was pacing up and down the street. Wow this was worse than I thought, I rode up with an air of nonchalance, trying my best to pretend I had no idea there was an urgency. "Where the fuck have you been ?!!" he demanded to know, "I had to sort something out with Fi," I said, actually beginning to feel a little bit unnerved. "Fuck Fiona !!" he said, "Get in the fucking car !" "What about my bike ?" I asked, "Stick it up your fucking arse for me," he yelled. I stood for a minute not really knowing what to do. "Get in the fucking car !" he yelled again. The chain, I thought, there was a chain in his boot for the bike. I went to the back of the car, flipped the boot open and took out the chain, I had it tied to a lamppost in around thirty seconds. Sam was so mad I was sure I must have done something wrong, I started to go back in my head through all the jobs I'd done recently, they'd all gone like clockwork, there was nothing, not one single thing I could think of that I had done wrong.

Chapter Thirteen

"We found them," he said, and out of that sentence all I picked up on was 'We' who were the 'we', I thought the 'we' was us two, who was this other 'we' ? Why that bothered me so much I don't know, but it did. "Who ?" I asked, still completely oblivious as to what was happening. "The guys who burned your fucking house down !" My jaw dropped, and my body weakened, I was unable to say a single word, I could feel him looking at me, waiting for a response. "I, I didn't know you were looking for them," I said it in a voice so quiet I wasn't sure he could even hear it. "WHAT ? You think we were gonna let them get away with that ?" he said, "We knew who they were, but they disappeared off the scene, till last Friday, then we got word they were back." 'We' again ? "Sorry Sam, I really don't know what to say, I mean, I had no idea." I was genuinely stunned. "We've had them in the shed all day, took them in, early hours this morning." What the fuck was the shed ? How can one conversation show you just how much you don't know someone, I mean I wanted them to pay, but now that it was an actual possibility, more than a possibility, an actuality, I didn't know what to do, I was fine running a few jobs for Sam, but I had no idea what he expected me to do with these guys, I'd dreamed of finding them, I'd even thought of all the very horrible things I'd like to do to them, even though I knew I couldn't, I'd eventually settled on calling the police. Well, one thing was for certain, that sure as hell wasn't going to happen now !

The shed was actually a huge barn, we'd driven for probably an hour out of town into the surrounding countryside, I had no idea where we were. It had been a strange and quiet journey, for me anyway, I had no idea what to expect, what I was going to find when we got there, who was even there, now we were here and all I felt was nausea. Sam jumped out of the car, he'd calmed down a lot now. I didn't move, all I could think about was mum lying in that hospital bed, suffering, in pain, knowing she was going to die, I knew it broke her heart that she was leaving me alone. That was enough to get me moving, I needed to remember what these 'dicks' had done, before I faced them again. I needed to remember the pain of being left behind.

I stood in front of two, massive, faded red doors, still trying to figure out whether or not I could go inside. Nothing could have prepared me for what I saw when I did walk through those doors, all I could think was 'who the fuck are these guys.' I had found my answer as to who the 'we' were, and I questioned what the fuck I had got myself into ! The 'dicks' were each tied to a chair, facing each other, although the state they were now in, I doubted very much they could see anything at all, my heart was racing at a million miles an hour as I tried to figure out if they were even breathing. I stood inside the door, looking at these two men, who were barely twenty feet from me, and whilst the sight of them sickened me, almost to the point of throwing up, it was simply because I wasn't used to seeing another human in that state, and not in any way because I was concerned for their wellbeing. Still, I didn't move from the door. There were two other guys in the room, the rest of the 'we'. I watched as Sam laughed and joked with them at one side of the huge empty space, and it dawned on me why it bothered me so much. I was jealous, I didn't know 'other' guys existed, I thought it was just me and him, he'd never once mentioned any one else, then again you'd think I'd have learned by now that I don't know anything at all.

The smaller of the 'dicks' seemed to be doing much better than the other one, he was sitting at least, trying to look defiant, the other guy was awake but slumped, I didn't feel sorry for them in any way, I couldn't, if Sam had brought me in and shown me two dead bodies, I'd have probably vomited my guts up, but I'd have also felt contented, like I did now, I was happy that this part of my life was going to be resolved. I finally pulled myself together, and walked across the room, hardly able to take my eyes off them. Sam stood, he put his arm around me, and introduced me to the other guys. "This, is Conal."

He looked at me with pride, like my dad would have, I realised that was the very first time he had ever called me by my full name, it was the first time anyone had ever called me by my name since mum died. It choked me up a bit, and I stared at the floor while I gained some composure. "This..." Sam said pointing to a young Asian guy, who I thought I might have recognised, but didn't, "...is Tatty," I looked and nodded, "And this guy, is Degs," as he looked at the guy I saw love there, there was respect, I looked from Sam to Degs and back again, trying to figure out the connection. They did look vaguely similar, so there was obviously some family connection there. Sam didn't say any more, but the older guy came over and gave me a massive squeeze, in the midst of the most bizarre of situations, this was the best I had felt in a long time. I had this overwhelming sense that I'd just gained myself a family.

The four of us stood, laughing about all the stupid things we'd done in the past, to be fair, I listened and laughed more than I spoke, I was so immersed in this feeling of normality, I totally forgot there were two pretty fucked up people sitting behind us. I was reminded when the little one shouted, "You fuckin enjoying your little reunion over there !" he yelled this whilst bouncing the wooden chair up and down in temper. To be fair I'd have been pretty pissed off too if I was him. "Oi mouth-piece, shut the fuck up," shouted Degs, then carried on as though no one had spoken, the skinny guy continued to bang his chair up and down, I half expected one of them to get really mad, but after a few minutes, of his continuous banging, Degs raised his eyebrows, looked to the skies, and calmly walked across the room, kicked the chair over, stamped on the guys leg, and calmly walked back, once again continuing his conversation like nothing at all had happened.

I liked this guy, I liked all these guys.

When all the frivolity was over, the other guys walked back towards the doors, I wasn't sure what to do, was I supposed to do something with the 'dicks', shit, surely they weren't going to leave me alone with them, panic set in, my heart racing and my body tensing, I mean I didn't have a problem with them giving the 'dicks' a good hiding, but I wasn't sure I could do it myself. I'd never been more relieved when Sam turned around saying, "Come on mate." Pheeeew, I looked back at the two badly beaten guys, caked in dried blood, one furiously trying to escape his bindings, and I didn't feel one tiny bit sorry for them. They'd felt nothing for my mum, nothing for me, now look at them, I couldn't help but feel smug as I walked away, back towards my new found family.

We went our separate ways once outside, I was treated to another of Degs squeezes before I left, and a warm smile from Tatty. I was on a high, I practically skipped back to the car with Sam, who himself was looking pretty damn pleased. I fidgeted non stop, unable to sit still with all the adrenalin still running through my veins. "How did all this happen ?" I asked, still grinning. Sam recalled with a great deal of excitement every thing that had happened in the last twenty-four hours. I sat and wondered why, why would these people who barely knew me, want to do this for me. "I'll always be here for you mate." I wondered if he'd read my mind. "And they're my family, if I care, they care, my dad knows all about you, I talk about you a lot, you know, I'm so proud of you kid, you've been through a lot, and you're still here every day, moving forward." Ahh so Degs is his dad, that made a lot of sense, as much as Sam had done some things, that still didn't sit well with me, I had always felt safe with him, I'd always known he would be there if I needed him, I could see where he got that from now. I smiled, remembering my dad, I was so young when he…well died, disappeared, doesn't really matter which, I didn't have him, and that hurt. Would we have been like Sam and Degs, I suspected that maybe we would.

I had so many questions about the 'dicks' and for once, Sam answered every one, more than likely because this was my business, and he was happy to talk to me about that. I just had to learn to keep my nose out of stuff that didn't concern me ! I was exhausted from all the information my brain was deciphering, so I was gutted when we pulled up at number ten and I realised I still had to bike it back home, back to reality. I unchained the bike, threw the chain in the boot, and said my goodbyes to Sam, well I tried to, he cut me off half way through, looking at his watch, he said, "Erm, where do you think you're going ?" I pulled out my phone and checked the time, it was dark out and it felt like we'd been gone for hours, shit, we still had work to do, I laughed it off, secretly devastated. Sam passed me a parcel and gave me the address. "Thank you Sam," I said, with the utmost sincerity, "No worries," he said. "I don't just mean for today, Sam," he took a deep breath, gave me a tight lipped smile and said, "I know mate, I know." He drove away, and for the rest of the day, things returned to normal, my normal.

Sitting in bed that night, I truly felt like I had achieved something, although I'd played no physical part in bringing those two down, I still felt a sense of accomplishment. This would normally be the point where my brain decides to tell me, beating people to a pulp is not a nice thing to do, and how on earth did you get into this mess, and what do you think you're playing at, and what would your mother think! Tonight…nothing. I was finally at peace with who I was, with what I was trying to do, and with the fact that people were inevitably going to get hurt along the way. Sadly, the reason I was in this game was, all the people I loved had indeed got hurt along the way.

Slowly opening my eyes, letting them adjust to a new morning, I knew instantly something about me was very different, there was no overwhelming sense of foreboding, the one which had met me each day as soon as I opened my eyes for as long as I could remember. The room seemed brighter, or maybe I was just seeing it more clearly than I had done, I noticed things I'd never noticed before, there was a picture on the wall opposite my bed, and yes of course I knew there was a picture there, but I'd never looked at it before, it wasn't some amazing piece of art, but it reminded me of being a kid, going to the beach with mum, dad and Joseph, it was a painting of a coastline, sand and sea, with a small fishing boat bobbing just offshore, it was bright and sunny, and gave the impression of being somewhere exotic. I felt more relaxed than I think I'd ever felt, maybe accepting my path in life, had taken away all the pressure of trying to change. I wondered what Sam's plans were for the two idiots in the shed. I mean surely they couldn't keep them there forever, could they ? Not that I cared, my mum died in the most despicable way imaginable, it was no skin off my nose if they did too.

When Sam picked me up, I expected some discussion about them, but he said nothing, we got on with work, just as we did every other day. When evening came and he'd still not mentioned them, I had to ask, "What will happen to them, Sam ?" "Don't know yet mate, depends on them I suppose." I tried to work out what he meant by that, when I couldn't, I asked, "What do you mean ?" "Well, the big guy, think he said his name was Mark or Mick, or something like that, he gets what's gone on, he gets he had to pay and he gets that nothing, and I mean nothing will come back on you." Oh, I thought, I get it, now, Sam went on, "But the other one, mouth-piece, don't know what we're gonna do with him mate, he's still being an arse at the minute, but hey, time will tell, you don't need to worry about any of it though." He ruffled my hair as he spoke, then punched me in the arm just to show he wasn't being too soft.

I went to the cemetery that day, because although I didn't feel the least bit guilty for what was happening to those guys, I knew it wouldn't sit well with mum. I tried my best to explain to her why it had to be that way, knowing full well she would be looking at me with that 'who are you trying to kid' look on her face, Joseph on the other hand would be shouting, 'YES ! Well done kid'. That's all I had now, imaginary conversations, with invisible people, but I have to say, I always left feeling like I'd been close to them, I always felt a connection, and I almost always left with a smile. With a deep breath I walked away, leaving my family there in the ground, again.

Thursday came round quickly this week, only because I'd already seen Fi, I'd text her in-between and she was doing ok, it didn't seem weird at all which was a massive relief. I always took my bike now when I went to hers, it used to be a two minute job, but now I was always there for at least an hour. It would have been longer if I didn't have other shit to do. I knocked and waited, she knew it would be me, I came around the same time each week. No answer. I knocked again, I shouldn't have been that concerned, it had been literally just a few moments, but I knew instinctively something was wrong. She was probably just on the loo, I told myself, I waited a minute then knocked again. Nothing. I knocked as loud as I could, my anxiety levels were rising by the second, I knew this feeling, I knew when things were wrong. 'You're always wrong about stuff' I told myself trying to bring some rationality to my thoughts. I went to the window, and squinted as I tried to see through the dirty net curtains, the kitchen door was open, so the light was coming in from the window in there, I could see the floor and one side of the room, it looked like maybe she was on the end of the sofa, I tapped on the window, there was no movement inside, in sheer panic now I started banging on the window shouting, "Fiona ! Fiona !" I swear I saw something move in the pile on the sofa. Then I saw her leg drop out from under the blanket, she was in there, I banged harder on the glass thinking maybe she was sleeping, but still she didn't answer. Without giving it a minutes thought, I went back to the front door, smashed the glass panel with my elbow, shoved my arm through the broken glass, my coat getting caught on the shards, in anger I ripped at the pieces, finally getting my hand in enough to open the door, I burst inside to see the tiny bundle on the sofa. My first thought was an accidental overdose, I had to think accidental, I couldn't bear to think she had wanted to leave.

I took out my phone ready to call for an ambulance as I pulled back the blanket covering her tiny body, before I knew what was happening, I was on my knees, the phone dropping to the floor. She was barely recognisable. Oh god no, I'm not sure if I said those words out loud or not, "Fi, Fi, it's me, Conal, don't you worry now, I'm here, I'm gonna get you some help." She had been beaten so badly, I could hardly find a part of her that wasn't covered in blood or bruises, why would anyone do this, why would anyone hurt her, everyone loved her. I snatched the phone back up from the floor and called 999. Waiting for that ambulance to come, felt like time had stood still, like someone had pressed a pause button, and all I could do was sit on the floor beside Fi and look at her, completely helpless, she hadn't spoken since I got there but she was breathing, and for that I was truly thankful, I couldn't lose anyone else, and especially not her. I heard the sirens in the distance, and covered her up before they came, her dignity was all she had right now. I kneeled on the floor and held her hand until the sirens were outside, soon they were there, asking questions about what had happened, how long she had been there, who she was, what her date of birth was, few of which I could answer.

They quickly moved her onto a stretcher and into the back of an ambulance, I jumped in behind them and sat watching her, I watched as her chest went up and down, 'you just keep doing that,' I thought, 'you just hang on in there.' I couldn't call Sam while I was in the ambulance, I needed to, but I would have to make do with a text. As soon as the text sent, my phone rang, 'Can't Talk Right Now' I text back. I knew Fi was just a little thing, but she was tiny lying on that stretcher, she looked so young, the paramedic kept on with the questions and I answered any I could, it made me sad as I realised just how little I knew. By the time we arrived, she had been connected to several monitors, checking heart rates, pulses, blood pressure, she'd had an IV fitted and was connected to a drip for fluids. Please make it, I begged, please don't leave me Fi.

    I didn't get a chance to absorb what was happening when we arrived at the hospital, doctors and nurses came running, and she was gone before I even had a chance to say goodbye. I was taken to a desk with a window above it, the lady behind slid it open and gave me a warm smile, I relayed all the details I'd already given, as much as I could with the little I knew. My phone started buzzing again in my pocket, it was Sam, I quickly asked the receptionist if we were finished, she nodded and directed me to a small seating area through the doors to her left. I thanked her, and answered my phone. "Where are you mate ? I've been calling for ages." He wasn't angry, he was concerned. "Erm, sorry, I, erm, it's Fi, I'm at the hospital." My brain wasn't working fast enough to form a coherent sentence, but I gave it a shot. Sam made as little sense as I did, "Shit, fuck, I've got to go mate, I'm gonna call you back in an hour, stay there," and he was gone. I had no idea what was happening in my life, nothing, nothing at all made sense to me any more.

Chapter Fourteen

True to his word Sam called that evening and I found out just why his call had ended so abruptly. Sam met me in the waiting room at the ER, I'd had very little feedback from the nursing staff, just enough to let me know she was ok, and they would let me know more once they'd carried out some tests. I was used to it, it wasn't so long ago I'd sat in this very same hospital, waiting for news of my mum.

One of them was gone.

One of the 'dicks' had escaped from the shed. Tatty had gone to check on them just before dinner time, the dirty, disloyal little fuck had left his pal, partner, whoever the fuck he was, right where he was. Mouthpiece was on the loose, and the urgency of Sam's calls were because he had assumed he would come straight for me. I was by far the easiest target, I was the reason he'd been tied to a chair, in the middle of no-where, and given a couple or twenty smacks in the face. It was obvious it would be me he would want to hurt.

In a cataclysmic burst of terror, my body turned cold, my hands shook, and my stomach was ready to empty itself, total panic kicked in as the truth hit home…it was him. Fi was in the state she was in, because of me, she could've died, because of me, because he would do anything he could to make me pay. Without even realising, I had fallen back onto one of the shiny, blue, vinyl chairs in the waiting room. I vividly remembered him that day at the fire, "Get my money or you're next." I was so caught up in these devastating thoughts, I didn't hear Sam's voice, I could see his mouth moving, but there was no sound. I stared at his face, he looked scared, did he know already, all at once the sound came back, so much so that I was almost drowning in noise, there were sirens outside, people talking, doors opening and closing, a TV was on somewhere, and Sam pleading with me to tell him what was wrong. "It was him wasn't it ?" I said. Sam was bent in front of me, one knee on the floor, he put his head in his hands, before turning towards me, with a pained look that told me it physically hurt him, almost as much as it did me, and he nodded. "It has to be, no one would hurt Fi, I can't think of a single soul out there who would do that to her."

He couldn't stay, he was meeting his dad and Tatty, they were out looking for Mouthpiece as we spoke, if he thought he'd had it hard before, it was nothing to what he was going to get. Before he left I had an idea, "Sam wait," he stopped and looked back, "Let the other guy go…" Sam was totally taken aback, "…he's just the sidekick, and… well, now, our bait for Mouthpiece." Sam nodded, he had that look on his face that teachers get, when you finally live up to their expectations. Once he was gone, I got straight back to wallowing in self-pity and guilt. I hadn't seen a doctor or a nurse come through here, there were other people waiting, but they were all chatting or laughing, supporting each other. Loneliness hit me hard, everyone in here had someone, and as usual I was here alone. Quickly I gave myself a figurative smack round the back of the head, to shut myself up. You are not alone I told myself, I tried to remember the feelings of yesterday, the warm feeling you get when surrounded by family, my new family. That gave me some resolve. I sat up straight, and told myself 'no matter what happens, you will be ok…you always are.'

It would be a further two hours, and several step ups to reception asking if they'd heard anything, before a nurse finally came to the door and called my name. All I could do was pray she was ok, and I did. I was taken through several doors, all the time taking note of which way we were going, a habit learned from never knowing what might happen next in your life. Three sets of doors, a left then a right and we were outside a room with the number 8 on it. The nurse smiled, she told me the doctor was inside, and he could answer any questions I had. I'd had to lie just a little and tell them she was my girlfriend and she had no other family, inwardly thinking…'I'm her drug dealer and she's here because of me'. Noticing how uncomfortable I was, the nurse asked, "Are you ready, or do you need a little more time ?" Shivers ran down my spine as I remembered the exact same words being asked of me, before I saw my mum for the first time after the fire. "No, no I'm good, yeh I'm good," I nodded away, my voice high pitched, my nerves getting the better of me, I took the deepest breath as she opened up the door. I didn't make it past two steps, "Oh god." I couldn't go any further, sobbing, simply no longer able to take the pain, physically or emotionally. I was comforted where I stood, by the nurse who'd brought me in, whilst the doctor and another man, brought over a chair which they helped me into. The other man, I'd soon find out, was a police officer. I didn't really see what was happening around me, the rest of the room was just a blur of machines and people moving, but in the centre clear as a bell there she was, swollen, battered, bruised, and bearing no resemblance to the Fi I knew, to my Fi.

Dr Weiss, had an accent to go with his very German sounding name, it was hard to sound empathetic with such a harsh accent, but he managed to pull it off, just, he smiled from time to time, trying to help me believe things were going to be ok. Although Fi had suffered a severe beating, she really was going to be ok, it would be several weeks before all of her swelling, cuts and bruises faded, she had a broken jaw, but that would heal, she had been given an MRI scan, to check for brain injury, which had come back clear, relief was just beginning to hit me, when my world was torn apart again. Dr Weiss guided me to the end of the room, turning his back to Fi as he spoke, in almost a whisper, he took my hand as he told me, "I'm so sorry Mr Doyle, there is no easy way to say this, but Fiona has asked me to give you some information, which you may find very difficult to hear. As well as all her obvious injuries, Fiona has also suffered a very serious sexual assault." I simply couldn't comprehend what he had said, but instantly my mind conjured up an image I never wanted to see, him, on top of her, while she fought for her life, ripping down her pants, and pushing himself inside her, I could see her face, screaming in pain and humiliation, and I could see his, contorted in pleasure and revenge, while her tiny body could do nothing to stop him. I needed to be sick, I looked around the room holding my hand to my mouth, the nurse guided me to the corner of the room and opened the door, I didn't shut it behind me as I raced to vomit, I kneeled as I spewed, my face a mixture of vomit, snot and tears, and then I screamed, like I had never screamed before, rage consuming me entirely. I left without speaking, without saying goodbye, my face still covered in remnants of my devastation. "Sam, tell me what's happening ?"

Sam was waiting outside the hospital doors, jumping into the car next to him, I filled him in along the way on everything the doc had told me, my revelation hit him hard, his only reaction was to bang his fists three or four times on the steering wheel, shaking his head, and putting his foot down. They'd not found Mouthpiece yet, but they had let his pal go, making sure someone wasn't far behind him. It wouldn't be long before he was tempted to come out from his cesspit, or for Mark to find him for us. Sam was taking us back to the place where they'd first found them, obviously there was no chance of them still being there, but we might just find something that could tell us where they might be now. Sam did have a couple of other people to see, they knew Mark and Mouthpiece, and they might have some clue as to where to find them. We came to a stop outside a simple terraced house, didn't look too shabby apart from the front door hanging off, courtesy of Sam, I presumed. Pushing the door to the side, we walked cautiously through the house, it was a simple two up two down, so there wasn't too much to see. It was sparse, and surprisingly tidy, there wasn't much around as regards paperwork, letters and such, and what there was gave us no clue whatsoever as to where they could be.

Sam was on his phone as we left, arranging to meet 'Charlie'. Soon we were pulling up on the high street, just outside my favourite little cafe, I waved through the window, as the old guy caught my eye, always with that little sense of guilt that I had neglected him, he never gave me any indication that he thought that way, all I ever got from him was warmth and a smile, I smiled back, before putting my head down and following Sam. At the end of the street, there was a tall, very thin, very pale guy, looking slightly unkempt, waiting for him, Charlie I presumed. They got to talking straight away, as Sam shook his hand. They seemed to be more than just 'drug dealer' and 'druggie', but maybe that was just Sam, he tended to treat most people with respect regardless of who they were or their history, guessing that came from his dad, he seemed that type of guy. I stood back, only a little, I didn't know this guy and he and Sam seemed to be doing just fine without me. Within a minute or two, Sam was on his way back to the car, showing me an address he had written on his phone. This was where Mark lived. "I thought your dad was following Mark anyway ?" I was a little confused, why were we looking for him if they knew where he was. " We're not looking for *him*."

Turning into the street where Mark was supposed to live, I started to feel uneasy, maybe it was just the adrenalin flowing, but something didn't feel quite right. "He lives here ?" I asked, "Doesn't look the type of house he would live in." This street was full of well kept houses, with perfectly manicured gardens, with several elderly people tending them as we drove slowly past. "His mum lives here," Sam said, "He lives with his mum ?" My heart sank, and I rubbed my face with my hands, trying to tell myself this was ok, but it wasn't, "I can't do this Sam, this has nothing to do with his mum." I was far too emotional for this right now. "Calm down mate, we're not gonna do anything nasty, just need to go and ask her a few questions, come on, you know me better than that." He looked hurt that I'd even questioned it. I nodded a couple of times, whether to myself or him I wasn't quite sure. "You can wait in the car if you like ?" I thought about it, but only for a split second. "No, no, I'll come with you, I need to do this." We parked a couple of houses away from the one we were going to. One thing Sam never did, was look out of place, he never looked suspicious, he never looked around him to see who was watching, he always looked for all the world like he fitted in anywhere. I put my head down a touch and followed his lead.

Mary was lovely, she could have been anyone's mum, she was a bit older than I thought she was going to be, slightly overweight, but well turned out. I couldn't really remember what Mark looked like, and so had no idea whether he looked like her or not, and why I was even thinking that, was a complete mystery to me ! "Hi, you must be Mary," Sam held out his hand, which she took, looking obviously puzzled as to how he knew her name. I hope she didn't notice me looking equally puzzled, "We're looking for Mark, he was supposed to meet us this morning, but he didn't turn up ?" Sam sounded so convincing, I'd have believed him if I didn't know better. She smiled now, "Oh, I'm so sorry, I've not seen him for a couple of days," she said, "Comes and goes as he pleases these days." She looked saddened now, "You know since he's been hanging round with that other one, what's his name ?" she thought for a while, then pointed saying, "That's it ! Karl !" She was pleased with herself for remembering. "Oh Mary, you want to keep him away from that one," Sam said, she beamed now, someone on her side, oh he was good, "He's bad news that one you know, listen Mary if I manage to speak to him, I will try to have a word, see if we can't make him see sense." He cupped her hand, which she welcomed, as she cupped his too. We said goodbye, and walked towards the gate at the end of the path, half way down Sam stopped, turned to Mary and said, "You wouldn't know any where else he could be would you," without batting an eyelid, she said, "He could be at Gregs house, they were always such good friends," Sam turned and grinned, winked at me and said, "We've got him." After waiting for

Mary to ' just pop that address down on a piece of paper' we were on our way to Gregs house.

My mind went into overdrive on the way to our next stop. Mary seemed like such a good person, nice, kind, just your average mum, who was worried about her son, it seemed to me that maybe Mark was just one of those damn fool people who got dragged into something they knew nothing about, and was now paying a very high price. Guilt started to kick in, he was a sorry excuse for a man, who'd got himself caught up in something he had no control over. I felt sorry for him, I knew I didn't have to, but it was becoming more obvious as the picture started to build that this was all about Karl, he was the ringleader, he was the horrible little fucker who had no respect for anyone, and it was his fault my mum was dead. I knew before we reached the house that we were finished with Mark, we just needed him to lead us to Karl, that would be enough for me.

Greg lived in a slum, there was no other word to describe it, he was obviously failing disastrously at leaving home, and taking care of himself, his mother must have been mortified. But he was an average guy, who at this moment in time, looked completely terrified, he was stood with his back against the wall, eyes wider than any I had ever seen, trying his best to string a sentence together. Mark wasn't there he told us, eventually, we knew that was true, there was no way he would have dreamed of lying. "Any idea where he is ?" Sam asked, "He was here, he just went out, but I don't know when he's coming back, he might be back soon or he might be back later, can't really say, I mean he didn't say, or I— " Sam put his hand up and shook his head, Greg took the hint and stopped talking, "Now listen Greg. Listen carefully, you are not going to tell Mark we have been, ok ?" Greg nodded, "We have no issue with you, so don't give us one, we will be back Greg, ok ?" Greg nodded once more, still glued to the same spot. That poor guy had no clue what had just happened, but I felt sure he wouldn't tell Mark we were looking for him. I felt so bad, I even gave him an embarrassed smile and a wave as we left, which left us both feeling very awkward.

Sam was quiet in the car, we sat for a good few minutes before I broke the silence. "What next ?" I asked, "Nothing," he said and grinned, "Degs and Tatty are at the other end of the street, and Buzz is still on Mark's tail." I laughed, I couldn't help it, how did he always do this without me even noticing. "We won't do anything till he's inside, we're looking for Karl, remember, I'm praying that's who he's gone to meet up with." Two hours passed and there was no sign, Sam had called his dad several times, no-one had seen a thing. Surely we couldn't stay there all day, Sam had stuff to do, this was a lot of time out of their day, in the strangest way, it showed me just how much I meant to them. I wish I could tell them how eternally grateful I was for the support they were giving me, but I didn't want to sound like a sissy, so I kept it to myself. Then it happened, there they were, I worried I wouldn't recognise *him,* but I did, hunched over with his hood up, trying to hide his battered face, in an instant I went from feeling the warmth of my replacement family to a rage I could barely control, my first instinct was to jump out of the car, sensing this, Sam put his hand gently on my arm, and shook his head slowly. I breathed deeply waiting for the time to come when I could let that rage out.

As soon as they were inside, and the door was shut, we made a move. I expected Degs and Tatty to be there too but it was just Sam and myself. I wasn't sure what to expect, were we going to kick the door in ? What I didn't expect was for Sam to whip a key out from his pocket and very quietly open it, it had barely opened enough for us to see in, when we saw him running through the house towards the back yard, I started to chase after him, and was promptly yanked backwards, "What the fuck Sam !" I yelled trying my best to get out from his grip. Before I finished arguing, Karl was being frogmarched back through the house by Degs and Tatty, I looked from Sam and back to them. While I had my chance, I ran at him and threw the hardest punch I've ever thrown in my life, not that I'd had the chance to throw that many. I was disappointed, I didn't feel better, I didn't hit him as half as hard as I wanted to, it changed nothing. "Hey mate, come over here," I walked back to Sam trying to wipe the tears from my cheeks before he saw them, while the others left with Mark and Karl in tow. I didn't know what they were going to do with him, and I didn't care. Nothing was ever going to make me feel better, nothing was going to make the whole situation go away, and nothing was going to make Fi not raped, or mum not dead. I sobbed into my hands, thankful that there was just Sam left in the room. I asked myself, how much more one person could endure.

Sam held me until I had cried enough, I straightened myself up, wiped away the remnants of the sorrow I felt, and headed for the door. "Where did they go ?" I asked, "Back to the shed, they'll be safe there till tomorrow." That's what they said last time I thought. "I need to see him," I said, climbing back into the car. I was running purely on adrenalin now and getting real high pitched, and very over excited. "You will," said Sam, "But not tonight," although I stopped to look him dead in the eye, I didn't argue, I didn't have the strength for one thing, and for the other, I finally trusted Sam, I knew he would do what was best for me, it seemed he always got everything right, and so tonight I would go home, to lay on my bed and let my mind take me to places I never want to be.

Chapter Fifteen

I slept, but not well, I had a horrible dream, my mum was running away from me, she was holding someone's hand, but I couldn't see who, it looked like it could be a child, she kept turning, with such a pained look on her face, she was terrified of what might happen, then she stopped running, I stopped chasing, she turned slowly to reveal the face of the person she was shielding, a smirking Karl. I started to run again, anger spurring me on, when she turned once more, I thought she was fleeing from me again, but she stopped, this time she turned and gave me the most wonderful smile, as she pushed Karl off the edge of the cliff we were now standing on. I woke, gasping for breath, my arm outstretched trying to reach for her. I did what we all do, I tried to make sense of what I'd just seen, and of course I couldn't, she obviously wasn't trying to save him, she was trying to save me from doing something I might regret. Was she telling me not to do this, or was she telling me he should die, I mean, dreams were just jumbled up thoughts, not premonitions or advice lines, weren't they? I tried to push it away, but that was easier said than done.

At some point I would need to visit Fi, I was putting it off, not because I didn't want to see her, simply because I couldn't bear to see her like that, selfish I know, I didn't even know if I could face her knowing I was responsible, but I couldn't stand the thought of her thinking I was ashamed of her, or worse, that I didn't care at all. I would go, but we had something to deal with first. I was up and ready at the crack of dawn, having not been able to get back to sleep after that dream. I'd decided mum was telling me I shouldn't do anything to him, but she understood if I felt I had to, I didn't know the answer to that yet. Sam was already on his way, it didn't seem to matter what the time of day or night, he was always there, always available, when did this guy sleep, I mean I'm assuming he did, unless he was a vampire, which doesn't exist, so obviously not ! Now come on now brain, let's stick to debating the real shit in the world ! I was feeling really skittish this morning, didn't quite know what to do with myself, I made a cuppa I couldn't drink, I needed food but didn't want it, I swapped my jacket twice, I'd sat on the sofa, sat on the chair, I'd been up and down to the window at least ten times in the last five minutes. I guessed it was the unknown, I still had no idea what their plans were for Karl.

We pulled up outside the shed, somehow it looked bigger today, my fresh morning eyes taking everything in more clearly. It was huge, and parts of it were falling apart, the doors were barely hanging on, but once they were locked from the inside they fitted quite nicely in their hole. But it didn't matter how big it was or what it looked like, it was where it was that was important, out in the middle of nowhere, surrounded by fields, an abandoned farmhouse, and some dilapidated out buildings. Degs and Tatty were already there, and by the state of Karl, they'd already made a start on today's business. Poor Mark, I swear he had no idea about half the stuff that had happened, he'd been there at our flat when they came asking for cash, but I'd never known whether he played a part in setting fire to our house, and I'm 100% certain he had nothing to with the... I couldn't even think the word again, let alone say it. He had nothing to do with what had happened to Fi. There was, it seemed, nothing much for us to do, Tatty had already managed to find out all we needed to know. Mark was not responsible for the arson attack, and he knew nothing of what had happened to Fi. Karl was in no fit state to answer any more questions, and so the only thing to do was to take a seat and start on the bacon sarnies Tatty had kindly brought. It may have seemed like a waste of time being there at all, but just seeing that bastard, tied up and barely breathing, was enough to make the whole thing worthwhile. Soon it was time to do what I'd been putting off.

I stood outside the hospital room door, taking deep breaths, trying my best to not look like this was the last place on earth I wanted to be. Practising my, you look fine, face. It would be so much easier to walk away, I mean to be fair, she wasn't my responsibility, I didn't owe her anything, I'm sure she wouldn't even expect me to be here, and of course I knew that was all a pile of crap, she meant everything to me, and the only reason for my hesitation, was the cowardice in me not wanting to see her hurt and not wanting to feel guilt. One more deep breath, accompanied by a fake smile, and in I went, I was shocked all over again to see the state she was in, she turned towards the door, and was obviously surprised to find me standing there, that on its own made my heart ache, for her to think no one cared, that *I* didn't care, to think that I wouldn't be there for her, hurt me deeply. But nothing could have prepared me for the destruction of my soul, that her tears brought. Rushing to her bedside I pulled her gently from the pillow, and cradled her head against my chest. "Oh Fi, I'm so sorry," I said and gently kissed her hair. I stayed that way for hours, most of them spent in silence, her in my arms, I could have stayed that way forever.

The moment was disturbed by the ping from my phone I'd been waiting for. "Listen, next time I come, we need to talk ok ?" She nodded, and gave me just the faintest of smiles, sitting with her head slightly bowed, her shoulders hunched, and her hands clasping each other in her lap, she looked so frail, wow, I thought, she is so strong, for all she has been through, here she is, still standing, well sitting, but you get the picture. I kissed her head once more, lingering just a little longer than I should, then I was gone. As always, Sam was there waiting. I felt good now, stronger, I suppose seeing her after what she had gone through, still fighting, still trying her best to smile, made me realise I should get my big boy pants on, pull the fuckers up, and do the same !

Karl was awake. Sam turned and looked at me, concern for me, his only worry, "You sure you want to do this ? We can take care of him, you know ?" "I know that Sam, and I truly can't thank you all enough," his concern turned into a smirk, "Eh, don't go getting all soppy on us mate," he was laughing now, and I had to too, I knew that was exactly the reaction my thanks would get, but I needed to say it all the same. "I need to see him, I'm not sure how I feel about what's going to happen to him, I've never had someone's life in my hands before, not physically any way." I suppose, maybe, I was asking him for some sort of guidance. "And you're not responsible now mate, the only person responsible for 'this', is him, he made his choices, now he has to pay the price, and listen, decisions don't have to be made today, ok ?" I nodded again, I had nothing else to say, but wanted him to know I acknowledged and was thankful for everything he'd said.

Here we where again for the third time in a week, sitting outside a giant ramshackle building, facing those faded red doors, the first time, I was crapping my pants, the second time, I hadn't known what to expect, now I was excited, there was no hesitation this time, I was out of the car and straight through the door, adrenalin was pumping so fast, the ends of my fingers and toes were burning, every nerve in my body was on alert, watching, waiting, knowing something was coming. Mark was nowhere to be seen, Karl was tied to the same chair, but now that chair was tied to some sort of left over farm machinery, each of his legs was tied to the chair leg, and his hands were tied behind his back, a piece of rope was tied around his neck, twice, the other end was attached to the old machine. He was bloodied and battered, neither of which I had any problem with, what I didn't like so much was the stupid fucking smirk he still had on his face. "What do you think you're gonna do kid?" he yelled, looking in my direction, I said nothing. He waited just a moment before snorting and saying, "No, didn't fucking think so, arsehole !" I couldn't believe what I was hearing, surely he must have understood the enormity of the situation here, I was dumbfounded, what did he think was happening here. This wasn't a lesson for him to learn, this was payback. This man had no respect whatsoever, while I stood watching him, astounded by his behaviour, he continued to throw insults at everyone, not that anyone gave a shit, they barely acknowledged him and when they did it was only to laugh. I had to wonder why we were even here, what could we do to him that they hadn't already done, maybe they would just keep him forever, giving him a daily hiding.

Degs and Tatty had put together a makeshift table, and grabbed some old crates to sit on, the other guy Buzz, I'd not met before, as I walked over to where they were sitting, he stood up and shook my hand eagerly, "Nice to meet you son." My face must have fell as he spoke, it had to have by the look on his face, "You ok son ?" he said still holding my hand. Buzz was about thirty-five, he was chunky, and not so tall, had a full beard, and shaved head, but what had stunned me into silence was his wonderful Irish accent, every time I heard one it shook me, it brought so many memories and emotions flooding back to me, all flying through my mind at a million miles an hour. Realising I'd still not spoken, I shook my head trying to shake away my thoughts, and shook back the hand that was in mine, with a huge, wondrous grin on my face.

I sat with my 'family' completely forgetting there was a half beaten guy in the corner, who had now, thankfully, shut the fuck up ! There was talk of what everyone had been up to, all the 'remember when's', talk of old friends, but eventually the conversation came back to why we were all there. My heart sank, I didn't want to remember why we were there. I'd enjoyed forgetting, listening to them reminiscing, catching up and making plans, and I still wasn't sure I could be part of what might happen next. Sam sensing my anxiety, put his hand on my shoulder and said, "Don't be worrying mate, no one is going to do anything you don't want them to, and you don't need to play any more part than the one you want, Ok ?" I nodded, "Yeh, yeh thanks Sam." He rubbed the top of my head and I pulled away laughing, to flatten it down. "Right, let's get this show on the road," said Sam as he stood, and pulled a gun from the back of his jeans. Oh holy fucking shit ! What happened to nothing will happen that you don't want, I didn't want him to get shot for fuck sake. "So, Mouthpiece, want to tell us what you've been up to lately ?" He was standing next to Karl with his gun in his hand, quite casually, he wasn't waving it around screaming and shouting, his arm was hanging by his side. For a change, Karl said nothing, SMACK the gun hit him in the side of the face, oh shit, shit, shit, I don't think I can watch this I thought, even so, there was this small part of me that needed to see it, to see that he had been made to pay. "Want to have a think about that, Mouthpiece," he said. Karl laughed, BANG, he smacked him again, a full back hander the noise was horrific, knowing it was made by a human face, made it all the more sickening. Without even realising, I'd stood up and walked halfway across the room, I looked back to where I had been and was baffled by the sight of the other three, still sitting chatting away about the good old days. I stood in this kind of no-man's land, somewhere between crazy and afternoon tea, thinking what the fuck, what the absolute, actual fuck. This was the most surreal thing I'd ever witnessed in my life. I heard that noise again and grimaced, I doubted it was something I could ever get used to. "Not ready to talk yet, Karly? No ? Cool, I've got all the time in the fucking world." He put his gun back in the waistband of his pants, rejoined his buddies and that was the end of that. I was dumbstruck, I swear I must have been standing there with my jaw dropping to my chest. After giving my head a good shake, and my face a good rub, I walked back to my crate and sat totally gobsmacked.

I'd kind of got myself all psyched up to come in, to not quite enjoy seeing him get another good hiding, although it's what I wanted and what he needed, and then we would all go on our way. But I guess that's what we did first time round, and look what that achieved, I could in all honesty, walk away and leave him there, forget about all of this, forget he existed at all, I can imagine that would be a horrific death for him, but I wouldn't have to see it, or even think about it if I didn't want to. That was definitely going to be the better option for me. It was so horrible though, I was too ashamed to voice my opinions to the other guys. "Come on mate," Sam stood up, and I automatically did the same, "Where are we going ?" I asked, "Still have work to do mate, come on." This day just got stranger by the minute, goodbyes were said, including a sarcastic, "Byyyye, love you," from the Mouthpiece, fuck, this guy was seriously short of a brain cell or two, I could only shake my head and raise my brows, yet again, as we left for a day at 'work'.

Chapter Sixteen

Visiting Fi at the hospital had become part of my daily routine, I'd told them I couldn't get in at visiting time, due to work commitments, so they'd very kindly turned a blind eye to my early morning visits. She was doing great, mentally and physically, she amazed me more every day, we'd still not had *that* talk, each time I thought I was ready she'd given me the most wonderful smile, or reached out for my hand, a moment I couldn't ruin, with what I needed to ask. The first time I'd seen her in that bed, I'd told myself she would be the one who decided what would happen to Karl. I questioned at first whether I was just being a coward, not wanting to shoulder that burden myself, but after a long and arduous debate with myself, I knew it was because she deserved that choice. Now the time had come for that decision to be made. I pulled up a chair next to her bed, took both of her hands in mine, trying my best to get up the courage to look her in the eye. "Conal ? What's wrong ?" she asked, sitting herself up straight, fear in her eyes, "It's not that there's something wrong, it's just…" I paused, I'd thought of so many ways to say this, but none of them sounded right, so I suppose it didn't really matter which one I used, "…the thing is, the guy who, well, you know, the guy who did this to you, well we erm, we know who it is." She pulled her hands from mine and used them to push herself up even straighter on the bed, before wrapping them around herself. After taking a moment to compose herself, she took a deep breath, "Go on," she said. I explained who he was, and why he had attacked her, making sure she could tell me what he looked like, just to confirm for my own peace of mind that we had the right guy. She looked me in the eye the whole time, whilst I glanced from side to side, feeling more and more uncomfortable. "I'm so sorry Fi, I had no idea he even knew who you were." She looked horrified, "You don't think I blame you, do you ?" I paused, stunned, "But Fi, he wouldn't have done this if it wasn't for me." Reaching for my hand again, her face softened, and she smiled, "Oh Conal, it's not your fault, you couldn't have known what would happen, you were only trying to get justice for your mum, please don't worry, please don't blame yourself." Placing my forehead on our hands, I asked myself 'where the hell did you find this woman', I lifted my head to meet her eyes, I needed to see her reaction, "The thing is, we've found him."

Her body tensed, her grip on my hand tightening, I could see she was trying not to show any emotion, but her body and her eyes betrayed her, of course they did. I went on, "And you see, the thing is, I need to know how you feel about that, I need to know how you want this to end." She looked totally horrified now, unable to control her feelings any longer. I spoke quickly, "I know this is hard, it's confusing, and scary, I could just decide for myself, I know, but I really do think you deserve a say in this." She leaned her head back against the pillows, and breathed deeply, shaking her head, "I don't know what you want me to say." I knew how she felt, this was not a situation any one expects to find themselves in. It was hard to find any sort of balance, if he got a good beating, would it be enough ? From what I had seen of him the answer to that was a resounding NO, should he be killed, now this sounds like a great idea, until you realise you have to live with the responsibility of deciding that, my idea sounded good still, leave him there to rot, but even that didn't sit well, I had no idea which was the right way to go with this, and here I was expecting her to make that decision at a moments notice. The silence became awkward, both of us I imagined, thinking of a million different ways to end this nightmare. "I can't say I want him dead," her voice was low but strong, "But, I have to know he won't come back." The dilemma was of course, the only way to be 100% certain he wouldn't come back, would be to do exactly what neither of us wanted.

I didn't see Karl at the shed for the next three days, and I had no idea whether any one else did, I didn't ask and they didn't offer the information, we continued to work, I visited Fi, who by the way was so amazing she totally blew my mind, this girl had giggled and laughed her way through the last few days, she was looking great physically too, the swelling had gone, and the bruises were beginning to fade. She had been on morphine for her pain, amongst other things, this could be a great break for her, if she could go this long without the drugs, maybe she was ready to get the help she needed to stop altogether, she'd made me beam with pride, she was due to go home today, and I knew that was going to be difficult for her, it was difficult for me too, I didn't want her there alone. I thought of asking Sam to find her somewhere new, but what I really wanted to do, was pick her up and take her home with me, where I knew she would be safe, where I could see her every day, where we could both be there for each other, I did after all, need her just as much as she needed me. After another battle with myself, I made the decision to ask her to come stay with me, even if it was just for a little while, just till she was strong enough, or felt safe enough to be on her own again.

I'd been sitting on the end of her bed for almost an hour when she said, "Come on, spit it out !" I gave her that 'don't know what you're on about' look, she laughed, "You're forgetting how well I know you Conal !" Oh this girl melted me, she can't have possibly known how much that meant to me, it told me how close she felt, how close we were, and that felt good. "Thing is, we've fixed your house up, and I know you'll be just fine there, but you know how much I worry about you, and I know my place is small, but..." she cut me short, holding her palm up to stop me, "If you're asking me to come stay with you ..." my heart was beating so fast by now, nerves, anticipation, you name it I felt it, ".... I'd like that." Oh shit ! She said yes, oh holy shit, she really did say yes, I'd prepared myself for the rejection, for feeling let down and hurt when she said no, but shit, it took a second or two to sink in, then she was in my arms, I squeezed her so hard, she could barely breathe, when I released her I revelled in the sound of her laughter ringing in my ears. "I'll be back around five to pick you up." I left feeling completely overwhelmed with love, brimming with happiness, right there and then, in that moment, life couldn't have gotten any better.

Today was judgement day, today we were going back to the shed, anxiety was rearing its ugly head once again. The thought of walking in there to find him gone again, filled me with terror. I wasn't sure having him on the loose again was something I could deal with. I'd made some decisions over the last few days, I couldn't be the man who condemned someone to death, but I could be the man who allowed him to suffer for as long as it took for us to break him. Sam was waiting as always, "You ok mate ?" "Yeh, yeh I'm good," I couldn't hide the bloody huge, ridiculous grin on my face, as I remembered Fi was coming home with me later that day, which set me up for some stick along the way. "So, what's got you so happy today ?" he said, wiggling his eyebrows, "Nothing !" I couldn't help laughing at the sight of him smirking at me, waiting for me to spill. "Aww did Fiona make you smile," he teased, "Shut it," I said, still unable to stop smiling. "Come on mate, spill the beans." I didn't know how he would react, but there was one way to find out, "I asked her to come stay with me for a while, you know just till she feels better, it must be hard for her, she must be scared, and I'd rather..." he stopped me, "Hey mate, you don't ever have to explain yourself to me, if that's what makes you happy, go for it," I nodded, "It does, I need to know she's safe Sam," "Course you do mate, now let's go make sure she stays that way !" I took a punch to the arm, which always frickin' hurt like a bitch, then sat back and watched the world go by as we made our way out into the countryside.

Degs and Tatty were waiting outside when we got there, my heart skipped a couple of beats, I couldn't decide what that meant, were they waiting to break the bad news ? As I climbed from the car I could hear them talking, they didn't seem stressed or concerned, so I allowed myself some relief. Sam went straight to his dad and hugged him, just as they always did. "How's he doing ?" said Sam gesturing towards the door with his thumb. "Still mouthing off," said Tatty, looking very bored with Karls behaviour. "You'd think by now he'd have at least learned a bit of respect, but nope, swear there's no brain in that lads head !" "Tatty's already give him a fucking good dig, he just laughs it off, you know what they say, where there's no sense, there's no feeling !" Degs added, "Gonna be a long one this son." Sam agreed, "You all ok with that ?" he asked, there was a unanimous yes, hands were shaken, hugs were given and I was totally blown away, these people barely knew me, and yet they were committing themselves to god knows how long, to make sure justice was served.

It was time to go inside, I followed behind the others warily, not having much idea what we were going to find. What we found was, Tatty had given him much more than a good dig, so much so I wondered how he was speaking at all let alone mouthing off, as if he could read my mind, he proved he could do just that, "Oh here he comes, how's your little slag doing ? …Mate !" I was already making a run for him, when I was stopped by Tatty's arm swinging out in front of me, "Rule number one, he gets a dig when we say so, not when he asks for it." He started to laugh, but it worked, Mouthpiece turned his fury on him instead. "Yeh you're hard aren't you ya shithouse wouldn't be so tough if I wasn't tied up would you ?" How they had sat and listened to this shit for any length of time was beyond me. I was still furious, pent up and sickened from that one remark, I was on edge, full of adrenaline once again, how on earth did they stay so calm. I wondered just how many times they'd done this before, obviously more than once or twice, that's for sure. Now I got where the saying 'like a walk in the park', came from, they really could be taking a walk in the park, it was that easy for them.

"So what are we doing with him ?" My stomach turned as Degs asked the question, he was looking straight to me for an answer. I wanted to tell him what we had decided but it felt so stupid now, I could feel my face burning, flushed with embarrassment. "Erm, well the things is, I, We, me and Fi that is, we were saying like, how, like we don't really want him dead, but obviously we don't want him to be able to just go back and do the same again, so I just don't know what to think." I realised I was rambling, so I stopped when I could. "Yes you do," Degs was looking at me again, "I do what ?" I said, confused, and a bit concerned, "You do know what you want, and it's ok to say, we're not barbarians here son, and there's no rush, we just need to start making a plan, you know, people here have jobs to do, and whatever's gonna go on here needs to be factored in to that." Right here goes. "Well we were kind of hoping we could just keep doing this till we break him, I mean I don't know if that would work, or if that's possible, or like if you'll have the time, I mean I understand if you don't, it's just…" "Jees son, take a breath !" said Degs, pulling me to his chest, "We told you son, whatever you want, as long as it takes, if that's what you want to try, then that's what we will try, but remember things change with time, you might feel differently, next week, next month." God the relief of finally getting that off my chest, was breathtaking, I mean I quite literally felt as though I had no breath left in me.

Things change, like he said, and no one knows when that will be, could be over time or it could be in the blink of an eye. Mouthpiece was off again, and it seemed that Sam had finally had enough. He walked over and asked one simple question, "How long have you got ?" Mouthpiece spoke through bruised lips, staring, as much as it was possible through half closed eyes, he spat in Sam's direction, forcing Sam to take a step back, and said with a grin, "Got all the time in the world me." Sam backhanded him, and as usual Karl laughed. This time Sam punched him full force in the face, he hit him again and again, until Karl stopped laughing. I don't think I'd ever seen Sam lose his temper, he'd been angry, but he'd always had complete control.

Walking back to the little makeshift table, he rubbed his fist and said, "Little fucker." They all burst out laughing when Tatty added, "Can't believe you forgot Rule number one !" Karl was quiet for a while, although not by choice, there was a welcome break in the high levels of testosterone in the room, everyone was calm again, soon it would be time to get back to work.

I still had to pick Fi up, so we needed to leave soon. I'd quite literally just begun to relax, and he was off again. "Hey arseholes, why don't you just wank each other off and have done with it." What the fuck was up with him, I mean I get he wasn't happy, but purposely trying your utmost to piss off the very people who are more than happy to hurt you, seemed like a really fucking bad idea to me. No one moved, but Sam wasn't happy, I could see he'd had enough, and I wondered whether I was being fair to any of these guys, keeping this going indefinitely. Sam lasted approximately five minutes, which was four longer than I expected given how hyped he was, "Sorry guys," he said, "I'm just not in the mood for this arsehole today, his voice grates on my nerves !" I fell into step with him, back to the other side of the room, I should do something I thought, this was my fault after all. I glanced back at the others, and was thankful that they still had no concerns whatsoever, in fact they didn't even look up to see what was happening, 'walk in the park ! ' "What the fuck is it you want ?" Sam asked him as we got close, "Wouldn't mind fucking your little friend here," he said. Even Sam looked taken aback by this comment. I started to panic, and looked back again for some sort of reaction from the others, I was right to be worried, they'd stopped talking now, and we're watching.

The energy in that space was so strong it was like a physical force keeping me on the spot. All of us waiting to see what would happen next, it felt like forever, but I know it had been just seconds, Karl was laughing again, "Yeh I could fuck him good, see if he's any better than his little crack head mate." I was moving now, too fast for Sam to stop me this time, the blows came from some guttural place deep inside of me, and I made every blow that rained down on him count. No one stopped me. And for that I was thankful. When I stopped and took a step back, and looked at the mess of blood that was his face, I was shocked by what I had done. I started to heave and stepped to the side while I emptied my stomach contents onto the dirt floor. No one spoke, no one came to me, and I wondered if they were disgusted with me too. I wiped my mouth on the back of my sleeve and looked over to Sam, he gave me just the faintest smile, and nodded. It was all I needed, I stood up straight, and walked back to his side. Through all of the blood and spit, and the swollen lips, incredibly he started again. "Pity your little slut didn't fight that hard." I didn't have the strength to hit him again, I was physically and emotionally exhausted, Sam took a step forward, but now it was my turn to stop him, I grabbed his arm and shook my head as he turned to face me. "Fucked her for hours, your little slut, did she tell you how much she loved me licking her out." Without a seconds thought, I took a step to the side, reached into the back of Sam's jeans, pulled out his gun, aimed, and fired, the sound reverberating around the room, as the bullet shot Karl straight through the head. I could hear people moving and someone shouting "shit" but I couldn't tell who it was. I turned calmly, handed the gun back to Sam, and walked towards the door. I didn't feel bad, I wasn't disgusted, I wasn't ashamed, I was fucking delighted. "Problem solved."

Chapter Seventeen

Well, my problem was solved, although I was more than a little certain I had just created one great big one for the others. But, they'd manage, I'm pretty sure it wasn't the first time they'd had to deal with this. Leaning on the car, I didn't have to wait long before Sam followed me through the door. "Fuckin' hell mate, you could've give us a fucking clue or something!" He was serious, but not pissed off, not that I gave a shit either way. In an instant I knew I didn't have to worry about him hurting me or Fi or anyone else for that matter, ever again. As far as I was concerned I'd done a massive, great service to the whole fucking community ! As I climbed into the car I checked my watch, shit it was already four o'clock. "Sam I need to pick Fi up at five, you reckon I'll have time to get home and get a quick wash and change before we go," He gave me a look that said, 'that's all you have to say', he shook his head, smiled and said, "Let's see what we can do." With that, he slammed his foot down hard on the accelerator, and we sailed through the countryside. I was home washed and back at the hospital, just in time to take her home.

You know when you wake up, and you forget for a minute where you are, or what's going on in your life, then in a split second, it all hits you at once, that was me. Last night was the best night ever, it felt so good bringing Fi home, knowing she was safe, knowing I could keep her safe every day, it felt like we'd always been together. It wasn't a we, as in a couple, but it was a 'we'. I'd offered her the sofa bed, which meant, obviously there was no sofa for me to sleep on, the floor would've been fine, but she insisted she would be good with us sharing. That must have been hard for her, or maybe she needed someone close to feel less scared. Either way, I held her through the night, and watched her while she slept. She slept peacefully, she was so quiet I had to keep checking to make sure she was still breathing. I realised this was the first time I had spent the night in the same house as someone else, since my mum had died. It was the first time since then, I hadn't fallen asleep feeling alone. Life was good, and that was a strange thing to say considering what I had done yesterday. Now, either it hadn't hit me yet that I had killed someone, or I'd been through so much shit, I really couldn't be affected by it any more, sadly I think it was more than likely the latter. It wasn't that I didn't have feelings for people, I had Fi, Sam, Degs, Tatty, there was very little I wouldn't do for them, but outside of that, I didn't really give two fucks for anyone.

Fi was still sleeping. Sitting on one of two chairs in the kitchen, drinking my cuppa, I couldn't take my eyes off her, she looked so peaceful, so beautiful, and still so frail. I couldn't imagine how, right now, life could get any better. I'd never been more content, in fact I don't think I'd ever been contented, there had always been some issue in my life causing some sort of underlying anxiety, but today ….none. The only thing playing some sort of game with my head, was whether or not to tell her what I'd done, I didn't want to keep secrets from her, and of course knowing he was gone would mean she didn't have the worry of ever seeing him again, but I couldn't bear for her to think differently about me. I couldn't stand the thought of her thinking I was some sort of monster, especially given the fact that I really didn't give a shit. She didn't need to know today, I had time, time to figure out what was best for both of us. I had just under an hour before Sam would arrive and I couldn't decide which I wanted more, for her to stay the way she was, looking like she'd never had a care in the world, or whether I needed to see her awake before I left. Just a little over ten minutes later she took care of that decision for me, she opened her eyes, but didn't move, blinking as she woke, puzzled for a moment, probably trying to work out where, exactly, she was, then there it was, the realisation came with a grin, and she quickly looked around the room to find me. I must have looked like a love struck fool, sitting gawping at her with my own massive grin plastered on my face. "Hi there," I said, "Hi," she spoke so softly, it was like it blew across the room, on the wind. "Tea?" I said, lifting my cup up in case she'd not heard, she nodded, and I jumped up to put the kettle on. We talked about how well we'd slept, how comfy the bed was, she thanked me for letting her stay, I of course told her it was my pleasure without it being a word of a lie. It was the most natural, wonderful experience, waking in the morning, to talk about your night, talk about the day ahead, discuss what we would be doing and what time I would be back. I loved this, I could only sit, and thank whichever god had brought her into my life.

I didn't want to say goodbye when Sam came to pick me up, Fi took my jacket from the hook by the door, and handed it to me, she told me to be careful, take care of myself, I told her I would be home after lunch to check on her. I walked towards the door, she followed close behind, as I turned to say goodbye, she stood on her toes to kiss my cheek, partially touching my lips, resulting in a really awkward lingering moment of, should I go for it or not. Her cheeks turned a perfect shade of pink and we both gave a short embarrassed laugh. Bowing my head to hide my delight, I left quickly before I could make more of a fool of myself.

By the time I'd reached the bottom of the stairs, I could feel shame kicking in, I'd not had time to think about what Sam would say today, or what was going to happen, I'd been too wrapped up in home life bliss to even care. Now it was time to face reality. I got in the car as slowly as I could, lips pursed, waiting for the shit to hit the fan, when nothing was said, I turned still moving slowly, waiting for some sort of reaction from him. He seemed his usual self. This was more unnerving than him having a go at me, was that it now, it was over, we all just got back to normal, got on with our lives ? I tested this theory out, "So what are we doing today ?" I asked, as cheerful as I could muster. "What do you think ?" he answered, I wasn't sure but there may have been a sneer in there. "Well, it's Tuesday, so Number 10 ?" He burst out laughing, making me smile in the process. "Seriously mate ?" he asked with a sudden dead pan face, I had no idea what he was getting at, had I got the day wrong, no, it was definitely Tuesday, "That's what we usually do on a Tuesday," "Fuckin' hell mate, that's what we do on a Tuesday when you didn't kill someone on a fucking Monday !" I felt my face redden, and had no idea how to respond to that. I also couldn't quite figure out why I had thought for one minute, we all just carried on as normal.

Shit ! I killed someone. Oh fucking shit ! Panic had finally hit, all the calm of yesterday was purely a delayed reaction, and now I couldn't breathe, I needed to be sick, I needed to get out this fucking car. "Pull over Sam," "What ?" said Sam, looking confused. "Pull over quick, I'm gonna be sick." I saw him glance quickly in his rear view mirror before pulling into the pavement. As I stood, yet again heaving on the side of the street, I realised I hadn't even looked at Mouthpiece after I'd….Oh fuck I killed someone, fuck, fuck, shit, I heaved again, what the fuck had I done ! Nothing was coming up, but I couldn't stop. Sam was watching, looking super nonplussed, waiting for me to finish with the dramatics.

As I took my seat again beside him, wiping my mouth as I did so, Sam asked, "You finished ?" I nodded, feeling like utter crap, slumped in my seat, wondering how the hell I ended up being a drug dealer *and* a murderer. "Right, time for you to go clean your mess up mate," he said. I sat bolt upright now. "What ??...I can't go back there !" he looked at me in disbelief. "You don't get a choice mate, you clean your own mess up, you decided to be one of the big boys, now you gotta act like one." Oh god I needed to be sick again, I practically curled up, holding onto my stomach, trying not to see the visions in my head of what Mouthpiece might look like now. Why did I do it, fucking idiot, absolute fucking arsehole. The journey out to the barn took nowhere near as long as I wished it had, and when we got there, I actually physically could not get out of the car. "Listen mate," said Sam, "I know this is gonna be tough for you, but you need to do it, you need to put an end to it, finish the job so to speak." I nodded and as he left the car I managed to whisper, "I'll be there in a minute." I sat curled up, wanting desperately to cry, to stay curled up in a ball and let the tears flow. I knew I had no choice, although if I could have stood, I'd have seriously considered getting out of the car and doing a runner ! I also knew behind those barn doors, where three men who were expecting me to do the right thing, I couldn't let them down, and if there wasn't also a very dead body in there I'd have been there in a flash.

I don't know exactly how long I sat there, and give them their due, they didn't harass me, they didn't even check to see if I was still there. But finally I was ready to face the mess I had made. I stool on jelly legs, taking deep breaths, and shaking my hands to get rid of the pins and needles in them. I tried stamping my feet a couple of times to bring my legs back to life, and when I was convinced my body was almost working again, I stood myself up straight, rubbed some colour back into what I guessed was a deathly pale face, ran my fingers through my hair, I straightened my top, and walked into the shed with my head held high. I was met by a round of applause from the three of them, sitting at our little makeshift table where they'd waited patiently for me to get my shit together, and thankfully, together it now was.

Once again they had made me smile in the most adverse of times, I was immediately comforted by them. I'd managed not to look in the corner, just the thought of it had my stomach turning again. As I neared the table, Degs stood and came towards me, "Come here son," he said, wrapping his arms around me, holding me tight, ah crap he was going to make me cry. I tried desperately to stop any tears escaping from my eyes, blinking them away as fast as I could. When he pulled away I spoke to them all. "I'm so sorry guys, I've put you all in a terrible position, I just don't know what happened, I don't really remember that much to be honest." Degs told me to sit down, and as I did, Sam patted me on the back, and Tatty leaned across the table, palm open waiting for mine, I shook his hand and looked at the faces of my family, a family I was truly privileged to have.

"Conal," I hated that, no one ever used my name unless shit was getting serious, my heart lurched, missing more than a beat as Sam said, "Are you ready mate ?" There was no more time for cowardice, he was right, I'd made my choice, whether I was conscious of it or not, and now it was time to, quite literally, clean up the mess. He stood, leading the way to the corner of the shed, I walked solemnly behind him, staring at the floor, still terrified to look up, I'd had a million different visions in my head of how he looked. I was so close to Sam, he must have felt my breath on the back of his neck. I don't know if that was because I needed him close, or whether it was to block the view of a dead man in the corner, I guess a little bit of both. He stopped, I stopped, he stepped to the side, I instinctively shut my eyes, I really couldn't bear to see what I had done. Come on ! Get a grip, it'll all be over soon, I told myself. My body was shaking, I couldn't manage to keep a single part of me still. Slowly I opened my eyes, my legs gave way and I dropped to my knees and broke down, I didn't care who was there or who could see me, I sat on my heels, with my head in my hands and sobbed. On the chair in front of me was some frayed rope, and some blood stains, there was no Mouthpiece, no dead guy with a bullet hole in his head, barely any evidence of something barbaric having happened at all, just the remnants of a nightmare. Sam was kneeling beside me, there was no physical comfort from him, but it wasn't needed, his face said it all, they had done their bit, they had cleaned up my mess, he handed me a bucket, and lay some sponges and towels on the floor. "Never, ever do anything you're not prepared to live with," he said, walking back to the others he turned with a smile and winked. I nodded in acknowledgement of what they had done for me, and got on with the job of cleaning up what remained of my mess, eternally grateful that I didn't have to see the worst of it.

There was just one part of this mess, still left to clean, I had to tell Fi. I had no idea where we were going, but wherever it was it had to be based on honesty, I had to tell her the truth, and face whatever consequences came with it. It was a long ride home, a quiet one, part of me wanted to ask Sam what they had done with him, and part of me really didn't want to know. Maybe it was just a question that needed answering some other time. So much had happened in the last twenty-four hours, I'm sure I could save some of the drama for a later date ! Sam gave me the rest of the day off, so although I was a little late getting back for dinner, it meant I could spend the rest of the day with Fi, if, and it was a big IF, she decided to stay once I'd confessed to her what I'd done. My life appeared to be one long drama interspersed with these tiny moments of bliss, like playing wrestling with our dad, having long chats with mum over a cuppa, like spending my first night together with Fi, beautiful moments, surrounded by heartache and madness.

Just putting the key in the door was an effort, I was emotionally and physically exhausted, and it wasn't over yet, I wished it was something I could put off, but this needed to be over, this was the last day I would give over to that vile, sick bastard of a man. All I could do was pray that she understood. Fi was getting better every day, the bruises were all but gone, she looked happier than I'd ever seen her, and walking in to see her sitting curled up on the sofa, watching tv, truly melted my heart, it was like all my worries disappeared when she smiled at me, like there was nothing in the world but her and me.
"Fancy a cuppa ?" she asked, jumping up and stepping into the kitchen, "Yes, thanks," I said as I joined her, I was surprised when she kissed me on the cheek again, surprised and ecstatic, I always had this big, stupid bloody grin on my face around her, but she didn't seem to mind. She took the two cups back to the sofa, and sat them on the glass coffee table in front of us, and went back to her curled up

position on the sofa, looking for all the world, like that was just where she belonged.

Just get this over with I told myself, just tell her, she picked up immediately on the negative energy I guess. "Hey, Conal whats up ?" She touched my arm so gently, so warmly, that for a split second I almost changed my mind, but what use would that be, it would only leave this hanging over my head, I'd only have to deal with it some other day. No ! There was no putting this off, It had to be done.

I took a sip of tea, burning my tongue in the process, my mind not working for anything other than getting my story straight in my head. "Come on Con, tell me," she looked worried, and that was something I never wanted her to be. Here goes I told myself. "Well, you know I told you we found the guy, the one who, well you know…" I still couldn't say the words, especially to her, "…well the guys, they took him up to the shed, and they gave him a real good hiding," " Good," she said with absolute resolution, "He deserves it." God this is going to get tough. "Well, the thing is, he wasn't sorry, not at all, he said some stuff that none of us wanted to hear." She was listening intently, hanging on every word I said. "He said things that I couldn't handle, things I couldn't bear to hear, and I don't know how it happened, I don't know where it came from, I was just so angry, I can't even really remember what happened, one minute I was standing there, and the next minute I was handing Sams gun back to him." My rambling only stopped when I felt her flinch, pulling herself back, into the corner of the sofa. She couldn't look at me now, she was looking into her lap, with one hand on her chest and the other over her mouth. I couldn't stand it, had I made a mistake telling her, I knew the answer was no, I couldn't live with her, knowing I was keeping something so huge from her. I knew if she ever found out she would never forgive me for not telling her, I wasn't sure which was worse, devastating her now, or doing it later. I waited for a moment, waited for something from her other than horror. "Fi, I'm so sorry, I don't know how it happened, my mind just went blank." She started to shake her head, "I'm ok, " she whispered, it's just a shock, erm, I don't know what to say, I can't tell you it's ok Con, I can tell you I understand, sort of, I think."

The very little colour she had, had now drained from her face completely. I hadn't expected anything more from her, in fact this was a better reaction than it could've been, she hadn't gone running for the hills...yet. "Listen I'd understand if you'd rather not be here, I've spoken to Sam, and he can find you somewhere to stay, if that would be better for you." My heart was pumping so fast waiting for that answer, it seemed to take an eternity, and my heart ached that there was no automatic 'No, I want to stay' but given what I'd just told her, it was hardly surprising. "I don't want to leave Con." Yes ! Oh god yes ! Thank you Lord, I said to myself. I had to control myself, this really wasn't the time for celebrations. "It's gonna take a bit of time to get my head round this," she said, "Of course, I understand, I can only keep telling you how sorry I am, you've been through enough shit without all of this." She placed her hand on my arm, "I think we both need some time to get our heads around this, don't you ?" She was trying to smile, but it wasn't coming easily. The evening was spent almost completely in silence as we both came to terms with yet another catastrophic event in our lives.

Chapter Eighteen

Things changed, of course they did, but not entirely in the way I'd thought they would. Me, and Fi became even closer, like she trusted me completely now, like I had made the ultimate sacrifice to prove to her I would protect her at all costs, and whilst most of the time that felt so good, a little part of me was sad, sad that the closeness I craved had been brought on by the most hideous thing I had ever done, it tarnished what should have been a beautiful step forward in my life. I could only hope that with time, the memory of that night would fade, and I could just enjoy being with her. Not surprisingly there were still more obstacles to overcome, since being in hospital she had been prescribed methadone for her habit, but I knew it wasn't satisfying her. The first couple of weeks she seemed fine, but now she was struggling, and I had no idea why, maybe monotony had set in, while she had so much on her mind, and was still full of adrenaline, she may not have needed as much, I didn't know, all I knew was I needed to help her. It was time to ask her what I could do.

I wasn't sure what I expected her to say but 'I need my stuff' wasn't it. She told me she was desperate, that she hadn't wanted to ask me, she was embarrassed and ashamed, and didn't want to let me down. I tried my hardest to get her to see her GP but she was having none of that, she told me they just wouldn't understand. In the end, all I could do was tell her I would speak to Sam and see what we could sort out. That, for now, seemed to placate her, and she went back to watching tv and eating the toast she had made for breakfast. Bliss, it was sheer, twisted, f**ked up bliss.

Sam as usual, had an answer, he could get more methadone but he would only get her small amounts at a time just when she was really desperate, he knew how dangerous it could be for her to have unlimited access to it, I didn't like the idea, I suppose a part of me dreamed I'd be her saviour, and now that dream was crumbling. Thinking about it, I had been kidding myself, I just didn't want to see it, I'd been ignoring just how hard this had been for her, but now we were in such close proximity, it was obvious she was in pain, she was nauseous, she was agitated, she tried her best to hide it, but she couldn't do that forever. It must have killed her to ask me, but she had to and I had to help. So here we were, not knowing where this would take us, not knowing what the next step would be, the only thing I knew for sure was, I would be there for her every step of the way.

Sam gave me a new job today, I didn't know the place, but I checked it out on my phone and it wasn't too far away, probably about fifteen minutes on my bike. I took my parcel, stashed it in my jacket, and got on my way. It took just about the fifteen minutes I'd thought it would, my heart was racing, not just from the bike ride, but because as I got closer I realised where I was going. This was the street where The Clinic was. Shit ! He's sent me to the clinic, shit ! This is fucking amazing, my adrenalin levels went through the roof, I'd convinced myself from day one, that this was where all my answers lay. My excitement though, was short lived, when I realised I was actually going to a hair salon, about three doors down from the clinic ! So frickin' close !

Surely this wasn't a coincidence though ? Then again maybe it was exactly that ! I was gutted, I'd been dying to have a look inside, see what was going on, figure out who it was, who was running the show, well not today mate ! Walking through the doors of the salon, I felt completely out of place, it was a nice place, everywhere was white, the fixtures and fittings were high spec, and all the staff were in pristine white uniforms, not the type of place I went to get my hair cut, but they all smiled, and one of the young girls came from the back of the room, and took her place behind the reception counter. "Hi, can I help you ?" she said with the biggest smile, she only looked about fifteen, her hair was perfect, her make up was perfect, and she'd obviously spent some of her wages in the clinic up the road, from what I could see of her oversized lips. It had always puzzled me why girls do that, still does. Anyway, back to the job in hand. "Yeh I'm looking for Brad ?" It didn't look to me like there were any Brads here, but she didn't seem surprised or bewildered by what I'd said. "I'll be right back, why don't you take a seat." It was the first time I'd ever been on a job where I'd been asked to take a seat, was I going to have to wait ? She went to the back of the salon, and picked up a mobile phone, she turned her back for a moment, then told me Brad would be along shortly. And so I waited, feeling more than a little uncomfortable and a lot out of place.

The girls carried on with their work, occasionally looking over in my direction, and smiling if I caught their eye. I was fidgety, I always was when I was out of my comfort zone, where the hell was this Brad guy ! Five minutes passed, and the only person who had come in was the woman standing at the counter now, she was dressed designer from head to toe, indicative of the type of place we were in, she wore a long trench coat style mac, six inch heels, she looked about thirty five, maybe, she had her hair up with some sort of clip keeping it in place, I have to say she looked amazing, she was stunningly beautiful, with that air of confidence, that reminded me of Joseph. You can imagine my surprise, when she turned to me and said, "Hi, I understand you have something for me ?" "Erm, I err, I…" I stumbled over the words, one because she really intimidated me, and two because she very obviously wasn't Brad, "I'm sorry, " she said holding out her hand to me, I took it automatically, "You look a little confused, I'm Brad." All I could muster was, "Oh." She laughed a little, I still wasn't sure I should be handing anything over to her, but she seemed to know why I was here. I took out the parcel, it was bigger than the usual ones, but wrapped in the same brown paper. Keeping her eyes firmly on my face, she took the parcel, and placed it in her bag without even glancing at it. She gave a nod, "It was nice to meet you Conal." She turned and walked away, leaving me standing there even more confused than I had been before. What the hell had just happened. I watched her through the window, not moving from the spot she had left me, she climbed into the back of what looked like it could be a Jaguar, and before I'd even had a chance to compose myself she was gone. Glancing around the salon, I was surprised to see that no one else was even the slightest bit concerned with what had just happened, of course, they didn't understand that she couldn't possibly have known my name.

I called Sam as soon as I could, "How did she know my name ?" There was a slight pause before he answered, "Who ?" "The woman, Brad," why was that not obvious I thought. "What ? You're making no sense mate." He did sound genuinely confused, and thinking about what I'd just said I could see why. I tried to explain, speaking as clearly as possible to avoid any more confusion. "Brad ?? The one I took the package to yeh ?" I was checking he was following before I continued, "Yes," he said, "Brad is a she, right, which was a bit of a surprise to say the least, gave her the package, she was very polite, then she said, 'it was nice to meet you Conal' what the fucks that about ?" "Mate I've got no idea what you're on about, I didn't know Brad was a woman, and I've got no clue how she'd know who you were." I knew he was telling the truth, for one reason and one reason only, he wouldn't lie to me, would he ? The whole situation had really thrown me, and reminded me of all the reasons why this whole escapade had started originally, it wasn't that I'd forgotten about it, but I seriously hadn't been working as hard on it as I should. I was no closer to finding out what had happened to Joseph, but to be fair to myself, there had been a whole heap of shit that had happened in the meantime.

I couldn't get it out of my mind for the rest of the day. I finished all my jobs about an hour earlier than I expected, normally my first instinct would be to go home to Fi, but I was still pretty uncomfortable with what had happened. I needed to know more, I parked my bike outside the old guys cafe, it was the end of his working day, so I knew he'd be cleaning up now, getting ready to go home for the day. And as I also knew, the minute he saw me outside, he waved with the same enthusiasm he always had. He made me realise just how lucky I was, there were people out there who had no one, and I may have lost a lot, but I had good people in my life, like George. I sat at the table nearest the counter, where he was cleaning down the work surfaces, he already had the tea on the go, a few minutes later he was sitting down with a tray in his hands, fresh tea, cake and biscuits, he never let me down. Talking with him was good, I mostly told him all the things that were going well in life, top of my list was Fi moving in, of course I didn't tell him why, or what had happened since, and there was definitely no mention of guns or dead bodies ! Didn't really seem like a tea and cake type of conversation. His family were doing well, and he beamed as he told me they were visiting him next week, he was so excited, he'd been into town buying gifts for them all, especially for his new granddaughter, who I learned was called Kitty, after his late wife, this thrilled him no end, but I could see it was also very emotional for him, whilst he smiled the biggest smile, his eyes betrayed him just a little.

Too soon it was time to get home and face the music.

Fi was on the sofa when I got home, the Tv was on, and for all the hurt she was going through, she still managed to smile and welcome me home, "Tea ?" she asked, "Yeh that would be good, thanks," I said, not wanting to tell her I'd literally just finished one. She was in obvious discomfort today, and although I knew what I had in my pocket could ease her pain, I couldn't bring myself to give it to her. I was trying to convince myself that if she just worked through this she would be fine, I mean if she asked for it she could have it, my mind was on fine form, having the usual argument with itself over what was the right thing to do, I knew she would hate to have to ask again, yet I wanted so badly for her to be strong enough to go without, that I told myself, I would wait until she did just that. I felt like an absolute shit for doing it, but she might have changed her mind ? I tried my best to shut myself up, took the tea she had made, and joined her back on the sofa. There was an awkward silence, as we both waited for the other to speak, I really couldn't say it, if she wanted it, she was going to have to ask. "You had a good day ?" I asked. She nodded and smiled, but that was it, shit, this was going to be harder than I thought. It dawned on me that she always sat with her arm across her stomach, this wasn't because she was comfy like that, it was because she was in pain. I wavered just a little before telling myself I was only doing this for her, I had it there if she needed it, but right now she was coping. I hoped she could make it long enough to realise she could do it, she could last a little longer, maybe cut down till she was off it all together. She didn't ask for it, and I went to bed feeling like a total gobshite for sitting by and watching her suffer !

How she still managed to greet me with a smile when I woke the next morning, I don't know, but she did, it should've been so welcomed, but it just made the guilt kick in even harder. I tried my best to act 'normal'. Today, I made us tea and toast, and we sat at the kitchen counter and chatted before I left for the day. I was meeting Sam at number ten, there were only a couple of jobs that had an early start, and that was one of them. I took our dishes to the sink, washed them and left them on the drainer. I wasn't sure how this was going to go today, given that she was expecting something from me last night, something I couldn't bear to give her. But it changed nothing, she took my coat from the hook, and once I'd put it on, she kissed my cheek and smiled, I loved that slightly embarrassed smile she gave, I couldn't help myself, I wrapped her up in both my arms and held her tightly. When I needed to leave, I cupped her cheek with the palm of my hand, slowly leaning towards her, gauging her reaction, I kissed her so gently, it was barely there, I held my lips to hers for a moment, not wanting to stop, she didn't pull away. My heart was beating so hard I could feel it throughout my whole body. It was time to leave. I leaned my forehead against hers and whispered, "I'm sorry." She knew what I meant, and she, being Fi, simply smiled and said, "It's ok, I understand."

Number ten was a write off, I flew round the corner into the street, only to be met by the flashing lights of several police cars, Sam was nowhere to be seen, either he wasn't here yet, or he'd arrived the same time as me, I knew this because, if he'd been here earlier he would most certainly have warned me off. I text him to do the same. Five minutes later, we were back on the high street, waiting for some of Sam's regulars. "Am I alright to take some time out this afternoon," I asked, "Sure mate, got to do the Posh fella, but after that I should be ok for a couple of hours," "Cheers Sam." I knew he'd be fine with it, but as my mum used to say, 'it's always nice to be asked'. Sam never asked what I was doing, where I was going, where I had been, I afforded him the same level of privacy, it worked. By two we were done, and it was time to put my investigative skills to the test. I was going back to the hairdressers, or Salon as they called it, it was a hairdresser when my mother went ! I thought I remembered seeing a cafe, just a little further up the road, although my mind was on other things at the time, so I could be completely imagining that. I was hoping to figure out the connection between the 'salon' and the Clinic, there had to be one. I was sure of it, I'd felt it last time I came, and I could feel it now. I was right about the Cafe, it wasn't like Georges, it sold lots of posh coffees, and fancy sandwiches, it smelled amazing though, and for a few minutes I got totally distracted while I ordered an Earl Grey and a goats cheese and beetroot sandwich. Remembering the reason I was there, I checked for a seat near the window, there was one right in the corner, perfect for what I needed. Then I watched, and waited. I stayed for about an hour and a half, not really long enough to see what was going on, but it gave me the chance to get a feel for the place. What I did notice was, a lot of people came and went, some didn't look at all like they were there for treatments of any sort, and the fact that they were in and out within minutes, kind of set me thinking I was right. The sandwich was amazing, best thing I'd eaten in ages, and I was gutted on the way back to meet Sam when I thought I could've picked a couple of those up for me and Fi for later. I'd do that next time.

And so I went back to work, I'd be home for tea time, then back out later in the evening. Every time I thought about going home, that sick feeling in my stomach returned. I arrived home to find her crying on the sofa, I was horrified, I had the means to stop her pain and I had walked away and left her. I went straight to her side, but that just seemed to make her worse, she wouldn't look at me, she didn't want me to hold her. "No," she sobbed, pushing my hand away, "Don't be nice to me," "Fi, please," I said, wanting desperately to comfort her. When I tried again to take her hand, she quickly leaped up from the sofa to get away from me. What the hell could have happened since I'd left this morning to have her in this state. "Fi, I'm sorry, here," I took out the small bottle I'd had in my pocket since the day before. "Here, I should've given it to you, I'm so sorry, I thought you were doing ok." Everything I said just seemed to make things worse, she was almost at the point of hysteria. "It's not you !" she screamed at me, "It's not your fault, it's me, I'm just fucking useless !" God, I'd never seen her in this state before. "Don't say that, please come here, you have a problem that you can't sort on your own." "You don't understand," she said, she put her hand into the pocket of her jeans, and pulled out an empty see through plastic packet, I stopped where I stood. "Oh," I said, "I see."

I didn't see. I was hurt, I was devastated, she had gone behind my back, she had gotten drugs from someone else, and worse still it was all because I'd taken it upon myself to take the moral high ground and withhold the drugs she needed, I had put her in a position where she felt she couldn't ask me for help, and that was devastating. I don't know who I was more pissed at, her or me. I didn't really want to accept the blame for any of it, but, obviously sitting back and hoping for the best wasn't the best option to take. I should've talked to her, I should've let her know I had something that could help, that she could have it if she wanted it, but that I really didn't want her to. That ! Would have been the grown up thing to do. That ! Would've been the right thing to do. So the problem was, where did we go from there, we needed to talk, but I doubt either of us could do that at the minute, emotions were running high, we both needed some time to compose ourselves.

I put the kettle on, like a good Englishman, and sat on the sofa, in my usual place. Fi was still standing, arms clutched around her tiny waist, looking down at the floor, full of shame. "It's ok, come sit down, I'll make us a cuppa, we can get through this, come on." I gestured with my head for her to come over, smiling as much as I could through my own pain, to make her feel better. She walked slowly back to the sofa, and placed herself as far into the corner as possible, her feet were up on the seat, she sat with her arms wrapped around her knees, keeping herself as small as possible. I knew that feeling, the one where you think if I keep on going, getting smaller and smaller, I might just disappear all together, and all my problems would disappear with me. Our night was spent using up a lot of tears, making plans and unmaking them, trying to figure out the best way forward, for both of us. The only decision we could come to, was that I would supply her drugs, and she would do her utmost to reduce her intake, there really was no other option until she was ready to accept outside help. We climbed into bed, friends again, that momentary kiss all but forgotten, this friendship/relationship was definitely a case of two steps forward, one step back.

Chapter Nineteen

It wasn't the life I had ever imagined having, selling drugs, supplying them to my best friend, trying to forget I actually murdered someone, shit, I really did do that ! But it was the one I had, and if nothing else came of it, it had introduced me to some of the most important people in my life. Degs continued to be the father I'd missed out on for so many years, and Sam the brother who was also one of my best friends. Tatty and Buzz had been there for me over and over. And slowly but surely they were helping me find my way in the world, and without really knowing it, helping me find the answers I'd spent so long looking for too.

So it seems, Tatty knew 'Brad,' before she was Brad, her real name was Collette, and in Tattys own words, 'she was always up her own arse.' Seems she changed her name five years ago after her husband disappeared, he being the original Brad, which seems on the face of it, a remarkable tribute to him, if you leave out the fact that most people believed she was the person responsible for disappearing him ! She didn't look at all like she could be responsible for offing someone, but then again, I suppose most people would say the same about me. Now she was supposedly running the hair salon, and the clinic amongst 'other things' there was one small, and to Tatty, very unremarkable detail in what he said, and that was, 'no one really sees her'. So the big question was, why, when I went that day, did she feel the need to appear in person. I needed to go back, it was the only way I would find the answers.

The next time Sam and I were alone in the car, I asked who had been doing the hair salon lately. He told me he had been a couple of times, and he had asked Buzz to go once. "Did you see Brad ?" I asked, "No," he said, "I just dropped the money off and left, that's what I get paid to do mate." I couldn't help but wonder why things had been so different when I was there. "And Buzz, did he see her ?" I knew I was pushing it, he didn't like questions, and there was no way he would answer for someone else, right on cue he said, "Well you'd have to ask him that wouldn't you ?" he said it with that, you should know better look on his face, and he was right. I did have one last question before he ended the conversation altogether, "Can I do the next one ?" He looked at me for a moment, trying to weigh up what I was up to, before deciding. "Yeh sure," he said, I know he wanted to ask why, but give him his due, he stuck to his own rules. I wanted to ask when, but decided not to push my luck any further, so, now it was a waiting game. I'd been back to the cafe near the clinic twice now, but it hadn't revealed anything more, there was definitely a delivery service going on, but I'd not seen Brad again, and from what Tatty said, I probably wouldn't. There was little more I could do now until I got the chance to go back.

And so life slipped into a real comfortable pattern, Fi was doing ok, she still had ups and downs but she was coping, work was going well, it kept the money coming in, and it was easy money to make, on the whole. I was usually home for dinner, could get away if I needed to, I mean I hated evening work, the nights were always so long, and it was often early hours before I got home again, but like I said, it paid the bills, and some.

Life was good, strange, but good, surreal, but good, so many things it shouldn't be, but it was good. Going home to Fi was by far the best part, sometimes she cooked, sometimes we ordered takeaway. We lived, for all the world, as a couple, but behind closed doors, we had never quite managed to make that leap from friends to lovers. I hoped this evening, that would change. We were going to have 'the talk,' the 'where do we go from here' talk, the 'what does our future hold' talk. And to be perfectly honest, it scared the shit out of me ! Part of me was psyched up, excited to finally get this all out in the open, but there was also that little part of me that feared she was happy as she was, always having the hope was fine, but knowing there would never be anything between us would be a virtual kick in the gut.

The day flew by in a blur, I was on autopilot, doing as I was told, going to places I hardly remembered getting to, all I could think of is what she would say tonight, I went through a hundred different ways she was going to let me down lightly, it's not you it's me, I'm just not ready, I'm not sure it would work, I don't want to spoil our friendship, the list was endless, and worse still, each and every one of them made sense. I'd hate to lose her solely because I wanted more of her than she could give. I was home for five, and as always she was sitting on the end of the sofa, curled up watching TV. And also as usual, as soon as I walked in, she was up, putting the kettle on, asking if I'd like a cup of tea. It was awkward, I so wish it wasn't, maybe that was telling us something, if we couldn't even discuss the future without feeling awkward, maybe this really wasn't a good idea, or maybe everyone felt like this, I'd never been in this situation before, so I had no way of knowing. Right brain, time to shut up and let your mouth do the talking. "So have you had time to think ?" I asked, she blushed and nodded, making me smile, "And ?" I asked, "You first," she said, she was crippled with embarrassment, and couldn't even look at me, but she was smiling, and I decided to take that as a good sign, it gave me just the hint of confidence I needed, to tell her, in no uncertain terms how I felt. I sucked in a little more air than I needed, and almost choked on my first word, quickly composing myself before telling her how I felt. "Fi, I love you, I think I knew it from the first time I saw you, I felt something that day that changed me, from the moment

I saw you, I wanted to protect you and care for you, and always be there for you, and even if you tell me you can't love me the same way, I will always be here for you, I will always do all of those things, because I can't forget the way I feel." Phew, I finally drew in another breath. Now I couldn't look at *her*, I looked at the floor, sitting on the edge of the sofa, my hands resting between my legs, waiting, praying for her to love me back. I felt a hand on the back of my neck, then another taking my hand, I looked up, she was looking right into my eyes now, I held my breath, knowing this was it, in the next few seconds my life would change irrevocably, one way or another. "Ah Conal, there has never been any doubt in my mind that you loved me, it's all that has kept me going for these past few months, but I had to wait, not for me, but for you, you had to know what you were getting into, no matter what has happened, or what you've learned of me, you have loved me regardless, and now I feel safe telling you, that…I love you too." Shit ! Oh holy fucking shit, she loves me ! She really loves me. She was in my arms in a second, and this time I kissed her for real. I kissed her like it may be the only time I ever got to kiss her, with no doubt, no worries, no fear.

That night was a night I would hold in my heart for eternity, but it was also a reminder of how far we still had to go. Knowing she had been raped, and in such a violent way, by the most hideous man, meant there would be obstacles for us to overcome before we could even think about a more intimate, physical relationship. We talked about it, and both agreed it was something we needed to take slowly. She was concerned this would be a problem for me, but she couldn't have been further from the truth. I would wait until the end of time for her, and longer if she asked me to. For now, knowing she was mine, knowing she loved me, was enough, the rest would come, in time. To the outside world it would seem like nothing had changed, but mentally, emotionally we were both in a place we never dreamed of being, having someone who cares for you, who thinks about you, who values your opinion, and who you can confide anything in, is the most wonderful feeling. The world was a better place, I told her I'd known from day one, and it was true, from the first time I saw her I knew there was something between us, that feeling never left, and here we are, reaping the benefits of never giving up, never giving in and following your instincts, they're there for a reason !

Sam had given me the news I'd been waiting for, tomorrow I would be going to the salon. He'd text to let me know in case I needed some extra time, I wasn't sure what he meant by that, but I punched the air, "Yes !" as I text back a, 'Thanks.' The morning came, and we were having a late start, which meant breakfast in bed with my girl, I loved saying that. I made toast, scrambled eggs and tea, it wasn't much, but she loved being made a fuss of, I suppose she'd not had that much experience of it in her life, at least I'd had the joy of a loving family at some point, even if I wasn't aware of the grim reality of what was going on around me. She shuffled up into a sitting position as I took the tray to the bed, fixing the pillows before I handed her the tray. I quickly threw back the duvet and jumped in next to her. This, is what mornings were made for.

I didn't have to be at the salon until around three, but still had a few jobs to do before then. I'd expected to be going on my bike like I had done the first time, but Sam had text to say he would be taking me today. It didn't make much difference to me, but I did wonder why. Leaving the house now was amazing, long kisses at the door, I love yous, and that overwhelming need to stay. One last peck on the cheek, and I was outside, grinning from ear to ear.

The morning was slow, or it might have just seemed that way, when you're waiting for something, time always seems to drag. But, eventually it was time to go. Sam had been quiet today, I mean he wasn't the biggest conversationalist in the world, but there was usually something to talk about. He wasn't annoyed, just not quite himself. It wasn't long before we reached the street with both the salon and the clinic on, Sam drove past the salon and parked the car near the end of the street, he passed me the package for the Salon, "I have a few things to do," he said, "I won't be long." I was expecting him to drive away once I was out of the car, but as I shut the door, he appeared on the opposite side, shutting his too. "Where are you going ?" I asked, puzzled, "Just have a few things to check on, nothing for you to worry your pretty little head about." With that, he grinned at me, raised his eyebrows and walked in the opposite direction. He was freaking me out today, all that silence in the car, taking me to jobs he had no reason to take me to, and now he was 'walking' to do some sort of god knows what, god knows where. Less than two minutes later I was gutted to be standing next to the car waiting for Sam. There had been no secret phone calls today, no personal pick up from Brad, just a regular handover, and a 'thank you' from the receptionist. I was in there less than thirty seconds. And now I was bored, leaning on the car waiting for Sam to get back.

  Where the hell had he gone ? I'd checked my phone for the time at least ten times in the last five minutes, it felt like it had been at least double that, I was pissed off, fed up, and just wanted to go ! It was another five minutes before he came walking around the corner of the street, about a hundred feet away from where we'd parked. It was obvious nothing untoward had happened, he seemed happy enough, it was strange seeing him walking, I'd only ever seen him go a few steps before, to or from the car. He unlocked the car from a few feet away, I climbed in and waited. "Everything go ok ?" he asked as he was putting his seat belt on. "Erm yeh," I said, "Good, no problems this time ?" he questioned, "Yeh it was fine, there weren't any problems last time, I just thought it was a bit odd that's all," I told him, feeling like I needed to explain myself. As we pulled away and drove toward the end of the road, I couldn't help but look into the road he had come from, hoping it would give me a clue as to where he had been. My eyes widened, and without having time to stop myself from making it so obvious, I swung my head back to look at Sam, he turned to me with a wink and a wry smile. What the fuck was going on ? In the street to the left, parked just a few metres along the road, was a black Jaguar, I recognised the driver straight away, he was the same guy who'd been parked outside the salon last time I was there, the same guy who'd picked Brad up when she'd left.

"Sam, what the hells going on ?" he was shaking his head, as he put his finger to his lips, "Not yet mate," was all he said. What the fuck, I thought, I could usually form some semblance of rationality to what was happening, in my less than 'normal' life, but I had absolutely no idea what he was up to right now, or how this impacted on me. I knew from experience, there was no point in questioning him any further, he'd said all he was going to say on the subject, and now I just had to wait until he was ready to fill me in. I realised, once I was over the shock, that I was more than a bit pissed off with him. This was my thing, this was my quest, it was mine, and if he was going to come in and start playing some part in it then I think he should at least have the decency to tell me what part that was. I also knew he would never do anything that would purposely put me in danger, and he would never tell me anything that would do the same. And so, as I always did, I trusted his judgement and left it at that.

And I was right to do so. A little less than a week later, Sam text and asked me to meet him on the high street, nothing new in that, so, I took my bike and got on my way. Things changed in a very unexpected way that day, things that would change the direction of my life completely. Sam was waiting in the car as per usual, I opened the boot, took out the bike lock and locked up my bike, as usual, climbed into the car as usual. That's where the usual stopped. "You'll be needing your bike soz, thought I'd told you," Sam said, laughing as I climbed back out of the car. "Are you messing, why didn't you say before I locked it up ?" "Sorry mate I was on my phone, didn't think till you sat down." He was still very amused with himself, which didn't impress me one bit. I unlocked the bike, threw the lock back in the car, and went to his open window, "Where am I going ?" I asked still very unamused. "Straighten your face mate," he said, trying hard not to carry on laughing, "You're gonna love me in a minute, promise you." He took the parcel from the seat next to him and handed it to me through the window, it was heavier than usual, a little bigger too. "So where's it going ?" I asked, intrigued now at what I was going to be so pleased about. He looked at me for a moment or two, then said, "The Clinic." Holy shit, so that's what his little venture the other day was all about. Holy frickin' shit. "Seriously ?" I asked, "Yes mate, now I think you get what a big deal this is, and it did take a bit of persuasion, you don't need to know the details, just don't fuck it up !" he said. His grin disappeared, and he became deadly serious, "Listen mate, I don't know for sure what's going on in that teeny, tiny, little brain of yours, but I have an idea, and you need to be careful, just remember, think before you act, and only act when you're certain." I wondered what he thought he knew, it was something I really wanted to ask, but right now wasn't the time. I stood speechless, until he said, "Well, go on mate, that thing won't deliver itself !" "Thank you Sam, like really, Thank you."

Chapter Twenty

I felt a little underdressed, if I'd have known where I was going I'd definitely have dressed for the part, as it was, all I could do was fix my hair with my fingers, and straighten my clothes, I had no clue what to expect when I arrived, and I knew there was every possibility this would be like any other drop off, in, hand it over, out. But I prayed as I pedalled that there would be something, anything that could point me in the right direction. I stopped at the end of the street to catch my breath, I'd been riding as fast as I was thinking, and had made it to the Clinic in a fraction of the usual time. Once I'd composed myself again, I pedalled slowly till I came to the cafe I'd stopped at previously. I couldn't leave the bike, in all my annoyance, I'd flung the lock back in the boot, so I took it and leaned it against the railings outside of the Clinic doors, although the lower half of the window was frosted, I would still be able to see if anyone was near enough to pinch it.

One last deep breath before I went inside. I was excited, exhilarated and eager to get inside, and a bag of nerves as I pushed down on the handle, the door was locked, taking a step back I looked around for a sign or a bell, there was both, a sign asking visitors to ring the bell ! I did so, and waited, within a few seconds a voice came through the intercom. "Hi, can I help you ?" It was a young woman's voice, "Erm ,yes, I have a delivery for Brad." "Push the door please," said the intercom lady. Oooh very nice, it was amazing, everything here was white too, the walls, the furnishings, the flowers, literally everything.

Before I'd even had a chance to say who I was or why I was there, I was ushered through a white door into a white corridor, and back through another pristine white door. Jees this must take some cleaning I thought, when what I should have been thinking is where the hell is this girl taking me.

She had in fact taken me to an office, which may or may not have been near the back of the building, it seemed we had gone in that direction, I made a mental note to take more notice in future. I was offered a seat, and she left with a smile and a wave as she said goodbye. I waited, feeling extremely vulnerable. I assumed Brad was on her way, this was so similar to what had happened the first time I'd delivered to the Salon a few doors away. I was surprised when a door I hadn't even noticed, it was hard to differentiate between doors, walls and decoration in this place, opened at the opposite side of the room to where I'd entered. It was in fact Brad, now whilst this was just what I wanted, it also bothered me, I remembered Tatty telling me how she barely dealt with any of her own business, so the unease I was already feeling suddenly became even more profound. "Conal, how nice to see you again," she offered her hand to me, I took it and shook it lightly. I had to ask, "I don't want to sound rude, but how do you know my name ?" She smiled, softly, looking away like she was remembering something, as she turned back to face me she said, "From your brother of course." I'd stood to shake her hand, but now I needed to sit again, my legs giving way, I could feel the blood drain from my face, my stomach was churning, and my mums words came back to haunt me again, 'be careful what you wish for son, you just might get it'. I managed to speak, even though I could barely think, "I don't understand," I whispered. "Oh Conal, you don't need to understand dear, suffice to say Joseph and I were ...hmmm, shall we say...*very* good friends, when I heard you were on the scene, I wanted to meet you," "But why ?" I asked, I was over the initial shock now, and needed answers. "Purely curiosity Conal," she said, "Now, I believe you have something for me ?" She held out her hand, I automatically placed the parcel in it, and with a nod and a smile, she took herself back through the door from where she had come And once again I was left in a state of utter confusion, and total disbelief.

Thankfully my bike was still there, I'd totally forgotten about it whilst I'd been inside, but soon I was on my way back to the high street to meet up with Sam. I know he didn't like questions, but I had a few for him anyway ! I locked up my bike, climbed in beside Sam and said, "Well ?" "What d'you mean, well ?" he said, "I mean, well, tell me what just happened ?" "Mate, you never make any sense, I was gonna ask you that." He was laughing now, "Mate, I'd love to have seen your face when you got in there," he laughed out loud, "Sam it was nut's, it's made me even more determined to figure out what's going on." Sam was serious now, "Listen mate, I know you have a lot of questions, and I get why, if I was you I'd feel the same, and I won't insult you by saying you don't know what you're dealing with, cause I'm pretty sure, given the reasons why you're looking, you're more than aware, but if they get even a sniff of what's going on, you do know you'll be joining your brother, right ?" He was right, I did already know all this, and in the past I'd always thought, I've got nothing to lose, but now I did, now I had Fi, and there's one thing I couldn't bear to do, and that would be to leave her alone in the world. My next sentence should have gone a bit like this 'so I'm going to forget about the past and concentrate on the future' but what I really thought was, 'I'll just have to be real careful then'. I still wasn't sure what Brad wanted with me, if she was being honest, then she really was just curious, but from what I'd heard, that was highly unlikely and the investigator inside of me suspected there was a lot more to it that met the eye.

I'd not yet confided in anyone about how or why exactly I'd got into this game, but I was so excited now with all that had happened I desperately wanted to share it with someone. I didn't want to burden anyone and especially Fi, but I knew she would want to know, in fact I knew she would be disappointed if she thought I couldn't tell her. And so that evening, with our takeaway on trays in front of us, sat on the sofa like we did every evening, I told her everything. I told her about my dad, about Joseph, about my lovely mum, about all the watching and planning and conniving I'd done. She listened and hung on to every word, munching her way through her chicken fried rice, "Wow !" she said, I let out a short laugh, I'd just filled her in on my whole life, all the dramas, the heartache, the ups and downs, and all I'd gotten in return was one word, to be fair to her it was a truly appropriate response. I couldn't help but smile, "Is that all you have to say ?" I asked, she burst out laughing, spitting rice all over her tray and the floor. Soon the two of us were laughing uncontrollably, maybe there was a touch of hysteria on my part at finally getting everything off my chest. When we finally calmed down, she said again, "Wow." She placed her tray on the coffee table, and took both of my hands in hers, "I'm so glad you told me, it makes me so sad to think you've been through all of that alone, and I totally get what your doing, don't get me wrong, it scares me too, but I get why you have to do this, and just so you know, I'm with you every step of the way." If I thought I couldn't love this girl any more, I was wrong, so very, very wrong.

And so the cat was most definitely out of the bag, Fi knew everything, and it was more than likely Sam did too. I'd always thought keeping this to myself was the best thing I could do, and probably the safest. But I have to say, it felt good having a couple of other people on my side, knowing I was not alone only made me feel even more determined to find the truth. It was going to take the one thing I had in abundance…time. Another of my mums sayings was, 'all things come to those who wait' and so I would wait, until I was 100% certain I knew it all, who was responsible for Josephs murder, who did it, and who if any one helped along the way, I wanted to know it all. Before I went any further, I needed to know what Sam thought, and what part exactly he was willing to play in all of this.

We had been driving around for a couple of hours, done all the usual jobs, and I'd started to ask the big question about a hundred times, quickly changing my mind at the last minute, and talking about something random, like what was on the news last night, or where we had gotten takeaway from. I tried once more, "Hey Sam…" he stopped me before I said another word, "Right listen mate, if your gonna tell me what you had with your cocoa before bed or what colour undies you've got on today, don't bother, you obviously have something to say, so just say it, this is me mate you know you can tell me anything, ask me anything, not saying I'll give you the answer, but you never have to be afraid to ask, ok ?" I nodded, of course I knew, it was just, every time I put the words together in my head I sounded like some plastic gangster trying to take the underworld down, in all honesty it sounded completely ridiculous, even if it was, in some sense, all true. He pulled into the kerb, brought the car to a standstill, and sat with his back to the door, "Right mate, I'm all yours." In about half the time it took me to tell Fi and using half the words, I didn't have to try so hard with Sam, straight and to the point was good for him, I told him what I was trying to do. "Hmmm," he said, nodding away looking through the windscreen at nothing at all. "And what do you plan to do with all this information when you have it ?" I couldn't answer, after all these months of thinking about this constantly, that was the one thing I had no answer for, maybe knowing would be enough. As if he could read my mind he said, "You and me both know, just knowing will never be enough," he was being serious, he wanted serious answers, and I didn't have one. "I don't know Sam," I told him, "Well, you know what mate, before you go any further, you better make sure you *do* know, we've been here mate, you've seen what happens when you don't make decisions, when you don't have a plan, things go wrong mate, you make mistakes, and with these people you can't afford to make mistakes," he was right. "I know, I know," I said, feeling the pressure, "I know you do mate, thing is, I also know, you already made the decision, you already planned what you're gonna do, you're just not comfortable saying it yet, and that's ok, we've all been there," he spoke softer now, he knew how hard this was for me, I wasn't like Joseph, I wasn't like him or his dad, or the rest of them. "I want them to hurt Sam, I want to take everything away from them, let them know how it feels to lose everything." I slumped back into the seat, relieved it was finally out in the open. "Ok, so you made a decision, it's some sort of plan, things change, but it's a start, and it means you're serious about this, I'll have your back mate, I'll be there for you as much as I can, let's see what we can find out eh ?" That gained me the customary punch to the arm that meant this little heart to heart was over.

We usually saw the Posh guy in the afternoon, but today we were going after dinner, Sam was picking me up around seven which meant I had a few hours to spend with Fi, it meant we could get on with something we'd been discussing for a while. She'd not been out since the attack, but we had made a plan to start on her recovery, nothing big, today we were going to have a cup of tea on the steps of our building, there were only three of them, but they were separated from the sidewalk by three foot of railings, meaning she should still feel pretty secure. I was back at home for three thirty, so we had loads of time to work up to it, she knew it would all be at her own pace, there was no pressure, the only reason we were doing this was for her.

During the time she had been here I'd learned so much more about her life, not all of it, I could tell there were things she couldn't tell me yet, but one thing I found really sad was, she had barely been outside her door in over two years, she'd had food delivered, she'd not bought new clothes in all the time she had lived there, she'd never been to the park, or to a cafe, it saddened me that she had lived just half a life. She'd not confided completely in me about her home life, but I did know she had left home when she was fifteen, she'd had to, that was as much as she'd said. And so this, today, was a massive step, and if she could do it great, if she couldn't, then we would try again another day.

I arrived home excited, eager to see what she would achieve today, and I reminded myself that just the fact that she was even considering this was a huge achievement for her. I walked up the stairs feeling so proud. I couldn't wait to see what the day would bring. I was surprised to see her, fully dressed, shoes on, hair tied up, standing by the coffee table waiting to go, she was hopping from one foot to the other like a boxer ready to take on the fight of their life, and above all else, she was smiling, she was positive, she was really up for this, every time I thought I couldn't love her more, she proved me wrong. I took her in my arms and swung her around, "You're amazing, do you know that ?" Her cheeks reddened and she replied, "So are you." "Right," I said, "Are we doing this ?" She nodded quickly with genuine enthusiasm, I'd assumed we would be talking, eating, getting ourselves psyched up for this, but the girl was ready to go, so, go we did.

She had two cups of tea ready, I carried them downstairs, she followed slowly behind me, she was still trying to smile, but things had gotten real now that we'd left the security of our little home. I stopped and turned to her, just in time to see her glancing back towards the front door, weighing up whether she should make a run for it or not. She chose not to, and although we didn't quite make it to the steps, we made it to the bottom stair in the hallway, I handed her a cup, and went to open the main door. I wanted her to feel the fresh air, to still see the world going by, we were just ten feet away from where we'd planned to be, but she was smiling, she was excited, this was a major step for her and I couldn't have been more proud.

I was ready for Sam at seven, he was waiting in the usual spot when I got outside, I was still on a high from seeing Fi so pleased with herself, Sam on the other hand was not. "So, why we going to see Posh so late ?" He didn't answer, but shook his head slightly, it was the 'don't ask' shake, okaaaay, so we don't want to talk, I always felt so awkward when he was like this, thankfully it wasn't too often, usually only when…oh shit ! "Sam ?!" I shouted, it startled him, "What the fuck mate !" " You're not going to kill him are you, seriously mate, why do you have to take me, not like I drive and I'm a quick getaway or anything !" My little outburst didn't improve his mood. "Oh for fuck sake mate, calm your tits down, we're not killing anyone." I blew out the air I'd been holding on to, "Sorry Sam, just don't know if I'm up to another one just yet." I didn't usually ask, but somehow, this time it felt right, "So what's up ?" He was shocked, he turned to look at me wearing the 'what the fuck' face again, I went on, "Sam you're always there for me, and it's obvious something's not right," I was sincere, and I hoped he realised that. "Listen, Posh guy is safe, we're only late cause I had something else to do, and that something is not something you can help me with," he was being sincere, but not totally honest. "But hey, thanks mate," he said, once again I gained a punch to the arm, but it put a smile on his face, so this one was worth it. "One more question," I said, he shook his head and looked to the skies, "Did you kill anyone else today" "No! Jees mate I'm not a fucking psychopath." Thankfully he was still smiling, "Okaaaay, just thought I'd check." I was being sarcastic, and he knew it, but it seemed to have helped bring him out of whatever state of mind he was in, which meant I could get on with loving life.

No one knows what path life has planned for them, none more so than me, I could never, ever have foreseen any of the things that had happened to me, therefore the only thing I could ever presume for the future was, to expect the unexpected, a saying which always served to puzzle me, as once you'd expected the unexpected it was no longer unexpected, was it? Anyhow, the point of the matter being, I couldn't have expected what had happened today. The Clinic/Salon jobs only happened once a week, for us that is, I'm sure they had 'deliveries' everyday. Each one of these days had to count, which was difficult to say the least, I never knew who I would see or how long I would be there, I could only ever make the most of what I had. Today I was at the Clinic, sometimes it was a simple drop off at reception, sometimes I would be taken to a treatment room near the back, I'd only been a handful of times, so it was far too early to figure out if there was any set pattern. So when I arrived today and my parcel was taken at reception, I was disappointed, but not surprised to be doing a straight in and out job, they were always the least productive. I handed over the parcel and began to walk back towards the door.

"Excuse me, Sir," I assumed she was talking to someone else, but I turned anyway, to see the young receptionist looking at me, she glanced down at the desk in front of her, she was obviously checking something, "Conal is it ?" she asked, looking at me, still smiling. I'd turned fully to face her now, "Yeah, I'm Conal." I returned to the desk, waiting for her to explain what she wanted. Miss Langley would like to see you." "Who ?" I was puzzled, who the hell was Miss Langley. "The proprietor ?" she suggested, ohhhhh, I thought, my eyes lighting up, suddenly standing a little straighter, appearing a little keener. "Oh, ok," my voice was saying nonchalant, although I suspect my body language was not. "Follow me," she said and walked off through the white doors, down the bright white, well lit corridors, but not to the same room we were in last time, this one was just a few doors away, but on entering, it could have been any of the rooms in here, I guessed they were all pretty similar. "She'll be with you shortly." She left with the same smile, the one that looked like it could possibly be hurting her face, and closed the door behind her. I sat on the white leather sofa and waited, approximately thirty seconds, she was keen today. I stood as she entered the room, being respectful to women was something I had learned from my dad, it had always stuck, even though he'd been absent for the majority of my life. "Please sit," she said, herself taking a seat at the desk near the window, there was a filing cabinet nearby, and a treatment table to the left, there was also a large ornate, wardrobe-come storage cupboard, all of course in white. "How are you ?" What the hell was this woman playing at, I'd like to say I had no time for pleasantries, but where this woman was concerned, I had all the time in the world. "I'm good, thank you, and you ?" she smiled faintly, "I'm very well, thank you," she paused for a moment, "Well, that's the pleasantries over with," shit can she read my mind too ! "I have a proposition for you," she said, I waited, expecting her to continue, she took some paperwork from her bag, and laid it out on the table in front of her. What could she possibly have there that would interest me, I thought. She went on, "I would like you to come and work for me, it would be in just a small capacity to begin with." I almost choked as I began, "Sorry, erm, Miss Langley…" she interrupted, "Please, call me Brad," "Sorry Brad, but I have a job." "Yes, of course, and by all accounts you're very loyal to your employee, and he to you." What the hell was that supposed to mean, she was freaking me out now, and as much as I wanted to stay and get to know her better, a small part of me was saying, run for the hills mate, before it's too late.

She didn't speak now, I knew the way it worked, she was giving me time to get freaked and it had worked well. Did she know something, or was she taking a guess, gauging my reaction, well if I looked anything like I felt she must have been right on to me. "Sam's very good to me, I'm happy doing what I'm doing, sorry you've wasted your time." I stood and headed for the door. "I fully expected this reaction, but I'm sure you could come to some arrangement with Sam, like I said nothing that would take up too much of your time." I didn't know what else to say, she wasn't coming across as someone who would take no for an answer, and let's face it the reason I was here was to find out who the big guys were, and if she was the way in, then I might just have to take her up on her offer. "Can I get back to you ?" I said, before I turned the handle of the door, "Of course Conal, I look forward to hearing from you, soon." I nodded, opened the door and was about to leave, brainstorm ! "How do I contact you ?" she laughed out loud, "You don't Conal." She sat back in her seat and went back to the paperwork she'd set out earlier. I guessed it was time to leave. Wow, how could this all be happening so fast, in fact it was too fast, I needed to speak to the guys, I needed to know exactly what her interest was in me, and there obviously was one, and what exactly had happened between her and Joseph. I didn't want to give any one the heads up, I needed to see their faces, what their reactions were when I asked them, I text Sam 'any chance I could meet up with you and the guys, need a little help with a decision'. It wasn't unusual for Sam to take a while to answer, and it was about half an hour later when he returned my text, 'course mate, gonna be next week though, Buzz is out of town, that ok ?' 'yeh sure, no hurry' I was gutted I'd have to wait, but it gave me time to think, and rethink, and then think a little bit more !!

Chapter Twenty-one

There were mixed emotions today, I was meeting the guys and hopefully getting the answers I needed, for now, but they wanted to meet at the shed, just the mere mention of it turned my stomach, and the thought of going back there filled me with absolute dread. Sam was picking me up at nine am, I'd already asked if there was anywhere else we could go, his answer, 'you can't hide from your demons mate, gotta face them straight on'. I knew he was right of course, but all the same, knowing what I'd done there made me feel sick to my stomach. And so, like I was once told, some days you just have to put on your big boy pants, and do your big boy shit !

The guys were already there when we arrived, sitting at our makeshift table, this time though it was filled with some sort of takeaway food, cups of coffee, and a tea for me. The food it turned out was a sausage, egg and bacon on toast, with a couple of sachets of brown sauce. I hadn't realised how hungry I was, until I'd finished, and everyone else was just half way through. "That girl not feeding you son ?" said Buzz, which immediately put me on the defensive, "Yeh course she does," they all laughed, "Oh, don't be having a go at his young lady !" said Degs, laughing even more. I laughed too, I'd surprised myself by how quickly I'd reacted. As soon as the last person had finished eating, Degs said, "So what's the problem son ?"

What was the problem ? Well, where do I start, someone killed my dad, mum and brother, and only one of those has been dealt with, granted it hadn't turned out the way I'd planned, but it WAS dealt with. "Do you know my history Degs ?" I wasn't sure how much Sam had told them, if anything. "Not too much son, you know Sam, plays his cards close to his chest, he'd only share if you asked, or it was necessary, right son ?" He patted Sam on the back, whilst Sam nodded in response to his question. "Right, I said, "In that case, this might take a while." I went on to tell the whole story just as I'd done a few weeks earlier with Fi, I always felt I needed to tell it all, to make them understand just how desperate I felt, just how much that desperation had built up, each time I'd lost someone else. "So what is it you need from us ?" Tatty sat up in his chair as he spoke, he was a big man and always looked so uncomfortable on his tiny little box, at that tiny little table. "Thing is…" it was hard to ask for this kind of help from these kind of people, the overwhelming urge for all of us, was to say nothing, and stay out of other people's business, "…I want to know who killed Joseph, I mean ideally I'd love to figure out what happened to our dad, but I reckon I may be out of time for that one. "I watched their faces, they glanced at each other, and at the floor, then they waited, they needed to know what I wanted from them. Here goes. "Obviously I don't for a minute expect you to do anything, I just wondered if there was anything you knew, anything you might have heard, something, anything, to point me in the right direction," I stopped for a couple of seconds, then went on, "And I know there was something going on between Joseph and the woman who runs the clinic, I mean she's obviously got a little side job going on there, and I get that it goes against everything you stand for, to tell me, but I had to ask, it's just been…" I was cut short, "Whooaaa, jees kid, you're making my ears bleed, calm yourself down." Buzz's accent still made me smile, each time I heard it.

Once again they looked at each other, each trying to gauge what the other wanted to do. "Listen guys, I can see there are things you want to talk about, I'm gonna take a walk." I'd managed to get in there and sit down without seeing 'that' corner of the room, but as I stood I totally forgot where I was, I turned to leave, but instead came to a sudden halt, the chair was still there, there were no other visible signs that anything untoward had happened, but I knew, and I was replaying the whole scene in my head. "You ok ?" Sams voice brought me back to my senses with a jolt, "What ? Oh, yeh, yeh I'm fine, let me know when you're done." I realised walking out of there I'd never paid much attention to the surrounding area, there were a few other buildings around, but I'd never really looked at them, I just knew they were there. I walked to the left of the shed, following the wall all the way round till I came back to the door, this time I took it all in. There were three small buildings that looked just like the shed, but smaller. Then there was what must have been a farm house at some point, it had been big, but was now derelict, most of the slates were missing from the roof, and the old wooden window frames were rotted, there were remnants of the windows, jagged leftovers from a long abandoned home. I could see there was another building a little further the other way, but I could only see the gable end of it. Curious now, I walked towards it, keen to see what this had once been. It wasn't in bad shape, it had been stables, I imagined how it would have looked, when it was up and running, it seemed sad to me that this had been a place of so much activity at some point, probably had the same family living there for decades, and now it was gone, deserted and abandoned. I heard a whistle coming from behind me, Sam was beckoning for me to return to the shed, I put my hand up to let him know I'd heard, and made my way back, nervous but hopeful.

    I prayed as I stood outside those barn doors, prayed there was something they could tell me, something they would tell me. I would understand 100% if they felt this wasn't something they could get involved with, but still I hoped. But, I was never going to find out by standing looking at that shed door, I took a deep breath, pushed it open and walked inside. At first I couldn't look at them, I was scared I would see on their faces that they couldn't do what I'd asked. I looked at the floor till I got real close, then stopped and raised my head, hoping one last time, I would see what I needed to. In front of me were four of the most deadpan faces I have ever seen, I looked from one to the other searching for even the faintest of clues. They said nothing, and I was becoming more and more uncomfortable by the minute, I shuffled from one foot to the other, looked around, looked back, when I couldn't take any more and my patience was failing, I said, "What ?" Still they sat and stared. What the hell was going on, had I overstepped the mark ? "Listen guys, if I've offended you or something, I'm really sorry." That did it, they couldn't keep up the facade any longer, Degs burst out laughing, followed closely by the rest of the guys. It was only then I realised, I'd been stepping backwards, and was now about six feet away from where I'd started. Laughing with my nerves, I said, "Fuckin' hell guys, I shit myself then, thought I'd really pissed you all off." They were so impressed with themselves, high fiving each other, with I told you so glances. "I mean it though guys, I know I'm asking a lot, and it goes against all the rules …" Buzz interrupted now, "What rules son ? We stick by our own, they're the only rules we need, right boys ?" They all nodded in agreement, "Come and sit back down now," Sam said, "Let's see what we've got for you." By the end of the day I'd learned a lot, some I'd suspected already, and some that really shocked me. Tatty knew more than the other guys but they all had something to put in the pot, some of it was fact, some was hearsay, but it all had to add up to something, didn't it.

So it seems. Brad is in her late forties, something I found hard to believe, she could've passed for early thirties easily, when I raised my eyebrows in obvious disbelief, Tatty said, "Remember where she works mate ?" " Ohhhh," I said, realisation hitting home. She had met Brad, the original Brad, when she was sixteen and he was twenty-nine, he'd always been a player and had several girlfriends, woman, partners all on the go at once, they all knew about the others, but they didn't care because he came from money, drug money, and they loved the lifestyle he could give them. But when he met Colette, as she was back then, everything changed, he was besotted with her, she was sweet, naive and beautiful, all of which he loved, by the time she was eighteen, they were married and living the high life. He gave her everything she could ever want, or need, clothes, houses, holidays, cars and she, by all accounts, lapped it up, soon forgetting her friends and family. His father adored her, and her mother hated him, she blamed him for taking her little girl away from her, but if what Tatty said is true, no-one ever stopped her from seeing her family, that was solely her own doing, maybe the sweet, innocent little girl, really wasn't so naive after all. Before long she was taking an active role in the family business. Time passed, and eventually the girl Brad loved no longer existed, he soon reverted to his old ways, with several girls on the go at once, Colette couldn't have cared less, she had what she wanted, and as far as she was concerned he could do what he liked so long as he didn't upset the status quo. Unfortunately for him, five years ago, he attempted to do just that. He found a young girl, early twenties, who was sweet, sensitive, naive, just like a girl he once knew, Brad obviously had a type. The rest is just hearsay, but by all accounts, he asked Colette for a divorce, she agreed, but before anything could be finalised, he disappeared. She was distraught at the loss of her 'soulmate' and that, it would appear, was that.

Now this was all very interesting, but didn't really help me in any way, it didn't tell me anything that could give me any idea who had killed Joseph. It seems it was well known that Joseph and Brad were having a bit of a 'thing,' it may have been well known in their circles, but I had no idea he did anything but 'work' ! Had she gotten rid of him the same way she had Brad? Or was it a simple drug deal gone wrong. At least I knew I was on the right track, still didn't fully explain her interest in me of course. Not to the extent that she would want me right where she could keep an eye on me.

The next little bomb shell…so, you remember how much Brad's dad liked Colette, well, it seems he may have liked her a lot more than he should have, and the feelings were mutual. Did his own dad get rid of him ? I felt like I was finding more questions than answers, but it did throw light on so many things. Was Joseph being used as a cover for Brad's fling with her father-in-law ? I knew nothing about him, and neither did it seem, anybody else, people knew of him, but nobody seems to have met him, or even seen him, he was like some sort of urban myth. Degs could tell me a little more about him, he had known someone close to the family when he was younger. Brad's dad was called Mike, he had built up a cleaning business when he was younger, hiring young girls, paying decent wages, he'd then gone into the property game, then started buying salons, that's where Colette came in, she dealt with the salons for him, and she did a great job by all accounts, but then Mike was always impressed with everything she did, in his eyes she could do no wrong. I'd asked if Mike was still alive, and the general consensus was yes, but no one could say for certain, a little bit of mental maths would've put him in his seventies, so it was perfectly plausible. My next question, was she involved in the drug side of his business, they were all in complete agreement, the general consensus being…she was running the lot !

Now it was time to fill them in on what I knew. She wanted something from me, I had no idea what, but the only way I would find out was to do as she had asked. "She's asked me to do some work for her," I looked around waiting for their reaction, they looked at each other, but the surprise I'd expected wasn't there. Degs turned to me, "It would seem like the smart thing to do, if she thinks Joseph may at some point have divulged some information to you, then she would want to keep you close." Buzz chipped in, "You know what they say son, keep your friends close and your enemies closer, all you gotta do now son is figure out which one she thinks you are." I nodded in agreement, she obviously wanted to keep a close eye on me, I just didn't know why. "Listen Sam," I turned in my seat to face him, "I want to do this, not because I want to work for her, but because the closer I am, the more I will find out, but it's only a few hours each week, so if it's ok with you, I'll take some time off to do it ?" Sam answered immediately, "Hey mate I know what this means to you, and yeh, so long as you don't slack off on me ?" He was grinning as he said that last bit, and I needed him to know how much it meant to me. "If you're not ok with this Sam, I'll find another way, it's really not a problem." Bam ! Punch to the arm, "Hey kid, can't do us any harm to have someone on the inside, eh ?" They all nodded in agreement at that one, "Too right son," said Degs, that kind of made it all seem ok, a bit like I was doing them a favour in the process.

I looked around at the people I barely knew, but who had seen me through some of the toughest times in my life, and it suddenly dawned on me, I had no idea who they really were, like, I knew they were good to me, but what did they do ? Where were they from ? How did they get here ? How deep into this game were they ? And how much of a favour would I be doing them ? My final question to them was… "So do you think I'm right, do you think she will lead me to whoever killed Joseph ?" There was a resounding agreement as Degs said, "Without a doubt son, without a doubt." He patted me on the shoulder, being the father figure he always was, "We'll be here son, if you need anything, anything at all, you know where to find us." I was overcome with gratitude, they'd no reason to help this kid who turned up out of the blue and caused them a whole load of grief, but they did it willingly, and with affection, and with loyalty, and when they said they'd be there for me always, I believed them with every piece of my being.

Chapter Twenty-Two

Back at home, I filled Fi in on where we were up to. She listened eagerly, asking questions, and giving her opinion, given the subject matter it was strange that I loved watching her so enthusiastic about something, but I suppose for a long time she'd had very little purpose in her life, and having something, anything to think about, to focus on then it surely had to be a good thing ? When I'd finished all I had to say, she suddenly leaped from the sofa, "Wait there," she said walking to the kitchen. While she was waiting for the kettle to boil, she asked more questions about what I was going to do about Brad. Then she stopped talking, handed me a cup, and walked towards the front door. "Come on," she said, nodding her head towards the door. I was puzzled now, what was she doing ? She looked so pleased with herself, but I knew how much she loved watching the world go by so I guessed she just wanted to sit on our stairs and watch the world go by. Reaching the bottom of the stairs, she turned to me and grinned, she gestured for me to follow her, and turned back towards the door, when two seconds later she was standing in the street, raising her cup to me I almost dropped the one I had in my hand. "Seriously ?" I said, "When did this happen ?" In that moment, the pride I had for her bubbled over, they were such small steps, and yet for her they were like climbing mountains. "Just now," she said, "We were talking, and I realised just how much I love you, and how much you love me, and how much I can trust you, and know you'll always look after me, and I thought, this is it, the time is now." "Come here," I said as I walked slowly down the steps, watching this beautiful, smiling, wonderful girl waiting for me. She was my everything, she stilled me, everything was calm around her, I was never more relaxed than when I got home to her, my heart swelled, but beat more evenly, it was like my life, my mind, my body all realigned when I was with her. I'd left my cup at the top of the stairs, knowing I'd need my arms when I reached her, as I got close I took hers from her hand and placed it on the steps. "Fi, you are my whole world, you make everything in my life better, you make me so proud of you, and I'm the luckiest person in the world to have you in my life." I wrapped her in my arms, and held her so tight, I held her like the world might end if I let go.

Although I'd made my decision already, I would be working for Brad in some capacity, I still ran the pros and cons through my head, over and over, ok, so I was going there in the hopes of learning something new about Joseph, but I was also playing into her hands, she obviously wanted me where she could see me too and I had no idea who was going to come out worse in this situation, these feelings always left once I was actually doing the thing I was arguing with myself over, so it was a relief to finally be sitting in Brads office, waiting to find out just what it was she wanted me to do. To keep things easy, I'd suggested I could give her a couple of hours each week when I bring her delivery, she was ok with that, although her somewhat disgruntled reaction told me that *she* was much more comfortable being the one who made the decisions. It did give me a kick to know I'd gotten one over on her already, she obviously needed, or wanted me there much more than I realised. She returned to her desk, opened a drawer to her left, took out several large books and some paperwork, it looked a bit like receipts, invoices, stuff like that. "I have a guy who does my books," she began, "I also have a guy who 'fixes' my books, do you understand ?" Of course I understood, I nodded and she continued. "Your job will be to make sure they're both doing the job well, do you think you can manage that ?" I'd not done any sort of academic work for over a year, but I was good at maths, so pretty sure I could check this over. "Listen, I can take a look, but obviously I can only check the figures I have, and depending what length of time you're covering, this could take a very long time." She was happy, she couldn't hide the smile although she tried to, "One thing I have plenty of Conal, is time." She picked up the books she'd removed from the drawer, "This is what you will need," she said, handing the books over to me, she explained which was which, both were green, one slightly darker than the other, otherwise identical, she then pointed at the paperwork on the desk, "You may need these, plus there will be some bank statements coming along shortly." As I picked up the paperwork, she walked towards the door, "Follow me, I'll take you to your office." Ooh my own office, can't be bad, "Oh and one more thing…." she stopped and turned, it was unexpected which meant I almost walked into her, and was now standing just a few inches from her, face to face, she was so close I could feel her breath on me, she was taller than me in her heels, and not for the first time since I'd met her, I felt just a little bit intimidated. "Nothing, and I mean nothing, leaves these premises, do you understand ?" There was no smile now, no kindness in her voice, I hadn't answered, trying to figure out how she could look exactly the same, but feel so very different, "Do you ?" she said, snapping me out of my daydreams. "Erm yes, yeh of course." She gave a very large, very fake smile, "Good," and then she was gone. Wow, imagine poor Brad when he realised what he'd really married.

Her obvious need to be in control, and the fact that she was still smarting from my decision to tell her how much time I could give her had incited Brad to change the day of her delivery, hence changing the day I would work for her. She hadn't actually told me this herself, Sam had sent a text filling me in on the change of details. I did laugh when I read it, knowing exactly what she was playing at. Made no difference whatsoever to me to be fair, just meant Sam had a bit of shuffling around to do. My day for delivery would now be Wednesday, which meant I would be there tomorrow, I'd given her just two hours initially, I told her we would see how that went. She didn't like that either, little Miss Brad did not like anyone telling her what would be happening, not in any way, shape or form. I kind of liked knowing I'd pissed her off and fully intended to do it as much as I could get away with, let's see what happens when someone rubs her up the wrong way I thought. I had just a day to wait before I got my chance to see exactly what I was dealing with. Although I probably shouldn't be, I was excited. Wednesday really couldn't come round quick enough.

And just like that I was standing outside of my new office, which was tiny, with the smallest window I have ever seen in my life, but it was big enough to do the job, everything I needed was in the drawer of the desk, which was far too big for the tiny room, it was all still white in keeping with the rest of the clinic, there where fresh white flowers in a white vase, to the far right of the desk. She had given me the code to the desk drawer last time I was there, I quickly put the code into the keypad, and took out everything it contained. There were the two green books, the receipts she had left, all neatly placed together in date order, and a stack of bank statements, also in date order, everything was done to ensure the utmost efficiency. I took them all and placed them alongside each other on the table top. I actually, for all my eagerness, wasn't that sure where to start, after a few moments staring at the contents of the drawer, I decided it was best to go with the most legitimate copy, then see how things differed from there. Over an hour later, I looked up at the clock surprised to see how much time had passed, it literally felt like I'd been at it for about twenty minutes, and even more surprisingly I was really enjoying myself, I had forgotten just how much I enjoyed numbers, and it was really good to be doing something which actually stimulated my brain cells ! I could have stayed longer but I was determined to do no more than the two hours I'd promised. Everything up to now seemed in order, I moved everything back into its place in the drawer, picked up my phone from the table, and left, feeling extraordinarily fulfilled.

My weeks flew by, looking forward to one Wednesday after another, thoroughly enjoying doing something so different to everything else in my life, but, determined to piss her off I never went past the two hour mark, and some weeks, just because I knew she hated it and just because I could, I told her I could only do an hour. I was only checking the last three months of her accounts, for now, so something had obviously gone amiss in those few months, maybe somebody got greedy, or maybe there were just mistakes being made, either way, from what I'd seen so far this first set of accounts was pretty straight forward, everything was accounted for, there were no discrepancies that I had seen. It's really hard to find what you're looking for, when you have no idea what it is ! I'd asked Brad whether there was anything in particular she was interested in, or whether there was something I should be looking for, but she simply said with a wry smile, "Let me know if you find anything."

And so, I continued each week, assuming that I would find nothing until I reached those second set of accounts. I was right. I'd taken out the ledger, knowing she wanted me to check the last three months, I turned back the pages to start three months earlier. I guessed she suspected someone of skimming money from her profits. I began, setting my alarm for exactly two hours, two hours came and went, I'd cancelled the alarm, and carried on, something wasn't quite right, but for someone to be taking money from her, there would have to be large amounts of money unaccounted for, surely it wouldn't be worth pissing someone like her off for the odd couple of hundred quid here and there. But that's not what was happening here. These accounts were supposed to find a way to incorporate the extra cash made from her extra curricular activities, namely the narcotics business, more commonly known to you and I, as money laundering. Now I can only assume, she would have found, given her status, someone who was more than capable of the job, someone who may have been recommended by a friend or acquaintance. Whoever was doing these accounts knew exactly what they were doing, cash was coming in from the regular sources, all being accounted for as it was in the first set of records, in this one there were extra invoices, extra expenses, all accounted for with the relevant paperwork. Except, and I have to think this was done purposely, purely because it wasn't a one off, each time one of the imaginary invoices was inputted, there were mistakes. Whoever had done this, was making it very obvious that this was a money laundering operation. Sometimes there were mistakes in amounts, mistakes with names, this was not something that could be done accidentally, and how someone could ever think they were getting away with this was beyond me. No one was stealing from her, someone was trying to set her up.

I was there for over four hours, I got so carried away trying to get to the bottom of it, that although she'd told me to only go back three months, I'd gone back further, for my own curiosity, I wondered when this had started, or whether it had always been going on. It was eight in the evening when the door opened, it was Brad. "I assume you found what I was looking for ?" she said looking at her watch. I looked at the clock on the wall, "Oh shit, I need to get home." I jumped up from the chair, grabbing my jacket and phone as I did so. "Yeh I found what you need, are you here tomorrow, I'll call in and go through it with you ?" She looked stunned, "Oh, ok, thank you Conal, that would be perfect."

I left quickly, almost running through the clinic back to my bike, cycling home as fast as I could. I was usually home by six, Fi had sent a couple of texts, but I'd been so wrapped up in my work, I'd not heard a thing. Before leaving the clinic, I had text her back, apologising, and letting her know I was on my way home. She was at the door waiting for me when I got there. I was hot and sweaty and exhausted, but I didn't care, as soon as I saw her standing there smiling, all my concerns and worries about being so late melted away. She was wearing her coat. "Where are you off to ?" I asked. "I thought we could go pick up a takeaway, I don't fancy cooking now, and the state you're in, I doubt you do." She started laughing, I knew I looked a mess, I gave her the biggest, longest, sweatiest kiss, before running upstairs to change my top and rinse my face. We had started off with short walks to the shop at the end of our road, the takeaway she liked, a Chinese chippy was a few streets away, but just about a ten minute walk. It was a perfect end to a very fulfilling day.

Chapter Twenty-Three

Sam had been great about the time I was spending with Brad, I'd tried as much as possible to ensure it didn't interfere with my work for him, and if it ever came to choosing between the two of them, then there would be no choice. He picked me up Thursday morning ready for the day ahead, it had become so much a part of my life, I didn't question anything we did anymore. All the jobs in the morning were the usual, straight in, straight out, drop offs and pickups. I asked if it was ok for me to go to Brads around four, and explained what I was going for. He seemed more interested than usual, he was never one for asking questions, he was more of a listener, but when I'd finished telling him what I'd found, he asked, "Who was doing the accounts for her ?" "No idea," I told him, "She didn't say," "Do me a favour, see if you can find out for me." I was surprised by his interest, but of course I gladly agreed to do that for him. "We have a new job tonight, won't be till around nine, so you'll have a bit of a break later," "Great," I said. I could get to Brad for four, be home for five thirty and have the whole evening with Fi. Not noticing how much I smiled when I text her, I was soon reminded, "Awww look at you," I hadn't realised Sam was watching me typing away with that big inane grin I always had when I thought of her. I could feel my cheeks redden, "Shut it you," I laughed as he made smoochy faces at me, always reminding me how much they all meant to me. How special it was to have a brother in my life again.

Four o'clock came round quickly, Sam dropped me off at Brads, and offered to pick me up afterwards, nothing new, if he was staying in the area he would often pick me up again, but I knew this was more to do with his interest in Brad's accounts, than doing me a favour.

Brad was waiting in 'my office,' the receptionist had told me to go straight through. When I arrived, she was sitting in my chair, books and paperwork spread across the table, I'd separated some of the invoices and receipts, and she noticed me scanning the table top, "Don't worry," she said, "Everything is just as you left it," I couldn't help but smile, she always knew just what I was thinking, she probably knew just what anyone was thinking ! As I walked towards the desk, she stood and offered me the seat, with raised eyebrows I sat down, and arranged the books and paper work in an order that would make sense. "So, when you asked me to look at these I assumed you thought someone was stealing from you, but it's pretty evident that there's something more going on here. I'm guessing you already have an idea what's happening ?" Of course she did, and god help whoever it was who was responsible. "I did have an idea, you're right, what I need from you is confirmation," she was walking away from the desk now, but stopped and turned when I didn't speak. "So ?" she said, oh, she wants me to tell her. "Right, so each time there is an entry for something that needed 'fixing' there is an obvious discrepancy, a lot of the numbers don't match, along with dates, so obviously if you were to have an audit, then it would become evident very quickly that you were doing a really bad job at laundering money." I waited for her reaction, "And am I to presume, given the amount of time you put into this, you went back a little further than the three months I requested." I wasn't sure I wanted to answer that question, but she needed to know, and if she didn't like it then we didn't have to see each other again, simple. "Yes, I know you said not to, but there were some things I needed to check, numbers I needed to check against the more recent entries,"   "And what did you find ?" She was deadly serious now, I guess this was going to be a big tell in who was responsible and why they had done it. "So I went back to July as you asked, but I needed something to compare it with, so I took it further back, there were the same discrepancies, going back until May, before that it was clean, no one would have been able to detect anything dodgy in there ."

She took the book from my hand, "Show me the exact date when all of this began. She held the book open as I leaned over to find the date in May when things had changed. I flicked back through the pages to the 2nd May. "There," I said, pointing to an entry regarding £20,200 worth of clinical equipment. She nodded, as though that in itself had answered all her questions. "Can I ask you something ?" I said, I needed to find out the information Sam has asked for, and although I'd tried to think of some other, less forward way to ask, I realised it was best to come straight out with it. "You can ask Conal," she said, with an obvious tone of, I may not answer. "Who was doing these accounts ?" "I'm not sure that's something you need to know," she was curious, she was one of those people who needed to know everything, and if I was asking questions, then she wanted to know why. "You're right Brad I don't need to know, but I want to, and I'm asking out of courtesy, I could find out for myself, but I'd rather it came from you." This amused her no end, I could see a twinkle in her eye as she tried hard not to smile, she failed miserably. "He is, or rather was, it seems, a very good friend of mine, his name is Gerard Long," "Thank you," I said, and she could see I was being sincere. "Can I ask *you* a question Conal ?" "Of course, you can ask," I answered, in the same I may not tell you tone. "Why is all of this so important to you ?" She was being straight with me, and so I afforded her the same, "I told a friend I would ask," "Not that, " she said before gesturing around the room, "This...why did you make so much effort to be here Conal." Should I tell her the truth ? I thought about it, and whether she knew or not wouldn't alter the fact that I would find what I needed to know, eventually. Before I gave it any more thought I told her, "I want to find out who killed my brother."

Her reaction didn't surprise me in any way, there was none, she purposely made absolutely sure she gave nothing away, but that in itself told me more than she could imagine, firstly she already knew why I was there, and secondly, she either had me here to ensure I didn't find out, or she wanted me to do just that. Of course she was never going to let me in on which of those it was, and of course it made no difference, I would carry on regardless, watching, listening and waiting, to quote Brad herself 'time is something I have plenty of'. She didn't comment any further on the subject of Joseph, and I had nothing more to say. "So Conal, how would you feel about taking over from Mr Long ?" Wow, *this* I was not expecting, she must have seen the look of surprise on my face. "It would be the same time, same hours ?" she waited patiently for my answer, I needed time to think, I really wasn't sure I was even up for the job, I wasn't that sure how these things worked, I mean they had to look really legitimate, and I didn't really know how you did that, I had to be honest with her. "I'd like to say yes, but to be totally honest, I'm not sure I'm up to the job." She smiled genuinely now, not trying to hide it, or smirking, "Maybe take a trial period, see how you go, let's face it, you can't do any worse than *our friend* Mr Long can you ?" I've no idea when he became 'our' friend, the fact she had said it made me feel slightly uncomfortable, like she was making him 'our' problem, and not hers, maybe I was reading too much into one tiny word, but that's how my mind had always worked. "Ok, I'll give it a go." I think we both knew this was just a way for both of us to keep the other just where we wanted them.

Sam met me outside just as he'd said he would, I was glad I'd been able to get the information he wanted, although I had no idea why he wanted it. I climbed into the car next to him, he nodded to greet me, and drove off back towards home. "So the guy who was doing her accounts is called Gerard Long ?" "Cheers mate," he said with a nod and a smile, signifying his appreciation, "You know him ?" I asked. "I know *of* him, I'm guessing Brad wasn't best pleased ?" "She already knew, she didn't say so, but I could tell," "Wouldn't like to be in his shoes now," Sam was shaking his head, I really wanted to know what his interest was, and normally I wouldn't ask, but this time I felt it was ok, given it was my good self who'd given him the information. "Why did you want to know ?" I asked, even though I still felt I shouldn't, he didn't seem to mind, but gave the somewhat vague answer of, "Just like to be prepared mate, that's all." That statement concerned me, more than a little, what did he need to be prepared for? How did this affect him in any way? And what was the connection between Brad, Sam and Mr Long ? I'm sure when the time came, he would let me know. For now, I would just have to wonder ! It was time to get home to Fi, I'd just remembered, I had an extra couple of hours with her this evening.

I couldn't wait to see her, but that was nothing new, she was the one person in my life guaranteed to make me smile. Today was no exception, she'd already put the kettle on, and had two cups waiting to be filled when I walked through the door. And I smiled, I smiled because she cared, I smiled because she made me happy, I smiled because I made her happy, and a little part of me smiled at the memory of my mum doing exactly the same thing whenever I got home. She couldn't have known how much this small gesture meant to me. And, as usual I wrapped her in my arms, pulled her close and kissed her tenderly. That feeling each time you kiss someone you love, or hold them gently, when your body tells you they are part of your actual being, when their touch physically affects you, and you can feel their energy coursing through your veins, it's that point when you know, you know you will never ever function as a human without them in your life. That is exactly how I felt, we were connected, on another level, always had been, from day one, I loved it, I loved her, I loved how simple our life together was, which sounds bizarre given all the obstacles we have overcome.

Takeaway was ordered, and Fi searched for something to watch on Tv. As we curled up together on the end of the sofa, she turned her head towards me, and kissed me, gently at first. Instantly I felt the vibes from her surge through me, setting my nerves on edge, and stirring things I knew I could do nothing with, we never had got round to having the conversation about sex, so it had always been off the table as far as I was concerned, but when she kissed me like this, it was all I could do to stop myself succumbing to all of my urges, every masculine part of me wanted to be inside her, craving her body, like my life depended on it. She kissed me harder, it almost didn't feel right, this was doing nothing for my resolve, it felt strange, alien to us, she had never kissed me this way before. She turned her body to mine, pushing her hands through my hair, her kisses were electric, passionate, carnal, I was losing control, part of me wanted to run away for fear I wouldn't be able to control myself, I was confused, excited, elated and horny as fuck.

Jees Fi what are you trying to do to me. When she reached down, took the edge of my t-shirt and lifted it, I stopped kissing her and pulled away, maybe a little too quickly, shit what was I doing ! What was she doing ! She shook her head, "No! Do not do this, no questions, no thinking, nothing." She pulled me back in towards her, and I kissed her more passionately than I thought was ever possible, I could sense her in every part of me, my whole body was waiting for her, waiting to know how it felt to be inside her, to be together like we had never been before. When her hands touched the bare skin of my chest, my breath stopped and the thought of touching her almost made my heart explode, I pulled her t-shirt over her head, and stopped, in awe of the beauty before me, I placed my hand on her waist and slowly slid it round to her back, drowning in every moment. Her skin was like nothing I'd ever felt, silk under my fingers, I pulled her to me needing to feel her body on mine, the moment we touched any thoughts of control were lost, she'd already undone the button and zip on my jeans, I slid my hands down the back of her jeans, my body now desperate to be with hers. We fell to the floor, never moving more than a couple of inches apart. I never, ever wanted this moment to be over, this woman I adored beneath me, moving as one until eventually I could take no more, I called out her name, the force of me now moving her up and down, her clinging on, kissing my chest, my neck, and then I came, straining to be as deep inside her, to be as close to her, as any human had ever been to another, bursting inside her, over and over, until we were spent, together, a hot, sweaty, breathless, wonderful mess.

Chapter Twenty-Four

Sam can't possibly have known, I hope, that would just be weird, but those extra few hours he gave me this evening, were the best damn thing he ever gave me. When I'd finished kissing every part of Fi's body and telling her a million times, to her amusement and giggles, just how beautiful, amazing, sexy, wonderful she was, we warmed the takeaway, and ate it, naked on our sofa. I was exhilarated, I could not imagine, in my life, ever feeling any better than I did in this moment, I was exhausted, physically and emotionally, I was elated, and so totally chilled it was unbelievable. I was always sad to leave Fi and go out to work, but today, well, I didn't want this to end, I wanted to stay feeling this way forever.

Sooner than I'd wished, it was back to reality. Sam had text to say he was on his way, and my heart sank. "I wish I could stay," I told her, "Me too," she said, "I love you Fi," "I love you too Conal." She kissed me again, it was short this time, not because she stopped, but because I did, I had to, it was already going to be difficult hiding my excitement from Sam, without the very obvious physical evidence to show for it ! She giggled, knowing exactly why I'd pulled away shaking my head with a smile.

Just a few minutes later, I was on my way down the steps, and jumping into the car. I knew he was looking at me, he always knew just how I was feeling, he knew if there was something wrong, and he knew if there was something right ! I tried my best to avoid eye contact, but I could feel his eyes boring into my soul. He didn't even drive, he just sat staring until I couldn't help grinning and asking him, "What ! ?" "Ohhh Conal, you dirty boy." My cheeks were so hot I could feel the burn, "Are you serious," I said, "Is nothing sacred with you," I couldn't help laughing, "You know me mate, nothing gets past this." He tapped the side of his nose, and then his face was straight, "Seriously though mate, I'm made up things are going well for you, if any one deserves it, you do, both of you." I thanked him, even though it drove me mad that I could get nothing past him, it felt good to know he was always there for me.

"So, where are we going ?" I asked, "We're going to the clinic." What the fuck, was he serious, "Like THE clinic ?" "Yes mate THE clinic," he seemed amused with himself, he liked knowing I was puzzled by his behaviour. I knew he wouldn't give up any information unless I asked him, but I also knew he was waiting for me to ask, so he could tell me ! Slight impasse coming up ! Even though I knew who would give in first, I wanted to make him wait, just a little while, just to make myself feel better. I lasted less than five minutes. "Go on then," I demanded, "Go on what ?" he asked, "Tell me why we're going." I turned to face him, waiting for a reply, while he grinned, making me wait. "We have something to pick up, then something to drop off, then we're gonna watch, and wait." He was being purposely cryptic, either to piss me off, or because he didn't want to give any more information than was needed. I left it there, I would find out soon enough. I puzzled all the way, over just what might be happening. Was it just a late pick up for someone who couldn't accept an early drop off, but then why would Sam need me, the watching and waiting was new though, not something Sam usually did, well not that I was aware of anyway.

I'd been thinking so much, I'd not even realised how close we were, when I looked up we were pulling into Renshaw Street where the Clinic was located. It was almost 10pm now and although the clinic was closed to clients, the shutters were still up, and there was a faint light coming from the corridor at the back of the reception, somebody was still at home. "I'll be back in a minute," Sam said, climbing from the car. And he was, he'd barely made his way through the door, and he was returning with, well nothing that I could see. He climbed back into the driver's seat, and set straight off. "Where to now ?" I asked him, not knowing if I'd get a straight answer, "Kings Road," he said. Kings Road was on the same side of town as the clinic, but about another 15 minutes, going away from the city centre, it wasn't far from 'posh guy'. I knew the way, we'd been many times before, but I didn't know Kings Road that well. It wasn't long before we were pulling up outside a huge house, very modern, loads of glass and grey frames, it was actually a little boring for me, I prefer something a bit more homely, but you could see there was a lot of money here.

Generally whenever Sam came to these types of houses, he parked just a few houses away from his destination, but today he parked right outside, only for the fact we had just picked something up to bring here I'd have been a little concerned for the life of the person inside ! I had a great view point from where we were. I waited as Sam walked up the short drive, knocked and stood back waiting for the occupant to open the door. I was surprised when it did, I'd actually seen this guy before, he'd been at the clinic a couple of times while I'd been working there, and he was not happy to see Sam at his front door, he was edgy, twitchy, he looked over Sams head, looking up and down the Road, he focused on me for a couple of seconds then turned back to Sam. Could this be Gerard Long ? And if it was, what did it have to do with Sam. Sam was speaking, but obviously my lack of lip reading abilities meant I had no idea what was being said. He handed a simple white envelope over to the guy, then walked away. The guy stood, looking stunned, as he watched Sam walk back down the drive. He didn't go back inside, in fact he was still on his doorstep when we left.

We didn't get far, Sam reached the end of the road, did a u-turn and headed back towards the guy's house. "Is this Gerard Long ?" I had to know, "It certainly is mate," was the short answer. "What's she gonna do about him ?" he looked at me like I was asking too many questions now, but he answered any way. "I really don't know, only time will tell, for now, she's not our concern, we watch and wait."
"What are we waiting for ?" I knew he was getting pissed off now, I normally didn't ask so many questions, but this was a little closer to home than the usual suspects, and I needed to know. "I'll know when I see it, can't tell you much more than that sorry mate. "And so we waited, and waited…and waited, I was ridiculously bored, and after an hour and a half of me sighing, huffing and puffing, Sam reached behind the passenger seat and pulled out a carrier back, inside where crisps, biscuits, a pack of donuts, and drinks, he handed me the lot and said, "For fuck sake mate, stick one of those in your mouth will you !" Gladly ! I thought. I'd had my takeaway, but that seemed like a lifetime ago now, it was getting on for midnight and I was bored and hungry.

I was woken up by the car engine bursting into life. "What's happening ?" I asked, sitting up quickly, rubbing my face to wake myself up. I looked around, we were still in Kings Road, but we were on the move. "Nothing much. Enjoy your nap ?" he was being sarcastic of course, "I did actually," I said giving him some back. "Where are we going now ?" It was 2.25 am, I'd slept for over an hour, I was actually a little embarrassed, but he'd obviously not needed me for anything special, otherwise he'd have made sure I was awake and on the ball. I was expecting nothing more from him, so I was surprised when he said, "You missed it all mate." He wanted me to ask, so I wasted no time. "What happened ?" "Well, I think we've found who our friend Mr Long is working for, or scared of, one or the other," "Why didn't you wake me up," I said, fuming that I'd missed all the fun." Awww you looked so peaceful, I couldn't bear to disturb you," he was a sarcastic little shit when he wanted to be ! " So ?" I wished he would just tell me, I mean it had no bearing on my life, I don't think, but out of sheer curiosity I wanted to know. Sam took out his phone, pressed a few buttons, and turned the phone my way. I didn't recognise this guy, I was pretty sure I'd never seen him before," Do you know him ?" I asked, "Don't know his name, but I suspect Brad will know exactly who he is," "Are you going to tell her," I asked, wondering when he started 'working' for Brad. "Hell no, if she wants to know, she can find out for herself," I wasn't sure if he realised, but this had put me in a bit of a predicament, I now knew who the guy was, what would I do if Brad asked me, or was that why Sam had told me, I had no idea as usual. " Will she kill him ? " I asked, fearing I may become responsible for yet another person dying. He burst out laughing, obviously hearing the concern in my voice. I didn't find it funny at all, you just never knew with these people. "Let's have a late start tomorrow mate, how does 11 sound ?" It sounded frickin' perfect !!

It was more than a week later when he told me we were going to visit a guy called...Charles Barrington-Lowe, or Charlie Lowe for short. Names like that make you think, don't they, I mean Charles Barrington-Lowe maybe wears a monocle or something, a sweater around his shoulders, slacks and boat shoes, but he could be walking around like Derek Trotter, in his sheepskin coat and cap. Just shows how judgmental we all can be. I heard a clicking sound and realised it was Sam clicking his fingers in front of my face. "Wakey, wakey mate, where were you then ?" I smiled and told him I was miles away. "Right we have to stay with it today, you don't have to do anything except sit in the car ok ?" I wasn't ok this was all starting to sound extremely ominous, or very boring, "Yeh ok," I said. It was 8pm, it was dark and wet and cold, and I didn't even want to be outside, let alone going to do god knows what to god knows who. I knew this was the way it worked, I knew this was the game I was in, but it was never going to sit right with me, not the way it had with dad or Joseph, sad thing is Charlie Lowe knew it too. As my mother used to say, 'If you play with fire, sooner or later you're gonna get burned' and today

Charlie mate you're gonna get burned. Actually, I had no idea what was going to happen to him, but I highly suspected he was not getting a bunch of flowers delivered this evening ! I was still totally baffled by why this had become our problem.

Charlie Lowe lived about five minutes drive from Gerard Long, in Westwood Avenue, these were tree lined streets with long drives, and beautiful huge old houses, all immaculately kept and not a soul around. It was practically desolate, which explains why we were here at this time. Charlie lived at number 227, the numbers to most of them were neatly etched into the massive sandstone gate posts. Most of them had electric gates, which made me wonder how we would even get in to 'visit' Charlie. Sam knew exactly where he was going, of course he did, this wouldn't be the first time he'd been here. We parked across the road, almost opposite the drive of 227, then we waited. But not for long, less than 5 minutes later, the glare of two headlights came into view, Sam suddenly sat up straight in his seat, he looked so different when he was in work mode, this was serious, he looked older, maybe even a little cold. As the other car got closer Sam quickly pulled the car round almost up to the gates of 227, I thought he was doing a U-turn, as the other car pulled up nearby, Sam put his hand up to him, I couldn't figure out what the hell he was doing, but I trusted him, and so I let him do his thing, even if my nerves were getting the better of me. He reversed about five feet, put his handbrake on, got out and walked back toward the waiting car. Suddenly the lights went out, there was no fuss, and just a few seconds later the guy was climbing into the back of Sam's car, his hair was wet, and he was in shorts and a t-shirt, so my best guess was he'd just got back from the gym.

What I hadn't noticed, and was really pissed off with myself for, and which I wouldn't be admitting to Sam, was, the car that had pulled up behind Charlie's car. I saw it now, but only because I recognised the guy getting out of the passenger side. It was Tatty, I breathed a sigh of relief as he waved, and climbed into Charlie's car, then, we trundled along Westwood Avenue, and out of town. I really wasn't up to seeing the shed again, every time we went there which was mercifully not very often, it literally knocked the stuffing out of me, I don't know how, but on a daily basis I managed to forget I'd actually killed another human being, although I use the word human very loosely. I hated being reminded of what I was capable of.

We were at least twenty minutes into our journey before I realised we definitely were not going to the shed. I started looking out for road signs, for some clue as to where we were headed. All I could make out in the darkness was, we were heading out of town, but I had no idea in which direction, and to be fair it really didn't matter, the destination wasn't an issue, the end product of the journey was. Charlie didn't speak a word, and surprisingly he didn't seem too concerned either, if I'd have been in his shoes I'd have been shitting my pants ! Maybe he was used to this kind of shit, what the fuck, nothing ceased to amaze me in this world anymore. I was finding the silence ridiculously uncomfortable, but couldn't think of anything to say that didn't sound equally as ridiculous. So I stayed quiet, and let my mind run away with me. Maybe Charlie wasn't bothered cause he was setting us up, or maybe he had a tracker in his car and someone was following us as we speak or rather think, or maybe he was just a tough little mother fucker and really didn't give a shit ! Thankfully just another half hour passed before we pulled into a street and began to slow, we were obviously getting close now. Charlie sat up in his seat, looking out of the window to the right, Sam was watching him in the rear view mirror. I was startled when Charlie suddenly said, "Here, on the right," Sam smiled at him through the mirror and nodded, I was more confused than ever now, it hadn't crossed my mind for a minute that they were on the same side. There was no shed, no old barn, no middle of nowhere, just a very nice street, with a very nice house, four guys, two cars and yep, it made no sense whatsoever.

Chapter Twenty-Five

Sam and Charlie both climbed out of the car at the same time, as soon as they were out into the fresh night air, they shook hands and hugged, patting each other on the back as they did, smiles all round. They were joined just a few seconds later by Tatty, he too shook Charlie's hand, I on the other hand stood in the background wondering what the hell was happening. I was a bit pissed off at Sam, I understood there were things he couldn't tell me, but sometimes, times like this, I just looked like a bit of a prick who came along for the ride. As if hearing my thoughts, Sam turned, tapping Charlie on the arm as he did so, and gesturing for him to come to meet me. I always hated this bit, I mean to be fair, there was no pleasing me was there ! I was either the prick in the background or the awkward, embarrassed kid who hated meeting new people. Charlie walked straight towards me, "Hi, Conal isn't it ?" He actually did have a posh accent, well maybe not posh but he was very well spoken, not up his own arse, I liked him, I often made these impulsive decisions about people, and on the whole I was usually right. He seemed really pleased to see me, I only wish I knew why ! "Yeh," I said extending my arm out to him, I took the hand he was offering, and wasn't surprised at how firm his handshake was, he did it with purpose, I've a feeling if he didn't know you or like you, there would be no hand shaking, it was reserved for those he liked and trusted, but he didn't know me, so how did he know I was either. I dare say it wouldn't be too long before I found out.

Whilst everyone was reacquainting themselves, they walked towards the house they'd parked outside of, there was a car in the driveway, it was as I said, a nice house, perfectly turned out, with a deep red, almost brown, door, in its pristine white frame, as Sam approached it, the door opened, to no surprise whatsoever, Degs appeared from behind the it, he hugged his son, then he hugged Charlie, then he shook Tattys hand, then there was me, "Ah hello son, come here." I couldn't help myself he always made me smile, made me feel warm inside, and I loved those fatherly hugs he gave me, just like he did Sam. It was amazing how that felt, not only did it feel good to be part of this family, it soothed me, the anxieties I'd been feeling just a few minutes earlier began to drift, I couldn't put my finger on it for a moment or two then I realised what it was, I felt safe, I felt secure, and I felt wanted, all of the things any child, no matter what their age, needs and wants from their father. Rather than being confused and anxious, I was now intrigued, I was eager to find out just how these people were all connected, and what this had to do with them, Brad, and me.

Sam called me to one side once we were inside, "You may not get home tonight, so you might want to call Fi and let her know," "Oh … ok." I wish I'd known this before we'd left, I'd rather have told her face to face, I mean I was often late home, but not all night. Sam suggested I use the kitchen to make my call, I was grateful for the privacy. Of course Fi was fine, nothing much phased her, she wished I was home but she understood and asked me to stay in touch. As I walked into the hallway before going back into the living room, there was a knock at the front door, my stomach turned, I stopped in my tracks waiting for someone to come and see who it was, I could see the outline of someone through the frosted glass, but couldn't make out who it was. Tatty came from the living room, beaming his usual giant smile. I hadn't realised I was holding my breath until I let out a noisy sigh when there was only Buzz on the other side of the door. They shook hands and greeted each other in their usual excitable way, before making their way back into the front room. Finally ungluing myself from the spot, I followed them through the door thinking I really wasn't cut out for this.

Now that everyone was there, the party atmosphere came to a rather abrupt halt. I took a seat on the sofa next to Sam, sitting way back in my seat, feeling very out of place amongst these people who obviously knew why they were there, and I waited to find out exactly what my part was in all of this. Degs was first to speak up, "Well, first things first, I think we need to fill the boy in on what's happening, yes ?" Everyone was in agreement, but all I could think was BOY ! It didn't bother me as much as it would have if someone else had said it, but still, BOY ! I felt like all eyes were on me now, all waiting patiently to see how I reacted to whatever it was they were going to say. It was Degs who spoke. "Firstly Conal, I know you must be feeling like you've been kept out of the loop…" I nodded, because I had, " …and that was intentional, but not because we didn't trust you, we just know Brad, and if there was anything at all for her to pick up on, then she would have, so we needed you to be behaving as naturally as possible, the only way for that to happen was for you to be completely oblivious to our involvement, I hope we haven't offended you too much." Now that he'd put it like that, I didn't feel offended in the slightest, it made perfect sense. "I was never offended, Degs, more confused than anything, but of course I understand, it makes perfect sense, but I'll be more than happy to find out what the hell is going on here !" They all laughed, and I was kind of glad I'd lightened the atmosphere a bit. "This…" he pointed across the room, "…as you probably know by now is Charlie," I nodded again.

Charlie stood and walked across the room, holding out his hand for me to shake again, I did so of course, "Nice to meet you Conal, good to have you on board, Joey is very sadly missed." What the fuck, I'd definitely missed something here, I was getting more confused by the minute. Degs moved to the edge of his seat and looked directly at me. "I'm sure you know that Joseph and Sam worked closely together for a long time, but he started out pretty much the same as you, I guess you coming from the same blood, we trusted you sooner, plus he was a cocky little arsehole sometimes, and you, thankfully, are not." They all laughed now nodding in agreement with Degs. "Don't get me wrong Conal, we loved him as if he were one of our own, but jees he was hard work sometimes." Everything he said about Joseph was said with kindness and with affection, there was no way I could ever be offended, Joseph was in fact a cocky little fucker. "Brad, as I think you've already figured out, wants you where she can keep an eye on you, she's trying to find out what, if anything you know about who killed Joseph." My eyes lit up, and now I was on the edge of my seat too. "Do you know who killed him ?" I asked, almost pleading with them. "We should do, son, but no, not yet, we know she was behind it, she had to be, but in all this time, we've not been able to get a single name, no trace of anything that could throw some light on who did it." Tatty spoke up now, "The thing is we know she keeps a tight community, and people are scared to talk, but believe me there is always someone, or some way, but this…zilch, she had a soft spot for Joseph…" I noticed all but Charlie now gave him his full name, I was humbled by their respect for my feelings, "…but that means nothing, she had a soft spot for the hubby and look what happened to him !" I was still trying to soak up the revelation that Brad was in some way responsible for Joseph's death, whilst trying hard to stay focused enough to take in everything else that was said. Sam, as always, read me like a book and piped up, "Hey guys, we're gonna be here a while, how about we order in some food, I'm sure we're all ready for something to eat." I was thankful for Sam's efforts to give me some time to digest the small but devastating bit of information I had just received.

Food was ordered, drinks were handed out, and there were a few moments of chit chat and relaxation before they all got back to the subject in hand. I had some questions of my own now, I'd had a small amount of time to get them straight in my head, I thought, in this situation I would feel a little awkward but I had no hesitation in finding out as much as I possibly could, while I could. "Would anyone mind if I asked just a few questions ?" They all looked at each other whilst each individually nodding their approval. "Thanks," I said, "How certain are you that Brad was responsible ?" Charlie spoke up, "Like, probably a good ninety nine percent, she loved Joseph..." I didn't miss that, "... and she knew he worked for us, but if she'd have found out what he was doing, well we all know how that would, and did end." "What was he doing ?" "Brad runs the biggest crew in the country, she knows everyone, and everyone knows of her, but no one really knows her, most people have never seen her, most people still think she is a he ! So when she took a shine to Joseph, we used it to our advantage." Sam chipped in now, "The thing is, in this business like any other it's all about building it to be the biggest and best you can, and that usually involves taking down some other businesses along the way, the only way to do that is attack their client base, and that's where Joseph came in." "So Joseph was your inside man ? And now you want me to be your inside man?" I suddenly felt very used, and disposable, I'd simply been a convenient and dispensable commodity to them. "No, no, no son not at all, there was never any intention of you being there any longer than it took to find out if they were on to Charlie," said Degs, and for all my underlying uncertainty, I believed him, he'd never given me any reason not do, but I still felt used, what I had to remember was, they didn't ask me to do any of this, yes they took advantage of a situation I had put myself in, but this was all my own doing. It took a few minutes, but I did eventually get over myself and continued with my questions. "What exactly was Joseph doing ? And did he know what he was getting himself into ?" I was looking at Sam now, he was supposed to be Joseph's friend, and I'm not sure I could work with him any longer if he'd not been up front with him. "He was looking for the best clients, the ones bringing in the big money, it took him a long time, like we said Brad trusts no one, but eventually she let him in, we were working with those clients to take over, bring her down, and yes Joseph knew exactly what he was doing." I was relieved, glad to hear he had not been betrayed by those he trusted. "And Brad, what else do you know about her, not like her work or stuff but personally, her family, her friends ?" There was a short silence, I guess she really did keep her cards close to her chest, then Tatty spoke again. "She has three kids, no one sees them, they go to private school, they're picked up each morning, dropped off each evening, and spend the holidays abroad, I get the feeling she's not really the maternal type," he raised his eyebrows and everyone muttered in agreement. "How old are her kids ?" I wasn't even sure why I wanted to know this, I just had this overwhelming need to know as much about her as I could. "I'm not entirely sure," said Tatty, "The older girl I'd say was around sixteen, maybe seventeen, then there's two younger girls, eight, ten maybe," "Friends ?" I asked, "There's only one real friend she's had since they were kids, they still meet up once a month, but the fact she sees her regularly means she tells her nothing." I couldn't help but wonder what she got out of all this, she had no time for her kids, she had no friends, she went nowhere, kept herself to herself, with an army of people around her, who more than likely didn't even like her but definitely liked the money. What a sad existence, she existed only to be powerful, and that was it.

The food arrived, and the talk returned to general chat, they laughed and joked about what they'd been up to, reminisced and generally had a great time, it felt good, not being so serious for a little while, I had nothing to give to the conversation, but I was more than happy to sit back, eat the most amazing Indian food, and just listen. I took the time too, to text Fi, just to let her know I was ok. When dinner was over and the mountain of empty takeaway cartons and leftover food had been cleared away, it was back to business.

So, Charlie had paid Gerard Lowe for a list of clients. Gerard wasn't exactly keen on doing this, but by all accounts he had little or no choice. Gerard was not well liked by any of the people in the room, and it seems for good reason, he was a 'snivelling little grass' 'couldn't be trusted as far as you could throw him' and 'would sell his own grandmother if need be' he was a 'sleazeball' 'slime ball' and basically a 'snidey little shit' who no one cared for. And so, when it was suggested he could earn some extra cash, like he didn't have enough, then he was up for it, he used the accounts to distract from the fact he was passing on client information. "What will happen to Gerard ?" "Oh don't be worrying about him son…" said Buzz, "… he's long gone, got picked up that night you two were watching him, remember ?" I nodded remembering the night, "How would you know sleepy head !" piped up Sam, simultaneously punching my arm, god that always bloody hurt, and I always had to grin and pretend it didn't ! The thing is, Brad was obviously going to try to find out who was pulling Gerards strings, which meant Charlie could be in danger, and as Sam worked for Brad, she had asked him to find out exactly who that someone was, and deal with it ! Hence the reason we had just kidnapped Charlie and driven him out of town. Sam got a not very well hidden side eye after that bit of info !

So what happens now ?" I asked, "I mean what would happen to Charlie, surely at some point Brad would realise he was never 'dealt' with after all." "You worry too much son," said Buzz "You think we're just winging it here?" As soon as he said that I realised how stupid I sounded, obviously they had a plan, they'd been planning this for god knows how long, probably years ! I laughed a little, a result of nerves and the acknowledgement of the stupid statement I'd made. There was a lot happening as we spoke, maybe not here in this room, but across the city and across the country, at least fifty percent of Brads clients were coming together to form one giant conglomerate of drug dealers, one giant company, working together to take as much as they could from Brad, once they were up and running the chances were they would then be able to take over the rest of the city/country. Now this sounded great in theory, but in reality it all seemed a little ambitious for five men sitting in someone's front room. Every so often I wondered why I was here, nothing deep, like the meaning of life and all that stuff, but quite literally why was I actually here in this room, why did they want me around, they'd been doing this for years, and I'd known them just a few months, it just didn't make any sense. As always my thoughts travelled in some sort of miraculous leap of telepathy, Sam turned to me, " You know you saved Charlie's life."

Back to what really matters here ! BRAD had my brother killed !! And I would, at some point, make her pay, but I still needed to know who did it, and these guys here in this room were the only ones who could help me. "I know this isn't really your problem guys, and in the middle of all this it's really not important to you, but would you still keep your ears open for any hint of who killed Joseph." There was a sudden cacophony of all their voices together, "Hey mate, that'll never be forgotten," "As if we could forget," "Don't you worry mate, it's always top of our agenda." They were all ready to do their utmost to help me, and that quite suddenly and unexpectedly brought out a lot of emotion. The realisation that you are not alone on your journey, that your fight is not yours alone, is something that fills you with pride, humility, and love. Sounds a bit soppy and out of place given the circumstances of us being together, but I loved these guys, they'd been there for me every step of the way for months now, and I could never have come as far as I had, without them.

When they'd finished reassuring me that they would, one way or another, find whoever was responsible, Charlie left the room and came back with a stack of books. They were books full of names and numbers for people all across the country, including any details Brad held for them regarding their finances, each book had a slight variant on the code they used, which meant I would pretty much have to figure mine out for myself ! There were so many numbers in these books, I was completely overwhelmed. Degs, seeing my obvious discomfort, laughed and said, "Don't worry too much about it son, there's very little in there that you really need to know, but we wanted to keep you in the loop." Thank god for that I thought, I mean just out of curiosity I'd like to know what was in them, and the fact they trusted me with this information meant the world to me, but if I needed to rely on it right now…I'd be fucked ! Plans were made for each of the separate 'companies' to cease trading with Brad at the same time on the same day, therefore hitting her as hard as they could, it seems this takeover wasn't simply about money, although that was the biggest reason, they didn't like her, they didn't respect her, and they were all getting a massive kick from hurting what she cared about most …cash !

While they busily made plans, I was making some of my own, I'd carried on with my small talk and ascertained what school Brad's kids went to, what time they went, and who took them, I'd made a split second decision, one that, in that moment, made perfect sense to me, she took my family from me, and that's what I was going to do to her. Don't get me wrong I'm not some sort of monster, but just when these guys are taking all means of income from her, knowing she will have to have taken her eye off the ball, I will be taking the only other assets she had, her kids. Then I'll hit her where it really hurts, asking an extortionate amount of money to get them back. I wouldn't be able to do this alone, and when the time was right, I would ask the only other person I could, to help me out, Sam. It should be easy enough, she wasn't half as careful of protecting her kids as she was her business deals. The next few weeks would be important, I was used to watching and waiting, and that's what I would be doing again, time was never an issue for me, but coinciding with the big takeover would definitely be to my advantage.

My main goal was to pretend to become one of Brad's biggest allies, she would love to think she was distancing me from Sam. If I could gain her trust enough to allow me to take the kids to school, that would be the easiest option. There were two slight issues with this, one, she already had an obviously very trusted guy to do that job, and two, I didn't drive, and I honestly didn't see me getting three kids on my bike ! So now was the time to finally start taking those driving lessons Sam had been nagging about for months, I'm sure I didn't have long, but so long as I could drive confidently I wasn't too worried about getting an actual licence, I just needed the ability.

Listening to these guys, pulling figures together, talking about all the different factions coming together, talking about the risks, the advantages, who will be doing what, when, where and why, and all the while ensuring Charlie was staying below the radar until it was all done and dusted, well, it was remarkable to be honest. I'm sure most people assume drug dealers have very little intelligence, simply buying from one person and selling to another, but listening to this, to these guys pulling off this massive feat, it was fascinating. There where over 200 other people involved from all over the country, which gave you an idea of just how prominent Brad was, and what these guys were up against, keeping all of those people on side, having spent so much time building up enough trust that you knew they wouldn't impart any information to Brad, had taken years of ground work. And now they were at the precipice, pulling together those last pieces of the puzzle ready to strike when the time was right.

While they continued to talk about things I knew nothing about, I tried to follow the figures in my book, trying to make some sense of the rows of numbers, I couldn't, it meant absolutely nothing to me, but then I suppose that was the point, if I could work it out in one evening then it really wouldn't be much good to them would it ! So I took advantage of the fact that I had little to input right now, and I Googled 'driving lessons in Cohm'.

Chapter Twenty-Six

Sam had been right, morning had well and truly broken, before we were back in the car, and on our way home. Fi had gone to bed around 1.30am, hoping I would be home earlier. It would be good to see her, it felt like so long since we'd spent that amazing time together. I counted down the minutes until I was with her again. She was waiting on the doorstep for me, tea in hand, when we pulled up outside, Sam shook his head and smiled at me, "Might have to get myself one of those," he said, nodding towards Fi, who was beaming and waving eagerly, waiting for me to go to her. I didn't let her down, within a minute I had her in my arms, kissing her passionately not wanting to ever let her go. There was a beep, and the noise of a car accelerating, I waved behind me without taking my lips from hers.

This is where I belonged, always, I loved the guys, and they were my family, but Fi was something else, she was an integral part of my being, as corny as it sounded, I felt complete when I was with her. Usually I would fill her in on my day, but this time things were different, what had happened last night was not my story to tell, I could however fill her in on all the stuff I'd learned about Brad, I'd not yet found the courage to let her in on my possible plans for kidnap and extortion ! After not seeing her all night, I really did feel that was one small detail that could wait a while. We sat on our step, watching the world slowly come to life, with our warm tea in our hands. If this was all I could ever have in life, then I'd gladly grab it with both hands.

I had a driving lesson booked for two days later, it came round quickly, I'd discussed it with Fi and we'd agreed she would take lessons too, so the same guy was doing us both, which meant she could come along for the ride. Although my nerves got the better of me at first, I soon found I was pretty good at it, the hour passed in a flash, and it was Fi's turn next, she was a nervous wreck, I hated seeing her like this, stressed and panicked. "Fi, you don't have to do this now you know," I told her, "Yes Conal, I do, if I don't do it now I might never do it." She melted my heart over and over, she never gave up on anything, and this was no different. And, she was pretty frickin' amazing, never put a foot wrong, did exactly as she was told, and at the end of the hour, her confidence had gone through the roof, she was loving it, she was genuinely having fun, it was wonderful to see the transformation. I paid the guy and thanked him, he was coming back two days later to do it all again, I wanted us both on the road as soon as possible. We were both on a high, I don't think I'd ever seen Fi quite so excited, she couldn't stop talking, and I loved listening to every joyous word.

I was still working with Brad one day a week, and I'd gradually and purposely lowered my guard. I needed her to trust me, and I needed her to think our relationship was all on her terms, it was easier than I thought, yet another one of mums sayings slipped into my head 'if something seems too easy, it usually has to be done again'. It was hard to know who was kidding who, but I suspected she was just as wary as I was, and therefore neither of us had any choice but to trust the other. I had two weeks to get rid of the driver, *and* be capable of driving, the physical driving didn't concern me, but I'd tried to befriend Archie, and he was having none of it ! He was old school, fiercely loyal, and a stickler for the rules. I was going to have to take more drastic measures, and no I wasn't planning on getting him bumped off, but I was sure I could come up with a bit of diarrhoea, or a touch of food poisoning. I also needed Sam on board sooner rather than later, there was no way I could track their route to and from school on my bike. If Sam wasn't up for it, and I wouldn't blame him if he thought I was crazy, then there was no way I could make this work.

I needed a plan, and I needed it soon. I had the idea but quite literally none of the logistics, I had no where or when, I had nowhere to go with these kids once I had them, I was obviously still going to need to work, which means I needed Fi on board, she was the only other person I trusted. Now that I'd made the decision to actually go ahead with this it was a huge weight off my mind, yes it was replaced with another huge weight, but it was a start. I would talk to Fi first, she would be my biggest hurdle, if she wasn't up for this, then it was a non-starter, then I'd speak to Sam, if it was the most ridiculous idea I'd ever had he would have no problems whatsoever telling me. And so, it was Fi first, but not today, she was on such a high, I couldn't spoil it for her. But tomorrow, she had to know.

How do you even broach the subject, I mean it's not something you just bring up over your cornflakes and cuppa, 'Sugar dear ? Oh and how do you feel about kidnap ?' It really wasn't going to work. I tried a few different scenarios in my head, and only one worked, the park, I don't know what it was about being outdoors, but for me it made things easier, there was nowhere to escape from when you were out in the fresh air, no other room to escape to, no house to leave, it may not make sense to some, but to me it was the only way. Before I left for work the following day, I asked her would she like to go for a walk later on, I gave her the heads up and told her I had something I needed to talk about, and that it was serious, seeing her face suddenly change to one of concern, I quickly reassured her it was nothing to do with us, as in me and her, that it was all about Joseph, but that I couldn't do it without her approval. I could have done it there and then but it wouldn't have been fair to leave her to mull it over all day on her own. This way wasn't much better, but I could only ever go for the slightly better option in this situation.

Sam was outside at nine am, and I needed to give him the heads up too. "Hey Sam, I have something on my mind I need to talk to you about, I might, well I WILL need your help, if that's possible, but I need to talk to Fi before it goes any further," "Anytime mate, you just let me know when you're ready." There was no hint of hesitation, and fair enough he had no idea what I was planning, but that was exactly the point wasn't it, he knew it could be absolutely anything, and the answer was always going to be, I'm here when you need me. I thanked him, sincerely, he nodded and that was the end of the conversation, it was back to work. There was no mention of the last few days, there didn't need to be, plans had been made and were in the process of being carried out, and yet to look at him, you wouldn't think a thing had changed.

I couldn't decide how I felt getting home that evening, I was excited things could finally be moving, but the apprehension was nerve wracking, what if she was horrified that I was even thinking that way, I mean in all fairness she should be, it could change things between us forever, sadly it was a risk I had to take. There are some things in life that we just can't let go, even though we are fully aware of the damage they could do, and this was one of those things. Fi was not on the step to meet me, but she was waiting inside the door to greet me with the most amazing smile, and the most tender of kisses, passionate kisses were unbelievable, but these did something to my insides that I often wondered if I could ever recover from. "Are we going straight out or do you want to eat first," she asked, I needed to get this all off my chest, I couldn't eat knowing what I was going to be asking of her. "You ok if we go straight out ? We could get takeaway on the way home if you fancy it," "Sounds great," she said. I could see she was worried about what I had to say, but as always, she took it all in her stride and carried on regardless. She grabbed her coat, and we left.

We called into the garage on the way to the park and picked up hot chocolate from the coffee bar. Handing over her drink, I looked her straight in the eye, "You already know that what I have to say is serious, I mean I'm asking a lot from you Fi, and you have to be able to say no at any point, I've thought long and hard about the damage this could do to us, I mean I thought I was crazy myself when I first thought of it, but there's simply no going back now, this is the only way I can make her pay." I realised I was rambling without really telling her anything at all. "Who are we talking about ?" she asked, and, give her her due, she remained completely composed, and didn't sound the least bit concerned by what I had said. " Brad, she might not have killed Joseph herself, but he would still be alive today if it wasn't for her." I waited for a reaction from her, there was none, she was managing to keep total control of her emotions, and I knew that was for my sake, not hers. "I see," she said. We were almost at the park gates now, it was quiet and almost dark, she pulled her coat across her chest, trying to keep out the cold, "And do you have an idea how you want to make her pay ?" "Yes," I waited again, this girl was good, she gave nothing away, "Well, let's hear it." Just a few feet ahead was one of the wooden park benches, for a moment I thought we might sit down, but then talking on the go was always so much easier, so I kept on walking. "It's not great Fi, obviously I had to find a way to make her realise the damage she's caused, I mean I'm guessing I'm not the only one who's lost someone due to her." She looked to the side and caught my eye, she could tell how nervous I was, and her face softened, she smiled, took my hand and squeezed a little, instantly reassuring me. "Hey listen, if it's something I can't live with, I *will* tell you, and we will find another way, plus I may not be able to give you an answer straight away, I mean you've had time to think this through, this will all be new to me." Now I could tell her, now I knew she was prepared, and would tell me straight how she felt, I could tell her my ridiculous plans. I took a deep breath.

"Brad has three kids..." I couldn't look at her now, I was too afraid to see her reaction, she would let me know in good time, "... two younger ones, about nine, ten and an older girl who they think is about seventeen, they're all at the same private school, and I'm gonna take them from her." Now I needed to look. She was completely impassive, how she was managing to contain herself I do not know. I slowed and took her hand when she didn't speak, pulling her towards me, she didn't want to look my way, and I couldn't blame her. "Fi I don't want to hurt them, I could never do that, nothing will happen to them I swear, this is all about hurting her, from what I've learned she couldn't care less about the kids, but the fact someone has dared to do this will hit her hard, and when she has to pay to get them back, that will hit her where it really hurts." There were several more minutes of unbearable silence before she spoke, "How can you guarantee nothing will happen to them ?" Shit ! Now I have to tell her this is where she comes in. "Fi, there are few people I truly trust in this world, and top of that list is you, I'll be asking a lot from you if I can pull this off, I've not spoken to Sam yet, I wanted to run it past you first," "You didn't answer my question Conal." Shit no, I didn't, did I ! I could barely bring myself to ask her but I just had to grow a pair and get it done. "The only person I would trust with those kids Fi, is you ?"

She was more than a little surprised, how could she not have realised where I was going with this, it seemed so clear and very obvious in my head. Now we needed that bench, there was one a few feet away, and I pulled her across to sit down. "Listen Conal, there's not a lot I wouldn't do for you, you know that, I'll listen to all your deepest thoughts, I'll be there when you need advice, I'll keep all your secrets, always, but I can't make a decision like that on the spot, no one could." She was right of course, but it wasn't a no, god I could kiss her right now, but I didn't want her to think I was being presumptuous. "Of course," I said, hugging her tightly, "Of course, Fi I'd like to give you more time, but there's a lot going on, and there will be an ideal time slot in about two weeks time ?" "Just a day or so Conal, ok ? Listen, I may have been shocked for a moment, I really had no idea that was the direction you were heading, jees you hit me hard with that one," she was smiling again now, over the initial sledgehammer of a conversation, "...and don't worry, it doesn't change one iota the way I feel about you." She took my hand and squeezed it tight. Shit ! I was going to cry, I gulped away the tears that were trying their best to escape, "Where the hell did I find you ?" I asked her. "You dragged me out of a deep, deep hole Con."

I didn't have time to wait for Fi's decision before speaking to Sam, I had to get moving one way or another, if I didn't have Sam on board then it was still a non-starter. He knew I wanted to talk, and he probably knew vaguely what about, but I can't imagine for a minute he knew what I was about to ask of him. Sam picked me up outside at nine, he was upbeat, he usually was, I was quiet, as I usually was when I didn't know how to start a conversation, I thought maybe, 'hey fancy kidnapping some kids with me' was a bit too casual. I couldn't face hours of anxiety not knowing what to say, so I bit the bullet and went for it. "So you know I said I wanted to talk ?" "Yeh," he didn't look my way, just kept his eyes on the road. "Well, I have a plan, well I'm not sure you could actually call it a plan, maybe it's more of an idea, cause I haven't actually made the plans, but ...." He interrupted my rambling, "Right, let me put you out your misery, you want payback for Joseph, yes ?" As always he was on the right track, "Yes," I said slowly, a slight question to my tone, "And your first port of call is Brad, yes ?" "Yes," I said, it was like he could read my mind, and I always found this a little discerning, but his next statement had me flabbergasted, "And you think the best way to get to her is through her kids ?" "Fuckin' hell Sam, how the fuck do you do that ! ?" He laughed a little, "You're so easy to read Conal, I hope you're not this transparent when Brads around mate, she'll chew you up and spit you out." He had just made this so easy, firstly I didn't have to ramble my way through an explanation, and secondly he hadn't said I was being ridiculous, and that wasn't a no. "Hey, me and Brad are like that," I said, crossing my fingers like we were best buddies. "She likes me, and that makes it a lot easier, I'm a bit more comfortable around her

now, and I find the less I think about stuff the more natural I am around her, so that's exactly what I've been doing, when I'm with her it's just work, I shut all my personal stuff out of my head, I'm getting pretty good at it." He nodded with a smile, like a proud father would do, after learning his son was making his way in the big bad world.
"So what's your *idea* then ?" That was it, I knew he was in.

Chapter Twenty-Seven

I'd spent the rest of the day with Sam going from job to job, each job interspersed with making plans, he was invaluable of course, he had all the things that weren't available to me, cars, homes, the means to move quickly from one place to another, plus this wasn't new to him, he knew how to move people around without being seen, I could have figured it out of course, but you can't beat experience, and I didn't have time. By the time we were ready to finish for the day, almost everything was in place, I was amazed how quickly he could pull things together, this could have taken me weeks, months or even years to pull off, but in just one day almost everything was in place, there were just a few things outstanding, one was how we would stop Archie, and the other of course was Fi, there were other options, Sam was sure he could enrol the help of some other guys, but I wasn't comfortable with that, this whole thing didn't sit comfortably with me as it was, and the only thing keeping me from calling it all off was knowing those kids would be well looked after. It all hinged on whether or not Fi would be on board, and by the end of the night I would know for sure.

It never ceased to amaze me how so much can change in a day, yes I know I keep saying it ! And you'd think I'd be used to it by now, but one minute you have an idea, then the next, well, the next you're planning to kidnap your boss's kids ! I prayed all the way home for Fi to say yes, part of me couldn't believe I'd even asked her and I had hated myself for putting her in this position, but there was just no-one else I could imagine doing this. I often wished I could put all this away, forget about what happened to Joseph, forget about what happened to mum, and try not to think about what happened to dad, but life just doesn't work like that, and my mind sure as hell doesn't work that way. I knew without a speck of doubt that as long as there was someone out there to be held accountable, then I would do whatever it took to make sure that happened.

Sam dropped me off around 4.30pm, and there she was, waiting at the door, all wrapped up against the cold, with a warm cuppa in her hand, and a smile for her guy as he came home from work. "Say hi to Fi for me," Sam said, " Not spoke to her in a while, she's looking well mate, you must be doing something right," he wiggled his eyebrows up and down, in a very suggestive manner, and I knew a punch to the arm was coming, I quickly, but not quick enough, tried to protect myself, and the punch landed fully on the fleshy part of my upper arm, did he understand how much that hurt, surely he couldn't ! It made me smile all the same, I loved Sam, I loved all my new family, I felt so utterly grateful to have them in my life. None of this would be even remotely possible if it was not for them.

I walked across the road, and sat on the step just as Fi did the same, she handed me a cuppa and leaned in to kiss me. We talked about our days, she'd not been out, but she'd done a full clean through the whole place, made dinner, had a soak in the bath and was now really chilled. I told her we'd done the usual day's work, filled her in on a few of the boring details. Then there was an awkward silence, both of us not knowing how to bring the subject up, it was up to me of course, this was my problem, I was, after all, asking of her, things I should never be asking. "I spoke to Sam today, you know, about Brad," "And ?" she asked, "He was in, he was great to be honest, he has a place where I can have the kids, it's way out, and he said it's real nice, but real secure too. He's gonna provide transport, and arrange food deliveries, phones, all that sort of stuff." She nodded and pursed her lips, she was still thinking, she was obviously on the verge of deciding one way or the other, and so, I waited, it wasn't something I could influence, or rush, this had to be her decision. She took a deep breath then began. "You know I wish there was another way…" my heart sank, "…it just seems so very wrong, don't get me wrong I totally understand why, for you, this is reasonable, but it doesn't feel right at all …" I was gutted, but I knew I'd asked too much of her, " … that being said, I would hate for those kids to be left with anyone else, and for that reason, for my own peace of mind, that they will be looked after, I have to say yes." Holy frickin' shit !! I couldn't believe what she was saying, I almost knocked her down the steps, grabbing her, pulling her into my arms, "Fiona McGuire, I fucking love you, wow ! You really are something else." I held her face in my hands and kissed every inch of it, "You know I couldn't do this without you ?" "I know," she said, she was smiling, she was happy for me, she was happy that I might finally be able to put a part of my past to rest. I was on a high, in the space of just a few days, all the work I'd put in over the last year, all the long restless nights, all those days watching and waiting, had all come together and had finally paid off.

Five days later, I was being taken on a dry run. If all the prep worked out, Archie would be in bed sick, and Brad would be calling on me, the newly driving licensed me, to help with the school run, I'd already done this route on my bike a few times over the last week or so, just incase, so I knew exactly where I was going. Doing it with Sam was so different though, he showed me where all the speed cameras were, and which ones worked, he showed me where all the on road cctv was, and which ones to avoid, he gave me alternative routes at almost every junction, none of which I'd even thought of before, it made me realise just what an amateur I really was, this may have been my idea but it was Sams 'job' he had done all the groundwork, and was now making sure nothing would go amiss. "How you feeling about it ?" he asked, it was a tough one, it was a job I didn't want to do, and yet, it was exciting and exhilarating knowing I would be getting retribution for what Brad had done to my family, if she hadn't had Joseph killed, I'd still have my mum, so she may not have pulled the trigger so to speak, but she most certainly had all of the blood on her hands.

Sam had said the house we were going to was way out, but when we still hadn't arrived two hours later, I wondered just how far ! He must have sensed my unease, as he always did, "Not long now mate, needed to be a good way out." I nodded in agreement, he was right, I'd not seen a house for probably the last half hour, but within a few minutes we were turning off the main road onto a narrow country lane, it was actually really nice, it made me think about the future, how nice it would be for me and Fi to have a little bolt hole out in the country somewhere, maybe we would have kids one day, it would be great to bring them up outside of the city. I was shaken from my thoughts when Sam pulled into another country lane, this one was even narrower than the last, there was definitely no room for two cars on this one. We travelled for another five minutes before Sam nudged me and pointed to the left, into the distance, there, a mile or so into the fields was a house, it looked big from a distance, my excitement jumped up a notch, I was up in my seat now, taking everything in, eager to find out just where we were going. It took just five more minutes before we were driving through the gates, and down a long, winding drive, lined with trees on either side, when we reached the end of the driveway the trees opened up to reveal a magnificent country house, it was beautiful, I mean totally stunning. I didn't speak as I climbed out of the car for a better look." I knew you wouldn't want them kids staying in some dingy hovel, so…" He pantomime bowed, waving his hand towards the house, saying, "… Ta da." I was shaking my head in disbelief, this was so much more than I could have asked for. "Sam, I don't know what to say, this is amazing," "Hey, it's what you needed, so it's what you got." I took his hand shaking it hard, what I really wanted to do was to give him a massive hug, but I wasn't sure he would appreciate it, so a warm two handed shake with the most sincere thanks would have to do.

He took me inside and quickly showed me around, two huge living rooms, a study, a massive kitchen, utility room, cloakroom, and six bedrooms. I could see what he meant about security, there were sensors and cameras everywhere, everything was run on the latest technology, doors were keyless, windows where all opened from a keypad, one was located in each room, all were run from the central keyboard in the study, it was like nothing I had ever seen. I could only begin to imagine how much a house like this cost. "Whose is this place ?" I asked, "The least you know the better, we have it for three months tops, I'm not saying you'll need it for that long, I would've thought a week, two maybe, but you never can tell." I was so impressed, 'Who lives in a house like this ?' I thought to myself, very clearly in the voice of Lloyd Grossman, my mum used to watch it every week without fail, and I'd sit beside her as she tried to guess who *did* live in a house like that. So many things reminded me of my mum, and thankfully the majority of them made me smile with the wonderful memories they brought. It was time to leave, for the long drive home.

We had been travelling for about half an hour when Sam said, "You do know there's no coming back after this don't you ?" He looked sad, and it took a few moments for the realisation of what he'd said to kick in, and no, I hadn't realised at all, oh shit I'd given no thought to what I was going to do when this was over. "What if she doesn't know it was me ?" I asked, "Then what would be the point, Conal ?" The blood drained from my face, I was sickened and panic stricken, I didn't want to leave, I'd already lost one family, I couldn't lose another. Oh shit ! What the fuck had I done, for the first time since I'd started this journey I began to question whether I could actually go ahead with it. I'd gotten so wrapped up in the excitement of getting revenge, I'd only considered as far as payback, I'd given no thought to the aftermath. "Mate this doesn't mean we will be out of your life, we'll still be around, we'll set you up somewhere else, get you a place sorted, you and Fi will have somewhere nice to live, maybe we can even persuade her to go into rehab, it'll be a new start for you both, don't get me wrong mate, I'll miss you like hell, but you can't stay, it simply wouldn't work." I couldn't speak, I couldn't argue, I could barely stop the tears from falling, this seemed more like an end than a beginning to me. Sam squeezed my shoulder, "Mate believe me when I tell you, everything is gonna be ok, OK ?" I could only nod, my throat far too tight to speak, I looked out across the fields, careful not to make eye contact whilst I failed in my efforts to stop my tears.

It had been a long, quiet and sad journey home, Fi was not on the step waiting for me, she was curled up on the sofa, two cups of tea on the table in front of her, and as always that beautiful smile greeting me as I walked in the door, I barely managed to return it before she noticed my tear stained face. Before I took another step, she was next to me, "Conal, what is it, what's wrong ?" She threw her arms around my neck. Still barely able to talk, I managed to whisper, "I'm ok, I'll fill you in, I just need a minute, sorry Fi." I took myself off to the bathroom, swilled my face several times, and stood leaning over the sink looking at myself in the bathroom mirror, what a sorry arse mess, I thought. I'd often asked myself who the hell I thought I was kidding, but this time it hit home more than ever, I wasn't some big time gangster, and I didn't want to be, I'd only gotten to know Sam to find out who killed Joseph, why, why did I let myself get so sucked in, why did I get so involved, why did I allow myself to care, I should have known I'd never be allowed to keep them, I wasn't meant to have a family, that's just the way it was, then my heart sank at the realisation that there would come a time when I would lose Fi too, I didn't know how, or why, or when, all I knew was, this is what happened to me, I loved people, then they were gone. The sadness destroyed me, and I crumbled to the floor and sobbed, unable to stop all the pent up emotion from most of my life from pouring out, and then she was there, she said nothing, but held me gently until my sobs subsided.

Chapter Twenty-Eight

Day break brought no relief for me, I had, quite literally, a couple of hours to make the decision of whether to go ahead or to call it a day. Eventually, after I'd managed to pull myself together, I'd filled Fi in on what had happened, and what it would mean for the two of us, it was unlikely the police would get involved, Brad dealt with 'things' herself, but she would never forget, and that would mean big changes for me and Fi, it could be years before we had the chance to settle down in one place again. And what did she say…"Whatever you decide Conal, I'm with you, you are all I have in the world, and wherever you go…I go too." That should have made me feel better, but it didn't, I just felt more sad that she would so easily follow me into what could be the end for both of us.

Sam was picking me up at 9.30 am and he would need a decision by then, we were already pushing it for time and any delays could put the whole plan out of action. It was 6.30 and I sat alone at the work top in the kitchen, I'd quietly made one cup of tea, whilst Fi slept on. Still I'd made no decision, I could see this was going to be a last minute decision, one I wouldn't know the answer to until Sam asked the vital question. I'd thought often throughout the night, about how much fairer it would be to just leave, walk away from Fi now and let her have a life with someone else, but the flip side of that was, I knew just how she would feel if I left, I would rather be on the run for the rest of my life than live without her, and I knew she felt the same way.

Hearing Sams horn beeping outside sent my stomach into overdrive, and filled me with dread, Fi hugged me and gave me that wonderfully gentle goodbye kiss she always gave me, "You'll know what's right for you when you need to, try not to worry, and don't forget, I'm with you all the way." I hugged her so tightly, all I wanted was to stay there and never have to leave, never have to make decisions, never try to predict how I would feel in two years, five years, and that was what this was all about, I could give up today, but I doubted very much that it would be the end, it would just delay the inevitable I suppose, but how could I know for certain, maybe I *could* put it all behind me, I just didn't know. Moving on filled me with guilt about letting my family down, and going ahead with my plans filled me with guilt about letting Fi down. It was a lose-lose situation.

Sam nodded as I got into the car, I gave back a halfhearted smile, the mood was solemn, and I knew he wouldn't ask what my decision was, he would wait until I was ready to tell him, and I was more than a little aware that it needed to be soon. And yet I still had no idea which way it was going to go, I hated myself for not knowing, and craved the peace of mind of knowing where my future lay. My only relief was knowing it would be over soon. I wished Sam would ask, it would make it so much easier, trying to figure it out myself just seemed to be getting more and more difficult. "So Sam, I've had a tough night, you really brought home to me just how much this is going to change my life, our lives," I corrected myself, thinking of Fi and Sam, "And ?" he said, I knew I'd already made the decision, when I realised I'd said 'this is going to change our lives,' present tense, this is, that was the answer. "And I want to do this." In that split second of realisation, all of the stresses, all of the frustration, all the indecision, simply drained away and left me with calmness. A calmness I'd not felt for a while, this was after all what I'd spent so long working towards. Sam banged his palm on the steering wheel, "Good on you mate, I would never tell you what to do, but I can tell you now, I'd have done exactly the same if I was you." He couldn't have known, but him saying that, filled me with pride, I was proud to be avenging my family's murders, I was proud that I was doing what Sam would have done, I was proud to have them all on my side, knowing each and every one of them believed in me, and what I was doing. I was proud of myself.

"So everything is in place, just as we talked about, the times may need to be tweaked a bit, and just to make you feel real good, we have just over a week, then it's all go, the guys have a date for their move, theirs will be over five days, so for maximum impact I suggested the middle of those five days, she'll be so wrapped up in her business crumbling beneath her feet, she's got to take her eye off the ball for a while." This was amazing, and all the excitement I'd had at the beginning, when the idea had first formed in my mind, all came racing back again. Today I would tell Brad I'd passed my test, Sam suggested slipping Archie something two days before, that gave us a day to make sure it had the desired effect, and time to administer a second dose if needed, not sure what it was a dose of yet, but he'd be getting a second one if the first didn't do the trick ! It was hard to believe this was really going to happen, my only regret would be not seeing the look on her face when she realised what had happened. That alone would be priceless, and so worth the stress, heartache and guilt it was going to cause.

I'd told Fi I'd speak to her when I got home, but she insisted she couldn't wait that long, so I took the first chance I could, when Sam got out of the car to get a couple of coffees, and I called her. She didn't even pretend to sound patient by starting with the pleasantries, there were no hellos, or hi's just, "Well ?" I couldn't help but laugh, and she didn't need an answer, "You're doing it ?" she said, "Yes, if you're still on board then yes." I waited for her answer holding my breath without realising it, "Good for you Conal !" she said, I burst out laughing, and could hardly answer as she demanded to know what I was laughing at, she had said the same thing as Sam, and in one of those, universe talking, meant to be, happy coincidence kind of moments, I knew for certain I was doing the right thing. "Fi, you just make everything ok, like always, with you by my side I feel like I could take on the whole world, I *do* love you," "I love you too," she said. Sam was getting back in the car, so I said my goodbyes, I was working for Brad that evening, and things had to appear as normal as possible, I hoped I could pull it off, in fact there was no hope about it, I had to pull this off.

At four pm I was cycling up to the front door of the Clinic, I'd already practised, taking deep breaths and appearing as my usual self. Fortunately I would be telling her I'd just passed my driving test, so a little difference and some excitement in my behaviour wouldn't matter so much today. I'd already planned to be as cheerful as possible, I needed her to ask me why, and she would, she had an overwhelming, uncontrollable urge to know things. I locked my bike up across the road as usual, and walked inside, the girls knew me now, so the door was usually ready to open when I got there. I nodded, smiled and waved a hello to the young girl on the desk, I think her name was possibly Molly, or Milly, or something along those lines. She smiled back shyly and gave a wave too. I went straight to my office, how good did that sound, pity it was just a tiny room with the stuff I needed in there, but yes, it sounded good. I was totally gutted when I arrived full of smiles, all ready for my acting debut, only to find Brad was nowhere to be seen.

She was almost always waiting for me when I arrived, I checked my watch to make sure I wasn't too early, I wasn't. Feeling utterly deflated at the total anticlimax, I took off my jacket, hung it by the door, and sat at my desk ready to start. I was like a teenager who didn't want to do his homework. I huffed and puffed as I took out the pile of books and receipts that had been left in the drawer for me. After sitting back in my chair sulking for a minute or two, I had a swift word with myself, and got on with what I had come to do. I was there for two hours, I had two books to do this week, I've no idea why she needed both doing, it didn't matter, I just did as I was told. And as I've said, I actually quite enjoyed it, so the time passed quickly, I'd even forgotten how pissed off I was that Brad hadn't turned up, so, it was a perfect surprise, when just as I was leaving, she walked through the door. I must have looked surprised, "Aww did you miss me Conal."

Sometimes I had to laugh, and this was one of those times, she loved it when she made me smile, so apart from the fact that I did genuinely enjoy her humour, I was also trying to stay in her good books. "Of course Brad, just not the same without you," I said, joining in the banter. I had my best, cheerful 10 out of 10 smile on, hoping she would ask me why, and of course she did. "What are you so cheerful about ?" "No reason," I protested, still with the ridiculous grin, "Oh, ok, if you don't want to tell me that's fine." Quick as a flash I said, "Only went and passed my driving test today didn't I," "Ah I see, well done Conal, I hadn't realised you were taking lessons." That was probably a lie, not much got past her, but maybe I was wrong, who knew any more. "First go, too," I lied, I tried not to think about whether or not she believed me, it would only get in the way of my facade. "I guess you'll be wanting a nice flash car soon then ?" she asked, "I may do, kinda like my bike though," I laughed. It was time for me to go, the seed had been sown and there was no more for me to do today. "Well, time for me to get home Brad, see you next week,"
"Goodbye Conal," she was always so formal with goodbyes, she always gave me the feeling it would be the last.

I made my way back home, happy that my day was over, there was no work tonight, Sam always gave me the night off when I saw Brad. I was exhausted and emotionally drained from weeks of planning, making decisions, unmaking decisions, thinking constantly about what we should do, what we shouldn't do, I was desperate to get home, to our little bubble of some semblance of normality. I tried telling my brain I was having the night off, but as usual it didn't take well to instruction. I could only hope that sleep would come quickly and my mind would get the rest it so desperately needed. It seemed to me, my mind had been on this fast forward pace for so, so long...

too long, I could barely remember what it felt like to get up in the mornings, and face a day that didn't involve putting things right.

I woke, barely remembering getting home and going to bed, my mind was fuzzy as I tried to piece the evening together, I'd not eaten, but instead fell straight into bed, Fi had sat beside me watching Tv, holding my hand till I fell asleep. She was still sleeping now, I watched her as my head began to clear, thinking how wonderful she was, and how lucky I was to have her in my life. I felt chilled, although big things were coming, right now there was nothing more I could do, and it felt good, no planning the next step, no debates with myself over how to ask people for help, no concerns over who was involved and who wasn't, it was done, the decision had been made, and my mind was at rest. I imagined feeling like this every day, I also knew that in just over a week's time, I, or rather we may never feel that way again.

Archie had been slipped more than a couple of laxatives in his morning coffee, thankfully I didn't need to have anything at all to do with this part, I was never near enough to him in the mornings, so it would have seemed a little bit suspect if I suddenly appeared bearing his morning coffee. And so of course Sam used one of his many contacts, to arrange for the guy in Archie's favourite coffee shop to do the dirty work for us, Archie would never know, and of course there would be no trail back to us. It was just two days until the big day, and nerves were starting to show, I was getting more jittery, forgetting things, getting a little snappy. It wasn't like me, I often became anxious but I never acted out, but then I'd never planned to kidnap the local drug bigwigs kids before either ! Fi on the other hand looked for all the world like she didn't have a care in one, there was no change whatsoever in her behaviour, in her emotions, her manner, nothing whatsoever, I was a bit pissed at myself, surely if she could hold it together so could I? A swift harsh word with myself was all I needed, I pushed away the negativity and the what ifs, and told myself it would all be good. It worked, to a degree.

By five o'clock that evening complete panic had set in, when it became blatantly obvious that no one was calling me to pick up Brad's kids, who by now we had established were all girls, Elizabeth was seventeen, Josie was eleven and Phoebe was ten. I had no idea how Archie was, or whether someone else had picked the kids up, I hated not knowing. Sam tried to reassure me by telling me to 'calm my titties,' when I'd asked for the tenth time, 'I wonder if it worked.' Ping...talk of the devil, my text read simply ' it worked,' I jumped from my seat screaming, "Yes !" All to Fis absolute delight, she had been worried about me getting so tense. It wasn't the best news ever but it was a start, I desperately wanted to ask Sam who had picked up the kids, but I knew we couldn't talk over the phone. And we still weren't out of the woods, we still had to wait and hope Archie wasn't back tomorrow, in which case we would have to repeat the dose. It was crazy that this whole plan depended entirely on the ability of a seventy year old man's stomach to tolerate laxatives. He would be getting double tomorrow ! We couldn't risk him coming back the day after.

I slept for just a couple of hours that night, but the sleep I did have, was deep. I dreamed of myself and Fi running in the countryside, laughing and falling to the floor together, it was amazing, but when we stood up, there was just grass for miles in every direction, just grass and sky, no landmarks, no distinguishing features, we had no idea which way to go, turning and turning trying to decide, it should have been frightening, but it wasn't at all, we were still happy, still smiling, still excited for life. It would be a strange day, if things went to plan, it would be our last day in our little bubble, we would be leaving the only place we had that felt safe and secure, I could only hope that one day I could give that back to Fi.

Archie had been served another dose of laxative in his morning coffee, it seems the barista was more than happy to aid us, Archie it seems was a 'miserable old scrote' ! His words not mine. And Sam had also found out it was Brad herself who had picked up the kids from school, she hadn't trusted anyone else enough. This wasn't boding well for me, if she trusted no one, then this whole plan was going to fall flat on its face. Sam was trying his best not to be concerned, but I could tell it was a worry for him too, when three pm came round and still I'd had no call from Brad asking for my help with the school pick up, my stomach was in knots, I couldn't eat, I couldn't think straight, I was on edge, constantly checking my phone for the fear I'd missed her call. Five o'clock came and went again, that was it, it was all over, all the worry, all the stress, all the time Sam and the guys had put in, all for nothing. "I don't fucking believe this !!" I yelled slamming my clenched fist down onto the dash board, "I fucking knew it was too good to be true !" I was rubbing my face with both of my hands, trying to stop the tears that so desperately wanted to creep out onto my face, "Fuck ! Fuck ! Fuck !" I yelled again, Sam didn't murmur, didn't move, he sat and allowed me my moment of anger. When I finally took a deep breath, he said, "It's not over mate, the timing was always going to be tight, and that's the way we need it, if she's making last minute decisions about this, her guard is lowered, we know she's struggling, she doesn't trust anyone, that's when she will make mistakes, this will occupy her whilst we get on with the takeover, then we will occupy her while you take her kids. "He made it all sound so simple, but it just wasn't, it wasn't simple at all.

Chapter Twenty-Nine

      I arrived back home feeling emotionally drained, physically and mentally exhausted and unimaginably devastated, we were so close, so, so close. The takeover had begun as planned, and I would play a small part over the next few weeks.

      Walking through the door to our packed bags, which would now be going nowhere changed my devastation to anger, I ran at the bags, kicking them across the room. Fi didn't move from her spot on the sofa, she knew what had happened, I didn't need to explain, I knew she would be desperate to come to me and console me, but now was not the right time, and she knew it. Her face was a mixture of sorrow and pity, and I couldn't decide which I hated more. I sat in silence, barely even able to acknowledge this beautiful person who I loved with all my heart, because I knew if I took even one scrap of the pity she offered me, I would simply fall apart. Sam was picking me up at seven for the rest of the day's work, it would be just a couple of hours, and I was grateful for it. I couldn't sit like this all night, although she would never admit it, I knew I was hurting her. She had given me space, endless cups of tea, food and a warm hand, each time I thought I couldn't love her more, she proved me wrong. Still, it was a relief when Sam text to say he was outside, and I didn't have to feel guilty for putting her under even more stress than I already had. I was maybe a little too eager to get out of the house, I practically skipped out of the door, kissing her quickly on the way. I hoped I hadn't hurt her feelings, but I just so desperately needed to do something that would occupy my mind.

Sam was in a surprisingly good mood, "Cheered up yet ?" he asked, like I was pissed off that he ate my last Rolo or something, I looked at him in total disbelief, "Wouldn't you be pissed off Sam ?" I asked. "Mate what's the point in getting pissed, one of two things will happen, either you'll be picking the kids up tomorrow, or it will happen some other time, but it will happen, so, like I said, no point getting pissed." I knew he was right, but I didn't want to wait, I was too fed up to even be bothered arguing with him, or reciprocating the banter he was trying to throw out. I turned to look out of the car window, not in the mood for chit chat at all. "Hey mate," Sam said, "It will all be good, I promise, it'll happen when it's supposed to happen, Brad is gonna be all over the place the next few weeks, so you haven't lost your chance." Weeks ? I thought, that really didn't sound that bad, I'd waited this long, would a few more weeks really hurt. Yes ! Yes, it would, I went back to sulking, feeling desperately sorry for myself.

Our first stop was number ten, we had been many times, sometimes night time, sometimes day. This guy used a lot of drugs, but he also sold a fair bit for Sam too, and you never quite knew what you would find when you got there, there had been police, guys with baseball bats, some dubious looking men in suits, some even more dubious looking woman wearing barely anything, there was quite literally always something going on, today the music was blaring, and people were milling around the doorway. Sam text No.10 and we waited for him to come to the car. Just a second later he popped his head out of the door, looked up and down, spotted the car and gave the thumbs up. Sam nodded, and we waited again whilst No 10 slipped back inside to get his cash, that was what we were doing tonight, there were a lot of pick ups, just like that one. It felt good, after days of not knowing and waiting on someone else before your plans could slip into place, it felt good to have some sort of control. There were a few more pickups, before we went just outside of town to the shed, Degs, Tatty and Buzz were there waiting when we got there. They were all on their respective phones, looking deeply serious, none of the usual banter, no smiles or warm welcomes, there was no time for that tonight, there was too much at stake to take time out. There was little for me to do, I was here to watch and learn only.

Having a moment to myself, I suddenly felt very guilty about the way I'd left Fi. I stepped outside, took out my phone ready to text her, to apologise for being a sulky idiot, and to tell her I loved her.

There was a missed call and a text from Brad.

Shit ! How the fuck had I missed them. I checked the time, it was only half an hour ago, there was no reason why I hadn't heard. Shit ! Shit ! I fumbled with the phone as I tried to call her back as quickly as possible, terrified I may have missed my chance, adrenalin was pumping so fast the ends of my fingers became numb, the call rang out, it rang again and again, and it just kept on ringing. My heart was racing, I was pacing up and down, it went to the answer service, I didn't want to leave a fucking message ! I ended the call and immediately called again, still it rang, I quite literally prayed for her to pick up. "Oh, hello Conal, so you finally decided to return my call !" She sounded genuinely pissed at me, this was good. Play it cool, play it cool I told myself, after a couple of deep breaths I said, "Sorry Brad, not used to you calling me at this time, everything ok ?" I knew the answer of course, my nerves were in tatters as I waited for her to say the words I so desperately wanted to hear. "No Conal ! Everything is most definitely not ok ! Damn bloody Archie has food poisoning." "Oh, is he ok ?" What the fuck Conal, I asked myself, but hey isn't that what anyone would ask ? "What !!?" She almost squealed, "I don't give a shit how he is, he's left me in the bloody lurch. Twice ! Twice now I've had to pick those kids up from school." Boy, she was angry, like so totally pissed off. 'Those kids' I see what the guys meant about her not having time for them, she didn't even acknowledge them as her own. "Oh," I said, not really knowing what else to say to her. Go on I thought, go on, ask me, please for god's sake just ask me! "Well, that's not quite the response I was hoping for, but anyway, I'll need you to take the kids to school in the morning, and pick them up in the afternoon." There was a pause as I waited for her to realise she was supposed to be asking, not telling, "If you can of course." I needed to walk a fine line now, between playing it cool and ruling myself out, "Really Brad ? I mean I've only just passed my test." "Conal ! Can you drive or not ! ?" "Well, yes," I told her, "And do you have time to drop them off and pick them up ?" She was being particularly obtuse now. "Erm, well, probably yes." I kept up the pretence, "Oh for god's sake, you either do or you don't." Oooh I liked her like this all stressed and needy, it would be good for the guys too. "Okay ! Okay !" I said, "I can do it." I could hear her taking a deep breath on the other end of the line, "Thank you Conal, I will send you the details straight away," and she was gone, no goodbyes, just the buzz of an ended call.

I raced back inside, "Sam, Sam it's on !" I yelled, unable to contain my excitement as I ran over and jumped in the air and high-fived him, "See, told you," he said, I turned to face the guys, there was a collective thumbs up whilst they all continued with their calls. Now I just wanted to go, I wanted to be back home with Fi, from tomorrow we would start a new life, I couldn't give too many details over the phone so I decided on a quick text, "It's all good," she sent back two smiley faces and a heart, so I knew she'd gotten the message.

I paced the floor, the next day's plans running around my head, checking each one to make sure I had it right. Sam had made plans for Fi to be picked up early, before I left, once we left the house tomorrow morning there would be no going back, and as always when I thought of leaving, my stomach flipped. For all that had happened, and the work I did, I was truly happy, so to move on and start over was a massive risk, but it was one I had to take. Sam was talking to Degs, who had just finished his call, they looked over at me, and Degs came over and hugged me tightly, as if he could read my thoughts, just like his son could. "This is not the end son, it's just the beginning."

I knew he was right, and I could only hope that these people I loved and trusted so much, would always be a part of my life, I simply couldn't bear to lose them forever. "So, son, it's all go, she's gonna get a lot of calls tomorrow, dumping her arse, by the time school pick up comes, I doubt she'll even notice they're gone." He was right, 'those kids' as she put it, probably wouldn't even flash up on her radar whilst her business was going tits up.

At last it was time to leave, Degs and the guys would be staying, but Sam still had work to do, and I needed to go home and make a few last minute preparations before we left, for good.

It was gone twelve when I got home, Fi was sleeping, probably mentally exhausted, just as I had been, I tried my best not to wake her but I was barely through the door before she was sitting up saying a sleepy, "Hi," "Hey," I said, sitting on the end of the bed and taking her in my arms. "So, are you ready for this ?" "Sure am," she said with a smile so big I couldn't doubt her. "I've packed the rest of our things," she said, pointing across the room to a pile of boxes and holdalls, "I'll take them with me in the morning, Sam's sending someone to help." Sam was sending someone to pick Fi up at five am, I was worried about her being alone at a strange house all day, but she was so excited, I wondered why I worried at all, in fact this whole thing seemed to excite her, she seemed to be looking at it as one giant adventure, and I suppose in some ways it was. She had even bought some books, games and craft stuff for the kids to use, she was an angel, I swear it. There was little more for me to do, I'd come home ready to pack away the last of my stuff, and now that it was done, all I had to do was fall into bed with the girl I loved. There was in fact just one more thing I had to do before I left, tomorrow would be a difficult day, in more ways than one.

I woke to my alarm, confused and wondering what the time was, and why I had slept so well, I'd fully expected to be up half the night going over and over today's plans in my head. But sleep had come quickly and deeply, realising it was the alarm for Fi, I was up, wide awake and helping her get ready to leave. I must have grabbed her and kissed her a hundred times, I was going to see her in just a few hours, but it wouldn't be here, it wouldn't be in our home, and it would be in the most bizarre of circumstances, and still I couldn't help but be happy, there were no nerves today, today I felt calm, collected, ready, I was strong, ready to take on the world. Sam was right, it would all come good, and at just the right time.

At exactly five am, my phone pinged, it was Sam's guy coming to pick up Fi. I'd initially been worried about sending her off with some stranger, but when Sam explained I'd already met the guy, it took a little of the stress away. Just a couple of seconds later there was a knock at the door, Fran was a guy who did odd little jobs for Sam, ones that didn't really fall into any category, like I'm pretty sure there's no full time job for 'Guy Who Picks Kidnapper Up ' but he did lots of other stuff, like delivering food, dropping people off here and there, heavy lifting etc. I couldn't quite place him, but I definitely recognised his face. We were met by this guy, who gave me the firmest handshake, and the biggest grin, "Don't worry mate, I'll take good care of her." I guessed he'd spoken to Sam. I helped him down the stairs with the bags, he refused to let Fi carry anything, which gave me faith in him, he was obviously a gentleman, and he left me in no doubt she would be safe.

Saying goodbye to her felt like the end, my stomach was in knots, my mouth was dry, I desperately wanted to snatch her up into my arms, run back inside and tell her I'd changed my mind. But I held it together and let's face it she was handling this way better than I was, she looked like she was going on her hols she was so excited, a little bit hyperactive, I'd made sure she had enough of her 'stuff' to last a couple of days, just in case there were any last minute hitches. One last embrace, one last kiss, and I was waving as the car disappeared into the distance.

I stood staring into the empty space where the car had disappeared in the distance, loneliness washed over me, stood in the darkness, in front of a house that was no longer my home, I felt lost. The thought of going back inside, knowing she wasn't there filled me only with dread, and I realised, the only real home I would ever know would be one with her in it. I could only hope that we would have that again one day soon. Finally, dragging myself away from the street, and from my self pity, I walked slowly, solemnly, back inside.

Brads text had read, '7.15 am, no later, 333 Princeton Park Manors' that was it, I'd Googled it to see where it was and figured it was about a 45 minute ride, I was leaving at 6 to give myself a bit of leeway. Which meant I now had around 10 minutes before Sam picked me up to take me to the car, I was showered and ready to leave long before he arrived.

Once I closed the door behind me today, it would be for the last time. That tinge of sadness tried to creep in again, but nothing was keeping me down today, and as quick as it came, I chased it away. Ten minutes later we pulled up alongside a row of run down garages, there was graffiti on every available wall space, and I doubt it had seen a street cleaner in…well ever ! Everything seemed so quiet, like the world was just waiting for the shit to start, well…it wouldn't have to wait long. The kids were to be dropped off at school for 8am, then the calls to Brad, breaking off alliances with her, would start at 8.15, I felt kind of important knowing that all across the country people were waiting for me to play my part in this whole setup, or rather, how amazing it was that so many people were prepared to wait for me to get my plan up and running, before they started theirs, yes that was definitely more like it.

Chapter Thirty

Princeton Park Manors was exactly what I imagined it would be, a massive gated community, houses that were barely visible through the foliage, security cameras everywhere, security guys on patrol in their little vans, I mean I'd been to some posh places with Sam before but nothing like this. I'd pulled up in my nice new Mercedes C Class, at the gate I'd been asked for my name before being allowed through, once inside, a very smartly dressed, and very well built young man, came to give me directions, it was then another 10 minutes drive through the grounds of this massive estate, before I came to the house I was looking for, I was glad I'd given myself those extra fifteen minutes. On a huge granite stone at the side of the entrance to the drive, was written 333 Princeton Park Manors. I drove slowly, taking in the perfectly manicured gardens and the huge expanse of lawn and was suddenly transported back in time to my childhood, images of me, Joseph and our dad rolling around the lawns of our beautiful home, while mum sat and watched us play, her heart full, watching her boys together. Wow, how times did change, if only Brad realised just how lucky she was, or how quickly this could all be taken away from her, she may be a little more thankful for what she had. By all accounts, she had way too much cash and far too many connections to lose everything, but she was going to suffer, if only because she hated losing, no matter how small the loss.

I'd hoped to have had some pictures of the kids, just so I knew what to expect, and to give Fi an idea of who she would be looking after. But there didn't seem to be any to find, no one had found any way to access their personal lives, no social media, nothing on the school website, they seemed to have the most cosseted life of any kids I'd ever known, which seemed fine for the younger kids, but Elizabeth was seventeen, surely she can't have gone through her whole life with no outside influence whatsoever. How sad that in her quest to ensure the security of her business empire, her children had become mere pawns in her efforts to keep the world out.

Once I'd gotten through the cover of the trees, the house came into view and wow, what a house it was, it was magnificent, that was the only way to describe it, the drive would take me straight to the front door. I'd been asked to wait in the car when I arrived, I sat for just a moment, eyeing up what was so much more than a house, it was beautiful, it was huge and it had been maintained to the absolute highest standard, and knowing Brad the way I did, none of this came as any surprise. Another, very smart and very well built young man appeared at my window, I wasn't sure where he had come from, I was so pissed at myself for being distracted, I couldn't afford to be making mistakes, and getting sidetracked by a house was pretty much unforgivable. I was parked right outside the front door, so I knew he'd not come from there, he had to have come from behind me, I'd have seen him from any other angle, I'd have seen him from the back if I'd been paying attention ! Lesson learned, no more mistakes ! He tapped on the window, gesturing for me to open it, I did as he asked, there were no smiles, no friendly faces here it seems. "Keep driving till you reach the end of the house, do a right, then drive into the building straight ahead of you, the doors will be open." He pointed in the direction he wanted me to go as he spoke, and again I did as I was told, driving slowly, taking care to be a lot more observant than I had earlier. I turned to the right, and immediately saw my destination, about one hundred feet away, was what looked like a very well planned extension to the house, with one huge double garage door, which as he'd said, was open, I kept driving, adrenalin had kicked in, ensuring my senses were hypersensitive to everything happening around me, which was in fact very little. As I got closer to the doorway, I could see it was just a huge vacuous space, spotlessly clean, unlike most garages. I carried on, I assumed this was all for security sake, but there could be another reason, maybe the game was up.

My knuckles were white on the steering wheel as I gripped it tightly, driving through the entrance of the garage not knowing what was about to greet me on the other side, I had barely come through the door when it started to close behind me. My heart was beating out of my chest, and I knew I was breathing way too fast, deep breaths, deep breaths I told myself, sucking in air and breathing out slowly, it worked, soon I was in control and thinking straight again. I was now sitting in a car, in a garage, well lit, with one door to my right, which I assumed would be where the kids were coming from. I'd done a dry run to the school, so I was confident I knew where I was going, I'd always been pretty good with directions. Tapping my hands on the steering wheel, to wear off some nervous energy, I watched from all angles constantly. I couldn't have been there more than two minutes, but it felt like forever, and I wished so much they would just hurry up so I could get the hell out and be on my way ! The door to the right opened, two very small children skipped through the door laughing with each other, they seemed happy enough to me, maybe we had Brad all wrong. Elizabeth was different, she looked sullen, didn't smile, didn't acknowledge anyone, or anything, I doubt she even noticed I wasn't Archie !

They climbed into the back of the car, and all three became unnervingly quiet. As soon as they were in the car, the garage door reopened, I reversed, turned around and drove back the way I'd come, and maybe just a little quicker than when I'd arrived. It was a relief to be out of the gates, out of the estate, back onto the open road and back to normality. A few deep breaths later and my nerves had calmed, now I could take a chance at making conversation. None of them had uttered a word, Elizabeth had sat staring out of one side of the car, the other two stared out of the other, there was barely even a movement from them, it was all really quite unnerving and very, very, unnatural, I remember being young in a car with Joseph, we didn't shut up, and we certainly didn't sit still. I don't know, maybe it was their schooling, or their upbringing, or maybe this was how they had been coached to behave, who knew, in the land of Brad, anything was possible.

"So, you guys looking forward to school today," I tried, smiling into the rear view mirror, I waited...nothing, maybe they hadn't heard, I tried again a little louder this time, "So, you looking forward to school today ?" There was a faint notion of a shuffle in the back, I was obviously making them feel uncomfortable, and there was still no answer from them, although I did notice that the two younger ones had glanced at each other with a rather puzzled look on their faces. Archie was obviously not much of a conversationalist, either by choice, or more likely, by order from Brad. I couldn't help feel for these kids, had they never had a conversation with anyone outside of home or school, this was getting more bizarre by the minute, and part of me couldn't help but think we might actually be doing these kids a favour, once they got past the shock of being kidnapped obviously ! "So you don't talk ?" I figured if I just kept it up one of them might cave in, or at least answer just to shut me up. I carried on talking at the silence that greeted me, the little ones were curious, I mean I definitely did not get the memo about keeping my mouth shut. "So, if I've got this right, we have Elizabeth, yes ?" She did acknowledge that, I saw her brows lower a little, I couldn't quite figure whether she was annoyed, or intrigued. "And you guys are Josie and Phoebe." I got a smile that time, well to be fair, they smiled at each other not me, but even so, it was a start. "I'm Conal," I told them, "I'll be doing the school run till poor old Archie is back." Each time I spoke I glanced in the mirror gauging their reaction, there was little to that statement. Elizabeth continued to stare out of the window, but the little ones were definitely intrigued by my 'bizarre' behaviour. "Which one of you guys is Josie ?" I quickly peered into the mirror in the hope of discerning who was who, but they just smiled at each other again, giving away little in the process. "So that makes you Phoebe," Phoebe, quickly turned to her sister with a confused look on her face, wondering how the hell I knew who she was, Josie found this particularly amusing and let out a little giggle. I liked them, they seemed like nice little kids, living in a very strange fucked up world. Elizabeth…she was going to be a much tougher nut to crack.

Almost fifty minutes later, we arrived at school, which was pretty much like home, electric gates and security guards. Once I'd given my name, a guy in an overgrown golf buggy guided me towards the school drop off point, which was about a quarter mile from the entrance. The kids were met at the entrance by a member of staff, I presumed. "Bye," I shouted through my now open window…nothing, they walked slowly into school, the only thing I got was a somewhat disdainful look from 'Miss'. It was a relief to have them out of the car, I couldn't even begin to imagine the kind of life they'd had, I doubted there had been much interaction with Brad, the little ones had been more fortunate than Elizabeth in the sense, they had each other, hers must have been a life of solitude.

It had been just a couple of hours since I'd picked up the car and headed for Princeton Park, but it seemed like forever. Fi would be waiting to hear how things had gone, and I was eager to hear how she was doing too. I called knowing there was little in the way of facts I could speak about over the phone, but hearing her voice, and knowing she was ok would be enough to keep me going. "Hey Fi, how's it going ?" I inhaled, holding my breath for a moment, my fingers crossed, willing her to be alright, "Oh Conal the house is amazing, everything here is so lovely," she gushed. "How was the ride out there ?" I asked, "It was great, he was so nice, reassured me all the way, and wouldn't let me get a thing out of the car." She sounded good, better than good, what a relief, I'd hate to think she was scared, worried, feeling alone out there, it was good to hear her being so upbeat. After filling her in on my morning, goodbyes were said, love was sent and I continued on my way home, well back to Sam. I no longer had a home.

Today was not the usual day's work, and before I got started, there was that little thing I had to do before leaving for good. I took the car, through the city centre to the quieter side of town, it was only about fifteen minutes drive to escape the hustle and bustle, and there it was, Cohm and District Cemetery and Crematorium, it was time to say goodbye, for what may be the very last time, sure I could talk to them whenever I liked, and they would never be a distant memory, but I loved my visits here, it was the only place I felt truly close to them. Tears were flowing before I'd even managed to get out of the car. I'd come prepared, with my tissues and flowers. I reached the plot where both of them lay, a simple white headstone, my mum would've hated anything more. I knelt beside them and said what I'd come to say.

"Mum, I'm so sorry I'm doing all of these things I know you will hate, I know you can't be proud of me right now, but I have to do it, I have to have closure, to have peace of mind, for just once in my life, but one day mum, one day I will make you proud, I promise, I love you mum." I lay the yellow roses I knew she loved, on the place where she rested, tears falling where they lay. Joseph would be easier, he knew how I felt, so I had no explaining to do, "So Joseph, you weren't just being a little prick after all, sorry mum, seriously though, I'm doing all I can to make them pay Joseph, I love you brother, I understand now, I wish you could have told me, I really do, but I'll finish this, I swear, I'll do it for you Joseph." Walking away from them was one of the hardest things I had ever had to do, it was like losing them all over again.

I had just one more goodbye. I stopped at the cafe on the way back to Sam, I needed to see the old guy before I left. It was good to see him, plus, it gave me a chance to use his loo, and wash my face down before getting back to Sam, it would only be a quick cuppa, but it was better than nothing, I hugged him like I was never going to see him again, because in all likelihood, I wasn't. He knew something was wrong, I could tell the way he looked at me, but he asked no questions.

I met Sam on the high street, soon I was following his car, heading for the shed. There was a lot to do, given what was going down right now. Sam spent most of the day on his phone, checking that details were correct and that everything was going to plan, I could only assume the other guys were doing the same thing. The atmosphere was sober, but exciting. I was, which now seemed like my second job, adjusting figures, each time a contact called in to say job done, I would use the code I'd now learned, to take down numbers in preparation for the next few weeks of deliveries, suppliers were already lined up, and cash was already on hand, as far as I could make out, all their hard work was paying off, things were running like clockwork, there had even been a couple of calls from contacts who had not been interested at the beginning, but now, seeing the takeover take place before their very eyes, were more than keen to join the club. Time flew and before I knew it, it was almost time for me to get ready to pick up the kids. As soon as I thought about it, nerves started to creep in again, my stomach was turning, this was it, it would be just the kids and myself, Sam and the guys would be tied up with other matters, although, he had assured me he would be at the house tonight to update me on what was happening. I was grateful for that, I needed him, not only for the moral support, but for direction, he would make sure I was doing things right, that everything that should have been done had been done, and of course filling me in on what had happened the rest of the day would be just what I needed to take my mind off what I had done.

Sam hugged me tight as I left, "You've got this mate, believe me you've got it," he patted my back hard before releasing me. "Thanks Sam, for everything, I couldn't have done any of this without you," and I meant it, with all my heart, I meant it. "Too right you couldn't," he laughed, before saying, "You'd have got there mate, I just gave you a little nudge," we both laughed knowing, that may, or may not have been true, and if I had it would probably have taken years. "See you tonight," he said, as I was climbing back into the car, "The guys will be there too." I was both surprised and relieved, it would be good to have them around, in such strange times, I needed them more than ever.

Chapter Thirty-One

As soon as I climbed back into the car, my mind shifted into work mode, no more emotional crap, no more nerves, no more distractions, this time I would keep my eye firmly on the ball. I'd heard nothing from Brad, not even a text to ensure I was still picking 'those kids' up. But then I dare say her mind was occupied by other things at the minute. School ended at five, bit late if you asked me, but then the kids probably loved it knowing they had nowhere to go once they were home ! I was at school about ten minutes early, there were several other cars waiting at the gates, so I assumed there would be no entering until the time was right. At five pm precisely the gate opened, each car followed behind the other all following our little friend in the gold buggy, in a convoy of school pick ups. At the end of the drive, there were two men, well dressed, who were allowing the cars to continue, one at a time, staggered each time by about thirty seconds, I assumed this was for both security, and privacy. I waited my turn, followed his direction, and waited outside the doors where I'd dropped them off a few hours earlier. Elizabeth came out looking just as sullen, maybe even more so than she had this morning. The other two looked tired, but I did get a definite smile from Phoebe this time, I smiled back and nodded my hello. Once their escort had opened the car door for them, I think maybe I was supposed to do that ? They climbed into the back seat and immediately returned to the exact same stance they had that morning when I'd picked them up. This was going to be a long, long drive 'home'.

I was so chilled, so calm, I was actually freaking myself out a bit, and things my mum used to say kept popping into my head like, 'The calm before the storm' and 'The peace before the crisis'. I wondered how long it would be before one of them asked where we were going, or if they'd even ask at all. It was about an hour, an hour of silence, when it became obvious we were nowhere near their home, at a time when we should have been arriving. It was Elizabeth who suddenly sat bolt upright in her seat, looking around, either side of the car, and out of the rear window. "Where are we going ?" she asked, she wasn't just curious she was scared, I could see her face in the mirror, instantly I felt sickened, I knew this was going to happen, of course it was, there was every possibility I was going to feel like an absolute piece of shit, and I did. "Brad...erm, your mum has something on, she doesn't want you back at the house, so we're taking you out of town, till she can have you back home." I prayed that would be enough to appease her. "She has 'what' on ?" she asked, seeming a little less concerned, she had the sweetest voice, nothing like her mother, she didn't look like her either, Brad was an amazing looking woman, but Elizabeth was stunningly beautiful. "Don't know to be honest," I said, she sat back in her seat, seemingly appeased by my explanation. On the contrary, the other two had barely noticed anything out of the ordinary was happening.

Another hour of silence passed by, and finally we came to the driveway of the house in the country, I'd not noticed last time, but there was a small wooden sign, half hidden behind some shrubs, pointing towards the lane, which read 'Wayward House', the name couldn't have been more appropriate, given what it was being used for ! Elizabeth sat up again, looking all around, taking everything in, the little ones followed suit, obviously realising we were nearing our destination. Seeing the house looming in the distance I was taken aback again at how wonderful it was, I imagined how much money you would need to have coming in to be able to afford to live there. And I dreamed of the life me and Fi could have if we had that lifestyle, for now, that was all I could do, dream, as of today we were homeless !

As I stopped outside the front doors of the huge, beautiful, imposing house, all three kids shrunk back into their seats, this was going to be just as tough as I'd thought it would, I had no idea what was going on inside their heads, and I wished with all my heart I could make this easy for them. Fi would be good for them, especially for Elizabeth, they were real close in age, I hoped it would help. Before I could get the car door open, Fi was out the house, down the steps, and waiting eagerly for me to get out of the car. I couldn't wait to have her in my arms, it felt like forever since she'd been there last. "How are they ?" she asked, "Not so bad," I said, I think they believe me, Elizabeth is not so sure but the others are too young to really question it." She was so over excited, and impatient to have them out of the car, showing them to their rooms, cooking for them, playing with them, she'd missed so much growing up, and I seriously felt like this was her opportunity to prove to herself that she could do what her own parents never could, she needed to know she was capable of nurturing, when she'd never experienced that herself.

Opening the back door of the car, my heart was beating fast in my chest, none of them moved. "Come on guys," I said, "Let's get inside," they were still, and gave no sign they'd even heard what I'd said. Fi squeezed in front of me, and in that beautiful soft, kind voice she had, she said, "Hey guys, listen, mum just had a bit of bother, you know these things happen and she wants you here to keep you safe, she will be here with you in a day or two. "Elizabeth looked up towards her, "Hi Elizabeth, I'm Fi," she held out her hand and waited. Elizabeth slowly lifted her hand and placed it in Fi's, and I could have sworn there was a faint smile in there. "Come on," Fi said, gesturing with her head for them to leave the car, slowly and cautiously Elizabeth climbed from the car, as soon as she started moving, the little ones followed too. I let out a huge sigh of relief. Fiona, you little star you, I dread to think what might have happened if she hadn't been there, but she was, and all was good, Elizabeth was happily following Fi, with two giggling little girls close on her tail, this is exactly why I wanted her here. I leaned back against the car, folded my arms and watched them go inside, with a sense of pride, and more than a little relief at a job well done.

I knew Fi would be inside, showing them to their rooms, making a fuss of them, trying to make them feel at ease, and so I left her to it. I took a seat on the steps, and took the time to gather my thoughts, think about what happens next, and wonder why Brad hadn't tried to call. Sam had arranged for someone to contact Brad, tell her they had me and the kids, and that they would be in touch soon. The idea being to try as much as possible to keep me off the radar. Sam felt she needed to know it was me, to know it was payback, I on the other hand was sure her suffering was enough, and it was something I could drop into the conversation at any point, if I decided I wanted to. But as yet I'd heard nothing. I checked the time, and realised she wouldn't have even had the text yet, we still had fifteen minutes to wait.

Watching the minutes tick by was torture, I swear time actually slowed down. Then there it was, not the text I expected but the call I couldn't answer, it was Brad. My heart was racing as I listened to the call, it rang and rang, stopped for a moment then started again, she called five times in all, followed by three texts demanding to know what the hell was going on. Until now it hadn't seemed real, but now that she knew, the ante had most definitely been upped, shit had gotten real, and my mind switched straight back into panic, anxiety and a whole heap of 'oh fuck !'.

Just as I thought, Fi was upstairs with the girls, they were getting on like a house on fire, it was remarkable how they reacted to her, how quickly they had become so comfortable in her company, but I suppose having somebody so warm and nurturing looking after you, couldn't help but ease any anxiety you were having. I'd almost forgotten to text Sam, he needed updating when I heard from her. 'I heard' was the simple message. I sent it and slipped my phone back in my pocket. I was pacing the floor not knowing what to do next, even though there was in fact very little I could do right now, I was supposed to be 'kidnapped' along with the kids, so all I could do was wait, and nobody likes waiting.

With nothing left to do, I took myself up stairs to check on everyone, I didn't get too far along the corridor leading to the bedroom the kids would be staying in, before I heard the giggles, it wasn't the sound of kids playing, it was the sound of teenage girls giggling to themselves. I stopped in my tracks and smiled, my heart swelled as I listened to Fi and Elizabeth chatting away. And I wondered how long it had been since either of them had had this experience. Not wanting to miss any of it, or to intrude, I slipped to the floor where I'd stopped, leaned against the wall and just soaked up the sounds of two people simply enjoying being themselves.

With the fear of the unknown kicking in, I stayed where I sat, taking the only bit of comfort I had. It was thirty minutes later, when I heard voices getting closer, they were coming to the door. I stood quickly just before the door opened, wanting to appear as if I'd just arrived. Fi came out first, gave me the biggest smile, and walked into my arms, I kissed her like I hadn't kissed her before, she clung on to me like we could never be parted again. Remembering someone was watching, Fi quickly lowered her head looking a little embarrassed. "I think you two have met," she said, her hand outstretched towards Elizabeth, who was now standing in the doorway. I nodded and said, "Hello Elizabeth, it's very nice to meet you," she laughed a sweet little laugh at my attempts at sarcasm. "It's good to meet you too," she said, giggling again. It was so good to see the ice had been firmly broken, and it was all thanks to this wonderful girl beside me, I knew I couldn't have done this without her, I knew from the start, but I had no idea just how much of a difference her being here would make, not just to the kids, but to me.

Josie and Phoebe were sleeping. Someone, who at this point was nameless, had shopped for essentials, Fi had told me they were there when she arrived, so the little ones had been showered, put in their fresh new pyjamas, and settled into bed. Although there were two double beds in the room, the girls were curled up beside each other in one. It was a beautiful room, spacious and bright, the walls and furniture were white and the bedding and soft furnishings were shades of grey, someone had very kindly placed fresh flowers around the room, there were children's books on table, and the craft things Fi had bought sat beside them. Sam had suggested locking the doors and windows, and keeping them in their room, but all I could think of was mum in that fire, imagine if something happened and there was no escape for them, it may have been a risk, leaving the doors unlocked, but it was one I was prepared to take, if only for my own peace of mind. For now, and hopefully for the short time they were here, they would only ever think we were working for their mum, and that she knew where they were, if it stayed that way then there would be no reason to lock them up anyway.

Fi, Elizabeth and myself made our way back down the stairs to the kitchen, it was strange how quickly we had settled into our new 'home'. Fi knew where everything was, she'd put the kettle on, got out three cups and a pack of chocolate biscuits, and sat at the large kitchen table waiting for the kettle to boil. Elizabeth sat next to her, and the two of them picked up where they'd left off. I placed three cups of fresh tea on the table and sat with them, before long we were all three laughing and joking like we'd known each other our whole lives. More than anything I loved watching Fi getting so much enjoyment out of this lovely young girl, both of them catching up on lost childhoods.

My phone buzzed in my pocket, I'd not realised how quickly the last couple of hours had gone, it was a text from Sam he was just fifteen minutes away. I was so excited to see him, I'd heard nothing of how the takeover was going, I could only assume it was going well, it would account for the lack of contact from Brad. I tried to get Fi's attention, I needed her to get Elizabeth back upstairs before Sam arrived, the least people she saw the better, plus we had a lot to discuss, things Elizabeth definitely did not need to hear.

I managed to get Fi over to the sink, I explained what was happening, she nodded and turned to Elizabeth saying, "You ready to go back up ? It's getting late and it's been a long day," "Yes of course," she said, as polite as ever. It was too late, as we walked back towards the stairs, I heard the door open, Sam walked in, from the look on his face I made the assumption everything was going according to plan, he was of course though, very surprised to see Elizabeth very much not locked up in her room ! Fi quickly turned towards me, with a look of apology on her face, I shook my head at her and said quietly, "It's ok, you're doing great," Sam hadn't moved from the spot, and Elizabeth, who had one foot on the stairs when the door opened, was glued to the spot too, did they know each other ? They both looked like they'd seen a ghost. Sam suddenly came to his senses, jumped back to life and walked past me towards the kitchen. Elizabeth did the same and carried on up the stairs, which left both Fi and myself staring at each other, totally bewildered by what had just happened. I didn't usually ask questions of Sam, but he wasn't getting away with this one. If he knew her it could change everything. I kissed Fi goodnight, I had no idea how long it would be before I got to bed, "If you want to stay with the girls tonight that's fine you know," she looked surprised that I'd suggested it, but I guessed they had a lot more to talk about, "I've no idea what time we're going to finish, I'd rather you weren't alone, but I'll miss you," she beamed that wonderful smile, "See you soon, I'll miss you too," she was running up the stairs before I could say anymore.

Back at the kitchen, Sam had coincidently sat in the seat that Elizabeth had just vacated, given his reaction in the hallway just now, I thought it best not to mention it, I didn't want to make him feel even more uncomfortable than he was going to in about five seconds time. I took the seat opposite him and watched him as he used his phone. It took just a minute before he shouted, "WHAT ? !" I burst out laughing, "Hey don't be getting all tetchy with me, you're the one who was just taken down by a teenager ?" He blushed !! He actually blushed ! In all the time I had known him, this guy had never shown even a hint of embarrassment about anything. I decided taking the piss might not be the best course of action, "Seriously though Sam what's with you and the girl ?" He looked utterly incredulous, "Don't know what you're on about mate," "Oh come on Sam, I've never seen you look at anyone like that, do you know her ? Cause you know that could be a real problem, like a big one." "I don't know her, never seen her before, and I didn't look at her like anything ok," he was getting genuinely pissed off now, time to change tactics, let's see just how interested he really is. "Not heard much from Brad," I said, "What have you heard ?" he asked, "She called five times, text three times, then that was it," "You didn't answer ?" "No, didn't answer any of them," " Good," he said and went back to his phone. "Seem like nice kids," I said, watching him for the slightest bit of emotion. He barely nodded. "They wouldn't talk to me, didn't even acknowledge I was there," he nodded again, not taking his eyes off his screen, and giving away nothing at all as to what he was thinking, "But as soon as we got here Fi and Elizabeth hit it off straight away. "There it was, his eyes flickered, just for a split second from his screen, he may not know her but he sure as hell wanted to ! I left it at that, curious to see what would happen next time he saw her.

Chapter Thirty-Two

It was going to be at least another couple of hours before the guys arrived, and our conversation had made things a tiny bit awkward. I hated awkward, so it was time to break the silence, "Have you eaten yet Sam?" I asked, "I haven't you know mate, is there anything to eat ?" I walked over to the fridge and opened the door, "Ta da," I said, palm outstretched showing him the array of food inside, he laughed, "Fran I'm guessing ?" he said, I nodded, "So what do you fancy ?" He wasn't fussy so I went for the easy option, took out some eggs, cheese, peppers and onion, and made a pretty damn good omelette. He wolfed it down in no time, and I wondered how long it had been since he'd actually eaten home cooked food. I put on the kettle ready for a cuppa, and text Fi to see if she would like me to make one for her and Elizabeth, she did. I gave Sam his tea with a large slice of Victoria sponge cake, Fran really was a good'un. I could've saved Sam the embarrassment and took the tea and cake up to the girls, but I was far too intrigued by his reaction to let this pass. I sent another text to let Fi know their drinks were ready. We still had plenty of time before the guys were back, so them coming down to the kitchen wasn't going to be a problem. I knew I was playing with fire, but I really wanted to find out what this was all about. I sat with my drink, cake in hand and waited. I heard the girls coming down the stairs, still chatting away at just the same time Sam did, he looked towards the hallway, then back to me. I waited for the telling off I expected for having them back down stairs, it didn't come. Hmmm I thought to myself with a smile. Fi walked in, and flashed me that amazing smile I always got from her, she came and kissed me, I held her waist and pulled her as close as I could. Nothing felt better to me than having her in my arms, and although I was fully aware, that we had no home, we were kidnappers, we were more than likely going to be on the run, it didn't feel like any of that was happening at all, it didn't matter, I was happy, and she was too. I wasn't sure how we were going to feel when this was all over, Fi was going to lose someone who it seemed could become a good friend, and, well, I didn't want to think about how things were going to change for me. But right now I was more interested in what was going on between the other two !

The energy between them was culpable, and I mean I could quite literally feel it, it was so strong I actually felt like we were intruding on some sort of intimate moment between them, either I had this very wrong or their chemistry was through the roof, how the hell was this going to work, shit, this seemed like fun five minutes ago, but the reality was, this couldn't happen. Fi sat down next to me, and Elizabeth at the end of the table, so that she was now placed between Sam and myself, he looked up from his phone, his face flushed red again, and nodded in her direction, he looked across the table at Fi, and asked how she was. "All good Sam, we've had a great time haven't we Beth?" It was just a simple word, a shortening of a name, but it hit me like a ton of bricks, this wasn't just going to hurt Brad, there would definitely be casualties along the way, cause Sam had a thing for her, and Fi was her new best friend. I don't know exactly how it happened but an hour later the four of us were laughing and joking like we did that every week. I liked 'Beth' it was obvious from a few of the comments she had made that she really had led a sheltered life, but that she also had a great sense of humour, and that her mother was probably her least favourite person ever. They had a nanny, who Beth adored, she told us if it wasn't for her she'd have gone insane a long time ago. I gazed at us all sitting around the table, thinking of the less than normal lives we'd led, and wondered for a moment if the fickle finger of fate had stepped in to throw us all together. I loved Fi, and I loved Sam and I'd never seen either of them as open and happy as I had tonight, and so there was a part of me that loved Beth too for giving them that gift. Even if it was going to end in disaster !

Sam's phone vibrated on the table. Fi knew he was waiting for a call and took that as her cue to leave, "Well, I'm getting real tired now," she said, "Do you mind if we leave you guys to it ?" "Not at all," I told her, pulling her in for another kiss, the wonderful soft, lingering, barely there touch that left me craving more. "Goodnight Beth," I called as she walked away, I doubt she heard me, she was too busy watching Sam, waiting for him to notice she was leaving, sadly for her he was too wrapped up in his call. When he'd finished talking and turned the phone off, he punched the air yelling, "YES!!! We smashed it mate, we did it, we only fucking went and did it." He was leaping around the room punching the air over and over. Only now with this release, did I realise the real strain he had been under, they had all been under. He stopped suddenly and looked around at the empty room, "Where did the girls go ?" "They went up, wanted to make sure they were gone in plenty of time, if they're anything like you they'll say fifteen minutes away then turn up five minutes later," he laughed, a real belly laugh, he was on a high, the job, or Beth, I wasn't sure, but it felt like something very right was happening here. Maybe it was just wishful thinking, but the vibe was definitely a good one.

The rest of our evening was spent, both of us on our phones, sitting at the kitchen table chain drinking tea and coffee, interceded with occasional chat, it was chilled, it was calm, it was good, life was good, in amidst the chaos of takeovers, kidnap, murders, and loss, was this wonderful space in time of 'normality' of happiness, of friendship, of hope.

It was almost two am when Sam got a text from his dad saying quite simply 'DONE'. "They're on their way," Sam said, nodding as he said it, his subconscious telling him it was all ok. That means they wouldn't be back till around four am, "Think I'm gonna try grab an hour before they get back," I said, "Ok mate, might get my feet up on the sofa myself," "Cool, I'll set an alarm for an hour or so." I made my way up the stairs, onto the huge landing, and down the corridor which led me away from Fi, even the corridors in this place were amazing, they must have been five foot wide, bright, with fabulous art works along the walls, each one a totally different genre from the one before, I'd never realised I liked art so much, but I couldn't help stop and taker a longer look at a few. Had I known Fi was waiting in our room, I'd not have even noticed they were there ! I opened the door, to a sleepy little blonde head peering from beneath the duvet. "Hi," she said, in that sleepy voice we all have after being woken in the middle of the night. She pulled back the duvet and patted the bed beside her, I didn't even bother to wash, brush my teeth, I barely managed to undress, before falling into bed beside her. Curled up in the most amazingly comfortable bed I think I have ever been in, I was grateful, thankful for the life I had, it wasn't straight forward, it wasn't perfect, and it was probably going to get more complicated than it had ever been, but right then and there I couldn't find a single thing to complain about. Sleep came easy, albeit short.

    I swear the alarm I'd set for an hour and fifteen minutes went off after ten minutes. It seemed as though I'd barely laid my head on the pillow, and I was getting up again. Fi slept on, she must have been exhausted, not surprisingly, it had been a long, emotionally draining day for all concerned. I washed quickly and quietly, gave my teeth a brush they really needed, dressed and creeped out of the room, leaving her sleeping peacefully. I walked as quietly as possible back along the corridor, past the landing, opening the door to my right slowly, I peeked into the room the kids were sleeping in, all was good, closing the door as quietly as I'd opened it, I turned and made my way down stairs. Sam was still sleeping on the sofa, so I did what all these occasions called for, I put the kettle on, I filled it, there would soon be a house full of people who would want, at the very least a good cuppa or a very strong coffee. Before the kettle had finished boiling, Sam appeared at the kitchen door, stretching and yawning, and putting a thumbs up at my offer of a cuppa. It was strange how much this place felt like home already, or maybe it was just down to the fact that it contained the people I cared about most in the world. Sam disappeared to the bathroom, and reappeared just a few minutes later looking fresh. I felt like I hadn't slept for a week, and he looked like he'd just arrived back from a spa ! I really needed that cuppa to kick start the day.

It was three fifty when the guys arrived 'home,' I expected them to arrive slow and exhausted, they'd been on the go for days, but I couldn't have been more wrong, they sounded like they'd just got back from a lads night out, I had to quickly herd them into the kitchen, shushing them along the way, reminding them that we had kids sleeping upstairs. They'd obviously forgotten, the sudden realisation had them all shushing each other, fingers on lips, which were still grinning from ear to ear. I was keen to find out how their day had gone, I mean it was very obvious it had gone well, but I wanted details, and, it also dawned on me that we had still had no more contact from Brad, I had no idea whether that was a good thing or a bad thing. I dare say I'd find out more once the guys had calmed down, and were ready to talk. I took the orders for coffee and tea, and watched and listened as they took their seats and began to fill us in on the previous day's events.

Brad had lost upwards of 60% of her customers, and there were more in the pipeline, alongside those who had heard what was happening and decided to jump ship. Those 60% were from all over the UK, and probably involved god knows how many different contacts, no wonder this whole operation had taken years to come to fruition, the guys were so pleased with themselves, all the hard work they'd put in meant everything had gone like clockwork. I knew it wouldn't be good, but I had to ask. "How's Brad taking it ?" There was a chorus of laughter. "Not well by all accounts," said Degs, "She's already had two of her guys killed, for not knowing this was going to happen, she's a ruthless bitch, she really is, she's currently offering ten grand for information about who's responsible," "Ten grand ?" I questioned, "With all the money she has ?" Degs spoke again, "Yeh she'll start low, in the hope some little scrote who needs the money, knows something, she'll keep upping it till she gets a bite." "And the kids ?" I said, "You haven't heard from her ?" Degs looked confused now. "Well, she called and text yesterday, I didn't answer of course, but I've heard nothing since, and nothing from Fran, I thought he must have been in contact with you guys ?" "Fuck," said Tatty, "She's even worse than I thought, let me see if I can find anything out for you." He left the kitchen, I presume for a quieter spot to make his call.

The talk turned from how amazing their day had been, to how as a mother Brad had not given two fucks where her kids were. I was starting to get worried, what if she just didn't contact us what if she really didn't give any fucks at all about where her kids were, but then I realised, even if she didn't give any, she cared a hell of a lot about status, about her reputation, and even more so about someone getting one over on her. So she *would* be in touch, at some point, once she'd gotten over the shock of losing her empire, all we could do was hope it didn't take too long ! Tatty came back shaking his head as he did so. "Fran's had one text from her, it said, 'fuck you,' pleasant little soul isn't she !" He was laughing now, although I was finding it difficult to see the funny side, noticing I didn't laugh along with him, he explained, "She will be in touch, it'll just take an extra day or so, don't worry, you ok with the kids here ?" "Yeah, they're no bother," I said, "Then just go with the flow son, it'll be just fine." As always when these guys reassured me, I had complete faith in what he was saying. They really did always know best. The night digressed into banter about who'd done the best, most, more efficient work of the day, it was time for them to finally wind down, probably for the first time in a very long time.

An hour later, tiredness began to kick in, one by one they became quiet, there were plenty of rooms for everyone, but the guys slept where they sat, and I, seeing my family settled and well, took myself to bed. I didn't check on the kids again, I'm sure we'd have known if there were any problems. I opened the bedroom door quietly, creeping towards the bed in the dark, hoping not to wake Fi, I smiled as I discovered the empty bed, knowing she would be with Elizabeth reassuring *her* that all was good. I was emotionally exhausted, but my mind still had time to throw a few problems at me before allowing me to take a break. I worried about the kids being here for any length of time, I worried unnecessarily about how they felt about their mother, as this was obviously something that firstly, wasn't my problem, and secondly, I had no control over. I worried about how Fi would feel when they had to leave, I worried about what would happen when Brad figured out it was me behind this, so many things to worry over, but eventually exhaustion took over and my mind was quiet.

Considering how tired I was, and how late, or early, whichever way you look at it, I got to sleep. I was up and feeling good by eight thirty. Fi was back in bed beside me, I've no idea what time she arrived, I must have been out cold, but it felt so good to wake up with her, this was normal, the most normal thing I'd done in the last twenty-four hours. She was already awake, and laying on her side, that beautiful smile waiting for me. I leaned over to kiss her, she welcomed me, pulling me closer as she did. For a moment I worried about who was in the house, or who may disturb us, but the feel of those lips, of her tongue on mine, took me to a place where there was nobody but her. Her skin on mine drove me insane, in a second I was on top of her kissing her more passionately than ever, and she responded to every touch and every kiss in a way she had never done before, all inhibitions were lost, gone forever, the world forgotten. I could have stayed there, so close, we were almost the same person, and been the happiest I could ever be for the rest of my days. When we were both sated, that wonderful logy feeling washing over us, we lay in each other's arms and said nothing. There were no words to describe what had just happened between us. I was grateful for this time we'd had together. The uncertainty of our future, meant we may not feel that safety, that security, that warmth of knowing nothing can harm you when you're together, for many months, maybe even years. I loved her, and didn't want to leave, but sadly reality had kicked back in, and things needed to be done, people needed to be seen, and it was time for both of us to get on with the job in hand.

Chapter Thirty-Three

We crept down stairs after checking in on the girls, they were awake and watching TV, Fi asked them to stay where they were, and told them she would be back shortly with breakfast. The house was quiet, either everyone had left, or they were all still sleeping. Wrong on both counts, opening the kitchen door as quietly as we could, we were met by the guys, drinking coffee, reading notes, eating toast. "Tea you two ?" said Buzz, holding the kettle up. "Yes, please," said Fi. Degs stood, then so too did Tatty, they both turned to Fi with their hands out, waiting to greet her. "So good to finally meet you Fiona," said Degs, taking her hand in both of his, making her look even tinier than she already was. She was shy but loving it, which was lovely to watch, these people I trusted with my life, embracing the woman I loved, welcoming her into the fold, simply because she was mine. They trusted her implicitly, purely because I did, proven just a few minutes later as we joined them with our tea and toast, courtesy of Buzz, and they began to reel off facts and figures, names and places, all written down in their own private shorthand, recorded and ready for future use. Within the hour, their phones had started to ring, all four of them ringing constantly. Fi was back upstairs looking after the kids, I'd heard nothing from Brad or Fran, and so here I was feeling a little bit like a spare part, making endless cups of tea and coffee to keep the troops going. I should've been thankful for the fact that I had little to do, but it made me restless.

A short time later my phone rang, at last, it was Fran calling to fill me in on what was happening at his end, he was, at the moment, 'acting kidnapper' he was the go-between, between us and Brad, she had at long last been in touch, he had called her several times, making demands, each time she had made demands of her own. She wanted to know who he was, who he was working for, and how much he would accept to spill the beans on all of us, he was of course not for sale. More to the point, what she did not ask, was, where her kids were, and whether they were okay. I was beginning to feel bad for actually having to send them back to her at some point, I imagined a life where I'd not had my mum there to fall back on whenever I needed her, I couldn't, she was the one person in my whole life, who had always been there for me no matter what was happening in her own life, she had protected, she had loved, she had ensured my safety, and above all she had made me happy, so happy that I'd barely noticed all the terrible times she had been through. But then that's what being a parent is all about…isn't it ? These kids had been fed, watered and educated, and as far as I could see that was where the parental responsibility ended.

I ended the call, and filled the guys in on what was happening. "She's got a lot on her plate son, and she was never going to just pay up, that was never gonna happen," said Degs. "I know that, but I thought she would have at least give a shit that someone, god knows who, had her kids, I mean for all she knows, anything could be happening to them." I was angry, angry for them, angry that she'd shown such contempt for her own flesh and blood. "Mate, business is what she's interested in, the only part of any of this that concerns her, is the cash side." Tatty was trying to appease me, but it wasn't working, he chipped in, "…and of course her pride, which at some point means you'll get what you want, she has to win…always !" He was right, although taking the kids in the middle of this meant the job would be easier, it also meant she would have to divide her attention between fighting armies of deserters, and finding, not her kids, but the person responsible for taking them. Just that sentence made it all make sense, in that moment, I wanted to take Fi, the kids and myself and just run, stick the money, stick the revenge, sending those kids back to her wouldn't just be hard to do, it would be a tragedy. I spent the next hour trying to figure a way out of this mess that would mean the kids would be looked after properly before remembering they were not my kids, they were not my responsibility, in fact I barely knew them, they were here for a reason, and one reason only, to piss Brad off, and take even more of the cash she was at present trying so desperately to keep.

The guys were busy, I'd made them all fresh tea and coffee, so while they were occupied, I took myself upstairs to check on the girls. I knocked on the door, and heard a chorus of "come in. " I smiled and shook my head at how quickly Fi and I had accepted these kids into our lives and us into theirs. I opened the door and peeked around it before entering. Fi and Elizabeth were propped up in bed, watching TV, the girls were laying on the floor, each with a colouring book in front of them and felt tips scattered around. Fi paused the Tv, they were watching one of those teenage American sitcoms that Fi loved so much. I sat on the end of the bed, and as I did, the little ones noticed I was there and sat up. "Where have you been ?" said Phoebe, "Just downstairs, working," I answered, "What have you guys been up to ?" I asked, Josie grabbed her book and stood up, she came over to show me her creations. "Which one do you like ?" she asked, I took a look through the few she had done, and stopped at one of a butterfly, she'd coloured it in pinks and purples, with flashes of green. "I love this one," I told her, she grinned from ear to ear, "That's my favourite too." She tore the page from the book and handed it to me, "This ones for you." I took the page from her hand, my heart literally skipping a beat, she can't have known what a beautiful gesture that was, it was an innocent gift, from an innocent child, who had no idea of the terrible world she lived in. The saddest thing I took from this, was, in the half hour I spent chatting, colouring in, and tickling two little girls, they never once asked where their mum was, or when they were going home. Somehow fate had served me up a little lesson in thinking before you kidnap. Nothing could have prepared me for just how much I was going to like these guys.

Sam called to me just as I was leaving the girls room, "Hey Con ?" I reached the top of the stairs just in time to see the other guys leaving. "We're off mate, I'll keep in touch, call me if there's any probs, or if you hear from Brad," "Thanks," I called to him as I walked down the stairs. "Is there anything you need me to do ?" I shouted as he reached the door, "No mate, just look after them…" he pointed up the stairs, "… and stay vigilant." I wasn't sure why he'd added that, did he think Brad would find us here ? He was probably just making sure I hadn't forgotten why we were here, I did need to be on the ball though, as I already knew, things could change in a split second.

Knowing the house would be empty for a while, I made cereal for the kids, tea and toast for Fi and Elizabeth, then walked to the stairs shouting, "Breakfast's ready." Instantly my mum's voice shot into my thoughts, 'Joseph, Conal your breakfast is ready' she said the same thing every morning of our childhood. I missed her so much, if only things had been different, I wouldn't be sitting here right now, if I still had her none of this would have happened, but then I'd never have met Fi, I wouldn't know Sam, I couldn't imagine a life without them now either, but then there was a time when I couldn't have imagined a life without my mum too. There was a noise on the landing that sounded pretty close to a herd of elephants, thirty seconds later, Josie and Phoebe burst through the kitchen door, each of them shoving the other to try to be the first in, just like me and Joseph used to do. And I found myself suddenly understanding just why that used to make my mum smile so much. The girls were followed closely by Fi and Elizabeth, still chatting away like they were the oldest of friends. Fi came to me and placed her arms around my waist, leaning into my chest, I wrapped her in my arms and held her there, kissing the top of her head, she turned her head towards me placing her lips gently on mine, that beautiful soft morning kiss I couldn't imagine living without.

Then she was back to talking, I stood back leaned against the kitchen worktop and watched them all together, it was like they had always been there, and yet less than forty-eight hours ago, I couldn't get a word out of them. At some point I needed to speak to Fi alone. I wanted to know what, if anything the girls were asking about their situation.

My phone rang, pulling me from my thoughts, shit it was Brad, I know she couldn't do anything to me, not right now anyway, but when her name came up on that phone my stomach turned and my heart raced, and that really did send a shock reminder of why we were here. I let it ring out, it rang three more times, I waited for the follow-up text, it didn't come. Hopefully that was it for the day, I don't know which was worse, seeing her name on that screen or having no contact at all. I sent a text to Sam 'Had a call,' he text back, 'cool.' Hopefully she would be contacting Fran next. Fran was a strange one, he was a lovely guy, seemed super helpful, a bit like one of those older guys at the supermarket, who has old time work ethic and always goes the extra mile to help you, but there was something else to him, I couldn't quite put my finger on it, but there was definitely more to him than meets the eye. For one, why would Sam have given him such an important job in the whole kidnapping saga, the only reason would be, he was more than up to the job. I wondered if he'd done it before, and what else he had done. Like I said, couldn't quite put my finger on it. This time I was yanked back to reality, quite literally, by Josie tugging on my arm, "Can we play outside ?" she asked. It was grey and miserable outside, thankfully, so it was easy for me to say, "Not today sweetie, looks like it might rain." She didn't argue or fuss, she just ran back to the table and picked up the book she had brought downstairs with her and began to read. I wished I could have seen them outside in the sunshine, running wild enjoying life, like a kid should, and I wondered if they'd ever done that. "How about a game of I-spy," I shouted. The girls jumped from their seats yelling, "Yes, yes," "Who wants to go first ?" I asked, "Me, Me." shouted Josie. I was beginning to see, she was the much stronger character of the two little ones.

Phoebe wasn't quiet, she was just a little more restrained. "Go on then," I said, Josie looked at Phoebe, then at Elizabeth, who was now looking what seemed like embarrassed. She turned away when I looked in her direction, but said, "I don't know if they know how to play it." "No worries," said Fi quickly. "It's an easy one." She explained the rules of the game, to the absolute delight of the two little girls, who immediately began to take turns shouting, "I spy with my little eye, something beginning with…" Combined with the sadness of all they'd missed was the joy of knowing they'd learned something new, something fun, they'd enjoyed being happy, they'd loved joining in, and it was all because of us.

Together, the three of us kept the girls amused for the rest of the day, they had ice cream and cake for lunch, at their request. They seemed real surprised when they were asked what they'd like, and I wondered if they'd ever been given much of a choice before. By the end of the day we had played all the old favourites, musical chairs, musical statues, hide and seek, which to my terror, Phoebe was ridiculously good at, she took it to the extreme, until at one point we were all yelling, 'Phoebe the game is over', but jees the kid was not giving in, we eventually found her standing stock still, completely out of sight, in absolute plain view, behind the curtain in the huge front living room, there wasn't even a smidgen of foot showing, she had stood there for at least a good half hour, whilst my mind raced wondering if she'd left the house, thinking she could be anywhere ! It was then I decided, hide and seek was definitely on the no play list from now on. We settled after dinner, for a game of snap at the kitchen table before it was time for baths/showers and bed. They were shattered, the main reason for knowing this, was just how quiet they'd become, considering there was a time when I could barely get a word out of them, they now found it hard to shut up for more than five minutes at a time ! Today I learned the value of one of my mum's all time favourite games, 'Let's see who can be the quietest for the longest.'

Dinners were made, kids were washed, bathrooms were cleaned, comfy pyjamas were put on, and little children were put in bed, happy, contented little children who still had not asked after their mother or their home. It was finally time to chill. I'd sometimes see my mum fall into her chair in the evenings, and now, all these years down the line I understood why, kids don't have to be playing up, or doing something they shouldn't be, to be hard work, they just are hard work, they require your attention around the clock, and sadly, probably even more so, when they're not so used to getting it. Before dropping into my chair, I'd made three cups of tea, and put some biscuits on a plate, Fi and Elizabeth walked back into the kitchen looking just as shattered as I felt. It was quiet now, there was plenty of talk but it was just that, no excited chatter, no giggling children, just regular adult conversation, it was a wonderful contrast to an equally wonderful but very different day.

It was strange spending so much time with Fi, strange but wonderful. This time of the evening we would usually be filling each other in on how our days had been, I missed that, but it was just as good to look back over the great day we'd had together. It came as a bit of a shock when during a conversation about my nerves being shot to pieces when Phoebe temporarily disappeared whilst winning at hide and seek, that Elizabeth, totally out of the blue asked, "So what exactly is going on here?" I felt the colour drain from my face, I had no answer, well I did, but not one I was ready to share. After a moment's silence I answered, "You know why you're here, your mum wants you here," "Yes, but why?" she asked again. "Your guess is as good as mine," I lied. I tried to keep up eye contact, not wanting to be obviously avoiding it, and revealing my lies too easily, although I could tell she was way less than convinced. She wasn't giving up easily either. "She's never done this before," she said, "She usually keeps us at the house when there's trouble, she just recruits extra security." The fact that they were used to this helped me to breathe a little easier, and to my shame, to lie a little easier too. Shrugging my shoulders I told her, "Like I said, we just got told to bring you here for a couple of days." She wasn't satisfied, but I think she realised that right now, I had no more to give her. To my relief it was, for the moment, the end of that conversation.

Chapter Thirty-Four

I was very much more interested in Elizabeth's next topic of conversation, her relationship with Brad. "You do know…" she said with a faint smile, "…she may just forget we are here." She laughed half heartedly, like it was a joke that wasn't that funny. "I'm serious…" she said, looking from me to Fi "…sometimes we don't see her for weeks at a time, and even then it's usually just in passing." I didn't know what to say to her, she was so matter of fact, about something which was so unnatural, a child without parents is a great sadness. Even if they're not a biological parent, having someone in your life who is a mother/father figure is essential to becoming a fully functioning adult, and yes they had Agatha, but that was work, she looked after them because she got payed to do it, though they did seem to adore her, and her them. My thoughts turned to how hard this must be for her, for Agatha, as the only person with any true feelings for them, the worry must be devastating. I tried, as anyone would, to reassure her that Brad loved her. "I'm sure she loves you in her own way, I mean she sent you here to keep you safe, didn't she ?" "She sent us here so she had one less thing to worry about," she corrected. There was a bitter twist to her sweet voice this time, I guess it was only to be expected. I had a feeling there was much more she wanted to say, but for now, that subject too, was closed. In the words of my mother, when all else fails, "More tea anyone ?" I asked, standing a little too quickly, making the chair make that awful scraping sound across the floor. I took the cups, and walked to the sink, the silence in the room now becoming awkwardly long, making every little noise I made, seem like I was purposely trying to recreate a marching band whilst washing some tea cups. "I'll have a fresh cup, please," said Fi, it was a welcome voice in the deafening silence. "What about you Elizabeth ?" I looked across to see her staring intently at her hands, one on top of the other on the table. She hadn't heard me, "Elizabeth ?" I said a little louder, she looked up, still not quite in the room with us, "Yes ?" she said quietly, "Tea ?" I asked, holding up the tea cup, "Would you like another ?" Suddenly coming out of her daydream, she sat up straight again, back with us now, "Oh…oh yes please." It was pushing on for nine pm, and Sam was due back any minute, I had a feeling he would like to see Elizabeth, and so, we would drink tea and eat some very good Bakewell Tart flavoured cookies, until he arrived.

I was right to leave Elizabeth just where she was, when Sam walked in and saw her sitting there, his face lit up, he tried to hide it, his eyes darting quickly away from her, but I was watching and waiting, and that look told me I was right, Sam had feelings for this girl, and I highly suspected she felt the same. This was going to be a problem of course, there was no way they could have a relationship of any sort, we were her kidnappers for god's sake, the least she knew about us the better. He had to know that, well of course he did, thing is, as we all know, none of us can help how we feel about someone, when the feeling is there, it's there and nothing can take it away. Unfortunately for Sam, this was all on him, he would have to ensure nothing came of it, he would have to put his feelings aside, and he would have to make sure she knew that he wasn't or rather couldn't, be interested. The sad part was, I'd never seen him like this, and I always worried about missed opportunities, what if she was 'the one', what if neither of them ever felt like this about anyone ever again, what if they missed out on an eternity with their soulmate, as usual my brain went into overdrive and maybe, just maybe, got a little bit melodramatic, then again, I'd always been told, by my mum of course, if you get a chance at happiness then grab it with both hands. How horribly sad to be in a position, where grabbing that happiness was simply not an option.

Sam joined us at the table, "So what have you guys been up to ?" he asked, looking at Fi, but very obviously more interested in what Elizabeth had been up to. "Ah, we've had the best day Sam, literally been back to our childhood, playing games all day, well Beth was mostly a spectator, but we're gonna get her to join in tomorrow," she laughed as she looked at Beth who was clearly embarrassed judging by the emerging pink tinge to her cheeks. They continued to talk about the day they'd had, Fi filling him in on the different games we'd played and the drama of hide and seek. I didn't want to even make eye contact with him, I knew what he'd be thinking, the kids were not supposed to be out of their room, I glanced quickly from the corner of my eye, and could see him looking my way with his eyebrows raised. Just keep making the tea I told myself, in the hope Beth would have distracted him by the time I got back to the table. She had, she was telling him how well Fi had looked after them, and thanking us all for looking after her, I swore I could detect a slight hint of sarcasm in there, but maybe I was just looking too hard. No-one answered her thanks, guilty consciences kicking in all round. "Hey it's not a problem, you guys have made it easy, it's been a pleasure," I chipped in quickly, trying to relieve the awkwardness. She smiled, whether she believed the reasons for her being here or not, she knew I was being sincere when I told her we were enjoying having her around. I for one would be sad to see them go, and I knew Fi was going to miss them desperately, especially Beth, and as for Sam, we really needed this to be over sooner rather than later, before people started getting really hurt !

"You heard any more from Brad ?" I asked Sam, he was taken aback that I had brought this up in front of Fi, but if we were trying to make this look realistically like we were just glorified babysitters, then this is what we had to do, right ? Once over the shock, he said, "No, not today." It dawned on me that Elizabeth didn't have a mobile phone, I don't know why I'd never noticed before, and I definitely should have checked when they first came ! That was slack I told myself. I decided to check that out, did she have a phone, but not with her, or had she never had one ? "Have you not heard from her ?" I asked, looking at Elizabeth. "How would I hear from her ?" she asked, perfectly innocently. A seventeen year old, without a phone, was certainly a rare thing these days. "Oh," I said, feigning surprise, "I thought she might have called you." "We're not allowed phones, Brad said we don't need them as we don't go anywhere alone." Most teenagers would be furious about that, but she was so matter of fact it obviously didn't phase her at all. "But how do you keep in touch with your friends," said Sam, probably weighing up how he was going to keep in touch with her. I gave him the what're you playing at look, which he ignored. She paused before answering that one. "The only friends I have, are from school and Brad doesn't like us to keep in contact with them outside of school." Why did she keep calling her Brad, for a moment I thought I must have said that out loud, but it was Sam's voice I heard asking that exact question. "She doesn't like being called mum, mother, mom anything like that, never has, when we were little we called her Collette, but then when dad went, she told us to call her Brad." "That must have been so strange for you, losing your dad, then your mum taking his name ?" Sam was getting a little too chatty for my liking, just a little too personal, I tried to intercede, "Well I suppose you're just used to it now eh ?" "Not really, it does still seem very strange, but if that's what she wants, then that's what she gets, if you know her well, you'll know she always gets what she wants." Shivers ran up my spine as she turned and directed that last statement right at me, and I wondered once again whether she believed a word we had said.

Sam wasn't giving up on getting to know Beth, as he now called her, and the questions continued as he tried to build a picture of her life, to be honest, there was not a lot to tell. Their dad the original Brad had been about as good a parent as their mum, but she did say they'd had a special relationship with the paternal grandfather, up until Brad went, he was never allowed to see them alone, but he showered them with gifts and they loved his visits, he was kind, and always told them how much he loved them, something I think they'd never experienced from either of their own parents. I became more and more saddened the more she talked, and Sam became more and more angry, which wasn't good, one, because he would want to make Brad pay, and two, because it meant, in the short time he had known Beth his feelings had become strong enough to provoke the urge to protect her. He looked tense, he looked pained, and the more she talked, the closer he leaned towards her. I was thankful for the large kitchen table keeping them apart. Time for a rescue tea. "Tea anybody ?" I said, beginning to collect the cups up again, it was then I noticed the time, we had been at that table chatting away for almost three hours. "Actually…" I said, "…It's getting pretty late, don't you think ?" I was looking at Fi now, she had barely spoken a word all night, but had listened intently to Beth, eyes filled with compassion for the friend she barely knew. She knew immediately what I meant, stood up stretching her arms in the air, and said, "I'm ready for bed, you coming Beth, we can go check on the girls and watch some TV till we fall asleep." Beth jumped up with a smile, more than happy to join her friend, they waved good night, the lingering look between Beth and Sam, bothering me more than it really needed to. I followed them out to the bottom of the stairs, wanting a little privacy to say goodnight to the love of my life. Taking her slowly by the waist, I pulled her in towards me, looking into her eyes, I told her how proud I was of her, and thanked her again for all she had done, and of course she told me no thanks were needed, I kissed her, lingering were my lips touched hers, I wanted her, all of her, "Go…quickly," I told her, "Before I lose control altogether !" I may have told her to go, but my arms held tightly on to her, she giggled, knowing what she was doing to me, finally I let her go. She skipped up the stairs, waving and giggling as she went. While I was left to try to compose myself, before returning to the kitchen to confront Sam !

"What the hell's going on ?" I demanded, speaking to Sam like he was a naughty teenager. "What ?" he said, looking genuinely puzzled. "You and Beth ?" I saw the change in his face as he realised he had not been keeping his emotions a secret ! "Don't know what you're on about mate," he said, very obviously knowing exactly what I was on about. "Sam, you're building up trouble for yourself, and for her, it's obvious there's some sort of connection between you guys, but you know this can't go anywhere... don't you?" I felt bad now, who was I to tell someone they couldn't take that chance of happiness, I just couldn't see how this could work, I suppose, to some degree it was a moot point, once Elizabeth was back home, he wouldn't be able to see her anyway. That thought brought my anxiety levels down a little. But I hadn't quite finished with Sam. "Seriously though Sam, what's happening here ?" He wasn't going to answer at first, but when he looked at me and saw the concern on my face, he changed his stance, he relaxed, his face softened. "You're right mate, there is something about her, I don't know what, I mean I shouldn't even be thinking like that, she's ten years younger than me, but I can't stop thinking about her, she's on my mind all day, and tonight, I literally raced back, hoping she'd still be up so I could see her, and yes I get that it can't go anywhere, let's face it, when she finds out what we've done, she won't want to know me anyway, so you can probably stop worrying eh ?" He was right, I'd not even given any thought to how Elizabeth was going to feel when she found out how we had betrayed her. I felt sick to my stomach at how hurt she was going to be, at how guilty Fi was going to feel, this was going to be so much tougher than we'd first realised. I should have been tougher, I should have locked them in that room and kept them there, then none of this would have happened. Shit ! What a fucking mess !

Once again I realised I'd heard nothing more from Brad, it was strange how easily I could forget about her all day, given that's why we were there. I waited with Sam, for the guys to come back hoping that one of them could tell me something new. It would be a further two hours before they returned home. They were quiet tonight, streaming through the door looking understandably shattered, I hoped the quiet wasn't indicative of any disasters ! Thankfully it wasn't, they were simply exhausted, having gotten over the initial euphoria, and the adrenalin now running low, they were in desperate need of a battery recharge. I did my usual, and made them tea and coffee, I fed them, and I listened. When they'd finished filling each other in on the day's events, exchanging facts and figures, and discussing the next step, I asked the same question I had the night before. "You heard anything from Brad ?" Tatty stood up and walked round the table to where I stood, "No-one has had any direct contact with her, but I don't want you worrying about that, it's only been two days, these things take time, especially with people like her, who are more concerned with saving face, than saving people !" He held up his phone to show me some texts he'd had. "These are from a guy on the inside," he said, handing me the phone. I read them eagerly, desperate for any snippet of information. I felt a huge sense of relief as I read the last of the conversation. Brad was furious, furious that someone had dared to take something from her, she had no idea who was responsible, but was not giving in just yet, they suspected it would take about a week, before she made any counter offers, and although that was way too long for my liking, as it was out of my hands, I would have to accept it. She was however 'fucking furious with that little prick for allowing this to happen' that made me smile, it solved a big problem for me, she still blamed me, without knowing I was responsible, I could probably live with that, the plan had been to eventually reveal to her that it was me who had taken her kids, right from under her nose. But like Sam said, I still had time to make that decision, telling her and not telling her would have completely different impacts on our future, it remained to be seen, which way I would go.

I took myself to my empty bed, Fi had fallen asleep next to Elizabeth, I'd checked on them first, and of course I stopped and smiled for a while, at how amazing she was, and how lucky I was, I closed the door carefully, thankful now for the sleep I would soon get, but sad I wouldn't get to do it with her. I thought about the day's events, trying to figure out what would happen next, I wanted to worry about Sam and Beth, because that's what I was used to doing, but tonight sleep was my friend, and it came swiftly and deeply.

I woke not to darkness as I usually did, but to daylight, it was confusing for a moment, and I quickly grabbed my phone to check the time. Shit ! It was past ten, I leaped from the bed, grabbing my clothes as I did, and still dressing myself as I ran through the door, I went first to the girls room where Phoebe and Josie were happily playing with some lego, Josie jumped from the floor and ran to me, threw her arms around my waist and yelled, "Good morning," I held my arms out in front of me, looking down at this little person, now attached to my body, not knowing what to do, before my instincts took over and I returned the hug she'd given me, Phoebe looked on from the floor where she was playing, she waved and shouted good morning, and all I could think was, shit I can't do another week of this, I'll be trying to go on the run with a whole family at this rate !! Remembering the hurry I was in, I told them I'd see them later and rushed down the stairs, along the hallway and into the kitchen, there they were, like they'd been doing this their whole lives, sitting at the table with their empty tea cups. Fi came straight to me, "Hello sleepy head," she said, kissing me gently and snuggling into my chest, I closed my eyes, kissing the top of her head. Elizabeth's initial embarrassment at our embraces had passed, and now she looked on, happy at seeing the love between us, another sign of the growing friendship between her and Fi.

Obviously all the guys had left, they were always early starters. Sam had left a message to say he would be back at tea time, he didn't say why, but I suspect I already knew the reason, and I was guessing my pep talk had not had any effect whatsoever. I joined Fi and Beth at the table, I wasn't quite used to the shortened name just yet, but 'Beth' seemed to prefer it, and so I would go along with it. "Have the kids mentioned their mum ?" I asked Fi, "Or have they mentioned going home at all ?" "Not that I've heard," she said, looking to Beth to confirm her answer, "No, I've not heard them, but why would they, they're loving it here," she laughed, a proper laugh and I knew she was remembering the fun they'd had the day before. "Surely they must be curious though, wonder why they're here, and when they're going back ?" I asked, puzzled by this whole family set up. "Listen, I don't think I have made myself clear…" said Beth, so serious now, it was hard not to sit up and take notice "…our mother does not care, we could be here for years and she wouldn't care, she never has done, the girls go to school they come home they eat they do homework and they go to bed, that is that, there's no fun, no laughter, no one caring how they feel, and so, no, they won't ask when they're going back, because why would anyone want to go back to that ?" She was sad now, and it was painfully obvious she was now thinking of her own life, she was thinking how hard it would be for her to go back, she'd had this tiny taste of freedom, of normality, of humanity, of family, and she loved it, we were, in actual fact only succeeding in making life harder for all of them. Guilt hit me hard, the disruption we had brought into their lives was immense, I knew it would be, but I hadn't imagined it would be caused by them experiencing love and kindness. I was overwhelmed with sadness, and couldn't help myself, I walked to where she sat, took her in my arms and held her tightly. As hard as it was that she would lose all of this, she needed to know she was worthy of someone's love. She clung on as though her life depended on it, and when she finally let go, it was to wipe the tears which were spilling onto her cheeks. Fi was ready with the tissues, and a warm hand, Fi loved to hold hands, she said it always made her feel safe, and that is what she was doing for Beth right now, making her feel safe.

Chapter Thirty-Five

The joys of yesterday were gone as reality hit home. Instead of returning three kids to a loving home, we had merely shown them what life should be like, before sending them back to a loveless house. The guilt now, was not from putting them through the ordeal of kidnap, but for showing them how it feels to be loved. I prayed now for a swift end to this whole terrible situation, so that we could all get back to our own lives. This was going to cause far more hurt than I had ever intended, or imagined, and I wasn't sure any more, that it was something I could live with.

The atmosphere in the room was sedate to say the least, tea was drank in silence, everyone deep in thought. When I couldn't stand it any longer, I did what my dad would have done, I placed a piece of the custard cream that Fi had given me, on my teaspoon and flicked it at Beth. Fi was mid mouthful of tea, which spurted all over the kitchen table as she burst out laughing, poor Beth sat stock still in shock, she had no idea what to make of it, but Fi's laughter was contagious and soon the two of them were laughing out loud, each of them returned fire, as I tried to shield myself from biscuits flying in both directions. It worked every time, my dad had always used this on Joseph, it never ever failed. The mood had lifted, and for that I was thankful, and just like that, 'normality' was resumed, for now.

Seizing the moment to relieve myself from the emotional rollercoaster of the morning, I excused myself and took myself outside, it was the first time I'd had fresh air on my face in over forty eight hours, and god did it feel good, I breathed deeply, taking the cold air into my lungs, sitting myself on the steps at the front of the house, just as I'd done at my old apartment. I sat and I thought, not in the usual way, worrying about how things were gonna work out, but more strategically now, returning these kids home was much more complicated now, I really did feel a personal responsibility for them, what I needed to figure out was, how, or if, there was anything I could do for them once they were gone, I suspected not, but I had to at least try. There were a few avenues we could take, probably the only viable one being, to ensure that someone was put in place to work with the kids, who would do exactly what Fi and myself had done these last few days, treat them like the wonderful people they were, show them the love and compassion they deserved, and make them realise how amazing and wonderful they are, it wasn't a lot to ask, I could only hope that it was possible. I knew it was a long shot, but I had a group of guys on my side who would do anything they could to make sure wrongs were righted. I was happier now, happy that there was at least a glimmer of hope for these kids.

The day passed quickly mainly due to the fact I'd slept half of it, and although I knew Sam's early homecoming was only going to cause more issues, I would be thankful of the support he would give. I was hoping to get a chance to talk to him when he arrived home, before he got a chance to sit down with Fi and Beth. He was always the one who made me see sense, who brought me back to reality, and today I really did need that. I found myself back on the doorstep, at four pm waiting impatiently for him to get home, daydreaming about going to work, going home to our little apartment, Fi waiting for me with my cuppa, and of course I asked myself why, why had I thrown all of that away, just for a retribution that helped no one but me. I'd put so many people in danger, turned so many lives upside down, just so that I could fulfil a promise I'd made to myself. The realisation of my selfishness hit me hard, the realisation that the fall out from this pathetic act of revenge could damage all of us for years to come, maybe forever. And the realisation that there was no going back. I was left feeling deflated and empty, and full of remorse and regret.

I heard a car in the distance, and knew it could only be Sam, but the hair on the back of my neck stood up anyway, ultra aware of the danger that could be approaching. My eyes darted about searching the distance, waiting for the car I could hear to come into view, I sighed with relief as Sam's car came into sight. I hadn't even realised I'd stood, awaiting the unknown, prepared for whatever or whoever was coming. And now that I knew it was him, I sat again, relaxed, and waited for him to arrive. " What's this ?" he asked, as he climbed from the car, "Another lecture ?" he was smiling so I knew that, one, he was in a good mood and two, he was up for a bit of banter. "Do you need another one ?" I asked, he laughed as he said, "To be perfectly honest, I very probably do." I could only smile right now, I refused to make anyone else feel bad about their lives today. If Sam and Beth got just a few weeks of happiness from this, then who was I to deny them it ? One thing I had learned today is, there are many, many things of which I have no control whatsoever, and I really needed to concentrate on the stuff I could. Once again I thought of mum, her favourite prayer was the prayer of serenity, which went something like this... 'God, grant me the serenity, to accept the things I cannot change, Courage, to change the things I can, and the Wisdom to know the difference'. It couldn't have been more appropriate than it was right now, I would do what I could to help these kids, but I had to accept there was a limit to how much I could, in reality, actually do.

Sam took a seat next to me on the steps, "So what's going on ?" he asked, "I mean you're not sat out here alone for no reason." He always knew, always, I started to shake my head as I explained how things had gotten on top of me today, how much I'd fucked things up allowing Fi and Beth to become so close, and how bad I felt about sending them home. I was being super serious and emotional, I was pissed at Sams reaction, which was to laugh out loud. "Hey mate, they might not be going anywhere at this rate !" I'm sure there was more than a tiny part of him that hoped that was a possibility. I made no attempt to join in with his laughter. "Sorry mate," he said, "I couldn't help myself, listen, I know this will work out, and you know I'm always right...don't you ?" It was a fact, he *was* always right, and so I suppose I had no choice but to believe him. "Just one more thing ..." he added as we got up to go inside, "...if these kids have had such a shit life, let's make this time count eh ?" When he said it like that, it suddenly made perfect sense, why take something away from them that they may never get to experience in their lives again. Sam had just made this whole ordeal a lot simpler than it had been five minutes ago. I often wondered what I would do without him, I really couldn't imagine.

Back inside, Fi and Beth were still talking, I mean what the hell did they find to talk about that kept them entertained for this long, it was like they never ran out of steam, or stories, or topics, or gossip, but I loved it, I loved seeing Fi enjoying life to the full. I had only known 'us' as just me and her, but this was so different, she was enjoying being a teenager, the teenager she had never had the chance to be, she had someone to share with, in a way that we didn't, and whilst for some people that may have been a problem, I could only love Beth for giving her the opportunity to have something that should have come naturally, I suppose in the grand scheme of things they were both in the same boat, on completely different levels of course, but they'd both missed out on the childhoods they deserved to have.

Beth's face lit up as she spotted Sam walking in behind me, she immediately tried to hide her reaction, turning quickly to Fi and continuing their conversation as though she had not even noticed we were there. It amused me now more than annoyed me, now that I had accepted that there were things I couldn't change, and Sam was right, even if this was short lived, they should both have the opportunity to experience the happiness they brought each other. Sam actually put the kettle on, something I can't ever remember him doing, I had to laugh at his attempts to impress with his domestic prowess. "Anyone want more tea ?" he asked, pointing to the empty cups in front of them. "Yes, please," they said in unison, each taking their cup and holding it up for him to take, which of course he dutifully did, stopping at the table, with cups in hand to ask how they'd slept, and how their day had been, "It was much quieter today," said Fi, "The girls have been as good as gold, and we have basically drank tea and ate." Beth laughed out loud, "I'll be two stone heavier by the time I... go home," the last two words coming out slowly and quietly as she realised a point would come where she would in fact, go home. Her sadness was felt by us all, the sadness of that mornings events instantly hitting home again, there was nothing we could say to make her feel any better, she would have to go home, that was a fact, and because of that, it was difficult to find any words that could even begin to change how she felt. Sam sat at the head of the table in the chair to her right, "Listen, I realise things aren't great at home, but look, you're nearly eighteen, she can't make you stay after that, you can do what you like then, but for now, while we're here, let's all pretend it's forever, just for a short time, ok ?" Wow ! I'd never heard Sam speak like this, with such heartfelt compassion, he took Beth's hand in his and squeezed, until, with tears in her eyes, she nodded in agreement. And there it was, that look between them, staring into each other's eyes, hands locked tightly together, and I knew there and then, this was not going to end when this was over. Sam would be watching and waiting, for that very first opportunity to take her away from the life that had left her with such hopelessness.

It took some time for the mood to lift, but Sam, who may have surprised me with his compassion for Beth, also had the gift of banter, and before long laughter filled the air again, I was happy to be the butt of his jokes, as he chided me over losing a kid, in the whole hide and seek debacle, took the piss out of me for how long it had taken me to make a move on Fi, and how easy I was to read. I didn't mind any of it, not one bit, the girls thought it was hilarious, and it proved to me that he was always listening, always taking notice, and always caring. For me it was confirmation that he would always be there for me, and it was the reason I loved him just as much as if we had been born brothers.

For the first time in the last few days, me and Fi went to bed together, we left Sam and Beth at the kitchen table still talking, getting to know each other, flirting shamelessly to the point were I felt like I was intruding, I laughed and shook my head as I said goodnight, for it to be completely unheard by either of them. They were so engrossed in each other, Brad herself could have been here saying goodnight, and I doubt they'd have noticed ! We walked slowly up the stairs weary from such an extraordinary couple of days. It was so, so good to climb into bed with Fi, to hold her close next to me and talk over our day, like we'd done so many times before. Fi began to explain to me just how hard Beth was finding the thought of returning home, she hated her mother, she hated the life they had, but she loved her sisters and couldn't bear the thought of leaving them behind. She was in an intolerable position where she would soon be of an age where she could leave, but her overwhelming urge to protect her sisters meant she would have to sacrifice her own freedom for them. It was a pitiful state to be in for anybody, but for a seventeen year old, it was completely soul destroying. My plan to have them looked after once we were gone, seemed even more crucial now. My thinking slowed, and the full on conversation we were having became a trickle. The guys were not coming home tonight, and knowing I didn't need to be awake for them, coupled with the emotional stress of the day, meant exhaustion took hold quickly, sleep bringing a well needed mental reprieve for us both.

I woke at my usual time, with the sky still dark outside, a time I liked. I lay for ten, fifteen minutes maybe, going over the previous day's events in my head, and wondering what the new day would bring. Leaving Fi sleeping as I creeped out of bed, I left the room shutting the door quietly behind me. As I'd done the previous couple of days, I checked in on the girls before I went down stairs. The little ones were still sleeping too, and Beth ? Well, Beth's bed was empty, this was not good. I moved quicker now, still trying to keep the noise to a minimum, tiptoeing down stairs as fast as I could and heading for the kitchen in the hope they were still there ! I marched past the living room, still on my toes, the door was open, I quickly took three steps back to see if I really had seen what I thought I'd seen. There, curled up on the sofa, spooning like a couple of pros, was Sam and Beth. I breathed a huge sigh of relief, feeling once again like the father figure in this crazy scenario. I couldn't help myself, they looked so cute together, I took out my phone and took a quick pic, assured Sam would appreciate it later, before getting on with making my morning cuppa. I enjoyed the time alone with my thoughts, the calm, the quiet, they both helped me to stay in total control of them, for a change !

It was just half an hour before Fi was up, walking into the kitchen in her pink pyjamas, bare foot and stretching. I took full advantage of the moment we had alone, quickly moving to the door and pulling her into my arms, I kissed her softly, she responded immediately, slow sleepy kisses, that felt so good, it was hard to let her go, but the house was starting to stir, I could hear footsteps upstairs, which meant our little friends were up now, and by the sounds of it were racing each other round the room ! "I'm sorry I fell asleep on you," I told Fi, still holding on to her, "That's ok, you looked exhausted, I know I was." I kissed her quickly on the lips, knowing she was eager to go see how the girls were doing. She disappeared to check on her little charges. That's when I heard the giggling coming from the living room. I smiled to myself, just at the thought of how happy they were. I could remember that first morning I woke up with Fi by my side, I couldn't believe how lucky I was, I couldn't believe I'd finally had the nerve to ask her to stay. I made four cups of tea, and placed them on the kitchen table whilst I started on the toast. I was excited to pull my 'tut, tut, tut,' face at Sam when he walked in, maybe throw a little bit of shaky head in there too. I amused myself as I buttered the toast imagining him trying to figure out just how they were going to play this.

Fi was back just five minutes later, the girls had requested orange juice and cereal, which she immediately started to make, I took out a tray, ready for her to deliver her room service order. She was loving this, there was something different about her, she was more alive than ever before, she brought a whole new meaning to walking with a spring in your step, she was almost walking on air, her eyes were brighter, she was lifted, emotionally, physically, spiritually, these kids had given her purpose, and it was something I hadn't even realised she needed, but was eternally grateful she was able to experience now. We had of course had a long conversation about my concerns for her when this was over, but she'd assured me she was prepared, she was continually telling herself it wasn't forever, but she was going to soak up every tiny bit of it while she could. I'd pretty much heard the same thing from Sam, live for the moment seemed to be the motto of the moment, maybe I should take a leaf out of their book. Fi had barely sat down next to me, when we heard footsteps in the hallway, it was so hard to keep a straight face as I watched them walk to their seats. Somehow Sam's features seemed softer today, or was I looking too hard for the effects Beth was having on him. This whole situation it seems was having a major effect on all of us, people were changing, experiencing things they never had before, learning about themselves, about life, about what was important to them, the only downside to any of this was, it was all built on lies, at some point the shit was going to hit the proverbial fan, and the fallout was going to be completely catastrophic.

"Hey Sam, how about I go to work today and you stay at home and look after the girls," I joked, he actually paused, I couldn't believe he was actually thinking about it. He didn't answer, just laughed off the question, as Fi reminded me, "Excuse me matey, I think it's a bit more like we look after you don't you think ?" Of course she really had, she always had. "You've been amazing," I told her, kissing her again to remind her just how much I appreciated her, forgetting for a while we were still in company, "Oh for god's sake mate, I'm trying to eat my toast," Sam was waving his toast in the air in protest and Fi bowed her head just a little embarrassed, but still with that beautiful smile. I laughed at Sam, "Look who's talking," I said, reminding him that he and Beth had barely taken their eyes off each other in the last twenty-four hours. Instead of returning the banter, he pulled Beth to his side and kissed her head, my heart melted for them, *this* was real, this wasn't just infatuation, or lust, or a way to pass their time, they'd fallen for each other, big time. I tried not to think what the future held for them, I tried, as they'd all requested, to live for the moment, but it was hard, hard to pretend this didn't have to end someday soon, hard to know the people I loved were going to suffer so much heartache, I couldn't bear to think of the hurt it would cause, so as quick as it came, I brushed it away, and tried as much as I could to live for the moment.

Chapter Thirty-Six

        It would take three more days, five days in total before Brad gave in and offered to pay half of the ransom money, HALF !! I mean for fucks sake woman, you might barter for the price of your car, or the price of your drugs, but you don't barter for the life of your kids, what I had asked for was a drop in the ocean compared to the assets she had, and yet she still couldn't bare to be the loser in this, still she was trying to take a lesser hit, just to make herself feel better, to save losing face completely, to tell herself that she didn't give in. She had called my phone just one more time, then given up altogether instead conversing only with Fran, of course she didn't know it was Fran, he had been using burner phones to call her regularly, she had told him each time that she would be in touch, which both Brad and Fran knew wasn't possible. That wasn't an issue, Fran was in no hurry, and Brad would have to give in eventually, today she was trying to bargain for a payment of £50,000 as opposed to the £100,000 we had asked for, when Fran rejected her offer, her answer was 'fine,' nothing more. The good thing was we knew from the fact that she had started to make offers, that she still had no leads as to who had taken the kids, which meant for now at least, we were safe, bet she wished she'd given her kids a phone now eh !

    For the last few days life had gone on pretty much as normal, Sam and Beth had grown even closer, the little ones, well, I adored them,

I'd actually panicked a little at the thought of never seeing them again, but now, now that offers were beginning to be made, the thought of them leaving made me feel physically ill. At the start of all this, the thought of moving on, going on the run, starting afresh, had been terrifying, and I'd questioned whether or not I could go ahead so many times, but that compared in no way to how I felt now, the losses we were all going to feel were unimaginable. I could never have foreseen how much things would change, how this little family whose lives we had turned upside down would become such an integral part of our own lives, that the idea of leaving them would be so absolutely devastating. And if *I* was finding this difficult to comprehend, I could only begin to imagine how Fi and Sam were feeling right now.

The laughter of the last few days had been replaced by a sad quietness, we talked, but it was disjointed and awkward, poor Beth had no idea why her friend and this guy who meant so much to her, had suddenly become so quiet and distant. They had to stop, I had to make them see what they were doing. I waited for my moment, and when Beth left to use the loo, I told them straight. "I understand this is tough guys, but look what you're doing to her, she doesn't know why she's here, she doesn't know why you two are acting all weird on her, she doesn't understand what's changed, it's got to stop, remember what you told me ? This could go on for weeks yet, so come on guys, get a grip, live for the moment !" I felt like a dispassionate jerk, and I knew I was being the biggest hypocrite ever, as I was also fighting the urge to wallow in self pity, but they had to see that we still had a game to play, and as crappy as it felt using Beth as part of that game, that was the only reason we were here, and sadly for us, we would all have to learn to live with that.

Waiting for Brad to agree to the full ransom seemed like such a petty move now, given that I didn't want the money anyway, this was only ever about making her pay metaphorically not literally, letting her know that if I wanted to take her family, I could, that if I'd wanted to hurt them, I could, and if I'd wanted to take money from her…I could.

Now it all seemed so insignificant, my worries for Fi and myself when I'd initially hatched this plan bore no comparison to my fears for them all now. In reality I could have taken those kids home days ago, I'd have proven my point, we could have been miles away, Sam wouldn't be hurting, Fi wouldn't be so desperately sad, and I would not have even a fraction of the guilt I felt now. In my quest for revenge I had torn apart five lives. I tried, in vain, to see another way, but there simply wasn't one, there was no way of easing the pain I had caused, I would have to live with it, and so would they. I couldn't replace Beth, I could only be the best friend and boyfriend to them that they could ever need, and hope that would be enough. My heart ached for them, for Fi, for Sam, for Beth and her sisters, at this point I couldn't find it in me to justify the steps I had taken, no loss of life was worth ruining so many others. Damn !

A further three days passed, and the atmosphere at the house had just started to lift, when we received the news we had been waiting for. In those three days, relationships had grown, Sam and Beth were closer than ever, they needed each other, just like me and Fi, they brought to each other the things they had missed out on in life, so much so, it pained me knowing he couldn't keep it forever. Now Brad had agreed to pay the full ransom, plans had been made to make the exchange, the money, for the kids, one of the demands from our end was that Brad would bring the money herself and she would bring it alone, it had taken several calls for her to finally agree to all our demands. Fran was dealing with the logistics, and although he would be the one delivering the kids back to their mother, it galled me to even use that word to describe her, he would not be doing it in a way Brad would be expecting. We had just two more days, just forty-eight hours to say our goodbyes, to end the relationships we had built up and to resign ourselves to the fact that our lives would change forever. It had been decided that we wouldn't tell the little ones they were going home until they were on their way. I had no idea how they were going to react, and there was enough going on emotionally without dealing with two, either extremely over excited, or completely devastated kids. Beth was different, she needed time to get her head round the fact that she was going home to the life she despised, to the mother she hated, and would be leaving behind her only true friend and a man I suspected she had fallen in love with.

I slept that night on tear stained sheets, having cradled the woman I loved, crying desperately at the loss of her friend. She was crying not just for herself, but for Beth, for the life she would be returning to, knowing it was going to bring her only sadness. There was no comfort I could give her, words would mean nothing right now, and so I held her whilst she tried to explain her heartache, and her worries, until she cried herself to exhaustion, and finally to sleep.

When I woke and was immediately engulfed in dread, squeezing my eyes shut, I tried in vain to drift back to sleep, I wasn't ready to face this awful day. Too wrapped up in my own fears for what the day was going to bring I hadn't noticed that Fi too was awake, I turned to see silent tears running into her hair, "Oh Fi, come here," I took her into my arms, and I wished with all my heart I had made different decisions in my life, ones that would not have resulted in the pain she was feeling right now. I lay beside her, her head on my chest, which was soaked with her tears, and imagined how Sam must be feeling, his sadness would be a lonely one. I wished we could stay in that bed all day, all week, that we would never have to face the repercussions of what we had done, what I had done. But the reality was, we had little time, and so to allow all of us to make the most of the last few hours we had together, this would need dealing with, sooner, rather than later. "We need to get up," I told her gently, "You need to spend some time with Beth." She said nothing, but burrowed even closer into my chest, "I'm so, so sorry you have to go through this, I wish I could make it better Fi, I really do." She pulled away from my chest, wiped her tears and looked me straight in the eye, "Don't do that Conal, this is not your fault, I knew what I was doing, and yes, none of us could ever have imagined things would turn out this way, but this is not on you, please don't think that way." Now it was time for my tears to flow, here she was truly wracked with pain for herself and her friend, and yet she still tried to prevent me from feeling any guilt, I never needed reminding how much I loved her, she did it so naturally, all day every day.

Sam was sitting at the kitchen table, his face a mixture of fear and wild desperation, I was thankful Fi was still getting ready. He sat with his head in his hands, I wasn't sure he'd slept at all, he looked broken, his face was pale, his eyes dark. He glanced up as I entered the room, raised his hands in the air and shook his head, "What am I going to do mate ?" he asked, barely managing to get out the words before his voice wavered. He was trying desperately not to allow the tears that were collecting in his eyes to fall, he blinked them away, I could hear the gulps as he tried in vain to control his emotions. I wasn't sure he was going to appreciate it, but my instincts took over, I walked to where he sat, stood behind him, took him in my arms and held him, now he was no longer able to hold those tears in, with the support and comfort of his friend, he was safe to let his tears for his loss, fall. And so too was I.

Knowing there would not be much time before Fi and Beth arrived, I grabbed some kitchen paper, ran it under the cold tap, and gave it to Sam to put on his face, it made him laugh, "Thanks mum," he said, "Seriously mate, thank you." I was humbled as I explained, "You never need to thank me Sam, never." He took a good few deep breaths, suggested I put a kettle on, and we waited, he had already decided he would be the one to tell Beth, he felt he owed it to her, it wasn't as simple as 'you're going home and we will figure out a way to see each other' it was 'you're going home, and we can't ever see each other ever again'. It was utterly, devastatingly tragic.

As if knowing what she was about to hear, it was more than an hour before Beth joined us in the kitchen. Fi was finding it hard to look her in the eye, but she did her best to hold it together. Sam was amazing, he was in complete control now, as soon as Beth walked in, he jumped up to put the kettle on, "Tea Beth ?" he said, giving her the biggest grin. I suspect she had already picked up on the vibes in the room despite all our efforts to appear as normal as possible, she was cautious as she came to sit at the table, and although she returned Sam's welcome, it was easy to see she knew something was wrong. Tea for all was placed on the table, when Sam reached for Beth's hands, it was all Fi could do to hold herself together. I had been holding her hand under the table, and she squeezed tightly now, I knew that hand in mine was the only thing keeping her from falling apart. Holding both of her hands in his, looking her straight in the eyes, like he knew she deserved, Sam began to tell her what he knew was going to destroy her. "So, Beth, you know why you're here, yes ?" she nodded, her face showing her fear for what was happening. "You knew it would just be for a short while ?" he spoke with such kindness, such compassion, it was heart wrenching to watch, as he finished the sentence. Realising what he was saying, she pulled her hands from his, reeling back in horror. "No !" she yelled at him, "No! Please ! Just a few more days," she had backed up out of her chair and was backing up towards the kitchen units, fight or flight mode about to kick in. Sam moved quickly around the table, needing desperately to comfort her, as he got close, she pushed her hand out in front of him, he stopped dead. "Don't !" she said, "Don't you dare feel sorry for me," Sam looked completely distraught. "Beth, I don't feel sorry for you, I love you, I can't bear the thought of never seeing you again." Shit ! Holy fucking shit ! He'd said the 'L' word, I felt sick to my stomach, I knew their feelings were strong, but this was just too much, Fi fell into my arms sobbing uncontrollably, as Sam managed to take the girl he loved into his arms knowing he had just a few more hours, before she was gone forever.

Chapter Thirty-Seven

There were hugs, kisses, tears, and promises of remembering each other forever, there were what ifs and maybes, and finally a dark sense of acceptance, that this would all be over in just a few short hours. Fi had cooked pasta, the little ones had been allowed to come eat in the kitchen, given it would be their last day, we felt it was safe now to do so. I'm glad we did, they brought a much needed touch of normality back to the day, they were fun, they giggled, they asked a million questions, about the food, about their room, about the Tv programmes they'd watched, the list was endless, and still not once did they ask about going home, I prayed they would ask excitedly about when they would see their mum, but in my heart I knew it was never going to happen, they had little, if any attachment to the woman, their only saving grace, a wonderful person in their life called Beth.

They were exhausting, just watching their energy, listening to them ramble nonstop, was emotionally draining, but all too soon it was time to get them ready for bed. Beth and Fi did what they had done every night, ran them a bath, got them comfy in their PJs and tucked them into bed, knowing it would be the last time this would happen. This really hit home for me, I'd truly loved this time of night, winding down after a hectic day. I would never see this day again, I would never feel this feeling again, and I realised the emptiness, the pain and the heartache I was feeling, was grief, I remembered it from the many times I'd felt it before, but this was the first time I had grieved for someone who's heart was still beating. Losing someone and being unable to do anything about it, is soul destroying, but losing people when you could have done something, but you're not able to, or maybe don't have the guts to, well, that destroys you in a whole different way.

Those two little girls had walked into a room full of sorrow, full of loss and fear, and they'd filled it with joy and laughter and love, but now we were left once again to the desolation of what tomorrow would bring. I was sure of only one thing, we had been changed, irrevocably. The silence in the kitchen was no longer awkward, it was welcome, I was tired of trying to lighten the mood, tired of pretending everything was going to be okay, and I was tired, completely exhausted of trying to find a way out. When Fi and Beth returned to the kitchen they looked just as I felt, completely and utterly emotionally drained. They sat in silence with us two, all now in quiet contemplation of the new life tomorrow would bring.

We would sit that way for almost an hour before Beth said something that would shock us all back to reality. "I know what you did," she was looking at no one in particular. No one spoke, instead we all looked at Beth, waiting, not knowing if we really wanted to hear, what exactly it was that she thought she knew. She couldn't look at us, instead looking at the table top in front of her. The adrenalin crushing my finger tips, told me just how much I feared what she might say next. Still she didn't speak. I couldn't wait any longer, it was killing me. As I was about to speak up, Fi spoke quietly and calmly, her soft tones helping to calm us all. "What is it you know Beth ?" "Well I know my mother didn't ask you to bring us here," she stopped again, she waited a moment, then went on, "I know my mother well, and if she were sending us somewhere to keep us 'safe' we would have been with someone who practically imprisoned us. There would have been no friendships, no games with Josie and Phoebe, none of it, it took me a little while to figure out why this felt so wrong, but there you go, I got there in the end." I started to speak, but was beaten to it by Sam, "And why do you think you're here ?" he asked, his voice full of sorrow. "Well, if my mother didn't ask you to bring us here, I can only assume, you did that without her knowledge, am I right ?" Sam nodded, he could no longer lie to her, he was not about to try to talk his way out of this. "And, if you brought us here without her knowledge, I can also assume it was because there was something for you to gain from that." Shit, this was hard to listen to, it was excruciating listening to her explain that she knew we had used her, that her time here making friends, and finding love, was all based on deceit. I wondered how long she had known, but couldn't bear to ask. Sam took her hand, and I breathed an audible sigh of relief that she let him, "Beth, I need you to listen now, and listen very carefully ok ?" she nodded, her eyes full of tears, full of hurt, and pleading for answers. "This..." he said, circling his hand to include us and them, "...was never part of the plan." I hung my head in shame and pulled Fi close, tears still running silently down her cheeks, she held my hand tightly, needing me as close as she could have me. "This was supposed to be a couple of days, and you'd be home, I wish I could say it would've been better if I'd never come back early that day, if I'd never have seen you, but I couldn't even imagine now, never having had you in my life, I should've been stronger, I should have stayed away, and I'm sure I speak for us all when I say, if there was any way of taking your hurt away right now, we would do it." Sam's voice was wavering, and I knew he wouldn't be able to talk for much longer. It was my turn now, time to be honest, to step up to the plate, and give her what she wanted, what she deserved, the truth.

"Beth," I said, giving her a moment to make sure she was listening, like really listening, because of course she needed to know we cared, and of course she needed to hear we had never intended to hurt her, but above all, she needed to understand, if she could, why. "This is going to take a while, and I will be telling you things that you may not believe, and in fact have no reason to believe, but I'm going to tell you anyway." I asked Fi to make some tea, tea really did help, why, was an age old question I had no answer to. "You're right Beth, we brought you here without your mums knowledge." She physically dropped back into her chair, she knew, but she had also hoped it wasn't true. "Some months ago I hatched a plan to kidnap you and your sisters, you have to know there was never any intention to hurt you, not physically anyway." I needed to tell her that, but it seemed hypocritical now, given the damage I *had* caused. "The plan was for you to stay in that room for a couple of days, your mum would pay the ransom, and you guys would be back home before you even knew what was going on." Fi returned to the table with tea for us all, there were quiet thanks, and halfhearted smiles, before I continued. "Before I say any more, you need to know, this was never about the money, I was never going to accept the money." Sam gave me a puzzled sideways glance, and I remembered I'd not actually imparted that little snippet of information to him ! "Then things changed, I brought Fi along because I knew she was the best person I knew to take care of you, the only person I would have ever trusted to look after you, I could never have known how your friendship was going to grow, so fast and so strong." Now she sat up straight in her chair, she was indignant, "I really did think you were my friend," she said, tears streaming down her cheeks, "But now…" she couldn't finish, she could no longer speak through the sobs of aching hurt. Sam instinctively reached for her, but she pushed him away "Don't," she managed to say through her sobs. Sam was crushed, the woman he loved was suffering and there was nothing he could do to comfort her. "Please Beth," I begged, "Let me finish, maybe if you understand why ?" she said nothing, all Sam could do was watch, and allow her to feel her loss. "I don't want this to sound like I'm making excuses, I'm not excusing my actions at all, or any of ours." I took a deep breath before I continued, "Your mum had my brother killed, and the fall out from that meant my mother was also killed, the resentment that built up in me, resulted in me engineering this plan to try to make your mum understand what it felt like to lose her family, I couldn't have imagined for a minute that she didn't care." Beth had heard enough, she ran from the room, straight up stairs and into the bathroom. Fi was up and out of her chair in a second, ready to chase after her. "Fi, maybe she needs some time, I know you want to help, we all do, but she needs time to come to terms with all she's heard." She nodded and took herself to the top of the stairs where she sat, and waited for her friend.

Sam was destroyed, ruined, "Why the fuck didn't I listen to you ?" he said, pacing the kitchen with his head in his hands, "How the fuck did I let this happen, this is not me Conal, I don't let shit like this happen." I tried to be as calm as I could, with emotions running so high, one of us needed to bring them all down a little. "Sam, you're heart ruled your head mate, just this one time, you let your guard down just a little, and you know why, because your human, sometimes you meet someone and no amount of knowing what should be done matters, all sense of rationality goes out the window, you see them and only them, the bigger picture is at best faded, and at worst non existent, remember what you told me, live for the moment, we did, and it's been amazing, now we have to pay the price, and we will do that, together, this is not forever you said, and you can look at that any way you like, this what we're doing right now is not forever, but neither is her going home, that's not forever, one day you'll find her again, and I promise you Sam, I'll be there every step of the way to make sure that happens." It worked, all the rambling I'd done had given him a few minutes to compose himself, to recover from his emotional meltdown, and see things more clearly. The hard part was going to be convincing Beth that this wasn't over.

Fi sat loyally at the top of the stairs for the next hour, dealing with her own turmoil as she waited for her friend to appear. When finally she heard the sound of the lock opening on the bathroom door, she stood quickly, hoping her friend would accept some comfort from her. Seeing her outside, waiting just a few feet away, Beth stopped in her tracks, obviously still not ready for any sort of physical contact. Fi sat back down, and leaned against the wall, her face red and eyes swollen from the tears she had cried. "Is it ok for me to talk ?" she asked, Beth nodded, and Fi could see she was aching for someone to hold her even though she couldn't let her do it just yet. Fi patted the floor next to her, grateful and relieved when Beth joined her, still keeping her distance, afraid of letting herself get close, and opening herself up to even more hurt. "I can never, ever find the words to express how sorry I am, none of them seem enough, none of them *are* enough, I could never have known what a wonderful, kind ,caring, beautiful, funny, wise young lady I was going to meet, and I realise that does not in any way excuse what we have done, not even remotely, but I hope it helps you see what an amazing person you are, we came here to do a job, to help someone find the justice he felt he needed in life, then move on, but you, you changed that, you have changed us all in a way we never thought possible, it won't make you feel any better right now Beth, but what you have done in these last few days has altered three other people, forever, in the most wonderful way. You have been the only friend I have ever had, you've made me laugh, and cry, you've listened to me tell you things I've never told anyone before, you have given love to a man I have never seen show any real emotion in all the time I have known him, and you have helped another understand that no amount of revenge will ever stop the loss he feels. "Beth was silent for a while, taking in all that Fi had said. Fi waited for the rebuke she knew she fully deserved, what she was not expecting was for Beth to fall into her lap sobbing. "I don't want to go, Fi, please don't make me go." Fi was horrified, she had expected to be vilified for her behaviour, but *this*, this was intolerable. With tears falling again she held her friend, unable to make any promises, knowing she had no answers, knowing there was, in reality, nothing she could do to help.

    I had heard Fi talking, and knew Sam must have too, sitting waiting for at least one of them to come and tell us what was going on was excruciating. Knowing the women we loved were going through something so traumatic, and sitting at a kitchen table doing nothing was torture, and so the relief of seeing them walk through the door, tear stained faces, holding hands, was something that would live with me for a long time to come.

They sat next to each other hand in hand, unable at first to tell us what had happened upstairs. There was no hurry now, everything was out in the open, everyone knew what the following day was going to bring, and it seemed there had been some sort of unspoken, quiet acceptance of the situation. The silence was hard, but not as hard as being unable to hold Fi at a time when she needed me most, for now, Beth was our priority, the one who needed us, and everyone else's heartache must take a back seat, we would have each other, but soon she would have no-one.

Beth's bravery shone through when she started to tell us exactly how she felt. "I knew from day one that this wasn't something my mum arranged, as I said, she would never have thought about our welfare, there was no way she would have had someone like you, Fi, looking after us, she fears anyone having any impact on us, of course it took me until yesterday to figure out just what had happened here, and between then and now, I realise that for you three, things have changed, I understand that you are good, kind, caring, understanding people, but that doesn't excuse what you have done here, because whilst you were responsible for changing your lives, you were also responsible for changing mine, something I had no control over, no choice in, you made me love you guys, you've shown me what family means, you've shown me how family pulls together for the good of them all, how we're all there for each other, no matter how we're feeling, that we listen, we understand, we support…and tomorrow, you will still have all of that, and I, well, I won't, and whilst that thought terrifies me, I have to thank you for giving me something I will hold in my heart for the rest of my life." She didn't cry, unlike Fi and Sam, who's silent tears hurt me more than if I were crying them myself, she smiled, she hugged Fi, then she stood to go to the man she loved, now it was her turn to comfort. She stood by his chair and pulled him to her chest, the sobs he had so desperately tried to control came out in a torrent, and she cradled him, like a mother would a child, until his sobs subsided, and the room was quiet once more.

I doubt any of us would see our beds tonight, there simply was no time to be lost with sleeping. There was no packing to be done, just two amazing kids and a wonderful young woman leaving the same way they had arrived, physically anyway, emotionally they would never be the same. In the drama of the day I had given little thought to how Josie and Phoebe would react to going home. "Beth," I said, "Is there anything we need to do to make this easier for the kids ?" She shook her head, "What can you do ?" she said, shrugging her shoulders, "They don't know any different, they've had some fun, I dare say they will quickly go back to what they know, they'll adjust, kids do." She was being so matter of fact, and that in itself made me understand their lives a little more, their lives were 'matter of fact' and little else. I imagined a day when I could rescue them all, give them the life they deserved, and maybe ease a little bit of the guilt I felt for putting them through this ordeal. I knew that realistically that was never going to happen, but I had to believe that for them, something would happen to change their lives, I needed to believe it for my own sanity.

Chapter Thirty-Eight

Goodbye.

The night was long, but sadly, not long enough. Arrangements had been made for Fran to pick up the kids and drop them near to the family home, and only once he had been notified that the money had been dropped at the drop-off point, it was nerve wracking, and sickening, and heartbreaking, and nothing at all could change that. The money would not in fact be getting picked up, and the kids would not be getting dropped off at home. The drop off was arranged for eight thirty in the morning, and at that exact time, Beth, Josie and Phoebe would be arriving back at school. This was never about kidnap, or ransoms, this was only ever purely about making her realise what she could lose, that she was not untouchable, in reality it had served little purpose, if not for the fact that she had the overwhelming urge to save face, I doubt she would ever have acknowledged her the kids were gone.

Fran would drop the kids off before returning for me and Fi, to take us to the next safe house. It would be a while before we learned how much Brad knew, of course Beth knew all of us, she knew exactly what had happened, and whilst right now I couldn't imagine she would let Brad know, things change, feelings change, resentments kick in, anything was possible, but then we had always known that. As the minutes ticked by, creeping towards the deadline, my emotions began to run riot, panic set in, so much loss was being felt in that house, the air was thick with sorrow, a thick darkness that made it hard to breathe. There were no tears today, too many had flowed in the last few days, today was merely the terrible anti-climax to a badly played game.

We left Sam and Beth to say the saddest goodbye. I answered the door, while Fi went upstairs to get the kids. I opened the door to find...no-one, this was bad, more than a little bad, what the hell was going on, I called up the stairs for Fi to keep the kids up there for a minute. Walking slowly outside, looking all around, I pulled the door closed behind me, Frans car was out front, but he was nowhere to be seen. Cautiously, with all my senses kicking in, I walked first to one end of the house, looking through windows, checking all around me as I went. When I found nothing out of the ordinary, I took myself to the other end of the house, stopped at the corner, leaning against the wall, breathing deeply. I had no weapons, no way of protecting myself, but right now I needed to protect everyone in that house, that was all I cared about. I stood with my back to the wall, and took one more deep breath, before slowly peering around the corner. I couldn't believe what I was seeing, there I was, nerves on edge, fully expecting to see Fran with a knife to his throat, or a gun to his head, and what did I see ? !! Fran sitting cross legged on the floor with a damn cat in his lap ! "Shit, Fran, what the fuck are you playing at, I thought they were on to us, the door goes, I open it and there's no-one there." I was pissed off, and extremely relieved, and Fran ? Well, he had no fucks whatsoever to give. "Oh sorry, saw this little fella and couldn't resist." Was he fucking messing, like seriously, we're all inside, a gang of emotional wrecks, and he's out here playing with a manky fucking cat, I was so bewildered I couldn't think of a single thing more to say, shaking my head, I simply turned and walked back to the house, listening to the gravel behind me that told me Fran was close behind, with or without the cat, I had no idea.

Sam was waiting at the door, obviously wondering where the hell I'd got to, this was turning into more of a farce by the minute ! I shook my head as I walked up the steps, and told Sam, "Don't even ask !" Fran greeted Sam in a way that showed they had obviously known each other a very long time, the affection Sam had for this lovely older man was undeniable, they hugged, a long close hug, he was family, and if not family, as close as. Fi came to the top of the stairs, "Are we ok to come down now ?" she asked, "The kids are getting restless." The kids were obviously excited, and as soon as I nodded, they flew down the stairs, almost knocking each other over in their quest to get there first. "Whoaaaa," I said as first Phoebe then Josie flew into me. They were giggling away, still having no idea what the day would bring. The giggling and the girls stopped dead when they saw Beth with their coats in her hands. "Where are we going ?" they asked, with a mixture of excitement and trepidation. I kneeled in front of them, and pulled them close to me. "You're going home today girls." Nothing, there was nothing, no joyous shouts of 'Yes !' No eyes lighting up at the thought of seeing their mother, they turned to Beth, and Phoebe asked simply, "Why ?" Beth smiled, she was putting on the greatest act of her life, her eyes were large and she made herself sound as excited as she could, "Hey we have to go home girls don't we, won't it be good to get back in your own beds, have all your own toys around you, get back to school ?" She gazed at them hoping to have sparked some sort of yearning for home in them. It didn't work, "But we like our bed here," Phoebe said, looking back and forth between myself and Beth, "Can't we just stay for a little bit longer ?" Beth came and knelt beside them too, "I'm so sorry girls, we've had such a great time haven't we, and we've learned so much..." she looked around at all of us, once again emotions were raw, "...one day we will come again, how does that sound." Now, we had cheers, "Yaaaay." Only now, at the thought of returning to their kidnappers, were they filled with excitement, satisfaction and happiness. I could only hope that someday we could fulfil Beth's promise.

The time to say our last goodbyes came, I took the girls to the car, hugged them both tightly, before strapping them into their seats, "You guys be good," I told them, "And, above all else, be happy…Ok? They nodded. Their sadness and complete lack of any longing to return home was killing me. I gulped back the lump in my throat that was threatening to expose my heartbreak to them, shut the car door and walked away from them for the last time. Beth was in Fi's arms, I wasn't sure she would ever be able to let her go. Two of them wiping each other's tears away, but they managed a smile, and even a giggle at something they remembered, before it was time for Beth's final goodbye. The hardest goodbye of all.

Sam had kept his distance, still standing in the doorway while all of this was happening, giving Beth the chance to do what she needed to do, to make this as easy, or the least difficult it could possibly be. He waited patiently for a moment he hoped would never come, as Beth and Fi left each other's arms, the mood was solemn. She stood for a while unable to face the man she loved, head bowed, knowing it would be the last time she ever saw him. Sam walked slowly, sadly to the bottom of the steps, his face full of pain, his arms aching for her. Hearing his footsteps on the gravel, she finally turned to face him, and she was lost, lost in the turmoil of leaving behind the briefest insight into real life, real love, real family she had ever known. She fell to her knees, her face in her hands. Sam was by her side barely before she reached the floor, horrified at the sight before him, no words were spoken, the two of them kneeling in the gravel embraced in each other's arms, grief stricken by the cruelest of jokes life had played on them.

Fran had waited patiently, knowing that time was getting on he caught my eye and tapped his watch, I shook my head telling him I couldn't intervene, I couldn't put a stop to this one final act of love between them. He could, he climbed back out of the car, took to his knees besides them and gently told them it was time to go. There was no dramatic clinging on, no being dragged away kicking and screaming, just a silent sorrow as Beth took her place in the front seat of the car without looking back, without any more goodbyes. In just a few minutes they were gone, just the rear of the car in the distance. I watched, Fi's hand in mine, until they were out of sight, even then it was hard to move, hard to believe they were gone, and devastating to know it was forever. I turned to comfort my friend, only to find, not surprisingly, he was gone, gone to cry the rest of his tears and to feel the rest of his pain, alone and in private.

We had two hours to gather all our belongings, then we would be leaving too, leaving all we had ever known behind us. The fears for our future now completely eclipsed by the events of the last twenty-four hours, meant we were numb, no longer knowing how we should feel, no worries, no excitement, just emptiness. We worked on autopilot, slowly, silently, methodically collecting the few things we had unpacked, piling up our bags near to the front door, just as we had done a little over a week ago. Back then we were preparing for a new beginning, for closure from the lives we had led, for myself, a resolution to the years of hurt and injustice I felt I'd experienced. But now I was ashamed of the hurt I had caused just for the sake of my own retribution, a selfish act that had caused those I loved most, a pain they may never recover from.

Back at the kitchen table, a place I feel I had sat for the majority of the last eight days, a place were we had enjoyed banter, games, soul searching, given advice, and love, we now sat, lost in our sadness, unable to find any words that would comfort the other, knowing somewhere in that house our friend was feeling a loss he would never recover from. I willed the hours to pass quickly so we could leave this place behind, a place that would always have such mixed emotional memories for us. I had learned in the past that there are things that happen in life that change us, not that they just give us a different outlook on life, but really change us intrinsically, like every atom in our bodies now works in a different way, every molecule in our brains now thinks a different way, an irreversible change that means we can't ever think, feel or see things in the same way ever again, and that, in this last week, is what had happened to everyone who had stayed at this house.

Sam came back to the kitchen after more than an hour, his face still swollen and red, he bore no shame for the marks of his sadness, he wore them proudly, a tribute to a young woman who had given him a love for life he had not known. I was surprised when he walked straight to Fi and hugged her hard, his head burrowed into her shoulder, eventually pulling away to smile at her, a little nod to the love and support we had shown to him. He walked across the room to where I stood, I was about to make yet another cup of tea, he threw one arm around my neck, and fake punched me in the stomach, this I loved, this was my Sam, strong, positive, ready for anything life would throw at him, and whilst it would no doubt take a long time, if ever, for him to get over losing Beth, he would not go down without a fight, he would not curl up and die, and if there was any way, any chance at all he could be with her again, then I fully believed if anyone could do it, he could. "What time are you expecting Fran back ?" asked Sam, he knew the answer, but someone needed to break the ice and I would take that, "Should be around ten thirty, hour there, hour back," "Not long now then eh ?" he said, the conversation forced, but a million times better than the silence that had preceded it.

We were going to stay at Frans house, I had no idea what to expect, he was such an average man, with his average car and his average clothes, he'd given nothing away about who he was or where he lived, I imagine that was the idea, he was perfectly nondescript, and that's what we needed right now, we needed to blend into the background and fade away. Sam assured us he would be at Frans within a couple of days, "I've been slacking off a bit lately… " he said, then adding sarcastically "…don't know if you noticed," that brought a smile to both of our faces. He needed to get back to work, he'd 'slacked off' at a time when they needed him most, but I suppose, for the best possible reason.

Ten thirty came and went, fifteen minutes passed before I began to feel anxious, by the time it had gotten to twenty minutes, my nerves were in bits. Sam kept telling me not to worry, it was probably just traffic, there was no way there could have been any problems. The only other person involved would be the guy Fran had contracted to watch for Brad's arrival at the handover point. As far as I know, up to now all of this had gone to plan, the girls should be at school, Brad would be on her way home, and a large bag of cash would be floating around somewhere waiting for some lucky bugger to find it. If anything had not gone according to plan, we would have known about it. Ten minutes later, there was a knock at the door, Sam headed down the hallway, his hand placed at the back of his waistband, followed closely by myself and then Fi, it was a relief to see Fran slowly appear as the opening in the doorway widened. "Where have you been ?" I asked, trying not to sound too disgruntled, only because Fran was such a good guy. "We had a small problem," he said, although I have to say, he did not seem the least bit concerned for whatever this small problem was. Sam asked "What problem ?" Fran turned towards the car and pointed, just at that moment the back window moved slowly downwards, whilst we all waited patiently to see who was behind it. Sam leapt from the steps, clearing the lot as he raced across the gravel, swinging open the car door, and scooping up the back seat passenger into his arms.

I didn't know whether to be ecstatic or horrified, I couldn't even begin to comprehend what this meant for us all. Where would she go ? What would she do ? What would Sam do ? What would we do ? Shit, this really had thrown up one hell of a shit storm !! I was still standing open-mouthed at the top of the steps, the three of us watching 'the great lovers reunion' happening before our eyes. "What the hell happened Fran ?" I asked, turning to where he stood. In his usual fashion, without any recognition for the seriousness of the situation, he said, quite simply "She wouldn't get out," "What do you mean she wouldn't get out, she's a kid." This man never lost his cool, and in the same quiet tone he said, "I couldn't cause a scene outside the school, you know, given the circumstances, so I told the girls she wasn't feeling well." I was staring at him in complete disbelief, "So she said no and you just left it at that ?" "No, not at all…" he said, "… we went for a drive, we talked, I asked her was there anything I could do to change her mind, when it became apparent that I couldn't, she asked me to take her home, now from what I've heard, she most definitely did not mean her mothers home, and so here we are." I was somewhere between gobsmacked and flabbergasted, this man could not be phased, he had said all of this like it was the most normal behaviour in the world. I was dumbfounded by this man…yet again !

Chapter Thirty-Nine

Before any of us had time to gather our thoughts, and get our heads round what had just happened, the five of us were on our way to Frans house. It was just about then I remembered Brad, oh shit ! "What ?" said Fi, I turned towards her, I'd been lost in a world of my own thoughts, "What ?" I said back to her, "You just said, 'Oh shit,' she told me. Ohhh, I'd said that out loud. "Oh, I just remembered Brad," I said, waiting for her to be as concerned as I was. "You only just remembered Brad ?" she said with an air of disbelief. "Well yeah, I've been trying to figure out what we're going to do about these two," I said, pointing towards Sam who was sitting besides Fran, and Beth who was in the back seat with us. "Erm excuse me, we *are* here," Sam reminded me, "Oh believe me, I know !" I retorted. "What's going to happen when she finds out ?" I asked, hoping someone was going to give me an answer. No one did.

It was a few minutes later before Fran spoke up,"Beth being here makes no difference to the outcome of what you guys did, you'll still be on the run, this was never about kidnap or money, so that's not an issue, you made your point, and almost everything went according to plan, if I've learned anything over the years son, it's don't sweat the small stuff, and to be fair given what you've been up to these last few months, Beth being here is that small stuff." What the hell did he know about what I'd been up to ? Who the hell was this guy ? And where the hell did all those words of wisdom come from ? Fran was becoming a little bit of an enigma. "*Has* anyone heard from her ?" I asked, "We won't know till we get back to the house," Fran told me. I don't know how, but he really had calmed me, nothing about the situation had changed except for how I now looked at it. He was right I suppose, although what was even more certain was, there would be no 'IF' Brad came looking for us now, Beth had made sure we would be targets for as long as it took for her to make us pay.

I was surprised when, after travelling for just an hour, we turned off the main road into a one way, well I'd have to call it a track rather than a road, wherever we were going, Fran was not expecting anyone to be coming the other way, because he did not for a second slow down. We passed an amazing house to our left, it was beautiful, it looked as though it had been recently renovated, with that perfect mixture of traditional and contemporary, my thoughts were always drawn to Fi whenever I saw houses like that, what I wouldn't give for the chance to give her something like that one day. Ten minutes later we pulled into the long driveway of Frans house, and a few seconds later we stopped in front of that perfectly wonderful house we had passed on the way in. "What are we doing?" I asked, not to anyone in particular. "This is Frans house," said Sam, opening up the door. I didn't make any attempt to get out, this couldn't be Frans house, this unassuming, lovely man, who drove an old Volvo, looked like he barely managed to comb his hair some days and didn't seem to do any work apart from odd jobs for Sam, surely couldn't afford this, I was definitely missing something here. A moment later I realised I was sitting in the back seat of the car…alone. The boot was open and bags were being removed, and I was still sitting trying to figure out once again, what the hell was going on ! Fi and Beth did not care one iota how Fran got his house, they only cared that they were together and that they were safe, I so wished I could take a leaf out of their book, that I didn't have a mind that couldn't rest until it had been through every possible configuration of an issue.

Jerked into life by a loud bang, bang, bang next to me, I instinctively put up my arms in protection, only to find Sam laughing uncontrollably at my expense, "Arse hole," I shouted, trying to calm my racing pulse before joining them to take a look around our new 'home'. Fran had given us the use of his home for as long as we needed it, maybe if Brad never came looking for us we could just live here forever I thought. Of course I knew that was just a pipe dream, we all knew Brad would never let this lie, even more so now that Beth had defected to the other side, but, dream I would. I grabbed the rest of the bags from the boot, and followed the rest of them into the house, they had all stopped just inside the doorway, with no idea why, I stood up on my toes to see what the hold up was, a few seconds later they were on the move again, I took a step through the door and came to a standstill, as it became apparent just what it was that had taken them aback. "Wow ! Holy shit ! Wow !" This house looked like it had dropped straight out of Bel Air. The traditional old exterior had morphed into an ultra modern enormous open plan living space, it was stunning, I had never seen anything like it, not in real life any way. Every wall was white, offset perfectly by a huge oak staircase, the art work on the walls was some of the most striking I had ever seen, it was so good I had to assume they were all originals, the colours leaping out against the white of the walls. Now I knew for certain there was more to this man than meets the eye, but what ?

"Let me show you to your rooms, so you can get rid of those bags," said Fran, walking ahead like an old porter from some old British comedy series. I couldn't help but stare at him, trying to virtually bore into his mind and see what was going on in there, I was completely baffled as to who he was. On a plus note, I have to say living here for a while would not be the end of the world. I dare say it was something we could all get used to, very quickly. Even if there was a constant nagging question mark over Frans head, this really did feel like a fresh start, it was hard to believe how quickly things had changed, and how each change had so quickly affected our outlook on life, right here, right now, I was actually beginning to feel the faintest glimmer of hope. I realised I'd made so many mistakes over these past few weeks, months, ones I could never atone for, but I still had to believe it was for the best, people's lives had been changed, but maybe they were supposed to change, maybe that's exactly what destiny had in store for all of us.

The top of the oak staircase gave way to one long, wide corridor, with huge oak doors giving access to bedrooms and bathrooms along the way. "Fran, this house is something else," I said, completely blown away by the way the simplicity of its decor contrasted so dramatically with its grandeur. "It is a beauty isn't it ?" he said, "I can't take any of the credit for it of course, my late wife bought the house many years ago, we lived here just the way it was until a few years back, she had a massive brain storm and decided she want to redesign, top to bottom, this..." he said gesturing around him, "...is what she achieved, it's a very special place for me, and I hope it can be for you too." He always spoke of such emotive subjects in the simplest way, it was hard to explain, he didn't speak without emotion, it was more that he was calm and warm, with a depth to everything he said, I could feel the love he had for his wife, even without a huge outpouring of passion or displays of any strong emotion, it was so very obvious. I wondered, but wouldn't ask what had happened to his wife.

We passed two of the very large oak doors, coming up to the third, he turned to Sam, "This will be good for you and Beth," he stopped, paused for a moment, then said, "I'm sorry, I assumed you would be sharing a room ?" Sam turned to Beth, "What do you think? Is that ok with you ?" Her face reddened as she nodded shyly, ducking her head and leaning even further into Sam's chest, "Thanks Fran, you're a good man." Fran nodded a thankyou and opened up the door. I had never seen a bedroom so big in all my life, the bed was at least a super, super king, in fact I wasn't sure there was an actual name for a bed that size, if Beth didn't want to share, it wouldn't have been an issue they could have stayed about ten feet apart in that thing! There were two pale blue sofas either side of a huge fireplace, the mixture of the old and the new continued into the bedrooms, everywhere looked superbly modern, with touches of old warmth as in the big old fireplace, complete with logs piled up to the side. Beth ran to the bed, leaped in the air and landed flat on her back on the huge expanse of pale blue duvet. She was joined a split second later by Sam, the two of them fell into each other's arms laughing, still on a high at having this second chance at happiness. It was time for us to leave. Fran closed the door quietly and we continued further down the corridor, past two more of the huge oak doors, and into an almost identical room, the only real difference was the colour scheme, this was shades of white, beautiful, the only hints of colour coming from some art work, and the numerous displays of flowers, although they were still suitably muted colours. Fran said his goodbyes, explaining he had somewhere to be, and would return in the morning. For the first time in what seemed like forever, Fi and I were alone.

For a moment or two it really did feel strange, a little awkward even, it had been a while and it felt a little like going back to that first night Fi stayed over, but one kiss, one warm embrace and the awkward feelings were gone, it felt good to have her in my arms, not because she was sad and needed comfort, but because we were starting a new life, for now, in this wonderful place, we were happy, and any worries we should be having, and there were many, were forgotten, maybe just for a short while, but any reprieve from the stress of the last few days was more than welcome. The kiss, the embrace, the passion, took us to that perfect bed, where we made love, slowly and with more passion than ever before, each time we were together, we learned more about the other, more about our bodies, about what felt good, listening to her groan beneath me, knowing I was responsible for that moan of ecstasy, that me being inside her, moving as one, giving her the pleasure I desperately wanted her to feel, was one of the deepest feelings I had ever known. We didn't leave that bed for many hours, soaking up the intimacy of just the two of us laying naked, no inhibitions whatsoever, talking about everything from Tv to our childhood. In those few hours, naked and free, we learned more about each other and ourselves than either of us thought possible.

I listened as Fi told the story of her childhood, interspersed with memories of my own, not in any way to make comparisons, but merely because her tragedies reminded me just how fortunate my childhood was. I knew her life had not been a good one, she had given tiny glimpses into her past, dropped hints of the horrors she had lived through, all the time I had wanted to know more, but knew it was something she needed to do at her own pace, in her own time, I had to wait until she was ready. I suspected the week she had spent with Beth had given her the courage to tell me more, it was just one more thing I was eternally thankful to Beth for.

Fi had lived with both of her parents until the age of seven, both were alcoholics, her father was also a drug addict, for as long as she can remember he had sexually abused her, not wanting to face any further physical abuse she had told nobody, he had as most abusers do, told her she would be taken away from her mum, that her mum wouldn't believe her, and that she would never see either of them again, and also like many children who have been abused, she loved her parents, they were all she knew, and the thought of somebody, some stranger, anybody, coming and taking her away filled her with more fear than the abuse itself. Her dad left when she was seven, and whilst this was of course a huge relief for her in many, very obvious ways, her mum's life spiralled even more out of control, she drank more heavily than ever before, became verbally and physically abusive towards Fi, and blamed her for her father leaving. I could only imagine the confusion, the hurt and the pain she had been through. At just seven years old, already having suffered years of abuse and neglect, she was now caring for her alcoholic mother who was almost incapable of caring for herself. Sadly her relief was short lived, her dad began to return each week for 'visits' during those visits he would take complete advantage of the fact that her mother was usually in a state of near unconsciousness, and continued to abuse her in the most unimaginable ways. Everything changed one day when she was ten years old. Teachers who had already expressed real concerns to social services, became even more concerned. When Fi went to school one Monday morning, obviously distressed, and crying, she continued to do so throughout the morning, unable to tell them why she had refused to move from her seat, when teachers finally managed to persuade her to move to somewhere more private, the reason for her reluctance became painfully obvious, her clothing, her seat, her legs, were all smeared with blood, seeing the horror on their faces, sheer, unadulterated shame kicked in, and she had made a dash for the door, her class teacher scooped her up in her arms, hugging her tight and telling her, 'this is not your fault, this is not your fault', until she collapsed, giving up her fight completely and allowing herself to be comforted. Her dad had finally done it, the thing she had feared more than anything else, more than the abuse she had already suffered for so long, he had raped her. Although it was hard to hear, my love for this amazing young woman beside me grew and grew, my respect for her magnified a million times, for all she had suffered, so many indignities, so many betrayals, so much hurt from those who should have been there to keep her safe, she was kind, understanding, caring, she would always give before she would take, all of the qualities it would be so easy to understand her not having, it could so easily have gone the other way. We lay quietly in each other's arms, each absorbing all the other had said, and now the things I had done, the reasons why, they all seemed 100% worth it.

Our thoughts were disturbed by some knocking in quick succession, somewhere in the distance, knock, knock, knock, pause, knock ,knock, knock, pause ,we sat upright in bed, pulling the sheets up around us, then we heard, "Conal, Fi are you in there ?" It was Sam, phew ! Was this the way it would always be, always being startled and thinking the worst about every little noise. Fi, eager to see her friend, jumped quickly out of bed and began to get dressed, she opened the door, and looked down the hall. Sam and Beth were knocking two doors down, which caused Fi to have a fit of the giggles, and call "Yoohoo, we're over here," Sam and Beth both turned at the same time to face a grinning Fi. I'd taken advantage of the goings on outside to get some pants on, and just a few moments later the four of us were sitting on the huge bed, the girls talking excitedly about how fabulous the house is, whilst me and Sam complained about how hungry we were. "Fran said there was plenty of food in the kitchen, any one coming," I said, jumping off the bed, and pulling my t-shirt over my head. The other three jumped off together practically in unison, and we headed for the door.

At that minute it definitely felt as though we were on a luxury holiday, some top class hotel, where everything we could possibly need was on hand. The kitchen was immaculate, it looked as though it had never been used, it was a simple mix of black and white, black marble worktops, contrasting with high gloss white doors, it gave a sheen and a hygienic, slightly medical look to the whole place, and it was amazing, absolutely fabulous. I got to work looking for the tea and biscuits, that would do as a start until we'd cooked some real food. A good old cup of tea, around the kitchen table, was something I had done to solve problems, to enjoy company, to talk about my day and to laugh and reminisce, for as long as I could remember. Food was made and eaten as all four of us talked of our hopes for the future, of where life may take us next, there was no talk of the practicalities, today was a time for hope, for dreams, tomorrow would bring more serious issues, but for now we would forget, for tonight we would live for the moment.

Chapter Forty

Fran was sitting with his newspaper, and a hot cup of coffee, at the kitchen table. I had come down to make tea for Fi and myself, not expecting him to be back, it was six thirty am, and having slept early and well, both of us had been wide awake for the past hour. "Good morning son," he said, looking over the top of the glasses he now wore, "Kettles hot," "Thanks," I said, taking two cups from the cupboard beneath where the kettle stood. "How was your night ?" I asked, not sure whether it was appropriate to ask, having no idea what he had actually been up to. "It went as well as could be expected, and yours ?" It was good," I said, adding, "Thanks again Fran, for everything, we had such a great sleep, those beds, wow, I've never felt anything like it !" "The wife," he said, short and sweet, a little bit like his good self. It would have felt wrong now not to ask about his wife, he'd mentioned her a couple of times. "How long is it since your wife passed ? Hope you don't mind me asking." He folded his newspaper in half and placed it on the table next to his cup, "No, not at all son." I took a seat beside him, tea in my hand, and listened.

Fran had lost his wife almost two years ago, they had been together since they were sixteen years old, and before that, they had been best friends at school. They'd practically known each other their whole lives. Sadly they'd never had children, but they had ploughed all their love into their nieces and nephews, of which they had many, and obviously adored. Three years ago his wife, Nadine, had been diagnosed with breast cancer, and even more sadly the prognosis had not been good, just twelve months later she had passed away. When Fran spoke he was always so casual, but when he spoke about his wife, his eyes lit up, his whole body became awakened, he was alive when he talked of her, she was a wonderful woman by all accounts, so kind and generous with her time, and with her money. He took out his phone and showed me a picture of them, they looked as if they were in their late twenties maybe, she was beautiful, and even in the photo you could see he blatantly adored her. Whilst she posed for the camera, he gazed at her, absolute unadulterated love in his eyes. "Who's that ?" I asked, there was a younger boy standing next to them. He turned the phone towards himself, clicking on the screen to make the picture disappear. "That's my brother," and with that, he picked up his newspaper, took a sip of his coffee and returned to his reading. "It was lovely to hear about your wife Fran, you must miss her terribly." He looked up, smiled and nodded, then went back to his paper.

Back in our room, Fi had been up, showered, dressed and was just about ready to come and find out where I had gotten to, I handed her the cup of tea I'd made a while ago, "It might still be warm," I said. "Where on earth did you get to ?" I explained to her the conversation I'd had with Fran, of course her instinctive reaction was to run down stairs to be with him. I took her arm as she headed for the door. "He seemed like he'd talked enough," I said, "Maybe we should give him some time." For me, it explained his lack of urgency at making Beth stay at the school, he had lost the love of his life, for him it surely must have been difficult to deny her the opportunity to build a life with hers. I'd meant to ask him if there had been any news of Brad, but I'd completely forgotten, I'd become so wrapped up in the love story he was telling, it hadn't even entered my head. I would need to know at some point, we would all need to know, it was vital to our decisions of what to do next.

It seemed like every day brought a new joy, that was always tainted by a new sadness, today was a beautiful day, I woke next to the woman I love, after a night free from worry, free from sadness, and there it was again, always waiting to knock on my door, and it wasn't that I was feeling any sort of self pity, obviously it was Fran who was deeply saddened by the loss of his Nadine, but he was a good man, a kind man, he had looked after us, opened up his home and his heart to us, and I'm almost certain we were all on the way to becoming really good friends, they were all the same, he didn't deserve his loss. I thought of them all, Fran, Degs, Tatty, Buzz and Sam, all on the slightly wrong side of the law, well ok, the totally wrong side of the law, but they were good people, genuinely nice guys, guys I couldn't have gotten through this last year without. I remembered the hug Sam had given Fran and wondered again what the connection was.

A knock at the door startled me out of my thoughts, and of course Fi eager to see what was going on outside the bedroom door, was flinging it open just a second later. Unsurprisingly, it was Beth, the two of them hugged, Fi holding her hand pulling her onto the sofa by the fire. "Where's Sam ?" I asked, "He's just taking a shower," she said, "We're going to go down and make breakfast, you guys coming ?" Fi looked at me, I nodded and she said yes excitedly. I loved watching these two together, it was a wonderful, warm friendship based on shared experiences of growing up lonely, and different, and with feelings of hurt and neglect, they may have been in totally different ways, but if you feel your mother didn't care, it hurts just the same regardless of the reasons why. I sat back on the bed and took out my phone, the only people who ever text me were here in this house, and so as I expected there was nothing new to see. With nothing more to do, while we waited for Sam, I took a seat with the girls on the sofa and joined in the gossip.

Fifteen minutes later the four of us were making our way noisily down the stairs, laughter and banter the pick of the day. The kitchen was empty, no signs anyone had been there, once again it was spotlessly clean, no newspaper, no coffee cup, but there was a small note on the kitchen table, 'Be Back at Seven, Will Bring Takeaway, Fran'. "What a guy," said Sam, "Can always rely on Uncle Fran." Ahhh! I thought, so that was the connection, as I wondered about who's side of the family Fran was from, it suddenly dawned on me that neither Degs or Sam had ever mentioned a wife/mother, and although it seemed a bit strange to be asking, after all this time, I was so curious I had to. "So Fran's your Uncle ?" I asked, "Yeh." I was hoping he would expand on that, so waited a moment before asking any more questions. "Him and dad have been best friends since they were kids, that's how he met my mum." Wow, I thought, that's a long time to have known someone, that means Sam's mum and dad must have known each other their whole lives too, how wonderful. "Really ? Wow that's some friendship…" he was nodding as I added "…so your mum is Frans sister ?" He paused, took a deep breath and said, "Yeh, well she was, she died when I was nine." Ahhh shit, I'd assumed they had split up at some point and that's why there was no mention of her. "Ah Sam, I'm so sorry mate, I didn't think." "Mate it's not a problem, you couldn't have known, it's nice when I get the chance to talk about her, it doesn't happen often anymore." I thought how sad it was that he never got the chance to speak about her unless someone else brought it up. "It must have been tough not having her around," I realised how ridiculous that sounded, because it obviously wasn't fun.

Sam went on to tell us all about Fran and his wife Nadine, his dad and his mum, Jenny. Jenny and Nadine had been best friends in the same class at primary school a year below Fran and Degs, by the time they left senior school they had already paired up after spending most of their younger years hanging out together. Fran and Nadine had sadly never had children, although they both would have dearly loved to. Degs and Jenny had a son and a daughter, who were doted on by all four of them, and spoiled rotten by Aunty Nadine and Uncle Fran. In all the time I'd known Sam he had never mentioned any of this, and now he sat whilst the three of us listened intently, engrossed in his story. Sam's mum, and his sister, were killed in an arson attack on their house. His sister, Gracie, was just eight years old. The minute the words left his mouth, my stomach dropped, I felt physically sick at the memory of all that had happened when my mum died, he must have relived every minute of that horror through me. It was no surprise now, how both he and his dad had given me every inch of support they could to help me get revenge, it became even more understandable, when he went on to tell us they had never caught the people who had done it. It also made us all understand his connection to Fran and Nadine, with his mum not around and Fran and Degs working, Nadine became the mother figure in his life, it was obvious from the way he spoke that he adored her, she helped him through the most traumatic period of his life. And now with Nadine gone, it was just the three of them.

Then he said something that made so many pieces drop into place. "Fran was always the mastermind, all this, the takeover, all of it, was Frans idea." Fran, the most mild mannered, quiet, kind hearted man I had ever met, was a criminal mastermind. I almost laughed, it seemed so absurd. "So Fran planned all of it, like Fran with the Volvo, who picks people up and drops people off." He heard the question in my statement, he grinned as he said, "Don't underestimate people mate." I shook my head, still unable to quite believe it. He went on, "Fran is a very, very smart man, he's unassuming, no one knows who he is, he stays under the radar, does the menial jobs in public, but behind the scenes, we would have nothing if it weren't for him." I knew there was something about him, but I was convinced he must have had a lottery win or something like that. "Do us a favour," Sam said, "Don't mention any of this to him." All three of us assured him none of what we had heard would go any further.

Another day, another shocking revelation, it was hard to imagine what could happen next.

Fran arrived home at seven on the dot, with three bags of, by the absolutely delicious smell of it, Indian food. The table was set in next to no time, drinks were made, and everyone was tucking in to poppadoms, naan breads, mango chutney, there were several curried dishes, none of which I asked the name of, along with tandoori chicken, onion bhajis, chicken pakora, there was literally a little of everything and every single bit was as delicious as it had smelled. Hunger had set in and so for five minutes we ate in silence, only ready to speak when our stomachs were satisfied they were getting fed. There was then the obligatory ten minutes of gushing about how amazing the food was, before we all slowed, feeling ridiculously full, and began to talk again, about something other than food. Fran looked directly at Beth and said, "I have some information about your mum, it's not going to be nice for you to hear, so I'd like to give you the opportunity to decide whether or not you want to know." In a panic she asked, "Is she ok ?" Of course, no matter what happens between a child and their parent, that child would never want anything bad to happen to them. "Oh she's just fine," said Fran, holding up his hand and shaking it, reassuring her all was ok. He looked around all of us now, "So you know she left the bag of cash at the park, and I know Conal that you didn't want that cash, yes?" "Yes," I acknowledged. "Well, we had already decided, once the coast was clear, the money would be retrieved and given to our local children's hospice, it made more sense than leaving it for just anyone to find." I nodded in agreement, it really did make much more sense, and I told him that. "Well, yes son, it would have made more sense, but when the bag was retrieved, it contained a change of clothes for each of the girls, and this note," he placed the note on the table, in two inches letters across the paper it said, simply, 'FUCK YOU'. Beth physically withdrew, her hand on her chest, breathing heavily, "I'm so sorry sweetheart," said Fran. Fi was already out of her seat comforting her friend, whilst Sam was on his feet snatching up the paper, fury oozing out of every pore as he crumpled it and launched it across the room. He was already marching out of the kitchen towards the front door, slamming the door shut behind him, I was torn between staying to help with the chaos that had erupted in the kitchen, and making sure Sam didn't do anything stupid. Beth was covered, she had Fi and Fran, who was also up and kneeling next to her, giving words of comfort, although I couldn't imagine how any words could make this better. I chose Sam, he couldn't let his rage allow him to mess up everything we had done, for now we were safe, I wanted to keep it that way.

I raced towards the door, hoping I would make it before he took off, not expecting to find him sat outside, at the bottom of the steps with his head in his hands. I took a seat next to him, with barely an inch between us. "How you doing ?" I asked, "Mate I just can't believe how fucking cruel that woman is, I mean I knew she was a bitch but this … it took all I had to stop myself from going after her !" "I know mate, you've got some willpower, I'll give you that, you had me worried for a minute though mate." He laughed a little at that and thankfully the fury had subsided, and he was left with just an angry sadness he didn't know what to do with. "I don't know what to say to her mate," Sam said, almost pleading for help, "You've just got to be there for her Sam, let her know she can talk about it whenever she wants, no one can make her feel better, knowing how someone feels about you is one thing, but seeing it written in black and white, well, that's tough." That was another one of my mum's little words of wisdom, and it was true, seeing anything written down in front of you made it hit home so much more. "Something has to be done about her mate, what about them poor kids for fuck sake." I could try to dissuade him, but I wouldn't, he had been there for me every step of my journey into retribution, it would be pretty hypocritical of me to deny him the revenge he now craved. "We'll sort it, but not now, not while emotions are running high, let's do this properly eh ?" He nodded in agreement, and I knew normal viewing had been resumed when as he stood, he gave me a sly punch on the arm in the process, still bloody hurt, arsehole.

Back inside, Fi and Fran had managed to control the situation, and all seemed calm. Sam took Beth by the hand and took her out towards the back of the house, looking for somewhere private to talk. I was glad of the opportunity to quiz Fran a little more on what was happening, without the fear of upsetting Beth. He never seemed phased by anything, like nothing at all, but then I suppose after so many years in this business, nothing would shock you any more. "So what do you make of all this Fran ?" He put down the glass of red wine he had just begun to drink from, and after a brief pause he told me. "Well, the woman is a callous one, she always has been, by all accounts she had the hubby bumped off, she had an affair with his dad, then blackmailed him, I mean this is all hearsay, but from pretty good sources, she has never looked after her own kids, but I did think she would have fought harder to get them back, just out off the sheer principal if nothing else." And that was the part I didn't get, "How is she sitting back knowing someone had gotten one over on her, without fighting back ?" I asked, "The only theory I have come up with is, she's not told anyone the kids are gone, that way she has no fight to win, no-one to impress, she can concentrate on what matters most to her, and right now that's trying to save her crumbling empire." He was right, I would never have thought of that, if no-one knew the kids were missing then she had already won, she'd gotten rid of the kids she had no time for, and had no reason to save face at all. Fuck she really did come out on top every fucking time ! I had been warned about this, right at the very beginning, but I never imagined she would forfeit her kids, no matter what the game was. Damn she was good. Or bad.

Chapter Forty-One

Fran waited just over an hour until Sam came back, before saying his goodbyes and leaving for the night, I wondered where he went, this was his house after all. He and Sam embraced, Fran whispering something as he did, and Sam nodded. After several pats on the back, they parted company. Fran said goodbye to us all, then, turning to Beth he said, "You remember what I said, ok ?" she smiled, nodded, and Sam pulled her closer to his side. What did he say, I thought, I made a mental note to remember to ask Fi later. And then he was gone, the emotional exhaustion of the evening visible on everyone, my go to reaction kicked in, "Tea anyone ?" On automatic pilot they took their seats at the table, as I filled the kettle, took out some cups, and made the stuff that cured all ills. Beth was completely mentally drained, dark rings had appeared under her eyes, contrasting drastically with her now pale face, once again guilt drifted in, we had turned her life upside down, and confirmed all the fears she'd ever had about her mother. She was lost and alone, despite those around her, who loved her and cared more than any one probably ever had, she grieved for the one person who should have loved her. I looked at the three of them in front of me thinking of all they had been through, and I thought of myself, of all we had lost, and I wondered which was worse, losing a mother who loved you, or having no love from a mother you still had, I couldn't decide, both seemed equally devastating, heartbreaking and soul destroying.

"Are you ok ?" Fi was tugging on my sleeve, I'd been so caught up in my thoughts, the kettle had long since boiled, as I stood staring into an abyss of hurt and sorrow. "What ? Oh, yeh, yeh I'm good," I got on with making the drinks, and joined them at the table. In the long silence that followed there was no longer any awkwardness, each having complete understanding for the other, each needing time to absorb all that had happened, each taking time to consider the effects of those events on their friends and their partners, each couple becoming a mirror image of the other, Fi and Beth leaning into myself and Sam, all needing that closeness, that intimacy and the strength it brought us, knowing someone cared for us more than they cared for anyone else in the world.

The silence was shattered by the sound of Sam's phone vibrating on the table in front of him, he looked at the screen before deciding whether or not he was going to pick up. He did. Kissing Beth on her forehead, he squeezed her tightly before answering his call and taking it outside. He was back within five minutes, he didn't seem stressed, or angry, so I assumed all was good. "That was my dad," he said, it was odd hearing him calling Degs his dad, he'd always used his first name, I wasn't sure what had changed, but there had to be some significance behind it, or maybe as much as he adored Beth, he didn't want to reveal his dads name in front of her ? He went on, "They're verging on seventy percent of Brad's business, they always hoped they could take a few more along the way, but none of us could have expected this, we were looking at fifty to sixty, and they're still getting calls everyday." "How do you know who's legitimate ?" I asked. "In what way ?" he asked, "So they call one of you, to express an interest in moving their business to you, but what if it's just a set up, what if it's just Brad trying to smoke you out ?" "No one is on the front line, there are many, many people working for them, there is no paper trail, no direct contact, no traceable technology, unless one of us tells her, then she should never find out." That statement made me a little uncomfortable, if Brad ever did figure out what was going on, then one of us was going to be a suspect, and given I was the last man in, I would probably be way up on the suspect list, shit, I hoped to fuck she never figured this one out. I was relieved when Fi asked to go to bed, I had been past exhausted hours ago, but I knew how much it meant for her to be there for Beth, and no, none of us had spoken much, but just being there, feeling safe with those we loved, had been enough to build up that mental strength again, we would all live to fight another day, but for now, this one was over.

Once again Fran was sitting, legs crossed, with his newspaper and his coffee when I reached the kitchen. "Good morning son," "Morning Fran." I flipped the switch on the kettle, and took the seat beside him. "How was your night ?" I asked, "It went as well as it could son, how was yours, I'm sorry I had to leave you all at such a time." "It was tough, emotional, you know, but hey, it is what it is, and all we can do is deal with it and try to keep moving forward, Sam will be there for Beth, I can only imagine how she's feeling." "Well, yes, believing your mother doesn't care is one thing, I mean there's always that little bit of hope that your wrong, but knowing she doesn't care, well hey, that's a real hard pill to swallow, she's just a kid you know, she's gonna need a lot of support from you guys." I smiled and nodded, "She'll get it, I mean even if I didn't give a shit, there's no way on this planet Fi would ever leave her to deal with this alone, I've just left her sitting on the end of Beth and Sam's bed !" Fran laughed, it was like nothing I'd ever heard, it was loud and it was joyful, and sounded remarkable, coming from this very quiet, extraordinarily calm man, I was so surprised I started to laugh too, god only knows what the other three thought as they walked through the door to us two, with tears streaming down our faces unable to stop now that we'd started, I'd said nothing even remotely amusing, he had been brought to this state by his sheer elation at our love for each other, at the bond the four of us had, and the memories of Degs, himself and their much adored wives.

I was once walking into the city centre, to the left of me was a building site, where some high rise building of some sort was midway through being built. All around the site, boards had been erected, around eight feet high, which over time had been plastered with advertising posters and graffiti. I spotted some graffiti on there which has always stuck in my mind, it said, 'How can I go forward when I don't know which way I'm facing...' I hadn't realised at the time it was a line from a song by John Lennon, and never had it struck a chord more than it did now. We were in limbo, all four of us, not knowing what might happen from one day to the next, not knowing how long it would be before we had to move on, we had no Idea which way was forward, we had no idea which way we were facing, I could never, ever have imagined how incredibly difficult it would be to live that way. Not able to make plans, barely able to live for the day, not knowing what may happen in the next hour, let alone the next day, month, year. No one ever seemed to have any news on Brad, no one seemed to know whether anyone suspected us of kidnap or not, did she know who was behind the takeover, did she know anything at all, there was no moving in any direction in a world full of unknowns.

A week into our stay at Frans and all of these questions finally took their toll. I was jealous of Sam, he still got to go to work every day, still got to participate in life whilst I was stuck at home going slowly stir crazy. Too much time to over think had only led to more reflection, and subsequently frustration, resentment, anger, I hadn't won, I was merely in a prison of my own making. She had taken the life of my brother, inadvertently caused the death of my mother, and now, without my even noticing, without her even trying, she had taken my life from me too. There was one thing I had been certain of, since the day I found out it was her who was responsible and that was, I would make her pay, and as I saw it, I had not made her pay in any way at all, what I had done, had merely been an inconvenience for her whilst she had bigger issues to deal with. And so in this time of boredom, of restlessness, of reflection, I began to hatch a plan to free us all from this self made prison, if I didn't, then that is where I would stay as long as Brad was still around.

I wasn't sure I could cold heartedly walk up to a woman and kill her, in fact I was pretty sure I couldn't, although if anyone had asked me twelve months ago if I was capable of murder, I'd have thought they were crazy, even to this day I find it difficult to recognise myself as that person, and yet I know I am. I wasn't sure what I wanted, right now she was angry, she was furious her clients and business partners had betrayed her, but she wasn't hurt because of me, she had no feelings whatsoever about that. I wondered if knowing she was going to die would bring out any emotion in her, whilst I may not be able to snuff out another life, letting her believe that might happen, was definitely something I could live with. And so started a new chapter in my crusade, just in my head for now. Once I had things straight in there, the next step would be to roll it out to Sam, he was just looking for an excuse to take down Brad, I knew he would need very little persuading. Already, having a plan for the future was making me feel good, knowing there was a way forward, a purpose, no matter how fucked up or twisted that way forward was, it gave me a lift, it gave me a way of finding out which way I was facing.

I wouldn't tell Sam for a further few days, there had been so many times I'd had weird and wonderful ideas, only to realise days later just how ridiculous they were, this time, I didn't waver, all those old feelings of the desperate need for revenge had returned. All those feelings of injustice, how no one had ever paid for the loss of my family, a small part of me wondered if those feelings would ever go away, regardless of whether anyone paid the price. Only time would tell I suppose, and as always, time was something I had plenty of. There were still so many unanswered questions, the why's and the who's, why was Joseph killed and who actually did the killing, it may be I would never find the answers but no matter how far we looked, the buck always stopped with Brad. I suppose I thought scaring her would be enough...it wasn't. I waited for a time when Fi and Beth were busy, today they were doing each other's nails, it was perfect, they'd taken themselves up to Beth's room, and Sam wasn't out till the evening. "How's everything going Sam? No-one has really mentioned anything for a while ?" He put down his phone, and filled me in on what was happening out in the big wide world.

I'd felt like so much of an outsider lately, unable to attend any of their meetings, unable to work, unable to even socialise with them. It was hard, it was lonely and I'd had enough. I craved my old life, and the only way I could ever have that back was to deal with Brad. The takeover was going better than anyone could have expected, there had been a couple of bumps, namely people who were obviously just out to get information, they had been 'dealt' with, I didn't need to ask how, but I could guess a big old red doored shed would have played a part in it. "So, Brad's offensive is to try sending spies into the camp, amongst other things," he said. I sat, patiently waiting for him to expand, when he didn't I asked, "What other things ?" For a moment he looked as though he was deciding whether to go any further or not. "You know sometimes it's easier not to know all the details ?" he said, "And sometimes it's not," I added, becoming a little less patient now. "Me, and the guys, we did talk about this, and it wasn't because we wanted to keep you out the loop, but you know, we've all been there, stuck in a position were there's nothing you can do, and sometimes it's just easier not to know." I couldn't believe he'd just rambled on and still told me nothing, "For fucks sake Sam just tell me what's going on !"

"More tea ?!" Now I knew how they all felt when my answer to every damn drama was, 'let's put the kettle on' it was then I realised it was actually just a coping mechanism for me, not help or support for anyone else, it was a distraction from reality, and that's exactly what Sam was doing now. He used the time it took him to make the drinks, to get straight in his head, how exactly he was going to tell me, whatever it was, without pissing me off big time. Taking a seat with two cups in his hands, he explained. "Brad still has no idea who's behind the kidnap or the takeover, we have several guys on the inside, ones I would trust with my life, but…she has put out a £100,000 reward for information leading to your whereabouts, and £500,000 for information on who's responsible for the takeover, and my friend, as you pretty much fall into both camps, that means there's a whole heap of people out there seeking your arse." I was stunned, of course I knew she would have people looking, but I'd kind of forgotten, with all the emotional drama going on around us, so to be reminded in such a huge monetary way, was pretty frickin' mind-blowing. "Do you know why she's looking for me, does she suspect me or…" I didn't know what the 'or' was, so I just left it hanging there. "No one knows, sorry mate, although personally I think if she thought you were behind it, there would be a huge bounty on your head." I can't say that made me feel much better, even though there was a tiny part of me that hoped she did know it was me, I mean that had been the plan originally, but of course that's fine when you only have yourself to think of, but there were other people to think of now, and top of that list was Fi, I couldn't bear for her to be hurt because of me. "You don't seem the least bit bothered," I said, a little bit pissed that I was gutted and he gave no fucks. "Mate, if I got in a tizz every time I thought someone was onto me, I'd be an emotional wreck, permanently, this is why it's better when we don't know, you see ?" I did see, and I wished I'd kept my nosey arse mouth shut, but I hadn't, and now I had decisions to make, the only way to keep us all safe was to take Brad out of the picture, how, I had no idea, but we had to find a way. "I'm not sure I can just sit around and wait for Brad to catch up with us, she's gonna figure it out one day, if she hasn't already." Sam sat up straight, eyes wide, then leaned in towards me, looking over his shoulder to make sure no one was in earshot. "Well, I'm glad to hear you think that way mate, cause I have an idea." I had thought, and over thought, and thought a bit more about whether or not I should broach this subject with Sam, and the little fucker already had a plan.

I relaxed into my chair as he went through the plan he'd been hatching since Fran had come home with the note Brad had left instead of the cash. I remembered thinking at the time how quickly he'd gotten over his anger, he already knew, from that moment, that he would find a way to make her pay. His plan was simple, the best ones usually were, the only hard part I could see would be getting her alone, but as he had people on the inside, there could be a way. I didn't have many questions, but there were a couple that bothered me, nothing to do with the execution of the plan, but more about who that plan would affect. "What about your dad and the guys?" "They're cool with it, they've no use for Brad, in fact she's just a hindrance, a cruddy little hindrance." I nodded in agreement, "And what about the girls ?" I wasn't sure he had remembered Josie and Phoebe, he took a deep breath, "I've thought a lot about this, and it's going to be a tough one I can only hope there will be a possibility for Beth to take them, we will try our best to make that happen, but I really have no idea at the minute," and one last question, "Does Beth know what your planning ?" he came back quickly, once again looking behind him "No ! And she can't, ever, I know there's no love lost between them, and I doubt she will miss her, but she can't ever know what we're doing." I knew that meant not telling Fi too, it was a promise I wasn't sure I could make, but I also knew telling Fi meant telling Beth, she would never keep something like this from her. Reluctantly I agreed to keep our secret.

Chapter Forty-Two

       Fran was due back at seven, he was supplying dinner again, but this time Sam would have left before he arrived. "Does Fran know what you're planning ?" Sam turned to me surprised. "Of course he does, nothing happens without him knowing." I'd asked myself before 'who was this guy ' and I found myself asking again. Sam had gone to his room to see Beth and get ready for his night shift. Just a few moments later, Fi appeared. Each time I saw her my troubles melted away and I was instantly thankful for all I had. I stood as I saw her, she smiled that wonderful smile as she walked into my arms, it seemed like so long since she had been there, she was just what I needed, she was always just what I needed to make the world seem right. Everything slipped into place when she was in my arms, all the bad things I had done made sense, and if dealing with Brad kept her safe, then that too was the right thing to do. It was a pretty twisted way for a mind to work, but it worked, and that was good enough for me.

       Sam left at six thirty, and Fran arrived home at dot on seven, Chinese takeaway tonight, I've no idea where the food came from, but it was always good. It was a little bit like your dad coming home when Fran arrived, something I'd not experienced for such a long time, but was really enjoying. I wondered if it was like having the kids he'd never had, looking after us lot. I hoped we gave him something, I hoped he enjoyed the time we spent with him as much as we did. I also hoped I would get a chance to quiz him about Sam's plans. We'd no timescale as yet, a little advice from someone right in the mix of things would help me know we were on the right track. Seeing Fran interacting with the girls was wonderful, he was the father figure he longed to be, and they lapped up every minute of it, for the first time in a long time, or maybe ever, there was this man in their life, caring for them, asking about their feelings, ensuring they had all they needed, laughing with them, making plans with them, asking nothing in return, all the things they, and myself had missed out on for so many years. How on earth could he be in charge of all this, all the crime, drugs, murders, kidnap, I mean I could only imagine the list was endless and yet I couldn't imagine this man in front of me being involved in any part of that, but then I suppose that was the point, who would ever suspect !

It looked as though the girls were never going to leave, it was pushing on for eleven and that was around the time Fran usually left, I resigned myself to the fact that I wouldn't be getting any answers tonight. "What time are you leaving Fran ?" he smiled, "I'll be staying here tonight son, I think it's for the best." I wasn't sure what that meant, I was pretty sure we weren't expecting any trouble, Sam would have said, I know he would, maybe there was just safety in numbers, either way, if the girls left soon, it would give me plenty of time to pick his brains. As if they'd read my mind, Fi stood and said, "You ok if we turn in ? We're gonna go catch up on some TV." She stood and bent to kiss me, when those lips were on mine, the deep breath of self control I took was most definitely needed. I held onto her waist as she went to walk away, and loved hearing that giggle as she turned to kiss me once more. "I love you," I said, "I love you too," she said, looking back as she walked away.

I listened as they walked upstairs, waiting until the coast was clear to see what Fran had to say about our plan. He beat me to it. "So what's on your mind young man ?" I had no qualms about talking to him, he was so easy going, easy to talk to, I reckoned he could lull the devil into giving up his plans. "You've heard about Sam's plans for

Brad ? I mean I'm totally on board, but then we're both emotionally involved, and I know that impairs your thinking and impacts on your judgement, and so I just wanted to see what you thought." It would be a long night, we talked into the early hours, about almost everything and anything. Fran supported Sam wholeheartedly, no 'ifs' 'buts' or 'maybes'. And his suggestion for a timeline was…sooner rather than later.

I was too hyped up to sleep, I needed to make plans, I needed to set timetables, I needed Sam back so we could put things in motion. For now I would have to make do with laying in bed looking at the ceiling, adrenalin I couldn't use coursing through my veins, making it impossible for my mind to slow. But I didn't care, I had missed this, the excitement of the next move, the next part of the plan, it wasn't something I thought I would ever miss, but facts were facts, here I was impatiently waiting for my partner in crime to return home, so we could make a date for retribution. Turning to my side, looking into the face of the woman I loved, there was no guilt, I pushed back a lock of hair that had fallen onto her face, resisting the urge to kiss those lips, not wanting to disturb her, this was the only way forward for us, the only way I could make sure Fi was free to enjoy life, she had waited so long to be happy, too long, and there was no way anyone was going to take that away from her.

I woke, instantly wide awake, at six am, after just an hour's sleep. Leaving Fi to rest, I crept downstairs, and there he was, I wondered if he ever slept, Fran that is, he was there with his coffee and his newspaper, in the same spot as I'd left him the night before. "You not been to bed Fran ?" I asked, grabbing a cup, "I managed a couple of hours son, how about you ?" "Same," I said. I liked this time in the mornings, just me and Fran, it was quiet and calm, just like him, and much needed after last night. "Any idea what time Sam's back ?" I asked, "Probably not till around five, you thought any more about how you and he are going to progress ?" I'd thought of nothing else, right up till the moment I fell asleep, and again from the second I'd opened my eyes. "I suppose it depends on Brads schedule, until we figure that out, we can't really go any further," "Well you know son, I'm pretty sure that's all being well logged as we speak, and you've had the go-ahead from the guys, so in reality, you could go tonight if it took your fancy." Well, if that wasn't a way to make it hit home I didn't know what was. I imagined Sam coming home and saying, 'come on, let's go,' and I would, no questions asked. Fran laughed, "I'm not saying he will ask you to go tonight, I'm just saying it's a possibility, if you wanted to." Just the thought of it had my mind racing, five o'clock couldn't come soon enough !

The day dragged, Fran didn't feel the need to converse, although he seemed to enjoy it when we did, he rarely started a conversation. Fi and Beth were baking, giggling as always, they brought out so much happiness in each other, I couldn't imagine them ever being apart. And I did what I always did at a time like this, I had full blown debates in my head about the rights and wrongs of pretty much everything. The only thing I knew for certain was, Brad would know what she was paying for by the time we had finished with her. Two o'clock came after what seemed like at least twenty hours, I was restless, I was bored of not talking and bored of talking, I wanted to be out in the fresh air, until I was there and then even the air irritated me, there was nothing interesting on Tv, and I was sick to death of making, and drinking tea ! Roll on five o'clock, I wouldn't be able to rest until I knew 'when' and I wouldn't know 'when' until Sam was home, and then he would want to eat, and spend time with Beth, I couldn't wait that long, and so at four thirty I sat on the steps outside Frans big red door, and I waited. He was five minutes late, and it felt like the longest five minutes of my life ! Climbing out of his car and seeing me on the steps he shouted, "Aww you missed me babe," he was in a good mood, that was good for me. I laughed as I stood to greet him, "Always Sam," "So what's the reception committee for ?" he asked, getting serious. "Sorry mate, it's all this time I have, doing nothing, I haven't been able to stop thinking about Brad all day, and Fran said we could move at any time, and I, well I just wondered whether you had any idea of a timescale ?" I took a much needed deep breath, "Wow, you really do have too much time on your hands mate." I thought he was being sarcastic, but as he sat on the stairs, and I looked at his face, he was serious. "You've got no idea mate, I'm bored shitless." "I haven't got a date, as such…" I sat up quickly, "… but it will be soon, probably in the next three to five days, I just need to check some details with the rest of the guys, they're all coming over tonight, so we can get this all straight, don't worry mate, it won't be long now." I realised just then how much the isolation was affecting me, whilst it was good to see Fi enjoying her friendship, it also meant I'd been spending a lot of time alone, too much time to think, and too many unresolved issues to worry myself with, the problem was, I was bored, I felt bad saying it, given I got to spend time with Fi, but she had Beth, and I, well, I sometimes needed someone other than them.

A punch to the arm and a rub of the hair later and we were back inside, Fran jumping up to give Sam a hug as always, and Beth waiting to be in his arms. Fran had cooked with the girls, I had no idea what it was, but it smelled amazing. As we sat down to eat, Beth informed us we were having creamy mushrooms on sourdough bread and spaghetti carbonara, there was garlic bread too, and the whole lot looked amazing, tasted frickin' delicious too. For a while, all the stress was forgotten, all the thoughts of what was to come, and normalcy resumed while we enjoyed good food and good conversation in good company. I looked at Fi, so much had changed for us and yet here we were, in the strangest of circumstances, still happy, still enjoying life, and yes, today I had most definitely had a wobble, but I could see hope again now, see a future that didn't involve constantly looking over our shoulders, one were we could make plans, settle down, and have the life we dreamed of, simple and happy.

The guys were due back around midnight, and although I should have been exhausted from the minimal amount of sleep the night before, it had been overruled by the adrenalin that was starting to build, knowing they would be back soon to help make decisions, meant the chance of relaxing was nil. In fact there seemed to be a buzz in everyone tonight, like we all instinctively knew something was coming, I loved nights like this, laughter, banter, memories, listening to Fran tell stories of Sam growing up, everyone talking about their hopes and fears without any fear of ridicule, this was family, this is what made everything that had happened, all we had been through, worthwhile. Normally Beth and Fi would be more than welcome to stay, but given the topic of conversation, it was probably best if they weren't, I took them to one side, and explained, without lying as such, that we had some things about Brad to discuss, I gave them the option to stay or go, knowing full well Beth would not want to hear any more about her mother. I followed them to the bottom of the stairs, before taking Fi in my arms and kissing her, as always the urge to follow her was almost too strong to overcome, and her giggle told me she knew. I was left with my urges and the vision of her backside moving from side to side as she walked up the stairs. Wow, I needed a moment to myself. I opened the front door, stepped outside and breathed in the night air. I'd always preferred the night, the quiet, the darkness, it was so much easier to think when your senses weren't being distracted by noise and vision. I was about to go back inside when I noticed lights in the distance, a cautious excitement kicked in, it was almost certainly Degs, Tatty and Buzz, but there was always the small chance it could be trouble. I pushed open the door and called in to Sam and Fran, "The guys are here."

Thankfully it was the guys, and before long, they were all sitting round the kitchen table, several different conversations going on at once, the energy in the room was immense, and I loved it. Listening to the guys telling tales about their days, I realised just how much I missed work and how desperate I was to get back to it. Fran plated up the food he'd saved for the guys, produced a couple of bottles of wine and some bottles of beer, and for a while, there was silence. I'd never been a lover of wine, or beer for that matter, and so of course, I made myself a cup of tea, with a side of digestives. I'd dunked my first biscuit when Degs spoke, "So you and Sam are gonna deal with Brad

I hear ?" He was looking at me, and as no one else was so hell bent on dealing with Brad, it had to be me he was asking, still I looked around to make sure it couldn't be anyone else. "That's the plan, the idea was to make her pay, and let's face it, she didn't give a shit, if she'd never seen them kids again, it would've been too soon!" During the nods of agreement, I wasn't sure if any one else had noticed Sam's knuckles whitening around the beer bottle he held, a sign that the betrayal of Brad towards her kids was something Sam found impossible to live with. "That's true son," Degs said, "Well, you know, I've already told Sam, if there's anything you need, anything at all, we're here, you just let us know." I nodded, knowing every word he said was heartfelt and true. "Thanks Degs, I think we're just waiting for a time slot." Degs looked over at Sam, "We should have that sorted for you tomorrow, there are just one or two things we need her around for first, but we should be able to give you a date by tomorrow." Sam was nodding, smiling at his dad, it was a thankyou, and I love you, all rolled into one. The tinge of jealousy I always had when they were together flickered inside me, it never lasted long, and I never begrudged them their relationship, it was just a momentary sadness that I didn't have that too. It didn't seem much to have waited all night for, but it was enough for me, tiredness hit like a rock, I had no more adrenalin to keep me going, I was too chilled now. The guys were staying the night, and it was time for me to say my thankyous, and my goodnights. " See you in the morning guys."

It seemed like forever since I'd been in bed with Fi...whilst both of us were still awake that is ! She had still been sitting in Beth's room when I'd come upstairs, but must have heard me, because just a few moments later, she appeared with a smile. "Come here," I said, opening up my arms for her, there was no kiss, just the warmth of an embrace, that helped ease the stress of a very long day. I'm sure we could've stayed there like that forever, instead I kissed her forehead and excused myself to the bathroom. With the hot water of the shower pouring down my face I battled with the decision of whether or not to tell Fi what was going on, trying to figure out whether not confiding with her was worse than putting her under the stress of knowing, was almost impossible, added to that the fact that she wouldn't be able to tell Beth, my battle resulted every time in deciding I couldn't let her know, no matter how I tried to convince myself, no matter how guilty I would feel for keeping her in the dark, it couldn't be worse than asking her to do the same to Beth. My only reason for telling her would be to relieve myself of guilt. Shower over, decision made, and I was actually wide awake enough to really enjoy the rest of the night. Fresh and ready to make love to the most wonderful woman I knew. I opened up the door and walked back to the bed, there she was waiting for me, curled up, fast asleep looking as beautiful as ever, I told the movement in my pants that he would not be needed tonight, in the hope he would listen up real quick and disappear ! Curling up next to Fi and placing my arm over her so gently it couldn't wake her, I lay thinking of the life we might possibly have. Now that Brad would be out of the picture, the options were limitless.

Chapter Forty-Three

I woke to Fi sitting up in bed next to me stroking my hair, smiling, "I've been waiting for you," she said, slowly sliding her leg over mine, and instantly re-awakening last night's unneeded erection. Pulling her gently on top of me I held her waist, looking up into her perfect blue eyes, she leaned forward to kiss me, and that was it, I was gone, taken away into another realm, the need to touch every part of her completely overwhelming, I was selfish and selfless, using up all she offered, and taking her to a place where nothing else mattered except the touch of my hands, my lips, my body, where nothing else existed except us. Being inside her, feeling her pulsate as she came, sent me completely over the edge, passion almost turning to animal instinct, until both of us were spent, laying breathless in each other's arms.

"First one to breakfast wins," Fi shouted, leaping out of bed, heading for the bathroom, and swiftly locking the door. "You're a cheat," I shouted, laughing at the little girl so obviously still inside her. There was no reply, but suddenly caught up in the need to win, I raced along the landing to one of the other rooms to use their bathroom, I probably should've knocked, I hadn't realised the guys would make it to bed, and was met by a very startled Tatty, "Ooops, sorry mate, wrong door." I laughed even more as I walked back to my room, having no choice but to wait for our own bathroom. I picked out some fresh clothes for the day, the choices weren't huge, T-shirt and jeans was pretty much it, the only real option available was colour, blue or dark blue jeans, and black, white or blue T-shirt, I kept my options small, it was easier that way.

We laughed about my story of waking Tatty up, before Fi decided she would wait for me to go downstairs, she didn't really know the guys that well, and although they would have gone out of their way to make her feel welcome, she wasn't quite ready to go it alone. I was surprised when we made it downstairs to find, no-one, no-one at all, not even Fran who was always there with his paper and his coffee. It seemed kind of strange not having our morning chat, I guessed they'd had a late night, and must be sleeping. We took advantage of the empty kitchen to enjoy breakfast together, these were things we had taken for granted in the past, when it was just us two, I missed those days, and yet I loved the life we had now, I loved being part of this huge extended family, but yes, having this small amount of time, doing regular things, by ourselves, was pretty much priceless too. We were half way through our eggs and toast when the deluge began, Fran came in first, closely followed by Degs, Tatty and Buzz, I assumed they'd set their alarms, as it had to be more than a coincidence that they'd all arrived together, Fran got straight down to making breakfast, Buzz offered a helping hand, but Fran declined with a smile. Just five minutes later we were joined by Beth and Sam. The whole gang, chatting away, fresh and ready for another day of criminal intent. Fran did not decline Beth's offer to help with breakfast, he welcomed her with a loaf, ready for toasting.

I noticed, whilst watching them all laughing and chatting, that they rarely looked downtrodden, in fact I don't think I'd ever seen them truly troubled over anything, had they seen so much in life, suffered so much hurt that nothing affected them anymore, was that a good thing or a bad thing ? Fran plated up and Beth served, the only time these guys were quiet was when they ate, whilst they did, me and Fi got down to making tea and coffee all round, the guys were thankful for all they had, and before long they were getting ready to leave. All of them except Sam, I hadn't realised he was staying at home today, and I was kind of excited, it would be good to spend some time with him, and it would give us a chance to finalise some details, the guys were going to get back to us with a date today, I hated the wait, these things got me so hyped I couldn't think of much else, I preferred to have things done and dusted, when possible.

It wasn't a bad day outside considering it was winter, so with jumpers on, and the fire pit lit, we made the most of the chance for some fresh air. Frans garden was beautiful, and kept immaculate, just like the rest of the house, I imagined it had been his wife who had designed and managed the garden, and also suspected, the management was now the job of a gardener, although I'd not seen one since we had been here. Talk turned to what we all wanted from life. "Not too much," I said, "I hope to have Fi in my life forever, of course…" she smiled coyly, "…maybe one day, we will be able to settle down somewhere, maybe have a couple of kids." She raised an eyebrow, thankfully still smiling. "A simple, happy life will do me," I finished. Everyone nodded, surprisingly Sam spoke next, I'd not expected him to have much input in this conversation. "You know when my mum passed, and I saw how much it hurt dad, I told myself I would never, ever fall in love, not with anyone, losing someone you love causes so much pain, and I never wanted to have to feel that, but the minute I saw Beth, as soon as I walked through that door, that day, and saw her face, everything changed, knowing you loved me, even for just a short time, would be worth any amount of pain." Wow, what the hell just happened, for a moment he reminded me so much of Fran, it touched me, warmed me, knowing just how happy Beth had made him, and being someone he could open up to, well, it meant the world to me, in that moment I felt closer to him than I ever had before, and Beth, well she was glowing as she curled up even further into Sam's chest. I thought about those days when I'd warned Sam against getting involved, and wondered how I could ever have dreamed of denying him this. Fi turned to Beth, "Well, hell girl, there's no following that is there !" When Fi laughed, I knew exactly where the phrase 'music to my ears' came from, her laughter lit up a room, it was infectious, it was heartwarming, and made me never want to leave her side. Sitting there, on that mild winters day, talking about all we had to live for, I wondered if life could ever get any better.

The news we had been waiting for came over dinner, at around six that evening. I knew when Sam excused himself from the table, it had to be that, he had made the decision not to tell Beth, and in a lot of ways, I couldn't blame him, no matter the harm Brad had caused, the love she had refused to give them, the time she had never made for them, she was their mother, and as such they would always love her. I pretended to have no interest in his call, as I carried on eating and chatting, the girls thankfully, had no idea of its importance, and for that I was grateful. Just two minutes later Sam was back at the table as though nothing had changed, he made no attempt to inform me of anything he had just heard. I would have to bide my time, I knew, but the curiosity was killing me ! The urge to make some excuse to call him to one side, was overwhelming, but if I'd learned anything in these recent months it was to act normal, don't make a scene, don't be obvious, and so I took a deep breath and pushed those thoughts to the back of my mind. "What's wrong ?" asked Fi, I realised I'd breathed a little too deeply, "Oh nothing, just ate a little too quick, that's all," she gently stroked my shoulder, and we all continued with our meal, half of us totally unaware of the enormity of what was happening.

I was quite literally ecstatic when dinner was over, and Sam asked if I could go have a look at his car window with him, he lied that it had been playing up, it was good to know I wasn't the only one waiting, not so patiently to share the news. We were barely outside the front door when he said, "Day after tomorrow ?" Shit ! It always seemed so good till you knew it was really going to happen, then the real adrenaline rush kicked in, not the anxious one, or the excited one, the one caused by fear, because, although we both knew, for us and the girls this was the only way forward, what we were doing, taking down one of the most powerful people we knew, was pretty damn terrifying. Nothing, nothing whatsoever could be allowed to go wrong, and whilst I had total faith in my guys, who knew what fate, destiny or the frickin' Universe had in store for us. Realising Sam was still waiting for some sort of reaction, I quickly nodded telling him, "Yeah, yes, definitely, let's get this done eh Sam," he grabbed my hand and pulled me in towards him, pulling me to his chest and patting me, or rather pounding me on the back, "Is right mate, for the girls eh ?" "For the girls," I agreed, returning his embrace. "I've got Brad's timetable, let me show you," he was heading back inside, "Brad has a timetable ?" That seemed pretty unlikely, Sam laughed, "Not a regular timetable, she doesn't do the same things, same day, every week, but she still does certain things in certain ways, so on a Thursday, there are about three or four possibilities, and within each of those possibilities, there are several M.O.s, so we might not be able to make plans that are set in stone, but all that means is, we have to be ready to go at a moments notice, with the ability to change depending which option she takes. "Wow this all got very real, very serious, very suddenly… and I loved it, it made me feel alive. "So, Thursday I get out of here for the day?" I asked, "Yep, we need to be in town all day, that way it should only take around fifteen minutes to get to her before she reaches any of her destinations," "What about the girls ?" I was worried about them being alone, I had no idea how long we would be gone, and I still hadn't figured out what we were going to tell them. "Buzz has arranged for Dan to come and look after them for a couple of days, we might not need that long, but, well, just in case." I was hoping he would say Fran is staying with them, the concern must have shown on my face. "They'll be fine mate, you've met Dan before," I couldn't remember meeting Dan, I really couldn't, but I trusted Sam, I would worry about them either way, we still had no real idea what Brad knew about anything, the takeover, the kidnap, Elizabeth's jumping ship, but I know he would never leave them in any danger. "I know Sam, I trust you."

Back inside, Sam went up stairs to check his ledger, there was no point in me looking, it was his own, complex, coded journal, nothing in there would make any sense to me. She had three possible appointments that day. One was to a guy she visited once a month on any given day, she always had her nails done the day before she went there. She met at a different restaurant each time, there was always an exchange of a ton of paperwork, but the guy had no offices, and always went back to his house afterwards. Sam wasn't keen on this to take her out, all the restaurants they'd ever been to where in very public places, and obviously chosen to be just that, she would be finished there for one, her next appointment was at one thirty, and that would be one of two places, she would have an appointment at her bank, she went there once a month also, but always on a Thursday, since she hadn't been for the last three weeks, it would definitely be happening that day, if she didn't go at one thirty, then it would be around three pm, which would mean, her trip to visit her sister-in-law would be at the one thirty slot. Her sister-in-law was an inpatient, at a local hospital for people with mental health issues, she had suffered mentally for many years, and had been an inpatient for the last six months, Brad for some reason, known only to herself, had taken to visiting her every fortnight, now we all know, Brad had no deep feelings for anyone, let's face it, her own kids didn't get a look in, so her visits to this woman, would more than likely involve some sort of manipulation involving money. The reason they knew she was going today, she'd not been for almost two weeks, and her plans for the following couple of days, wouldn't fit in with her visit. It was complicated, and by no means foolproof, there were no certainties, we would be working on the tightest of schedules, where anything could change at any moment, why the hell couldn't she be like regular people, and have a regular diary, with a regular schedule !

We were all set, Sam had made the decision to wait until her last appointment, we would have more idea of where she would be then, and could easily plan for both. On a high, ready for whatever life would throw at us next, we went back to the kitchen and lied to the women we loved.

Chapter Forty-Four

Thursday came around way too fast, I'd spoken to Fi about how she'd feel if I went to work with Sam for the day. I didn't lie when I told her I'd been struggling being cooped up in the house for so long, and of course she was totally on board, practically pushing me out of the door, telling me not to worry, and to 'have fun'. I left her with a lingering kiss, a tight embrace, and a guilt trip I might never recover from. Dan had arrived at seven thirty, and despite Fi's protests that they did not need a babysitter, I assured her this was purely for my own peace of mind, and nothing whatsoever to do with her ability to look after herself.

And just like that we were on our way to kidnap the woman who had become the bane of our lives, and kidnapped she would stay until such time as we were assured she was no longer a threat to any of us.

The journey back to town was quiet and exciting and nerve wracking. I felt like I'd been stuck in that house for months, and being back out in the big wide world was hugely exhilarating. The closer we got to town the more I felt like I was going home, and it felt good, even though I had nothing to go home to, returning to this place were I'd spent so many years with Joseph and my mum, felt good, I'd never expected to be coming back so soon, or ever. In reality, if it wasn't for the fact I was still in hiding, it would've been a great day, but as it was,

I needed to stay under the radar as much as possible. There was one small request I had, one Sam wasn't happy about, but I needed to do, I wanted to see George, it would have felt wrong to come all this way, and not let him know we were ok. Sam reluctantly agreed. He was going to park outside, I could run inside with my hood up, head down, and check who was in there before speaking to anyone. We pulled up outside the little cafe I'd been to so many times, "Quick as you can mate, we're really taking a chance here," said Sam, "I know, and I'm grateful Sam, honestly, I am."

I'd caught him in the quiet spot, in-between breakfast rush, and the start of lunch, which was obviously great for me, there was one little old couple sitting at the window table, they had tea and cakes, and made me smile as they sat holding hands across the table, had they been in love for a lifetime, or had they found it in later years, either way it was a beautiful sight. I walked to the counter, and ordered tea and coffee to take away, I still had my head down when he said, "That'll be four pounds forty please." I took a ten pound note from my pocket and looked up as I handed it to him. His eyes widened as he realised who it was, and his hand shot out to take mine, clasping it, and shaking hard, in recognition of his joy at seeing me. "Oh it's so good to see you, how're you doing ? How's your young lady ?" I let out a little laugh, it was comforting seeing his reaction, knowing there was still someone here, in the place I called home, who would miss me. He came from behind the counter with my drinks, "I wish I could stay," I told him sadly, I had just a few minutes to catch up on how he was doing, how his daughter and grandkids were, he asked what I'd been up to, and I lied about my new job out of town, I couldn't help adding, "There's a chance we might come back here one day, you never know." All too soon it was time to leave, I'd not quite been prepared for how sad that made me feel, George was someone I would choose to always have in my life, if I could, but sadly right now, it wasn't an option.

Sam had several small jobs to do in town, whilst I'd been off the scene, he'd still had to carry on as normal, for the rest of the day I would be just a passenger, waiting until we had a time to start moving on our plan. At one pm Sam received a text, it read '1.30 bank' which meant our job had just become ten times easier. The hospital her sister in-law was in, was about half an hour outside town, a lot less populated, with several roads that were prime for a kidnap spot, no houses, no shops, just rows of hedgerow. The only traffic would be people visiting the hospital, and at three pm that would be practically nil. As Sam relayed the details, and went over the plan, I found out I had plenty of adrenalin left in me, the tips of my fingers were tingling to the point they were almost painful, my heart was beating too fast, I could feel it pounding in my chest, and I started rubbing my top lip, which was something I'd only recently realised I do when I'm starting to feel under pressure. Knowing the job was going to be at the hospital whilst making things so much easier, also meant we had almost four hours to kill before we could get the job done. It was going to be one hell of a long day. This time there was going to be no hiding the fact that it was me and Sam behind the job, this time she would know exactly what was happening, and why. We did need just one other person to help us out with this, and Sam had already put that in place.

By the time two o'clock came I was quite literally going crazy sitting waiting in the car, Sam on the other hand was so chilled you'd have thought he was waiting for his dry cleaning to be ready. "How do you do it Sam ?" I asked, "Do what ?" he said, "I'm in bits here, this day has dragged on forever, and I just need to get there and get the job done, and you're just sitting around like you've got nothing better to do," his answer … "I haven't." I turned towards him, looking at him in disbelief, "Seriously Sam ?" "Yes, seriously, I have nothing better to do than wait for that heartless fucking bitch to get what's coming, I'm feeling fucking great mate," and he really was. I remembered the day Fran had placed the handwritten note Brad had left at the park, in front of him, his reaction had been explosive, and he clearly had not recovered.

Two thirty came and at long last we were on our way, I couldn't sit still, I shifted in my seat constantly, my palms were sweating, my heart was racing, but it was good, I felt good, the thought of seeing the look on her face when she realised what was happening, was all I needed to keep me going. When she realised, there were people out there who loved her kids when she didn't, that there were people who would make sure she would never hurt them, or anyone else again, and on top of all of that, she would now tell me, whether she liked it or not, exactly who killed my brother, only then would all of this stress be worth it, a million times over.

At three pm, when Brad was entering the hospital, we were waiting, practically in a ditch off the country lane that led to the hospital entrance. Waiting almost twenty feet away, at the edge of a tiny lane that was no more than twenty feet long, and led only to a gated field, was Lenny. Lenny was waiting for the go-ahead, everything that happened from here on in, depended on his timing being absolutely spot on. Whilst I sat and worried over every single thing that could go wrong, Sam was still totally chilled, "Trust me," he said, laughing at my stressing, "Lenny has never let us down, he's done this a hundred times, his timing is perfect, believe me, I have total faith in him." I already knew this, and it wasn't helping in any way, I knew I wouldn't rest until Brad was safely in the back of this car. She didn't stay long at the hospital, they'd paid a guy on the inside to let us know when she was on the move. That meant in the next twenty minutes or so, I could, hopefully, begin to chill my arse out !

Sam was about to say something, when his phone vibrated, he picked it up from between the two of us with no urgency whatsoever, I, on the other hand, sat bolt upright, my heart was almost pumping out of my chest as I stared at him, waiting to hear what the text said, "It's a go mate, we're on." He rubbed his hands with glee, whilst I felt a mixture of excitement being slightly outdone by nausea, I could only hope the nausea didn't win out. In less than three minutes, we should see Brad's car drive past, she never drove, so it would be Archie at the wheel. I did feel bad that he may get hurt, but sadly for him, he was a small price to pay, to get our hands on her. I barely had time to think about him before their car flew past, the screech of brakes, and the explosive sound of an impact, told us Lenny's timing was most definitely spot on. Sam was on the move the minute he'd heard the collision, and just a few seconds later, we were pulling up behind them. Brad's car was on its side, Lenny was already out of his Volvo, and standing in the road, hands on hips, with a massive 'job well done' grin on his face. He nodded as we got out of the car, Sam shook his hand, and then we were back to work. Sam jumped up onto the side of the car, he gave me the thumbs up that told me Archie was ok, considering I barely knew the guy and by all accounts he was a miserable old git, I was relieved, no one else needed to be hurt, it would just be one more innocent person to add to the tally of the impact Brad had on their life. He had the back door open, and was reaching in, a slim, woman's hand reached out towards him, looked like Brad was ok too, I couldn't help thinking, 'more's the pity' let's face it, her being taken out in an accident wouldn't have been the worst thing to have happened !

He pulled up hard, before a blonde blood stained head appeared from the opening, shit, I don't know why, but I still couldn't help but feel bad. He helped her onto the top of the car, which was in fact the side. She sat, pushing her hair behind her ears, and wiping away the blood from above her eye, she was obviously dazed, shaken, something I hadn't actually thought was possible. I wish I could have saved a picture of the look on her face, when she realised it was me helping her down to the ground, it was a mixture of horror and fury, I could only imagine where her head was at. She hadn't lost her tenacity though, "What the fuck is going on ?" she demanded.

She had a gash on the side of her forehead, obviously caused by her head crashing against the side window as the car had gone over. All the anxiety I'd had, the nerves, even the rush of adrenaline, had gone. I was in work mode, I was here to get the job done now, and Sam had been right all along, I needed her to know it was me, and now we needed her to know it was Us. She yelled again, "I said what the fucks going on ?" Sam had already asked that I not speak to her, I could see why, not knowing what was happening was pissing her right off, she needed to be in control, and the loss of it was infuriating for her, it was quite amusing to watch too. I'd seen her mad before, but now she was livid, and there was definitely some underlying unease there too, and that, I'd never seen. Sam calmly walked to the back of his car, whilst Lenny and myself stood guard, I doubt she would try escaping, it really didn't seem like the type of thing she would do, I didn't ever see her running from anyone or anything.

Sam returned with a couple of zip ties, he passed them to Lenny, who moved behind Brad and demanded, "Hands !" she didn't move, looking even more defiant than she had before. "I said, give me your fucking hands," he bellowed, his voice was deep, and boomed as he spoke, I swear I could feel the vibrations hitting me, but still she didn't move. "Listen, you fucking little slag, last chance, or I'll do it myself, and I won't give a shit how I do it." Two seconds later, she was face down in the dirt with Lenny's knee in her back, her arms being dragged roughly behind her. "Now, I *was* gonna just tie your hands up but seeing as you're a goddamn bitch…" he didn't finish the sentence, but before she had a chance to speak, or move, both her legs were tied together, and attached to her hands. I cringed, what was it in us that no matter how hideous the person, watching a woman being abused and humiliated still felt extremely uncomfortable, and very, very wrong.

Lenny called an ambulance for Archie, before me and Sam unceremoniously dumped, a furiously protesting Brad into the boot of the car, the yelling didn't last long, Lenny quickly appeared from behind us, and gagged her, looking extremely pleased with himself he brushed the invisible dirt from his hands, to say 'job well done' and promptly slammed the boot shut, and I have to agree, it really was a job well done. I was surprised to hear Lenny comforting Archie in the softest voice, reassuring him that help would be with him soon, which was our cue to leave. After goodbyes, thank yous and handshakes, we were on our way to the shed with our not so precious load. Now the two of us were on a high, adrenalin pumping for all the right reasons. With the music turned up just a touch, we couldn't even hear Brad in the boot, which meant we could enjoy our achievements in peace. Lenny had left the scene of the 'accident' but had waited on the main road to ensure help was actually on its way for Archie. As soon as the blue lights were in sight and he was sure he would be safe, he left.

It was strange today, pulling up outside those big faded red doors, the last time I'd been here the memories of what had happened were still fresh in my mind. I'd struggled to push them away, but today, it was barely a passing thought, and not one that impacted on me at all. Sam had told me Fran would be meeting us, I didn't question it, although I wasn't really sure why he was needed. When Sam climbed out of the car, I'd expected him to walk to the boot, but instead he went straight inside, followed by my good self, wondering why he'd left Brad. As if reading my mind, Sam said, "It won't hurt her to stay in there a bit longer." He was looking very smug, which was something he'd often told me not to do, but then, I suppose when it was Brad you were dealing with, it was kind of understandable.

Chapter Forty-Five

Fran was sat at our little makeshift table, with a coffee and a newspaper, the place looked just like it had last time I'd seen it, there wasn't much call for change in a barn. I purposely made myself look into the corner, the place I'd taken the life of another man, I needed to know how I would feel, test myself, see how my emotions were holding up, I felt...nothing, no guilt, no nausea, no anger, quite literally nothing whatsoever, it wasn't as though I couldn't remember, or I was trying not to see it in my mind, I saw every moment, and it meant nothing at all to me.

Fran stood to greet Sam, in the way he always did, as he did so, there was a noise from the far side of the shed, startled I turned quickly, arms out to the side, my mind ready for combat if it was needed, it wasn't, it was only Degs, I hadn't been expecting him, and by the look on Sam's face, neither had he. Sam looked from Fran to Degs and back again. "Oh come on son, there's no way I was missing this, how did it go ?" Sam laughed, hugged his dad and filled him in on the events of the last few hours. The culmination of which was Sam gaining a pat on the back from his dad, who was beaming with pride. All of a sudden it seemed very bizarre, I tried to imagine my mum being utterly delighted, when I filled her in on my afternoons accomplishments of damaging and kidnapping the local drugs boss, I couldn't really see it going down too well at all. How times change eh ? It wasn't long before we were all sat around the table, drinks in hand, laughing at Fran and Degs as they reminisced about old times, I can see how they had remained good friends for so long, there was a lot of love between them. They enjoyed life to the fullest, again a rather bizarre statement considering what they did together, but hey, it worked, and as my mum would have said, 'if it's' not broken, don't fix it.' I loved listening to these guys, I could've sat there all night, but we had to remember at some point, we were here for a reason, and that reason was still stuffed in a car boot about twenty yards away.

Sam, I think, would have been happy to leave her there all night, but thankfully he listened to reason from all three of us and conceded that maybe we should bring her inside. It was another fifteen minutes, before he backed down, saying, "Come on then mate, let's get the dirty work done." I was up and at the door before he was, I was excited to see her again, for her to realise the mess she was in, for her to know why she was in this mess, and to make sure she knew in no uncertain terms, there was no easy fix this time. We didn't want her cash, we didn't want her allegiance, we didn't need her for anything, and the sooner she knew that, the sooner she realised she had nothing to barter with, then the sooner she would realise she was well and truly in shit street. And that was a moment I had waited a long time to see.

I was waiting impatiently at the boot while Sam took his own good time to walk over. He was enjoying this, having her just where he wanted her, it was beyond comprehension how the love you have for someone can cause the strength of your emotions, be they on the love or hate spectrum, to spiral so far out of control that they don't belong in the realms of reality any more. This wasn't normal, this wasn't what real people did, and yet I didn't feel I was a different person, more just the same person living a different life. And that life had led us to pulling a now semi conscious woman out of the boot of a car without it having any kind of emotional impact whatsoever.

We half carried, half walked Brad into the shed, I wasn't really sure what we were going to do with her once we were inside, not like we were tying this floppy mess to a chair any time soon. "Where's she going Sam ?" I asked as we got through the doors, "Here will do," he said, promptly dropping her. Not at all ready for him to let go, she slid from my grasp, she was a dead weight, there was no way I was holding her up alone. "You're just leaving her there ?" I said. "She's not going anywhere any time soon mate," I stood where she lay, a crumpled heap on the floor before me, and my humanity momentarily kicked back in, it just felt so wrong leaving her there in the dirt, hurt and unable to protect herself. A voice came from somewhere near the little table, it was Fran. "Son, remember why you're here, it doesn't pay to let your emotions get in the way of your work." He was right, and as quick as I could, I pushed my emotions to one side. I locked the barn door behind me, and took my seat back at the table. As I did so, Degs stood, picked up a holdall from the side of his 'chair' ruffled my hair, making me smile, and went to where Brad lay. "What's he doing now ?" I asked. "Well, we're not animals son, Degs is going to check she's still alive," said Fran. This man was so blazé about the most outrageous things. Degs opened up the bag as I watched, intrigued at what was going to be pulled out. Are these guys for real I asked myself, as Degs took out first a stethoscope, then a blood pressure monitor. He checked her pulse, I assumed it was ok, he said nothing, he listened to her heart, checked her blood pressure, and gave her the all clear, I mean he was no doctor, but the fact that he had all these things, and seemed to know what he was doing, suggested this was not his first time playing Doctor Degs. "She'll live," he announced, as he sat back at the table, and went back to drinking his coffee. "How long will she be out ?" I asked, turning back to them. "Erm, possibly ten minutes, possibly a couple of hours, of course she could be blagging the bloody arse of us, only time will tell son." Fran was right, she may in fact be faking the whole thing, shit, these guys really had been there, done that, and bought every frickin' t-shirt going.! "And in the meantime ?" I asked, "We wait," was the unanimous and very obvious answer.

It would take Brad precisely forty seven minutes to come round/ stop pretending. Before she moved in any way, Degs and Fran had her up off the floor, and tied to 'the chair,' before she knew what was happening. I wondered how long that chair had been in use, how many lives had been snuffed out or changed forever in it. It wasn't a good way for my mind to wander, and it always took a conscious effort to chase the thoughts away. But I managed it, and I have to say, it was getting easier with time. I could see, after all these years, just why it had little to no effect on these guys. Sam hadn't even looked up from his phone, whereas I had taken in every moment, maybe I should start taking a leaf out of his book, take a step back, and not get so involved. Within a few minutes, Degs and Fran were back at the table continuing the conversation they'd been having, as though nothing at all had interrupted them. I took one more glance over my shoulder at her, before rejoining the conversation too, and trying my best to forget she was there. Fran was telling us a story from when he and Degs were kids, they'd stayed over at Degs house, something they did a lot. Unbeknown to Fran, Degs had placed a fresh egg in the inside pocket of his jacket, he'd waited till they were about to leave, stood back as Fran put his jacket on, then promptly slapped him in the chest and ran, while Fran was left unimpressed, to clean up the mess. They both laughed as they recalled, no malice involved, no anger from anyone, they'd had a wonderful, life long friendship, and it was a beautiful thing to see.

All four of our heads turned simultaneously to the corner of the room, Brad was stirring. "Ahh the dragon awakes," said Degs, in full, story mode dramatics. He stood, pulled up his pants which had slipped slightly after sitting for so long, "You ready pal ?" he was looking at Fran now, "Always ready for you pal," said Fran with the most genuine smile. Sam hugged his dad, hugged Fran, turned to me and said, "Right come on mate." He headed for the door, I followed automatically, completely confused as to what was happening. I turned to Fran hoping he could give me some idea, but he and Degs were already focused on their subject. Instead I waited until we had left, closed the door behind me, and asked Sam why we were leaving. " What's going on Sam ?" He didn't answer till we were both back in the car. "She's a woman ?" he said, as though it were perfectly obvious, he looked more confused than I did, "I know that Sam, but why are we leaving?" "My dad would prefer if I never hurt a woman, he knows what that does to a man, and he would never want me or you to feel that way." I was really taken aback, I mean I understood completely what he was saying, but I suppose, being in this game all these years, I had assumed it would all just be part of the job. I actually felt a little guilty that my assumptions had led to me thinking they had totally forsaken any moral standards whatsoever. Of *course* hurting a woman would be an issue, and now that I'd thought about it, I was also pretty sure that hurting her was going to be a final option. "So what do we do now ?" I asked. "We go home," he said, I nodded, unsure of how else to react. Sam laughed, then said, "There's no quick fix for this one mate, you know what she's like, she's a stubborn little bitch, she's gonna be here for a while." It was true, there was no way Brad would give in easily, or quickly, but at least while she was here, there was one less thing to worry about. I might even get back to doing a bit of work, I thought, Sam had been subsidising me, to be fair, we'd not really needed to spend anything anyway, but it would be good to earn my keep again. The day had become a bit of an anti-climax, but on the flip side, I unexpectedly got to spend the night back home with Fi.

Having text Fi on the way back, I was delighted to see that they'd made dinner when we got back, I'd not realised how hungry I was, there was barely a word spoken until our plates were clean. Sams phone was busy throughout the evening, and whilst he didn't look overly concerned, there was definitely something on his mind, he was just a little quiet, maybe slightly distracted, or maybe he was just tired, emotionally drained, and maybe I should put away my psychiatrists cap now and just enjoy the rest of the evening. I did, we talked, we laughed, and as we had an early start, we had an early night. A night with my girl, on our own, in our own bed, was just sheer bliss, I was so grateful for the time we had together, I even agreed to watch some old episodes of Vampire Diaries with her, we couldn't watch the newer ones obviously, that was her and Beths 'thing'. I loved that they had a 'thing' knowing she had someone whilst I wasn't there brought me great comfort, and maybe in a slightly selfish way, it meant I didn't have to worry about her too. All the way home I had dreamed of spending the night with her, making love, intimacy, passion, the feel of her body, her reaction to my touch The reality was, falling asleep in each others arms half way through an episode, which incidentally, and not that I'd admit it to her, I actually really got into !

Dan was back at the house at seven am, and Sam and I were ready to go when he arrived. I took Fi in my arms, and kissed her as I always did, like we may never meet again. I don't know why I put myself through it, it killed me to leave her every time, maybe I should stick to a peck on the cheek from now on. Sam wasn't much better, he too was struggling to leave his girl behind, and I know just like me, he was thankful they had each other. The drive was quiet, early ones usually were. "Everything been ok ?" I asked, "Yeh, sure mate," Sam answered. He seemed sincere enough, and so I left it at that. We pulled up outside the sheds big red doors, just as Degs and Fran were coming out, I guessed they'd been listening out for us arriving. "Good morning boys," said Fran, he and Sam embraced, and Sam asked how the night had gone. "Not so bad
…" Degs said, "… she's totally pissed off of course, but her heads a lot more fucked up than I expected it to be, she's no clue what's going on, I'll leave that to you boys to fill her in." Oh, I thought, I was surprised at that, I assumed she'd have guessed by now what was happening, surely she must have some idea, but then again, she had done so much shit to so many people in her lifetime, she probably had no idea which pile of shit had pissed us off. "Well, she's about to find out," Sam said. Degs took his son in his arms, "You call me son, if you need anything, anything at all, you hear me," "Thanks dad, and you Fran, seriously, I don't know what I'd do without you guys." This was

all getting a little bit heavy, Sam had taken all of this so much more personally than I'd realised, I hoped it wouldn't influence any decisions he had to make, as he'd reminded me often, emotions make mistakes, and mistakes are costly in this game, sometimes even deadly.

Brad was sitting in the corner, tied to the chair, with a look of utter disdain on her face, I noticed she had what looked like some fresh bruising, and maybe a couple more cuts, but I couldn't be certain they hadn't been there yesterday. Sam picked up his box, the seat he used to sit at our table and said, "Grab a chair mate, follow me, it's story time." I did as he asked, and followed him to just a few feet away from Brad. He placed his box on the floor, and sat facing her, I followed his lead and did the same. "So, Brad, do you know why you're here ?" she stared at him, her eyes filled with fury, and even in her bound to a chair state, she managed to sit up straight. "Not in the mood to chat… no ?" Sam was so calm, I mean dangerously calm, worryingly calm. I sat beside him, saying nothing, I wasn't sure he wanted me to be part of this, whether I was here purely as a spectator or was expected to have some input at some point, I decided my best bet was to stay quiet, until he suggested otherwise. He went on, "Twice, your shit-house of a husband tried to have my dad killed, and twice I was prevented from doing anything about it. My dad is good at biding his time, but me, well, not so much." He stood now, and walked a few feet away from her, before turning back to look her in the eye, she had dropped a little now, the staunch stature disappearing, either from the realisation that Sam knew more than she thought, or the exhaustion of the last twenty four hours. "Do you know what the worst thing that happened to me in my life was ? Losing my mum, she adored me, and when she was gone, I was lost, a part of me was gone, a part I've never ever gotten back. And yet, your daughters disappear from your life, and you couldn't give a fuck, how the fuck does that work ? How can one person be a mother who would die for her kids, and another be a mother whose kids could die, and she wouldn't give a shit."

I understood now, this wasn't just about Beth, this was a lifetime of hurt, he had lost his mum, and Brad had attempted to take away the only other person in his life, he had been waiting for this moment for a long, long time, it explained his reaction to the note she had sent instead of a ransom, it explained just how hurt he felt for Beth, and in some ways this was a perfect form of therapy for him, he could confront and deal. How that was going to pan out remained to be seen. Sam took his seat again. "Do you even care where your daughter is ?" I wasn't sure whether Sam noticed, he was so wrapped up in getting his point across, but I did, Brad didn't know ! She did not know Beth was with him, she didn't know where her daughter was, and yet she had stayed home, trying her best to save her business, and she really hadn't given a single fuck about her. Brad didn't answer, but she was waiting for him to tell her, she wanted to know, she was curious now. "We took your daughter home to you, and she refused to leave, she refused to get out of that car, she refused to return home to a mother like you, she begged to stay with people she had known just a few weeks, rather than go home to you, how does that make you feel Brad ?" Well, if the look on her face was anything to go by, pretty fucking furious was the answer, she almost answered him, but quickly regained her composure, she had obviously made a very calculated decision not to respond to anything he said. "Do you have any idea what it did to her when she found out what you sent instead of cash ? Do you care ?" I hoped now with all my heart that he hadn't noticed the subtle change in her face, suddenly the fury was gone, and she wasn't trying to hide the smugness that had replaced it. It was too late, Sam had seen it. He stood again, walked back to our table, picked up his water bottle and swigged, until the rage he was trying to hide had subsided. This was all about control, he couldn't let her see any emotion, and give him his due, he was doing well, all things considered. He walked back to his seat, his composure restored, he spoke slowly now, softly, "I have your daughter, and I will have her forever, I will make sure by the time we are finished with you, you will never, ever have the opportunity to hurt her again, do you understand ?" The calmness with which he spoke was chilling, and if she didn't believe him, if she wasn't afraid, then the woman was a damn fool.

"Conal would like you to tell him who killed his brother, I'd prefer you did that now, simply because it would make things so much easier for him, but if you wish to do it the hard way, then later will do." He picked up his chair, took it back to the table, and sat calmly eating the croissant that he had bought on the way. "Oh, by the way, my dad and Fran are behind the takeover." I swiftly glanced back, my box still in my hand, just in time to see Brad's face turning red with rage, she rocked back and forth on her chair, pulling at her restraints. Not one tiny iota of emotion for her kids, but her money, well that sent her spiralling into insanity. Sam was smiling, well, smirking, he didn't need to look back to know exactly what his last remark had done to her. Brad was left to her fury, while Sam finished his food and drink, in sweet, unadulterated smugness. We talked for a while, about nothing in particular, simply passing time until he was ready to confront her again.

"So Co-lette …" he said, she threw him a glance that made me thankful she was tied to a chair, he was getting to her, which for now was all he wanted, he wanted to piss her off, he wanted her to feel the anger that he had felt, he wanted her to know just who was behind her life falling apart, and why she was sitting where she was right now, "… you ready to start talking ?" Once again it took literally a split second for her to regain her composure, she sat up straight, full of the arrogance she wore so well. "I guess not," he said, "You know, I've been using this shed for about ten years, and my dad for god knows how many years before that, I've never so much as seen a pedal bike come past here." He was letting her know the chances of someone coming across her one day were practically nil. She didn't flinch, she gave not one shit. Sam went on, "I don't care how long it takes, I have all the time in the world, and let's face it, people are not exactly queuing up to come looking for you, in fact, with you out of the way they're all free to join team Degs." There it was, the slightest of twitches in the corner of her eye, that told us once again, we were on the right track. She was saying nothing today, but Sam seemed happy enough, he knew he was playing the long game, and he was happy to do it, the longer she was here the more she would lose, he knew it and she knew it, and he had nothing to lose.

Chapter Forty-Six

Lenny, who was supposed to be a one hit wonder, then out of the game, was babysitting Brad tonight, which I assumed meant Fran was back home with the girls. I couldn't wait to get home, although I'd done pretty much nothing at all, I was exhausted, I needed my bed and my girl. I didn't know it at the time, but it would be almost two weeks before Brad gave up anything at all. I understood why he had her there, I knew he wanted to make her pay for hurting Beth, but there was something more, telling me who killed Joseph was pretty straight forward, but he hadn't made it clear what else he wanted from her. He'd asked vague questions about why she did things, why she hurt people, but there had been no specific question, that would all change. He bided his time, he waited until she realised that she could be there, in that shed, for an indefinite period of time, losing money every day, getting thinner every day, and gaining herself a few more cuts and bruises along the way. I'd always known she was a stubborn fucker, but I never expected her to hold out for this long.

We arrived at the shed on a Friday morning, relieving Degs and Fran from their night shift. By all accounts, the takeover was all but done, everything was running smoothly, and apparently if they continued on the path they were on, Brad would have no business to go back to, of course she still had a ton of assets, and therefore would always be a threat, I wasn't sure what that meant for her, would they let her go knowing there was a possibility of her retaliating ? No one had really filled me in on the long term plans, personally I'd have liked to see her staying in that shed, where she was no risk to anyone, but obviously that was not practical for anyone.

Brad was looking tired, she'd lost weight, that was part of the plan, weaken the body, weaken the mind. They had untied her twice a day to let her move around, to eat and of course relieve herself, but apart from that she had spent the whole two weeks on that chair, there was a tiny part of me, and it was only tiny, and only because I am my mothers son, that felt sorry for her, I was glad I felt it, I needed that reminder that I was still human, because what we were doing to her really was not. I also had to remind myself, she was a vile, wicked bitch of a person, a horrible mother, and a killer, who cared for nothing but money. Sam couldn't have given any fucks whatsoever how thin she looked, how tired she looked, or whether she lived or died, he was here to watch her suffer, as far as he was concerned, things were going pretty damn well.

There was no time for breakfast or coffee today, Sam was straight on it, he sensed her weakness, and was going to make the most of it. "So, Colette, ready to tell my friend here who killed his brother ?" Her arrogance was all but gone now, there was no derision in her glare, in fact there was no glare, as strong as she had always been, there was virtually none of it left. Still though, she didn't answer. Sam waited a few moments then repeated slowly, "Are-you-ready-to-tell-this-young-man-here, who-killed-his- brother ?" She didn't even return his gaze, she remained slouched in her chair, looking at the floor beneath her. "Not yet ?" he said, "I'll be back in five, you have a little think about it, see if you'd like to change your mind." I followed Sam to the shed door, which he held open for me, before stepping outside himself. "Today's the day Conal, I can feel it."

We stood outside for maybe five minutes, maybe a little more. Sam was psyched, he knew he was getting close and it had gotten him on a complete high, he was bouncing on his toes as he talked, his body trying to work off some of that excess energy he had. "Right, come on, let's get back to it. I expected that meant he was right back to asking the same questions he'd asked for almost a fortnight, but instead he sat back on his box, took out his phone, and started texting someone, probably anyone, anything that would make it look as though he had no cares, that his time was limitless, and her refusal to talk had not affected him in the slightest. Suddenly there was some movement at the back of the shed, Brad was trying her best to sit up straight. "Lenny Walker," she all but whispered. I wasn't sure I'd heard her right. Sam was up and off his chair marching in her direction, before I could even ask if he'd heard the same. My heart was racing as I followed him across the room, she couldn't have said that, she couldn't have. I was just a few steps behind Sam when his arm flew out, he backhanded Brad full force across her face, he hit her so hard, the momentum took her and her chair to the floor. "You're a fucking liar," he screamed at her. He had lost control now, and I knew why, it was the same reason I felt I could be physically sick right now, because if she was telling the truth, then the guy who killed my brother was sitting at home right now with Fi and Beth. "Why would I lie ?" said Brad. She seemed like she genuinely meant what she'd said, but who knew with this woman. "Sam…" I said, "…I need to talk to you for a minute, outside." Sam didn't speak, but marched towards the shed door. Once outside I reminded him that she knew Lenny was working with us, from the crash, "I know, I know," he said, "Do you believe her ?" I asked. He didn't answer, instead he took out his phone. Sam filled his dad in on what had been said, "So what do you think, is she telling the truth ?" he was hoping for some clarity from his dad, which unfortunately he did not get. He turned off his phone, and stood looking at the floor. "Well ?" I asked, hoping he would tell me no, no way would Lenny do that. He took a deep breath before answering, "He said Lenny would do anything for money, absolutely anything, and when he takes a job on he is totally loyal to that person, to that job, to getting the outcome they are paying for, but once the job is over all loyalties are instantly forgotten." "So what do we do ?" I asked, "No idea right now mate, but we've waited this long, we can wait a bit longer." We both knew the way Brad worked, there was much more possibility of her giving us a scapegoat, than her giving us the truth, and as exhausted as she was, it would still be killing her to even think about giving in.

Next stop…Lenny.

We spoke to Lenny, who was not the least bit phased by our questions, and very simply and calmly told us Brad was talking utter bullshit. "She offered me twenty grand to let her go, but you know me Sam, she could've offered a million, I keep my word, when I take a job, I finish the job, and besides, I like Degs, and I don't like many people, I can make you a promise, one I don't do very often, at no point will I collaborate with Brad, I don't like the woman, never have, never will, I have worked for her in the past, and… " he looked at me now, "…I'm sorry son, if she'd have payed me to kill your brother, I'd have done it, but she didn't, and I didn't, sorry I can't help you more." He was so sincere, it was hard not to believe every word he said. Sam thanked him, while I pondered the fact that there was a slight possibility I had just come face to face with the man who'd shot my brother.

I was fortunate I had my work with Sam to keep my mind busy, but it didn't stop the questions, the unease at not knowing for certain. At the end of another day, as we took the journey back to Frans house, my mind was full of what ifs and maybes once again. What if it really was Lenny, what if it was someone even closer to home, how would I deal with that, maybe I'd never find out for sure, maybe it was Brad herself, what would we to do with Brad if she never gave us the answer, how could she answer Sams vague questions, I wasn't even sure what he wanted to know, she had no chance. If there's one thing wracking your brain with a million questions does, it makes time disappear and before I knew it we were pulling up outside Frans front door. Walking in through the hallway, my mind still looking for answers, I was happy to see Fran sitting at the kitchen table, this time with a book in hand, and his usual cup on the table in front of him. "Good evening boys," he said, I was glad the girls were not there, we needed his advice, and there would be discussions the girls couldn't hear. "Evening Fran, how're things ?" I asked, "Not so bad son, not so bad." "I'm just going to see Fi, then do you have time for a chat Fran ?" I asked, "Of course son, I'm going nowhere tonight," "Great, see you soon."

Both girls were in Sam's room, and as often happened, all four of us sat on the huge bed, catching up on each other's days, missing out the bits they really didn't need to hear, it was a great way to wind down, and I think, just what both of us needed. Beth and Fi were like the audio version of a good massage, we were totally relaxed by the time we left the room almost an hour later. I'd asked the girls to give us an hour to speak to Fran, before we ate, and of course, with tv still to watch, they were totally fine with that.

Fran was waiting, three fresh cups of tea and coffee on the table, a plate of biscuits beside them, of course we presumed Degs would have spoken to him already, but hopefully, he could give us a bit more insight. "So boys, what can I help you with ?" We looked at each other, each waiting for the other to start. Sam took the lead, and filled Fran in on what had happened at the shed, what Brad had said, and what Lenny had said too. "So as you can see Fran, we have a bit of a dilemma." Fran put down his coffee, rubbed his chin and said, "Well, yes, it would seem you do." He took another mouthful of coffee before he continued, "I can't tell you who's telling the truth, I can only tell you what I know, and that is this, I've known Lenny a long, long time, and believe me when I say, he's nobody's friend, he's a bit of a lone wolf, looks after number one, but what I will say about him is, he's loyal to his customers, and I've never know the man to lie, if he did something, he'd have no qualms about telling you straight, Brad on the other hand, I wouldn't trust the woman as far as I could throw her, doesn't answer your question, but it's the best I've got I'm afraid."

Fran had said pretty much what I was thinking. "I don't know Lenny at all, but like you said, he would have had no problem telling me straight if it was him who shot Joseph, he has no reason to lie, and Brad wouldn't know the truth if it jumped up and bit her on the arse." Sam nodded in agreement, "I'm with you mate, I might have known Lenny a bit longer, but that tells me nothing, what I do know is, I would trust Frans instincts over Brad's lies, any day of the week." And so that was that, Brad was lying again, if she hadn't told the truth by now, I doubted she ever would. Sam must have sensed my feelings of defeat. "It's early days yet mate," he said, I gained myself a punch to the arm, I hadn't had one for a while and the familiarity of it brought me some comfort. He went on, "I told you this was going to be a long one, she's the one wasting away mate, we will just bide our time." Sam was back to his usual self, and his mood lifted me, we were home, we had lost nothing, and I got to spend the evening with my girl, life wasn't too shabby after all.

Another week passed and nothing had changed, all the highs of thinking Brad was about to talk, that she'd had enough, had come to nothing. I think we were both coming to the realisation that Brad was not going to give in, it wasn't even that she didn't want to tell us who killed him, she just couldn't, she would quite literally rather die than lose face and let someone get one over on her. The problem now was what to do with her, we couldn't just let her go, she was too much of a liability. It was time to get the guys together and decide what steps to take next. It had become obvious that Brad had been given quite a few beatings, the bruises were more obvious, there were fresh cuts to her lips, swollen eyes, no signs of any sort of torture, thank the lord, I'm not sure I could've coped with that. I'd wondered for a while what had been happening whilst we were not there. Sam had eventually filled me in, Degs wanted to know who had tried to kill him and who her contacts were in Ireland, it was the one side of her business they'd not been able to infiltrate, and obviously they'd kept up the heat on who killed Joseph. She had given up nothing, nothing at all, not one iota of information. I couldn't imagine what it would take to make her talk, although I'm sure she would find out real soon. Degs and Fran had been using the softly, softly approach, their words, not mine, but from what Sam had said, their patience was running low, and they were ready to take things up a notch. I wasn't sure I wanted to know what that notch was.

For the first time in a while, everyone had made it back to the house, it was good to have everyone together again, it gave me a sense of comfort, one that only family could, I was more at ease than I'd been for a while. Fi and Beth joined us for dinner, Indian takeaway at Tattys request, Fran ordered in from the same place he usually did, a small restaurant in the nearby village, called The Red Fort, and as always it was delicious. Beth and Fi knew there was business of some sort to be discussed, and they knew they did not want to know what that business was, and so, they very kindly excused themselves from the table when dinner was over. I followed Fi to the stairs, taking her by the waist and pulling her tight to my chest as I'd done many times, it always seemed such a long time since those lips had been on mine, and once again I made the mistake of kissing her a little too long, and a little too hard, it didn't take much from her to turn me on, I quickly pulled away, taking a deep breath. I would need a swift walk in the cold night air before going back to the guys. She, as always, giggled knowing exactly how that kiss had affected me. I smiled, laughed a little, shook my head, and headed for the front door, before making my way back to the kitchen. The guys were enjoying catching up, and for a while I sat happily listening to them, before all too soon it was time to get serious.

"First things first," said Degs, "So, after you spoke to Fran about Lenny, a few of us got our ledgers out, and suffice to say, it was in no way possible for Lenny to have killed your brother, but we did notice something in there, before I start, you do know Joseph and Brad were in a relationship of sorts ?" "I wasn't entirely sure, but I did have my suspicions," I told him. "Right, so, a couple of weeks before he was killed, there was a new kid on the scene, cocky little fucker by the name of Sean Matthews, now we looked at him before, but to be honest, he didn't seem the type, he wasn't around long, few weeks tops, turned up dead a few days after Joseph. At the time we assumed they must have been working together, it made sense that Brad had taken both of them out for the same reason, probably a botched job, although we couldn't find any evidence of one." He stopped for a breather and a mouthful of the beer that sat in front of him. There was a lot to take in, it was the first time I'd heard anything solid from the time Joseph was killed, I waited eagerly for him to tell the rest of his story, "When we spoke to Lenny, he told us about this girl Katy, he'd seen Joseph with her a couple of times, he couldn't be absolutely certain that the dates matched up, but he was pretty sure, now if Brad had gotten any inkling Joseph had another girl on the go, that would be more than enough for her to take him out, you know better than most, this woman does not like any one to get one over on her, looks to me like poor cocky little Sean was brought in to do the dirty work, then swiftly disposed of, and sadly young Katy was a little bit of collateral damage, you know how Brad hates loose ends."

    I sat, stunned into silence, all these months, all this time looking, searching for answers, all the pain I'd put people through, I'd even caused the death of my mother, and for what, a dead man. My chest was starting to tighten, my hands curled up into balls, it was a moment before I realised I was holding my breath. With nothing to say to anyone, I walked from the kitchen, and out of the front door, back into the night air, and I kept on walking, I needed to get away, I didn't know where I was going, I just needed to be somewhere where the air was clearer, colder, crisper. When I reached the line of trees, and knew I was out of sight, I stopped, I bent forward, put my hands on my knees and took long hard breaths. This was it, everything I had worked for, gone, I had worked toward this moment for so long, and now there would be no retribution, no payback, no justice, nothing. Who was I without this crusade for answers ?

I really didn't want to return to the house, knowing the guys would be sitting waiting, feeling sorry for me, it was embarrassing, I didn't want their pity, but there was little more they could give me right now. My plan was to stay out until I saw the lights of their cars leaving, but the fact that I hadn't brought a jacket, and it was the middle of winter, middle of the night, and felt like minus twenty, meant I would have to go home and face the music. I took a slow walk back to the house, stopping at the top of the steps, pretending to take in the night sky, whilst knowing full well I was just putting off the inevitable. The guys did me the courtesy of not falling into an awkward silence as I stepped back into the kitchen, Sam nodded and smiled to welcome me back, the rest of the guys carried on their conversation as though they'd not even noticed I had left. I stood at the kitchen counter, made myself a fresh tea, and asked the guys if anyone wanted one, they were all good. I took my seat back at the table, glad for the chance to have my mind on business other than my own. It worked for a while, but soon enough the subject of conversation returned to Brad, and what they needed from her, what the chances were of getting anything from her, and what to do with her after that. Tatty was getting a beer from the fridge when he asked, "So Conal, what are you thinking, do you agree that the likelihood is, this Sean guy killed your brother?" I'd thought of pretty much nothing else for the last couple of hours, and yes, I agreed with them. Brad was jealous of this girl, took Joseph out, then tidied up her mess. I didn't care who killed Sean, and whilst it was sad the young girl had to get involved too, I really had no feelings for her either. And right now, I couldn't care less what happened to Brad, although I still felt uncomfortable hearing them talk about 'getting rid' of her in such a mundane way. "I think you're right," I answered eventually. It seemed the most plausible scenario, plus it would explain why there had been no leads, the guy was dead within hours of Joseph, and in a different city, it was just a shame the connection hadn't been made sooner.

Chapter Forty-Seven

Sleep came sooner than I expected, and I was thankful for it, Fi held my hand tight, something she always did when she knew I had something on my mind, something she did when she knew anybody needed comfort or support, it felt good falling asleep hand in hand, knowing what that meant to both of us. Morning came all too soon, along with that feeling of loss I'd fallen asleep with, I should have been relieved it was now something I'd no longer have to deal with, but I didn't, I just felt I'd been denied the chance of retribution for my family, I felt cheated. I felt flat and empty, and even the gorgeous sleepy girl beside me couldn't snap me out of this one, it was something only time could heal. She did of course make me smile, how could I not, as she turned eyes still shut, lips pursed, searching for my mouth, for my good morning kiss, I helped her out, leaning in and cupping her face with one hand, gently kissing her. She cuddled into my side, and I slipped my arm under her head, pulling her close, she slept, as I thought. There was no one left to blame, no one to fight for answers, no justice to be found, it was time to move forward now, but I'd spent so long stuck in the past, I had no idea where to start.

There was a knock at the door, "Yes," I shout whispered. Sam's head appeared in the doorway, he was in a good mood, it was easy to tell, it wasn't just the ear to ear grin that gave it away, his whole body was energised. "Hey Sam what's up ?" I whispered, "You ok mate ?"

"Yeah, I'm good, thanks Sam." Far from feeling embarrassed that he thought I'd still be in a mess, it felt good, it was what I needed, because knowing I had the support of these guys, was exactly what was going to help me decide which path I took next. "You up for work today?" he asked. Sliding my arm carefully from beneath Fi, I climbed out of bed, and took our conversation out into the corridor. "What have you got on?" I asked, "Few jobs round town, then up to the shed," he said, "In that case, yes." Sam looked surprised, I guess he'd assumed I'd have had no reason to see Brad again, now that I had all my answers, but I wanted her to know that I knew, I needed her to know she couldn't hurt me anymore, and I had a few sly digs I wouldn't mind throwing her way too. "Great, I'll see you downstairs, we're leaving in about half an hour, that ok?" "Sounds good to me."

Showered and dressed, I had just enough time to have a quick cuppa with Fi before leaving for the day, Beth and all the guys were already in the kitchen when we arrived, seeing them all up and ready to go, I quickly checked my phone and was surprised to see it was almost nine thirty. "Sorry guys," I said, "Must have needed that sleep." Tatty rubbed the top of my head as he passed, and Buzz chipped in, "We all need it sometimes mate, not a problem." I was grateful for the understanding. Dan was already here, and by the half eaten plate of food in front of him, he had been for a while. I probably needed to start setting an alarm.

I was almost certain, having lost my family, I wasn't about to lose another one, this was where I belonged now, this was the life I wanted, my only obstacle would be Fi, and if she decided it wasn't for her, then I had a decision to make that may just be impossible.

Ten minutes later there was a convoy of cars leaving the house, with a plan to meet at the shed at two pm. It would be the first time everyone had been there together for a long time. I wondered what was going on that required them to be out in force, I was both afraid and intrigued. The convoy continued until we hit the outskirts of town, where everyone went off in their own directions. "Why is everyone at the shed today ?" I asked Sam, he paused before answering which only resulted in worrying me even more, I knew he wouldn't purposely hide things from me, but I also know he wouldn't want to worry me any more than he needed to, he knew me well. "Two reasons, one, this is the first time it's been possible to get everyone together, otherwise they'd have done it sooner, and two, hopefully it will frighten the living daylights out of Brad, and she will finally give up some info on the Irish side." Made sense I suppose, but I also knew this was not going to go down without any sort of violence. I didn't give two fucks for Brad, but I didn't particularly want to be a spectator !

There was barely time to fit a job in before we made our way out to the shed again, I was hyped, Sam was hyped, adrenalin and testosterone were in full force by the time we reached the big red doors. Someone was already here, there was a silver Mercedes parked at the side of the shed, I'd not seen it before so had no idea who to expect when we got inside. I wasn't prepared for the sight of Brad when I walked in, the excitement I'd had swiftly receded, leaving me with shame, nausea and horror. She was so gaunt now, and had obviously taken quite a beating, very recently. It hadn't been that long since I'd last seen her, but she had deteriorated rapidly in that time, my humanity kicked in, and regardless of the things she had done, and the woman she was, this felt so wrong, this *was* wrong, my earlier plans, and dreams for a future with these guys suddenly seemed abhorrent. I wasn't sure I could get through the day, never mind a lifetime of this. Fran, Degs and Tatty were sat at the table, chatting like they'd met up for lunch, they had no concerns for the mess of a woman behind them, for them this was the norm, they might not be doing this every day, but it was very much part of the job, and one they'd done many times before. Maybe in twenty years time I would be numb to it too.

I couldn't eat anything I was offered, feigning an upset stomach, so I didn't have to tell them, the sight of Brad beaten to a pulp had made me feel physically sick. And so I sat, sipping on a bottle of water, as they laughed and joked, taking the piss out of each other, and paying no attention to the huge elephant in the room. Only when they had finished with their food, drinks, and conversation, did they turn their attention to Brad. Several prayers for them not to hurt her while I was there, were answered, I remembered the conversation Sam and I had about Degs not wanting his boy to see a woman getting hurt, I was extremely thankful for Degs line of thought, and very relieved that I was not going to have to witness it today. Lenny was the one who spoke to Brad first, he took a box and sat himself in front of her, the room was quiet now, as we all waited to hear what he had to say. I looked at the faces in that room, she had pissed Lenny off accusing him of killing Joseph, she'd hurt me in the most unimaginable way, she had hurt the woman Sam loved in a way no mother should, we all knew she had tried…several times to have Degs killed, and so I had to wonder about Fran, Tatty and Buzz, had she done the dirty on them too. I dare say time would tell, but for now it was time for Lenny to have his say.

Lenny was cold, there was little emotion in his voice, but it was clear, and deep. "I don't care why you told this boy I killed his brother, none of my business, but you will tell him the truth now !" To my surprise there was no hesitation from her, no arrogance or attitude, she said simply and quietly, still managing a slight smirk, "Lenny didn't kill your brother…although he would have, if I'd asked him." She managed a faint laugh, still hell bent on getting the better of us all and probably thought that was news to me, but Lenny had already made it perfectly clear, if the job had been on offer, he'd have taken it. "Exactly what I told him !" said Lenny, swiftly wiping the smile off Brad's face. Lenny was done, he had a point to prove, and Brad had put up no resistance whatsoever. To be fair though, that was an easy one. Who would be next ? Lenny joined the guys at the table, nothing was said about his conversation with Brad, and just a few moments later Sam stood for his turn to confront Brad. He was joking with his dad just a second before he picked up his box, in just a split second his whole demeanour changed, he was serious, maybe even a little angry, and I highly suspected he would be a lot more angry before the day was out. He sat directly in front of her, much closer than Lenny had, "I have a lot of questions for you today, Colette," she flinched as he said her name, as though the mere sound of it caused her physical pain. The guys sniggered, knowing her reaction without even needing to turn around. This time the guys continued to talk quietly, giving Sam the privacy he needed to say exactly what he wanted to say.

"Why don't you care about your kids Collette ?" She looked surprised, surely she must have figured out by now that we were all involved in taking the kids, she knew Beth was living with us, surely she must have put two and two together. But I have to say the look on her face wasn't telling me that at all. She didn't answer, more than likely because she had no idea what to say, it can't have been a question she was asked very often, if ever. "Do you have any idea how much you've hurt them, damaged them, probably to a point where it will affect them for the rest of their lives, do you ?" I could see the cogs turning in her brain, she had not expected this at all, she was ready for questions about Degs and the Irish side, but she quite literally had no idea this was coming. I'd have liked to suggest that she come up with an answer pretty quick, but I seriously doubted she would have listened. I'd never seen Sam so wound up as he was when Beth was involved, all of his emotions were heightened where she was concerned, but he kept them in check. "Do you even like them ? Care about them ? Want them ?" Sam was so calm it was making me feel uneasy, I knew something was brewing underneath the calm facade, something was going to blow at some point, and if Brad didn't start answering questions real soon, then there was going to be one hell of a price to pay.

He continued this somewhat serene inquisition for some five minutes or so, not straying from his controlled manner, no change in his tone of voice, no change in his stance, and yet I could see the anger building inside, he was hiding it well but it was there. "Colette, I realise this came as a surprise to you, it was obvious you weren't expecting this line of questioning at all, you do know Beth lives with us…? "Brad's eyes were suddenly wide, had she not understood when we said we had her ? She didn't have the energy to be infuriated, but she wanted to, she pulled weakly at her restraints, having no effect on them whatsoever. "…you know she lives with ME, that I took her away from you, for myself ?" With the burst of anger she now had, there was enough adrenalin in her veins, that she found the energy to struggle to get to him. "You're a fucking liar," she screamed. Sam was delighted, finally he was getting a rise out of her, just like he wanted to, he needed her to lose control, that was when she would make mistakes, when she would give up information she really didn't mean to. When he'd finished laughing he told her. "We took her, we kidnapped her, then we took her back to you and she refused to go !" He was getting angry now, it was always going to happen. That's where the fun started. "I don't believe you, you fucking arsehole," she yelled. "Oh fucking believe me Colette, she never wavered, not even remotely." "Stop calling me fucking Colette you little prick, I know my kids and they would never leave me." Sam stood up so fast, no-one could have stopped him, he leaned into her face and laughed at her, she made a vague attempt to head-butt him, which only made him laugh even louder. "Why would she want to go home to you, you have nothing to give her, not your time, not your love, not your support, nothing, she got more of that in the short time she spent with us than she ever did in a lifetime with you." Exhausted by her outburst, Brad lowered her voice, "Where is she ?" Sam had her, he took his seat once again, and swiftly changed his topic of conversation. "Why did you try to have my dad killed ?" Degs looked up from his conversation, eyebrows raised, either not expecting the question, or waiting for the answer. "For obvious reasons," Brad said, "I know the reasons, I just want to hear you say it," "You may think you know…" she said, still with the indignant air she carried so often, "…amongst other things, I was simply taking out the competition, and before you ask, yes, Fran was next." It was hard to imagine, sitting in her seat, having been beaten and starved, having to have feared for her life at some point that she still managed to be an arrogant little fucker. What the hell happened in her life to make her the person she was today. From what I remember, when she was first married she was a sweet, innocent young girl, it seemed to me, greed had created a selfish, meaningless, heartless shell of a human. How sad, I thought, to think of the life she could have had. Or maybe, she had in fact been born a heartless fuck. Who knew !!

"So who was it ?" Sam asked, Brad had regained some composure, the arrogance had returned, she was once again just where she wanted to be, her fury at losing Beth to the opposition lost for a moment, replaced by the joy of holding all the cards. "Oh there were a few," she said, " Where would you like me to start ?" She was smirking, in an instant Sam was on his feet, and in a split second the back of his hand made contact with her face. Shocked by his son's violence towards a woman, Degs was almost ready to intervene, he was stopped by the gentle placing of Frans hand on his arm. Fran shook his head gently, telling him he couldn't, this was something Sam needed to do, he needed to release this anger she'd brought out in him, and let's be honest, she damn well deserved it ! Brad flicked her head up, trying her best to get her hair out of her eyes, it worked, sort of, I half expected her usual smirk, but there was none. She was tired, she had these little spurts of energy, the odd rush of adrenalin, remnants of her old self, then exhaustion returned, she had little fight left in her, but that didn't mean for a minute she was giving up. "Who...was it ?" Sam repeated. He waited for the answer, I doubt he ever expected one, but as often happens in these situations, things had gone way too far to go back, which meant all they could do was keep on asking in the hope she would hit a point where she wanted to live.

I was stunned when Brad began to laugh, "What's the point of me telling you ? Let's face it, I don't even believe myself half the time, I've told so many lies I barely know fact from fiction any more." Well, if nothing else, she was being honest now, and she was right, even if she told the truth, we couldn't believe her, but that's not what this was about anymore, it was all about winning.

In all honesty, it didn't matter, it didn't matter why she didn't care for the kids, it didn't matter who tried to kill Degs, none of it mattered, because no matter what the answers, no one was going to feel any better, not me, not Sam, not Degs, it would change nothing. I think I'd already realised, this was more about finding out her Irish contact, all this other stuff, well it was only happening because it could, it was an opportunity for answers, and a good way of grinding her down, but it wasn't the reason she was here, this was much bigger than my hurt feelings, or Sam's. Still it was good of the guys to give us the chance to put some ghosts to rest, get some shit out of our system so to speak. And Sam wasn't ready to give up yet. "Do you like your kids ?" he asked again, I prayed for her sake she didn't smirk again, I wasn't sure how many more digs she could actually take. I was stunned a moment later when she said, "I don't know them," she wasn't arrogant, she wasn't enjoying making him angry. If I had to guess, even though it wasn't easy to tell, I was almost certain she was sad. "You don't know your own kids ?" he said, his voice full of scorn. And then it happened, the only time I had ever heard Brad sound even remotely human. "I know that Elizabeth is smart, I know Phoebe is more studious than Josie, and Josie loves sport. I know all the things I could read on a school report, but I don't *know* them." As hard as it was to believe, I really do think she was being honest. "How does that even happen ?" Sam was curious now, the interrogation style questioning had stopped, he genuinely wanted to know how, as their mother, that could ever happen. "Brad adored the girls, but he also had a lifestyle he wanted to portray to the outside world, he wanted a nanny, and housekeepers, he wanted them to attend boarding school, I drew the line at that one, but from the day they were born, I wasn't allowed to be the mother I wanted to be, they were practically brought up by other people, we never had a relationship, my only regret in life is that I gave up too easily, fighting to be there mum." Sam was stumped, and so too were the rest of the guys, everyone in that room had stopped what they were doing and were listening intently to Brad. I'm pretty sure they were doing exactly what I was, questioning the sincerity and integrity of all she had said.

All was quiet, Sam had no answer for a mother who had supposedly been denied the opportunity of bonding with her children, Brad was waiting for a response from someone, and the guys went uncomfortably back to drinking tea, and pretending to check their phones. "I do love my kids, I would never want them to be hurt, but I don't know how to love them the way a mother does, will you tell Elizabeth I'm sorry." Once again all eyes were on Brad, I don't think this woman had ever apologised for anything in her life. A small part of me felt sorry for her, if what she was saying was true, then she'd been denied the one thing in life she dreamed of, and that would explain the cold, hard-hearted woman we had before us today. Unsure of where to go from there, Sam quietly picked up his box, and without saying another word, he returned to his seat. Brad sat with her eyes shut, a pained look on her face. It was a look you couldn't fabricate, it was the look of a mother who had lost her child, I'd seen that look before. Even knowing the woman she was, every part of my being wanted to go to her, to comfort her, to console her, I was my mothers son, and I couldn't ever leave someone to suffer alone that way. I shoved back the box I was sitting on, walked to where she sat, and knelt in front of her. "You are a terrible person Brad, you've done so many terrible things, but no one deserves to have their children taken from them, I'm sorry you never got the chance to be the mum you wanted to be, but there's still time," I lay my hand on her shoulder as I stood, the only bit of comfort I could give her without getting some very strange looks from the guys.

To my surprise, when I sat back at the table, I was met by a circle of nods of approval, my heart filled with absolute pride at that moment, in this awful situation, in these horrible circumstances, understanding who we were, and what we had all done, we still had humanity, we still had compassion, we were still beneath it all, nice guys.

It was hard to tell where things would go from here, just because Brad had shown a tiny shred of decency didn't mean she could be trusted in the real world, she knew too much now, there were very limited choices, she could either be killed, kept in the shed until she inevitably died, or a miracle could occur, and she would give up everything they needed to know and swear allegiance to them, that last one was never going to happen and even if it did, they would never trust her enough to let her walk out of there. I could imagine that usually in these cases there would be people to consider, kids, husbands, family, all those people who you knew her disappearance was going to have a devastating effect on, but in her case there was no-one, no-one would miss Brad, no-one would be hell bent on finding out what had happened to her, no-one would be distraught at the loss of their loved one, I couldn't even begin to imagine how that felt, knowing there was no one out there who cared whether you lived or died. Of course Brad's father, the real Brad, the original Brad, would be slightly pissed he would have to find someone to take over the business, although I highly suspect there would be someone waiting in the wings to jump into her shoes. I wondered if, right now, I was the only person in her life who was concerned about what would happen to her. Sadly, that was more than likely true.

Thankfully, when the time came for her, I knew I would not be around, I knew that would be something Degs and Fran would deal with alone, and for that I would be truly thankful. I also knew that as emotional as this was now, she would soon be forgotten, she meant nothing to me now, she was merely the route to my answers, I have those now. She will become what most people do, a blurred memory, destined to be stored way down in the depths of my mind, very rarely making it to the surface.

Thinking we were finished for the day, I was keen to leave, things had gotten extremely awkward, being cruel to a hard, soulless woman was one thing, but things had changed, there's never any excuses, another one of my mothers sayings, but there are reasons, she had a reason for who she was, and for me that did change things. It was not over yet though, as much as Fran and Degs understood how her past had moulded who she had become, it altered nothing for them, right now was what mattered, what she'd done and what she was capable of doing was what mattered, and that still had to be dealt with, like any professionals, they had a job to do, and they couldn't allow emotions to get in their way. Fran drew the short straw, it was his turn to try to get the information they needed, or wanted, I wasn't sure which it was. I had seen both sides of Fran, the wonderful gentle man, who would do anything for any one, and the hard emotionless robot he could become. He didn't sit, he walked to where Brad was still tied to the chair, he circled her several times, before stopping in front of her. "So what do we do with you now ?" He was quiet and calm, almost caring, but not quite. "Oh Francis, we both know I'm not leaving here." She managed a faint smile, which went down well with Fran, he actually patted her on the shoulder. "We still have some business to deal with though, don't we, why are you so hell bent on keeping it to yourself." Fran was walking back and forth, hands on his hips, no sense of urgency, he had resigned himself to the fact that he may not get the answers he wanted. Brad managed to pull herself up straight, flicked her head to the side, removing the hair that had fallen onto her face and said, quite simply, "Because I can." I actually jumped, at the sound of Frans fist making contact with her face, it was sickening, every single atom in my body wanted to walk away, but I stayed exactly where I sat, partly because I couldn't let the guys down, and partly because I was rooted to the spot with fear, I couldn't let them know I wasn't dealing with this. Basically I didn't want to lose face, which we all know is exactly why Brad was in the predicament she was in right now.

After the fourth contact between fist and face it was obvious Brad was now in no fit state to talk, even if she wanted to. It was hard to see Fran like this, the lovely, nurturing caring guy, who had looked after us over the last few weeks. I didn't want to believe he was capable of this, let alone witness it. Rubbing away the blood from his fist, with a tissue he had taken from his pocket, he returned to his seat, resuming the conversation he had been having with Degs about what they were having for dinner that evening, not a word spoken about what had just happened, not a question from anyone else in the room. It was surreal, they flicked back and forth, between their different characters, the line between good and bad so blurred it was difficult to see where one ended and the other began. I couldn't have been more relieved when Sam stood, grabbed his car keys and said, "Come on then mate, we've got work to do." I was at the door before him, just a quick goodbye called to the guys on the way out. I didn't even want to think about what was going to happen when we weren't there. My mind wandered back to hearing Degs say he couldn't be violent to a woman whilst Sam was around, but that had obviously all changed when they'd witnessed Sam smacking her in the face. Shit!

Chapter Forty-Eight

I raced back to the car before I exhaled in a woosh, Sam raised his eyebrows as he looked at me with, 'what the hell' written all over his face. "Ah Sam, that was full on mate, I'm no good with women, not when they're all sad, and pouring their heart out, I wish this had never happened, we could've all just got on with our lives." I wasn't comfortable knowing the outcome for Brad, it really didn't sit well, but I'd known this was a possibility, or rather a probability, before we started, and when I'd thought there was a chance of getting even with the person who killed Joseph, it definitely seemed worthwhile. "Mate she would be out of that shed less than an hour before she was wreaking havoc on all of us, she's emotional because she's undernourished, she's exhausted, pissed off, but believe me, she would very quickly recover and wouldn't think twice about taking you, me or anyone else out." He was right, and I knew it, I was just holding on to some slim hope that there was another way.

I text Fi, I just needed to hear from her, she always kept me sane at times like this, she was my strength, always there to lift me when I needed it, it could be as simple as the text she replied, 'I miss you, come home soon xxx,' she made me smile with one simple sentence,

I simply couldn't imagine a life without that. And that is why Brad, couldn't live.

It was good to get back to some sort of normality, regular jobs, with regular people, who weren't being held against their will. It didn't totally remove the vision of Brad from my mind but it helped. "Sam, is there anyone looking for Brad ?" "The father in-law has got a few guys out looking for info, but to be honest, no one is making much of an effort," "And the girls ?" I asked. I wasn't sure he even remembered Phoebe and Josie. "They're doing ok mate, the nanny, housekeeper, whatever they call her is doing what she's always done, and the kids like her, so there's no worries there," I had one last question, "Is anyone looking for Beth ?" He paused before answering, which I knew from experience was never a good thing, he was either about to tell me something I didn't want to hear, or he was going to try to make light of whatever was going on. "They are, but we have it all in hand, they're nowhere near close to finding her." I felt guilt seep in as he said it, my concern wasn't for Beth, I only cared about them getting too close to Fi. I nodded as I took in the information, staring at the road ahead as I did. "Don't worry mate, Fi will be just fine." I laughed, as always, at this guy's mind reading abilities, he never, ever failed. "How do you do that ?" I asked, "It's really not hard with you mate." Another reminder that I am my mothers' son.

Greeted with the news the following day that we didn't have to go see Brad, filled me with absolute joy, I couldn't have been any happier, I had been dreading getting out of bed, knowing we had to return to that damn oversized shed ! So when Sam announced "Day off today mate," I was quite literally ecstatic. I flew back upstairs to give Fi the good news. "How about we go out for a walk today ?" I asked, "Really ?" she said, jumping up onto her knees on the edge of the bed. I'd been so wrapped up in my own woes, I'd not given enough thought to the fact that both her and Beth had also been cooped up in this house for weeks. "We won't go far, there's no rain forecast so we can take a couple of sandwiches, bag of crisp or something eh ?" She was like a kid who'd just been invited on a day trip, she leaped from the bed, rummaging through her wardrobe searching for something to wear, after grabbing a pair of jeans and a shirt, she was off to the bathroom, but not before kissing me hard on the lips, and telling me she loved me. "I'll meet you downstairs," I shouted, as the bathroom door closed. I came out of my room just in time to see Sam returning to his, with a tray laden with drinks and snacks, obviously planning on spending a good deal of the day there, he gave his eyebrows a wiggle, and wore a massive grin as he saw me appear in the corridor. "Looks like you're ready for a good day," I laughed, "Oh you'd better believe it mate," he said. He disappeared back inside his room, the house was empty apart from us four and back in the kitchen it felt strange sitting alone, it seemed like a lifetime since I'd done it, and to my surprise, it felt good, I loved them all dearly, and I would give my life for Fi, but five minutes to myself felt like heaven. It was more like forty-five minutes by the time she appeared at the doorway, forty-five minutes of drinking tea and playing silly games on my phone, with no interruptions, no drama, no one getting hurt, I suppose what most people would call 'normal' maybe even boring, some days I prayed for boring, but it was very rare my prayers were answered.

    Fi looked absolutely stunning, I began to think Sam definitely had the right idea, but she was so excited I couldn't possibly change my mind. She grabbed my jacket, just like she used to do at home, and pulling my hand like a small child, she dragged me out of the front door and down the steps, before running off into the cold morning air, twirling as she went like this was her first ever experience of the world. I stood, taking in her beauty, watching her enjoying something so simple as freedom, fresh air and fun. She stopped to shout, "Come on," before running off once more. I took to my heels and chased after her, thrilled by her squeals of delight when she realised I was hot on her heels, as soon as I was close enough, I grabbed her by the waist and pulled her close, kissing her gently, I pushed a piece of hair behind her ear, as I told her I loved her and couldn't imagine a life without her in it, she was as always coy enough that it made her all the more wonderful. We walked hand in hand, talking like we used to do, it seemed like such a long time since we had done this. Before we realised it, we had been walking and talking for more than two hours, we had talked about everything, from our pasts to our future, eating our sandwiches as we went, it was days like this I would remember forever, just me and Fi, allowing each other a peek into our souls. As our walking slowed, the cold set in, I could see she was starting to shiver, it was time to return to the house. We made our way back through the trees at the end of the grounds of the house, as soon as we did so, I saw a car in the distance, outside the house. I wasn't sure whose car it was, but then they all had a different car every week, I guessed it would be Fran, it was his house after all. Five minutes later we were back inside, taking off our coats and rubbing our hands together trying to warm them up, it was quiet, it seemed Sam really was planning to spend the day in bed.

We were still chatting, laughing about the fun we'd had when we walked into the kitchen. Horror hit instantly, as I tried to take in what I was seeing, I could barely make sense of it, my eyes scanning the room as I tried to take everything in, Sam was bound and bloody on the floor, it was all I saw, before I had any chance to react, I felt a searing pain in the back of my head, that was the last thing I remembered for a while.

I woke with a start, instinctively trying to jump up and protect myself. Of course that ship had well passed, where I lay on the floor, I could see Sam to my left, he was face down, unconscious, and bleeding from a wound to his head, he was bound and gagged. I tried desperately to see if he was breathing, it was just too hard to tell. My eyes flashed around the kitchen searching desperately for Fi. I found her tied back to back with Beth sitting on the floor on the other side of the room, both of them with tear stained faces, both looking absolutely terrified. My heart ached for them, for Fi, I had promised her I would always protect her, always keep her safe, and here I lay useless on the floor in front of her, my guilt very quickly turned to anger. "What the fuck's going on ?" I yelled, I hadn't seen the person who had hit me, and couldn't see anyone from where I was. But a voice from somewhere behind me told me, "You'll find out soon enough." Whoever it was sounded young, they couldn't be alone, this wasn't some kid who'd done this, this was crazy, how could this even have happened, this wasn't like Fran or Degs, or any of the guys to be honest, how could they not have seen this coming.

I was angry and I was scared, not a great combination for anyone. I could only guess that they were waiting for Fran and Degs to get back, I wished with all my heart there was some way of warning them before they returned, or hoping they just wouldn't be as dim as me, and they'd have thought more about a strange car at the house, it was only five thirty, that meant there was more than likely at least a couple of hours before anyone came back, if they came back at all. I prayed they would realise something was wrong. All I could do was sit, terrified and helpless, while my mind raced with thoughts of what would happen next.

The waiting was long, and the only thing I was thankful for was the silence, and the fact they'd not hurt the girls...yet. The silence meant they were waiting for someone, and that meant we had a chance, I couldn't imagine for one minute, the guys wouldn't know by now.

They arrived with force, our saviours, our knights in winter coats, bursting through the door guns blazing, all I could do was stay close to the floor, screaming across the room, "Fi, get down, get down !!" I tried through the cacophony of noise, and the mass of legs, to see where they were, I looked desperately for them, but they were nowhere to be seen. I hoped beyond hope they'd managed to get themselves to safety. I still had no idea how many people there were in the room, then, as quickly as it had started, there was silence once again. The sound of gunfire gone, the chaos swarming around me gone, only the smell of gunfire in the air, and the fear within me left. The relief I felt as Degs knelt beside me to check on his son, was like nothing I had felt before, I prayed Sam was ok, I really did, but the only person I could think about was Fi. I started calling her name, "Fi ! Fi ! Are you ok ?" There was no answer, I began to shout again, but was stopped by the touch of Degs hand on my shoulder, the look on his face terrified me, my heart beating even faster than I ever thought possible, "Where is she Degs, is she dead ?" He shook his head as he said, "No son, no she's not dead," I couldn't find relief, he was trying to reassure me, but it wasn't working, I knew something was terribly, desperately wrong. Degs placed his hand on my shoulder, "They're gone son, there was so much happening in here, there were too many of them, we had to keep fighting, or we'd all be dead." Laying on the floor did nothing to stop me from collapsing even further, and my world along with it. I didn't hear anything after that, I lay in my catatonic state on the kitchen floor, my body paralysed with terror, my mind unable to compute what he had said, I kept hearing it over and over, but I couldn't absorb it, I was unable to accept it, until all at once it hit home, and the whole world came back to me in a rush of pain, anger, hurt and sorrow all of which were fighting to be at the forefront of my consciousness. Pain won out, heartfelt, terrible, agonising pain, I let out a roar, a noise I'd never made in my life before, a noise that scared even me, a guttural devastation at the realisation it was true, she was gone.

Still on the floor, hands bound behind my back, feet tied together, I struggled to release myself, I didn't mean to yell, but it was all I had. "Get these fucking things off me," I screamed, fighting with the ropes around my wrists, Fran was there in a second, his shirt covered in blood. "Stay calm son, let me get those off you," his calm tone didn't help, I settled onto my side as he undid the knots, as soon as the ropes were gone, I was up on my feet, rubbing at my wrists where they'd been bound, turning and turning, taking in the carnage. Fran continued to talk, he was telling me they would find them, they would get them back, they knew who it was, it was all good to hear, except I needed her now, I needed to know right now that she was ok, the thought of her being scared or hurt was terrifying, there was so much adrenalin in my system I was nauseous, before I had another minute to think about it, I was rushing to the sink barely managing to hold on, before vomiting into the basin. I was shaking, my head was spinning, in a panic I turned to Fran, about to ask him what was happening to me, it was too late, he caught me as my legs gave way, guiding me back to the floor, where I sat with my head in my hands till the feeling passed. "You need to stay there son, you're in shock, it's understandable, I can't imagine how I'd feel in your position." "I should've known Fran, I should've known," I said sadly. "We can all say the same son, but that's not how it works, sometimes nothing gets past you, sometimes it does." "But I saw the car outside, I knew it was a strange car but I just assumed it must be one of you guys, you know what Sam told me, a long, long time ago ?" I looked at him, full of sorrow, "He told me to never make assumptions, he wouldn't have, if he'd have been in my shoes, this would never have happened." I was completely and utterly devastated at the realisation that it should have been me who stopped this from happening. I wallowed in my sorrow.

"Is Sam ok ?" I asked, finally remembering I wasn't the only person here suffering. "Yeah, he's doing just fine, he's had a nasty knock on the head, but he's had worse, saying that, he doesn't know about Beth yet !"

As Fran spoke, I heard the same heartbroken, fear ridden sound that had come from me just a few minutes earlier, and I knew Sam had asked where Beth was. I had to go to him, trying to stand with my legs still weak was hard, but Fran was there to help. He guided me to where Sam was, sat on the floor in his dad's arms, inconsolable at the loss of his Beth. "We'll find them Sam, you know we will." Degs told us they had at least twenty people out looking for them, and it wouldn't be long before they had a lead. I knew they would leave no stone unturned until they found them. "Was this Brad ?" I asked, wondering why she would wait until now. Fran told us, "No, this is nothing to do with Brad, just a group of guys trying to do the same thing we did, but without the manpower, we knew about them, but didn't think they were capable of this, like the boy said, we shouldn't make assumptions, and believe me, it won't happen again." It was only then I began to see the rest of the room, it was absolute chaos, there were three dead guys in a pile in one corner, Buzz and Tatty were cleaning up, and there were at least three other guys there I thought I knew, I'm pretty sure there would be several more outside. Wow this had been one hell of a shit storm.

As the rest of the world around me continued to seep in, I noticed more and more, there were bullet holes everywhere, I knew I'd heard a lot of gunfire, but I had no idea just how much. Now that I'd sort of recovered from my wobble, I joined in the clean up job with the guys. It was a very subdued affair, no one was in the mood for talking, everyone seemed to be covered in blood, and I had no idea whether it was theirs or not. "Is anybody hurt ?" I asked, looking around at each of the guys. "Frans got a flesh wound, Degs will sort it, but apart from that we did pretty damn good," Tatty high-fived Buzz as he spoke, it was a feeble attempt at lightening the atmosphere, but sadly it wasn't going to work this time. Sam was up on his feet now, looking like absolute shit. He was agitated, walking back and forth, firing off question after question to his dad, Degs answered each one calmly. Who was it ? Where are they from ? Who got away ? Where will they have taken them, and the most important one, "When are we going to get them ?" Degs had an answer for every one. And less than ten minutes later all of us were heading back towards town.

Chapter Forty-Nine

It was an obvious assumption to make, that all those involved would have gone straight into hiding, the important thing was only to find the girls, that's all I was interested in and I'm pretty sure Sam felt the same way. Fran had an idea where they could be, the guy responsible was called James Furlong, he was currently laying in a heap on the kitchen floor of Frans house, very, very dead. Tatty had told us they owned a row of garages, they had been left standing after the council flats nearby had been pulled down, apparently it was where he did his dirty work. Each time I thought about Fi, my stomach turned, I was covered in a cold sweat, my body tensed, anger and fear fighting for prominence as they surged through my veins, and hearing the words dirty work associated with her, made all of that ten times worse. It was a long, eerily quiet journey, there was no use for small talk, we all knew exactly how the others were feeling. As we pulled into what looked like some wasteland, I saw what we had been looking for, about fifty foot in front of us was a row of old garages, both Sam and myself were out of the car before it had had a chance to come to a complete stop, Degs tried to slow Sam down, but he really wasn't in any mood to wait. Degs grabbed him by the arm, "Come on son, none of us have any room for any more mistakes today." Sam took a deep breath and nodded, we had to keep ourselves safe, we were of no use whatsoever to Fi or Beth if we were all dead !

There were five garages, and there were six of us, there was no way we could do one garage at a time, it was far too risky. Fran silently allocated us a garage each, pointing to each of us before pointing to one of the doors before us, he would stand back, keeping a lookout for anything unexpected. As I turned to walk towards my allocated door, Fran pushed something into my hand, I almost threw it to the floor when I realised what it was, "Come on son, we both know you can use this," he whispered, "Now come on, get your act together." Fuck ! I felt so sick, I knew the colour had drained from my cheeks, "Conal, come on son, get a grip, this is no time to fall apart, your girl is in one of these." That was all he needed to say. I tightened my grip on the gun he had thrust at me, clasped it in both of my hands and nodded letting Fran know I was good to go. And I was, within thirty seconds, I'd gone from a wreck who'd remembered how he felt last time he took a gun into his hand, to controlled, composed, strong, confident and determined, it amazed me just how quick we could go from one to the other. I've said it before, but it really is a wonderful thing, the human mind.

Each of us stationed ourselves to the left hand side of each of the doors, on a count of three we knocked, nothing happened, another count of three and we did the same, again there was nothing. On the next count we would be trying the doors to see if any were open, three of them were. The noise of them lifting meant that anyone inside the other two was now more than aware that we were there. Fran was on his way back to the car, the others moved to the sides of the two doors that hadn't opened, Fran was back seconds later with two hydraulic car jacks. They were slid quickly under the handle of the garage doors. Within a minute, we were in, guns poised, anything that looked like a man was going to die very quickly. No shots were fired, and my heart sank at the sight of the empty room, it was obvious the other guys had found the same thing. Sam started yelling, "Where the fuck is she ? This is a fucking joke !" "Back in the car !" shouted Degs, he was not happy, it was obvious he fully expected to find them, and he was not used to being wrong. I was terrified that whoever had them was a lot more dangerous than these guys had originally thought. It was just a fifteen minute drive to the next place, a house on the end of a short row, all of the other houses in the street, except these few, had recently been demolished, and, by the looks of it these were next to go.

There was no waiting this time, straight up to the front door, Sam practically walked through the locked door, kicking it off its hinges as he went. A guy appeared at the top of the stairs, Sam saw him and fired, no more questions, there were going to be no prisoners taken on this job, as Sam walked through the door at the right, another two shots were fired, with the enemy dealt with it was time to search for the girls. Sam and I made our way upstairs, there was little to search, this was a simple two up two down, and after quickly checking out the two small bedrooms, and the tiny bathroom, hearing a call from the guys that there was nothing downstairs, the only other place to check was the loft, Sam climbed in slowly using the torch on his phone to check the dark space above him, I knew, when his body slackened, there was nothing there, they weren't there, and that meant the chances of us finding them any time soon, were fading. Panic set in, I couldn't bear the thought of not knowing were she was, all the awful memories of her childhood, of her being raped, of being terrified to move out of the door, of being abandoned, and neglected, came flooding back to me, and as always the guilt of my part in all of this set in, it was unavoidable, if she hadn't met me, she would be safe in her own little world, in her own little house, with the comfort of knowing what each day would bring.

"Where next ?" Sam asked, trying his best to stay up beat, even though the stress he was under was obvious, the terror in his eyes gave it all away. "We're still waiting to hear, Sam, there's nothing we can do till then." Degs put his arm around his son's shoulders, doing the only thing he could…comfort him. "Dad there must be something, anything, anywhere," "Not right now son, let's get back to the shed, we can check in with the rest of the guys, and take it from there." It wasn't ideal, but we needed to keep moving, we needed to keep doing something, or was it more that we needed to keep feeling like we were doing something. I sat in silence in the back of the car, staring through the window, but seeing nothing, my head was too full of visions of Fi, her tear stained face, eyes filled with terror, pleading with me to help her, to save her, and I was out on the road with no clue as to where she was. I tried, with little success, not to think about what might happen, the thought of trying to live a life without her was not one I could ever begin to contemplate.

The atmosphere when we arrived at the shed was solemn, we all completely understood the danger the girls were in, and that tiny bit of hope we'd had, when we thought we knew where to find them had gone, and we were bereft of any emotion, left with just a huge pool of emptiness.

That mood changed in a split second, one that would change everything horrifically forever. Fran had walked a foot or two from the car when he began to run, he was followed closely by Degs, I'd had no intention of rushing inside, but their panicked state had me running behind them. As soon as I stood outside of the car I heard what they had already heard. "HELP, HEEEELLPPPP, SOMEBODY HEEELLLP, PLEASE ." It was Brad's voice, from the woman who had been barely able to speak last time I'd seen her, those screams came from one place, and one place only, a mother, a mother who was desperate and hysterical and terrified. And that could mean only one thing. Fran flung open the door and rushed inside, all had their guns drawn, Brad was pointing in the only way she could, using her head to guide them to the back of the shed. It was plain to see what her hysteria was all about, the sight that met us, brought Sam to his knees, and had me running in a blind panic towards the horrific scene we all faced.

Time slowed, in the time it took me to reach them, I had taken in everything I needed to enable me to do everything I could to free Fi.

There were three of them, Lenny, Beth and Fi, they had been lined up next to each other, each with a noose around their necks, and each with blood pouring from wounds to their legs. No longer able to hold themselves up after being shot in their knees they had slowly slumped onto their own noose and left to slowly suffocate. I couldn't help the others, I couldn't even think about them, all three of them looked like they were dead, but I had to believe there was hope, I had to.

I grabbed Fi in my arms, lifting her enough to remove the rope from her neck, I lay her on the ground in front of me, automatic pilot kicking in. I checked her airways, I checked her pulse, there was nothing. Instead of panic, I continued to do what needed to be done. I had no idea what was happening around me, just what was going on right there beneath my hands. Taking up the stance we had learned in school, I knelt beside her, hands entwined over her chest, and began, 1,2,3,4..., I knew that the recommendations for adults was that no breaths were needed, but I gave two breaths anyway, then on with the compressions, stop, check, start again, stop check, start again, I don't know how long I was there, I only came back to the real world, when a hand touched my shoulder, and I realised I was dripping with sweat, gasping for air. It was Fran, "Son, you've done enough." In fury, I shrugged away the hand that was trying to comfort me, and started again, 1,2,3... stop, check, start again, with tears falling, and my heart breaking I carried on until I could no longer hold myself up. Sitting back on my heels, gasping for breath, I looked at the beautiful young girl before me, at what I had done. I stayed beside her forcing myself to stare at the destruction I had caused, and something inside me shifted, I didn't feel sad, I didn't even feel angry, I just came to understand that I was never meant for this, I was never meant to be loved, I had no idea why, but now it all made sense, I had to accept it, this, if nothing else in my life ever was, was proof that I could never, ever feel this way about anyone ever again.

Remembering there were other people in the room, I glanced around, my eyes glazed, and my mind fuzzy, not really able to completely comprehend anything anymore. I was numb. Sam was cradling Beth, but I couldn't tell if she was alive or not, and I didn't care, Lenny must have been dead, he was flat out on the floor, and there were no signs of life. I felt nothing for them, none of them, not a thing. I left Fi where she lay and walked to where Brad sat. "Who was it ?" She was sobbing, she was a complete mess, for all the hardness she portrayed, she was still her mother. She shook her head as she said, "I don't know, there were two of them, they came in shot Lenny and strung him up." Lenny had stood no chance, he wouldn't have been expecting anyone to turn up at the shed, this place had been used for almost a decade without anyone knowing its whereabouts. Brad went on, "They had masks, I didn't know the voices, they didn't mention any names, nothing, nothing." She was hysterical, sobbing again, and I didn't care. I sat on my box, at our table and stared into space. There was little happening, I could hear Degs and Fran and Tatty on their phones, all of them looking for answers, all of them hurting. And then I heard it, Sams voice, "You're ok now Beth, it's ok."

Rage literally tore through my body, I flung my head around to where they were, eyes wide, they were still on the floor, in the dirt, her eyes still shut, I was devastated to see the faint movement of her chest. It took everything I had not to lose control, instead I screamed within my own mind, 'WHY ! WHY !' Why had she lived and Fi died, that wasn't fair, that wasn't right, I loved Fi, loved her more than he could ever possibly love Beth, I know I did ! Jealousy engulfed me, so much so I couldn't bare to look at them, I didn't want to see her breathing, I didn't want to see Sams relief, I didn't want to see them at all, I wanted Beth to be dead and Fi to be the one laying there with her chest still moving up and down, with me telling her everything was going to be ok.

I had to get out of there.

I headed for the door, but was stopped by Tatty, "Come on son, there's nowhere for you to go out there, not just now." With little emotion, and unable to look him in the eye, I spoke, "Tatty, please let me go, I can't be here right now." He knew with one look, that he couldn't deny me the time alone I needed. "Stay close son, we don't know who's out there remember." He was right of course, I hadn't even thought about that. The fact that he cared, brought a twinge of emotion to me, one I didn't want to feel, nodding, I quickly stepped to his side and outside the big red doors. It was cold and dark, there could have been anyone out there, anywhere at all, I wouldn't have known, and didn't particularly care. I had little to live for. I'd told myself so many times I couldn't live without Fi, and now I knew that was true, there seemed no point to any of this any more. I walked slowly along the road outside the shed, reached the end of it, turned and walked back. When the anger at Beth living started vaguely to subside, I battled with the emotions that were trying to push through, it was easier feeling nothing, emotions were too complicated, they hurt too much, and I didn't want to hurt anymore, been there, done that, and wore numerous T-shirts.

I needed just a few moments, hand on the door ready to go in, to prepare myself for seeing Fi again. Deep breath, door open, and there she was, laying just as I'd left her, I waited for the hurt to hit, for the panic to set in, but it didn't, still there was nothing. I loved her, and I didn't want her to be gone, but she was, and there was nothing I could do about it. Acceptance had kicked straight in, I'd missed denial, anger, depression and bargaining, and gone straight to acceptance, that would save a whole heap of heartache I thought. "So what next," I asked, to the surprise of everyone in the room. Degs stood up, and came towards me, I backed off knowing full well he was going to try to get me in some sort of embrace, he stopped a few feet away. "Son, I think you're in shock, sit down, give yourself a bit of time to get your head together." Simply and calmly I told him my head was just fine. I'd spent so much of the last couple of years, most of it in fact, trying to make people pay, this would be the last time. Degs didn't argue, he went back to Fran, I assume to continue finding information and making plans. I wasn't interested in the logistics, I just wanted them to let me know when they had the scum who'd done this.

Thinking I might like to go home, it dawned on me that once again, I no longer had one. I looked around the shed, from one end to the other, and high up into the rafters, it was the first time I'd really looked, it was high, like really high. Tatty joined me at the table, "How're you holding up ?" he asked, I shrugged my shoulders and put my hands up either side of me, in the classic 'I don't know' stance. I really didn't know, I knew I should be feeling more than I was, but I didn't.

Degs and Fran joined us a few minutes later, each of them patting me on the shoulder as they passed me and sat down. As they sat there was a voice from behind me. At first I thought it must be Sam. But quickly realised it was Brad, Degs backside had barely touched the box, before he was back on his feet, stomping towards Brad. What had she said ? What was happening now ? As he got within a couple of feet of her he said, "What was that Brad ?" "Ronan Doyle," she repeated, "The Irish connection, it's Ronan Doyle." Degs looked at her for a moment or two before saying simply, "Thank you Brad," "No Degs, thank you." I hadn't seen what had happened but I knew, I knew Sam had collapsed the minute we had walked in that door, which meant it was Degs who took Beth from that noose, it was him who had saved her. I waited for the rage to hit again, but there was none. All this pain, all this sorrow, all Brad had been through, and now, just like that it was over. Just one sentence, and she was done, I'd spent weeks backwards and forwards to this shit-hole, time I'd spent away from my beloved Fi. I thought about why she was here, the things she had done, not just to me, but to so many people, ruined so many lives. And yet here she was, feeling sorrow, hurt, relief, thanks. Even as I stood, I wondered where that person had gone, where had she been all these years, she could have saved so many families so much heartache, by just being *this* person, this person she was now. This person who understood grief, who understood loss.

BANG...BANG...BANG. Her head fell limp, her hair falling over her bloodied face. I looked at the gun in my hand, I looked at Brad, blood dripping from the hair she'd not brushed in weeks. I looked back at the gun, turning it over a couple of times, nodded with satisfaction to myself, a smirk or maybe a sneer, whilst I took in the sight of Brad, and a note to myself...no more...no more Mr. Nice Guy.

THE END

ABOUT THE AUTHOR

Susan Pritchard was born in Liverpool, England, and has been a budding author her whole life. After spending most of her adult life bringing up her children and fostering many others, she finally managed to do something for herself, pull it all together and put the book from her head down on paper aged 56, after more than a decade of dreaming!

Printed in Great Britain
by Amazon